# Emeralds of the Alhambra

A NOVEL

Book One of the Anthems of al-Andalus Series

JOHN D. CRESSLER

# Emeralds of the Alhambra





For information about special discounts for bulk purchases, please contact Sunbury Press, Inc. Wholesale Dept. at (855) 338-8359 or orders@sunburypress.com.

To request one of our authors for speaking engagements or book signings, please contact Sunbury Press, Inc. Publicity Dept. at publicity@sunburypress.com.

FIRST SUNBURY PRESS EDITION
*Printed in the United States of America*
June 2013

**Trade Paperback ISBN: 978-1-62006-197-8**
**Mobipocket format (Kindle) ISBN: 978-1- 62006-198-5**
**ePub format (Nook) ISBN: 978-1-62006-199-2**

Published by:
**Sunbury Press**
Mechanicsburg, PA
www.sunburypress.com

Mechanicsburg, Pennsylvania USA

# Praise for John D. Cressler's *Emeralds of the Alhambra*

"A deeply moving and enlightening novel on the co-existence of religions."

*—Shirin Ebadi, Nobel Peace Prize Laureate*

"...Cressler has woven an imaginative and intricately persuasive story...[a] vivid and gorgeous world of romance, intrigue, murder and negotiations between multiple religions in medieval Spain...[a] story of love between human beings, for God, and for the creation so graciously bestowed on us. A thoroughly gripping and engaging first novel."

*—Professor Susan Abraham, Harvard Divinity School*

"...Seamlessly weaves history, religion, passion, loyalty and romance into a compelling, beautifully-written narrative which brings [the reader] into the richness, majesty and complexities of this different, yet alluring world..."

*—Rabbi Rachael M. Bregman, Temple Beth Tefiloh and Rabbis Without Borders*

"... More than ever, we need stories like Cressler tells, confirming the transformative power of relationships. Cressler illuminates the beauty and meaning found in Islam, Christianity, and Judaism, reviving an important shared history..."

*—Eboo Patel, Founder and President, Interfaith Youth Core*

"...A work of honesty and sensitivity that renders in depth, and with painterly detail, the living contours of a great civilization that the modern world needs to re-discover...A moving story of love across boundaries, set at a critical point in history...with unmatched and vivid descriptions of place, lifestyle, manners and practices..."

*—Salma Khadra Jayyusi, poet, writer, and literary historian. Founder and Director of EAST-WEST NEXUS/PROTA for the dissemination in English of Arabic cultural achievements*

"[Cressler's] compelling characters and vivid imagery bring this tale of intrigue and barrier-breaking relationships to life in a way that even a visit to the Alhambra did not...[Celebrates] the power of love to forge human hearts into timeless bonds."

*—Cathy Devlin Crosby, Cofounder of Neshama Interfaith Center*

"A captivating love story that speaks deeply to the purest and most humane places of the heart. A highly enjoyable and enthusing novel."

*—Aytekin Erol, Lawyer Society of Cinematographic Work Creators, Istanbul*

"*Emeralds of the Alhambra* has it all – mystery, intrigue, duels and interfaith romance...Cressler artfully draws us into the fascinating lives of the novel's main characters with vivid prose. We experience the blows and blood of the fierce battles between enemies, as well as the luminosity and laughter of spell-bound lovers...Transports readers back to medieval Spain and offers them a peek behind *la Convivencia* and all the rivalry, romance and complex relationships that existed between Jews, Christians and Muslims."

*—Tayyibah Taylor, Publisher and Editor-in-Chief of Azizah Magazine*

"...A story of passionate love...and the spiritual quest for God...Cressler adds a most important element to the mix by weaving in the "problem" of how to reconcile interfaith concerns, [making] this wonderful novel especially prescient for the third millennium."

*—Marian Monahan, Cofounder of Neshama Interfaith Center*

"History, conquest, and a captivating love story...Dares us to engage in conversations with those of different faiths. This is more than a novel, it is a resource."

*—Angela Harrington Rice, Senior Executive Producer, Atlanta Interfaith Broadcasters*

"[Cressler] has a finely-tuned, sensuous capability to drink in and pass on exquisite sights, smells, colors, sounds and tastes...[At] the deepest level...Cressler helps [the reader] understand the... overwhelmingly powerful force that love truly is...and the role love plays in our experience of the Divine."

*—Father Gene Barrette, Missionaries of Our Lady of La Salette*

"...The novel's rich and descriptive narrative serves as a call from the past, challenging us to realize that more is possible than we dare imagine. In its pages are found nearly everything that makes us human..."

*—Professor John B. Switzer, Spring Hill College, Cofounder and Director of the Muslim, Jewish, Christian Trialogue*

## *Reader Reviews*

“Cressler weaves a beautiful love story between a man and woman who overcome the boundaries of language, religion and dogmas to form a union which epitomizes Andalusian civilization. I lost myself in this engulfing story and fell in love with [Cressler’s] own humanity and sense of tolerance. We need to come together, as he writes so beautifully in *Emeralds of the Alhambra*, as peoples of the world, to endure times that are becoming increasingly violent and fanatical.”

*—Acar Nazli*

“Seeped in a rich and sensual history, this is a tale of love and faith that transcends time...Cressler reminds us of the transformative power of a hope and courage rooted in love, a reminder that is essential as we face the seemingly insurmountable conflicts of today.

*—Anita Hall*

“...An eye-opening novel and a beautiful story full of daring, intrigue [and] love...It is a story you will not find anywhere else, and it must not be missed!”

*—Robert Wilhelm*

“...The riveting story line of battles, political and religious skullduggery, and the star-crossed love of William Chandon...and Layla al-Khatib...makes this...a real page-turner!”

*—Roger A. Meyer, MD*

“...Transported me back to [the] 14th century, where the landscape...looked different...but the problems of humanity were the same — How do we live together in peace?...[Cressler’s] painstaking research and his care for detail are evident. I would not be surprised if someone decides to make an epic movie based on *Emeralds of the Alhambra*.”

*—Kemal Korucu*

“With beauty and ardency, *Emeralds* captures the triumph of love over religious and social conventions, progress over history, and warmth over the chilling callousness of war.”

*—Sylvia Hall*

*For my Maria:*

*My lover.*
*My best friend.*
*My beloved.*
*Everything I know of love*
*I know from loving you.*

*I believe.*

**In Dreams and Love**
**There Are No Impossibilities.**

János Arany

## *Contents*

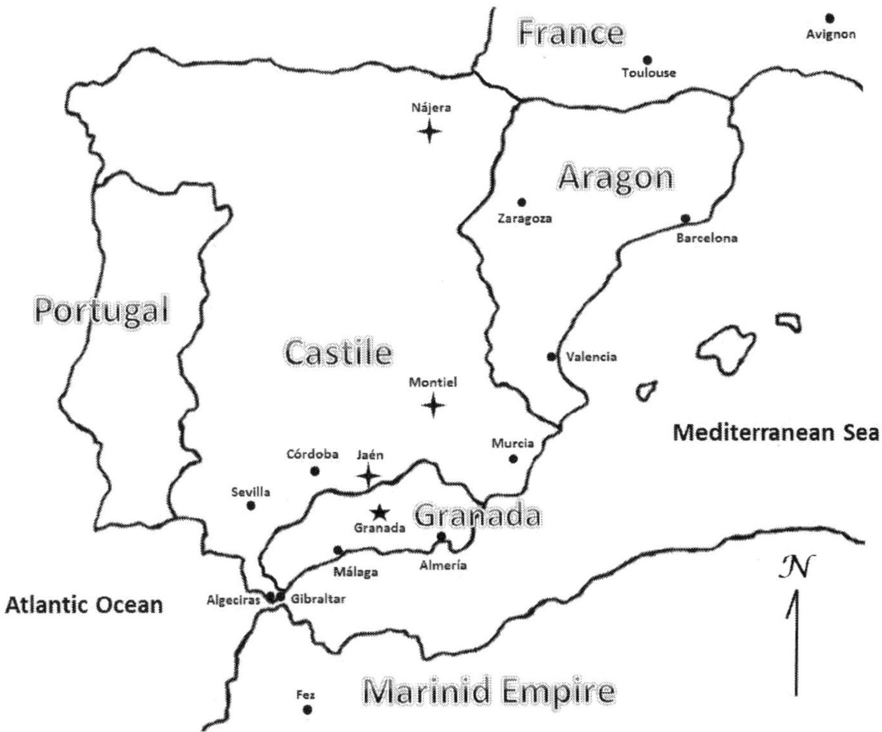


*Map 1. The Iberian peninsula in the spring of 1367, showing the borders of the Kingdom of Granada, the Kingdom of Castile, the Kingdom of Aragon, the Kingdom of Portugal, the Marinid Empire, and France, as well as important cities and battles (the latter are indicated with stars).*

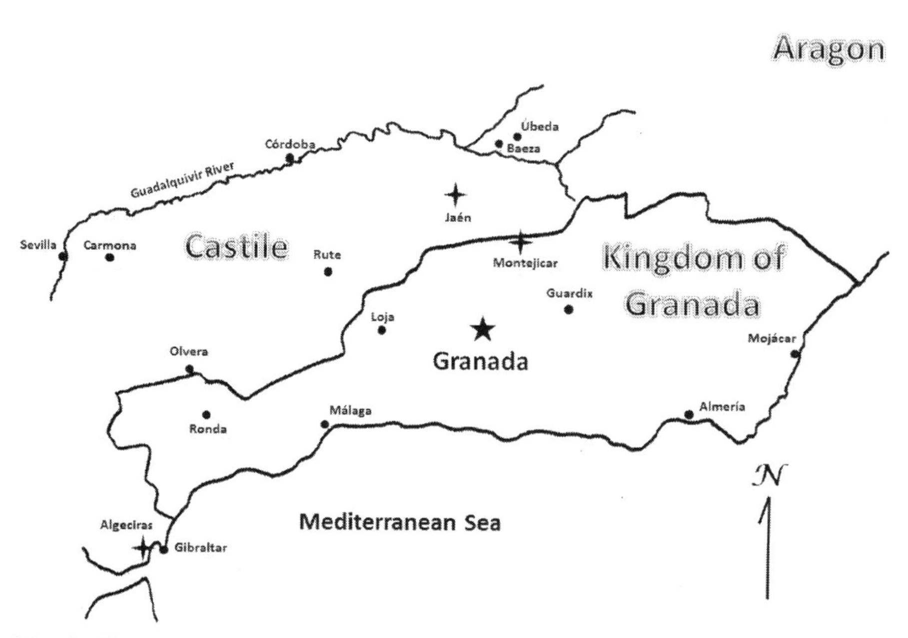


*Map 2. The Kingdom of Granada in the spring of 1367. Battles are indicated with a star.*

*Map 3. The city of Granada, showing the orientation of the Alhambra, the city walls, the Darro and Genil Rivers, and the Albayzín.*

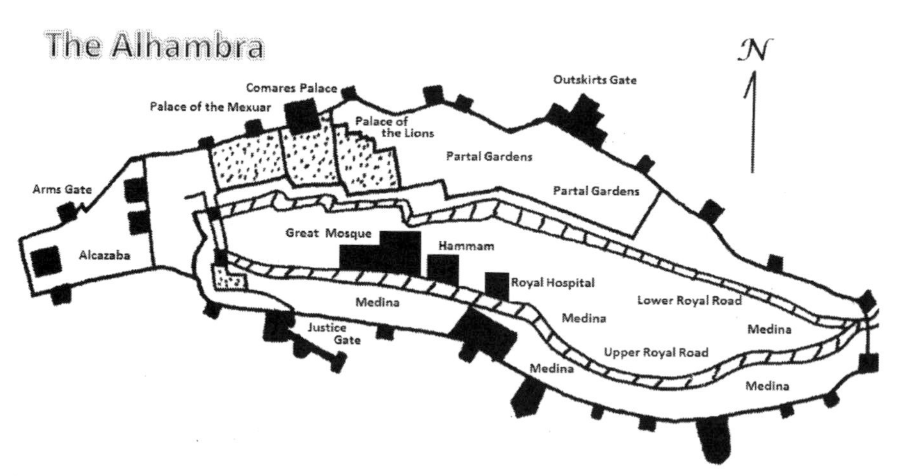


*Map 4. Layout of the Alhambra. The Alhambra is seven hundred yards long and one hundred yards at its widest. The dark objects at the perimeter wall are defensive towers.*

## *Characters*

***Abu Faris Abd al-Aziz*** - Sultan of the Marinid Empire
***Afán*** - Layla's Lusitano stallion
***Ahmad al-Mubarak*** - Royal Ambassador to the Marinid Empire
***Aisha*** - Layla's lady-in-waiting
***Alfonso*** - Salamun's young assistant
***Alonso*** - Member of the Sultan's Royal Bodyguard
***Antonio de Castrocario*** - Papal ambassador to Genoa
***Auria*** - Sultan Muhammad's slave-concubine
***Bashir al-Waziri*** - Military Vizier of Granada
***Bertrand du Guesclin*** - Mercenary, leader of the Free Companies
***Bishop de Hulhac*** - Apostolic Nuncio of Pope Urban V
***Bishop de Fonte*** - Apostolic Nuncio of Pope Urban V
***Blue*** - Chandon's Andalusian stallion
***Cardinal Coysset*** - Legatus a Latere of Pope Urban V
***Charles V*** - King of France
***Constancia*** - Head nurse at the Maristan Hospital
***Danah al-Khatib*** - Lisan al-Din ibn al-Khatib's dead wife
***Diego*** - Salamun's young assistant
***Don Alfonso Tello*** - Counselor to King Pedro of Castile
***Don Sánchez de Velasco*** - Commander of Castillo de Montiel
***Don Juan Duque*** - Counselor to King Pedro of Castile
***Don Perro Carrillo*** - Commander of the Portuguese forces fighting for King Pedro
***Don Ruy Mexia*** - Counselor to King Pedro of Castile
***Don Sancho Coronel*** - Counselor to King Pedro of Castile
***Don Gonzalo Ruiz Girón*** - Papal ambassador to Aragon
***Don Alfonso Méndez*** - Aide-de-camp to Enrique II of Trastámara de Guzmán
***Edward the Black Prince*** - Edward of Woodstock, the Prince of Wales, son of King Edward III of England
***Ernaud de Florenssan*** - Papal liaison of King Charles V of France
***Enrique of Trastámara*** - Bastard brother of King Pedro of Castile
***Farqad al-Bistami*** - Military Vice-Vizier
***Garcia*** - Servant to Sultan Muhammad
***Guinot de Diagon*** - Lieutenant of the Free Companies
***Hasan al-Nisawi*** - Knight of Granada
***Hugh Calveley*** - Mercenary, leader of the Free Companies

***Ibn al-Shatir*** - Astronomer from Maragheh, Persia
***Ibn Zamrak*** - Personal secretary to Sultan Muhammad, court poet and former student of Ibn al-Khatib
***Imam Abd al-Hamid*** - Grand Imam of the Mexuar Council
***Imam Abd al-Malik*** - Senior Berber imam on the Mexuar Council
***Imam Abd al-Rahim*** - Berber imam on the Mexuar Council
***Imam Abd al-Salam*** - Berber imam on the Mexuar Council
***Jabir*** - Boy in the Maristan
***Jalil al-Ghudari*** - Master of the Royal Treasury
***Johan*** - Salamun's young assistant
***John Templeton*** - English ambassador to Castile
***Juan*** - Male nurse in the Maristan
***King Pedro*** - King of Castile
***King Pedro IV*** - King of Aragon
***Layla al-Khatib*** - Grand Vizier's daughter
***Lisan al-Din ibn al-Khatib*** - Grand Vizier to Sultan Muhammad V
***Luis*** - Servant of Sultan Muhammad
***Majahid al-Khayyat*** - Chief Administrator of the Maristan Hospital
***Mansur al-Mussib*** - Sufi master at the madrasa in Granada
***Maryam*** - Baby in the Maristan Hospital
***Matar*** - Berber assassin
***Muhammad V*** - Sultan of Granada
***Musa*** - Member of the Sultan's Royal Bodyguard
***Nafi*** - Baby in the Maristan
***Nasr*** - Member of the Sultan's Royal Bodyguard
***Qasim*** - Head Eunuch of the Royal Harem
***Robert Cheney*** - Chandon's second in command
***Rodrigo de Palencia*** - Commander of Castillo de Santa Catalina
***Salamun the Jew*** - Royal Physician to Sultan Muhammad
***Sosanna*** - Chandon's dead fiancé
***Tariq al-Harish*** - Royal Ambassador to Castile
***Tahir al-Shashi*** - Layla's attacker
***Urban V*** - Pope
***William Chandon*** - English knight from Brittany
***Yazdan*** - Member of the Sultan's Royal Bodyguard
***Yusef al-Nur*** - Teacher at the Madrasa
***Zyad*** - Head of the Sultan's Royal Bodyguard

## *Alliances*

**Kingdom of Granada** (Sultan Muhammad V)
Kingdom of Castile (King Pedro)
Marinid Empire (Sultan Abu Faris Abd al-Aziz)

**Kingdom of Castile** (King Pedro)
Kingdom of Granada (Sultan Muhammad V)
England (King Edward III and his son, Edward the Black Prince)
Kingdom of Portugal (King Fernando)

**Enrique of Trastámara** (bastard brother of King Pedro of Castile)
Kingdom of Aragon (King Pedro IV)
France (King Charles V)
Republic of Genoa
Avignon Papacy (Pope Urban V)
Free Companies (led by Bertrand du Guesclin and Hugh Calveley)

## *Spain in the Spring of 1367*[1]

By the 13th century, the Christian kingdoms are mid-stream in their attempted *reconquista* (reconquest) of Muslim Spain, having conquered Córdoba in 1236, Valencia in 1238, Murcia in 1243, and Sevilla in 1248, slowly but surely pushing the Moors into the Mediterranean Sea. (The Muslims of Spain, regardless of ancestry, are known collectively to Europeans by the term "Moors".) The Kingdom of Granada is the final holdout of "al-Andalus" (a catch-all word for the lands of Moorish Spain), a mere one-hundred mile wide swath of land at the extreme southeastern tip of Spain, stretching from the coast north of Mojácar, through Málaga, to Gibraltar.

Under the moderate Arab Nasrid clan who rule from the Alhambra Palace, the kingdom prospers, wildly, and by the 1360s Granada, under Sultan Muhammad V, remains a stubborn bulwark against Christian reconquista. Improbably, Granada is allied with the Muslim Marinid Empire of North Africa and also is a tribute-paying vassal state to the Christian Kingdom of Castile, ruled by King Pedro from Sevilla.

Tensions that have for decades smoldered between Castile and her Christian neighbors finally boil over. Pedro's illegitimate brother, Enrique of Trastámara, is championed by the king of Aragon, who lusts after a unified Spain under Aragonese rule. Enrique is supported by King Charles V of France and even the Pope himself, presently in Avignon and itching to help cleanse Spain of infidel Moors. Enrique brashly declares himself the "true" king of Castile in 1366 and the Castilian Civil War, a death match between Pedro and Enrique, brother against brother, is afoot.

Enrique assembles a large army consisting of Aragonese, French, and Breton troops, supplemented by a diverse collection of mercenaries, and invades northern Castile from Zaragoza, the capital of Aragon, forcing the unprepared Pedro to abdicate the Castillian throne without a major fight.

Pedro gathers his meager treasury and troops and retreats from Sevilla to Galicia, in northwestern Spain, where he begins frantic preparations for war. Upon Pedro's departure, Enrique sets about expanding Aragon's boundaries southward into the lightly-

1 A historical primer of al-Andalus and Granada, a glossary of terms, notes on language, views of the Alhambra palace complex, and contemporary photographs are included in the back matter.

guarded underbelly of Castile, capturing Murcia, Lorca, Huéscar in quick succession. Cazorla, Baeza, Údeba, fall next, and finally the stronghold of Jaén. Enrique's conquest of the Castilian buffer lands traditionally separating al-Andalus from Aragon produces significant discomfort in Nasrid Granada, given Aragon's strong and vocal resentment of Sultan Muhammad over his alliance with Pedro and the perceived meddling by Moors in Christian politics.

Meanwhile, England's Sir Edward of Woodstock (Edward the Black Prince), in an attempt to head-off France's thinly-veiled ambitions in Spain, as well as attempt his own land-grab, weighs in behind Pedro, and the Hundred Years' War creeps south into Iberia.

Sultan Muhammad, as vassal to Pedro, walks a thin line between the warring brothers, but in the end, agrees to send six hundred of his best cavalry to support Pedro.

Pedro's ragtag army of twenty-eight thousand English, Castilian, Gascon, Aquitainian, Majorcan, and Muslim troops clash decisively with Enrique's superior army of sixty thousand at Nájera, in the Rioja region of northern Spain, on a fine spring day, the 3rd of April, 1367.

Among Enrique's officers is Sir William Chandon. A strapping twenty-five year old Chandon brilliantly leads the forces of Jean de Monfort of Brittany to victory over the House of Blois at the Battle of Auray in France in 1364, winning the Breton War of Succession, a linchpin in the Hundred Years' War. As a reward for his valor at Auray, Monfort appoints Chandon Viscount of Saint-Sauveur in the Cotentin, in Brittany, where he settles, a suddenly-landed, wealthy English knight living now as a Breton on French soil. At the request of the King of France, Chandon's cavalry rides with Enrique.

The famous English longbow makes its first appearance in Spain at Nájera. Edward the Black Prince's twelve thousand English longbowmen first overwhelm the French archers then train their arrows on Enrique's cavalry, to devastating effect. Enrique's Aragonese and French cavalry units panic and turn tail, leaving his flank and rear dangerously exposed. Edward strikes like a hammer. Chandon's Breton cavalry stands firm, stubbornly anchoring the suddenly sparse flank. With heavy losses, the Bretons are able to temporarily blunt Edward's charge, allowing Enrique just enough time to escape.

Enrique's force of sixty thousand is quickly routed, with losses of seven thousand dead to Pedro's two hundred. Enrique and his whipped forces limp back to Zaragoza to lick their wounds and regroup for round two of the fight. Pedro settles back into his palace in Sevilla, supremely confident.

Eight days later, on 11 April 1367, a Moor courier in transit from Granada to Sevilla is intercepted in Carmona and his throat slit. In his satchel is an official communiqué from Sultan Muhammad to King Pedro, declaring that Granada, empowered by Pedro's decisive victory at Nájera, will seize the opportunity to strike north through Jaén and invade the former Castilian border lands presently occupied by Aragon.

Made aware three days later of this bold and unexpected move by the Moors, Enrique, fearing a two-front war, summons Chandon and sends his elite Breton cavalry south to bolster the garrison of Castillo de Santa Catalina in Jaén, only forty miles north of the Granada. Enrique's instructions to Chandon are simple - send an emphatic message that Aragon is off limits to Moor meddling.

## Scarecrow

20 April 1367. The rough-hewn, gray-weathered monolith stands silent watch. Grim and imposing, it guards the valley floor against trespassers. Chiseled from an ancient Lebanon cedar two feet thick at its base, it stands forty feet tall, crossbeam notched and fitted then cinched tight with tarred hemp twine, visible from three miles on a scorching, heat-wrinkled August day, six in winter. Eerily backlit at night by pitch-fueled fires, it serves as a warning beacon to wayward Moors, the papal calling card of reconquista, a graphic reminder that the days are numbered for rich Granada. The giant wooden cross is perched high above the cliffs on the eastern end of the limestone promontory that anchors Castillo de Santa Catalina, castle-garrison of Jaén.

Chandon quickly picks his way among the boulders along the edge of the jagged cliff, arriving finally at the base of the cross, a stone's throw east of the castle walls. His six officers and the garrison commander trail behind him. He stops, rests his hand on the cedar scarecrow and glances skyward at the red and yellow striped Aragonese banner whipping and snapping in the stiff wind. He looks down upon the walled city to his left, then up to the backdrop of mountains defining the eastern horizon, the Sierra Morena. He turns to survey the valley floor to the south, five hundred feet below. He studies the landscape, a hawk pining for a jack rabbit atop a late spring updraft. Moments pass in silence.

"The Moors will attack from there." He points southeastward to the thin scrub-line marking a meandering stream running between two burnt-brown rolling hills dabbed green by thousands of silver-tipped olive trees. "See the worn cart path just west of the stream? It heads due south. Granada."

He points again, just to the right.

"We can easily hide our cavalry in those trees." His officers follow Chandon's finger to the eastern edge of the mountain due south of them, perhaps a mile distant. There stands a thick half-acre of oaks, a hundred yards from the stream. The span between the woods and the cart path is rough plowed and treeless, sloping gently downward to the valley floor. The path bends around the woods then escapes behind the mountain as it winds southward into the rising hills.

"The Moors will round the bend and their eyes will lock onto their prize. We will stand vigil in the woods, safely hidden. There is room for archers in the rocks just above the tree line. Loose the arrows and by the time the Moors realize what is happening our charge will be on them. Let the Moors discover firsthand the temper of Breton steel. Trust me, these heathen will think twice about invading Aragon."

Chandon's officers nod their heads in agreement. Robert Cheney, his second in command, says, "A good plan, William."

"Sir William, why not just stay in Santa Catalina?" Seven heads slowly turn to Rodrigo de Palencia, garrison commander. "We are safe here. Jaén cannot be taken while Santa Catalina stands. The castle was built by the Moors two hundred years ago. No army has ever successfully breached these walls, Moor or Christian. We have ample food and water. Why risk open battle?"

Chandon sighs, looks south once more, studying the landscape. "Because, Rodrigo, we must send a clear message to the Moors. We must crush their invasion before it begins. Here. The element of surprise is with us. The Moors expect only a garrison of a few hundred light infantry tucked safely behind the high walls of Santa Catalina, not a hundred-fifty of Brittany's finest heavy cavalry. My men were born for attack, Rodrigo." Chandon's officers grin. "We will quickly slaughter this lead element. Then the Moor commander will have to figure out just how many Breton cavalry he will have to face at Jaén."

"Sir William, you have not battled the Moors. They do not honor our code of chivalry. I was at Montejicar in '63. I have seen firsthand what Moors can do in battle."

"They will find us worthy opponents, Rodrigo."

Late that evening, inside the castle keep, an oak fire crackles and pops on a deep bed of blood-red coals inside the wide-mouthed stone fireplace. The mingling of the bright dancing light with the dim glow of oil lamps hung high above casts an uneven, modulated crimson hue.

The garrison is fast asleep. Sentries are posted on the ramparts, staring southward into the crescent-mooned night, struggling to bring the landscape into focus. A boulder or a crouching Moor? A horsed rider or a grazing goat? Sentries startle easily these days. Several false alarms a night are not uncommon.

The gentle breeze whispers through the pine trees. The scent of wood smoke is strong, comforting. A dog barks in the distance, then stops abruptly. Lanterns twinkle in the city below. A charger just outside the castle nickers then snorts, a pointed shush from a squire quiets him.

The cool blue stone of the castle is reflected by the moonlight, here and there brightly lit by sentry fires, walls dancing in tune to the fingered glow. Christian only in name, the castle has never confided the secrets of its Moor architects.

Chandon and his officers stand vigil in the keep, gathered tight round the fire, joined by Rodrigo and four of his men. After pleasantries are exchanged, standard chatter commences regarding troop strength, arms caches, complaints about food, lack of women. Cheney asks about the townsfolk and their loyalties. Rodrigo wants to know about the farms of Brittany, then probes Chandon about Enrique's next move in the Castilian chess match. No answer is given.

Conversation slowly dies as the night deepens. The silence slithers into the keep, stretching out. The air is heavy, tranquilizing. The eerie flickering light alternately illuminates then hides their faces.

Robert Cheney breaks the trance. "Tell us about the Moors at Montejicar."

There is a long pause, followed by a reluctant, heavy sigh. Rodrigo begins in soft tones, "I commanded five hundred infantry, a mix of archers and foot soldiers, under Juan Martínez de Palategui. Three thousand good men, well trained and fed. We were ordered to capture Montejicar. It was spring, nearly four years now. At sunrise we woke to face a thousand Moors at the crest of the low hill to the front of the city. Half were on horse, many of them turbaned in their Moorish way, wearing uniforms of bright colors, and carrying heart-shaped leather shields. We prepared to absorb their cavalry charge and then counterattack with our own to break their lines. The Moor cavalry wore only chain mail, no plate. Only broadswords and javelins. Their horses were undersized." He manages a pained, "We laughed," then falls silent.

A minute later he resumes, speaking slowly to the coals. "Instead of charging in force to break our front, they raced round us on both sides in a pincher move, then attacked at our flanks and rear. They charged full speed, throwing their javelins, then quickly retreating to safety out of easy bow shot, then charging again, over and over. Each time more of us fell. The infantry carried crossbows, not bow and arrow. I have never seen the like. Steel-framed and three and a half feet tip to tip, firing a foot-long bolt with a steel broadhead. Their crossbow infantry, supported by the light cavalry, moved to within fifty yards of our line but strangely did not engage us, instead targeting only our armored knights on horse. The Moor bolts tore into their plate and they fell, one by one."

"Impossible!" Cheney interrupts. "No crossbow can penetrate tempered plate."

Rodrigo looks up, meets Cheney's eyes. "Nevertheless, our knights fell. One, then ten, then hundreds."

"I said the same of bow and arrow until I saw firsthand what an English longbow at full draw can do," one of the Breton officers concedes.

As the silence stretches out, eyes bore into Rodrigo's shadowed face.

"Panic spread quickly. As we broke rank and scattered the Moor knights rode up, slid easily from their mounts and walked among our terrified infantry, challenging any soldier willing to a sword duel to the death. Those that accepted in a vain attempt to recover some honor were run-through and then beheaded."

Eyebrows lift in unison, glances are exchanged. Chandon's eyes reluctantly retreat from the coals, turn and lock onto Rodrigo. His expression is unreadable.

"We ran. I am no coward, but we ran. Juan Martínez brought three thousand to Montejicar. By late afternoon we were four hundred. The next morning we returned to recover our dead. We found Martínez nailed to a cross at the top of the hill. Naked and headless, crucified as a warning for all to see. The Moors still hold Montejicar." He offers an exhausted sigh. "I will not soon forget that day."

The room grows quiet. Only the crackle and pop of the fire dares speak as the dancing light punctuates the troubled faces of the knights.

Chandon offers, "There were rumors of Moors at Nájera, but I heard of no such stories or tactics."

"Perhaps. But I was at Montejicar, Sir William. I have no desire to meet the Moors again in open battle."

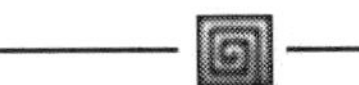

The squires and their attendants have already left their masters for the night, ambled to their tents to prepare their own meals, clean dishes and then bed down. The sun has set and the dark is slowly creeping in, unnoticed. Breton knights huddle around their fires in small groups, talking quietly. A bright burst of laughter springs up at a joke, then fades, then another round flares across the courtyard. One knight embellishes a battle yarn for his friends, eyes wide and excited by the memory, hands evocatively stretching and moving, his friends listening intently, smiling at the coals. A playful one-up challenge is offered, followed by more laughs.

Chandon and Cheney stroll through the courtyard, stopping now and then to visit briefly with their knights. Chandon is alert, trying to gauge the morale of his troops.

"It is good to hear the men laugh again," Cheney offers.

"Yes. Our losses at Nájera..." He shakes his head in disgust. "So needless. The cowardice of the Aragonese and French cavalry cost us the victory. My heart aches for our lost friends, Robert."

"Bretons are a resilient bunch, William. They will be ready to fight the Moors when the time comes."

They stop. Knights rise to offer their greetings.

"Sir William, when will we be introduced to the fine ladies of Jaén?"

A chorus of whoops and whistles echoes. Heads turn around the courtyard.

"Forget the Castilian women, boys, I have a bigger prize for you. They say that the Sultan's harem travels with the Moor army, hundreds of dark-eyed women in colored silks, long flowing raven hair and sweet perfume between their breasts. So beautiful they can freeze a man dead in his tracks at fifty paces with just a smile." He pauses for effect. "I hear that the harem grows tired of Arab boys. They need some Breton men to satisfy their lust."

The knights ring out in unison with bawdy cat calls and whistles, then gamesome teasing and shoulder slapping. The light-hearted moment harkens back to better days in Brittany.

Cheney smiles at Chandon.

"Rest, my friends. We will soon have our chance to prove our honor to the Moors on the field of battle."

Lusty whoops and hollers ring out in reply.

Chandon and Cheney walk on.

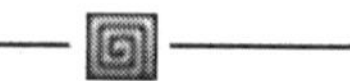

Three days later, the scouting party of the Moor invasion force has been sighted.

Two hours before sunrise, torches light the frenetic lower courtyard. Gleaming plate, nervous horses and killing tools litter the scene. Chandon's knights dot the courtyard, squire's assisting in the laborious process of donning armor.

Each cavalry trooper first dresses in heavy felt pants and gambeson, followed by a hauberk of steel-ringed mail. Then comes fifty pounds of thin, tempered steel plate, added one piece at a time, strapped and locked into place. Fitted chest and back plates, hinged plates for shoulders, groin, arms, thighs and shins, to allow movement. Lobster plate guards for gloved hands and socked feet. Last is the angular helmet with retractable visor. Tugged on, then strapped tight. Broadsword and either studded mace or battle ax are hefted, followed by short swings to test balance and fit.

Attendants work quickly to ready their master's charger stallions, nineteen-hand, two thousand pound monsters. Born anxious, gentle words and coaxes sooth the wild-eyed stallions. Occasional rears prompt whips to snap, garnering attention. Saddles are slung, girth's cinched tight, thick felt armor draped then tied on the horse's haunches.

Chandon strolls from the keep in full armor trailed by his two squires, exits the main gate, then enters the lower courtyard, surveying the scene. He seems satisfied with the progress. The promise of battle quickens his pulse. The man exudes confidence.

A short while later the Breton cavalry mount on command then exit the west gate two-by-two, begin their slow descent to the valley floor. The knights are all business now, silent, attentive to their mission, mentally rehearsing battle moves, offering prayers, strapping on their swagger. Next come the archers on foot. Squires on stock horses bring up the rear, followed by several two-wheeled carts carrying horse feed, water, arrows, spare armor and assorted extra weapons. The moon has set, rendering the scene opaque, the clanks and squeaks and clops all that mark the Bretons' passage.

The burnt orange sun breaks its beams over the distant mountains and begins its slow climb. Wispy clouds at the horizon exhale pinks and purples. It will be a fine, bright day. Warm. The air is still, but there is a faint, oddly pleasant smell of freshly tilled earth mingled with animal dung. A whiff of perfume from some unseen late spring wildflower tiptoes. Red oleander spills from the rocks. Foxglove, wild sweetpea and sandwort are scattered about in their riot of whites and blues. Gnarled, ancient olive trees dot the rolling hills as far as one can see, their tiny white blossoms ready to pop. Low, patchy grass rambles through the groves, clinging desperately to the parched earth, lusting after moisture. Busty warbling from a shrike echoes in the oak copse while a lone vulture drifts lazily, high above the valley floor.

Chandon's cavalry waits, impatiently, safely tucked back from the edge of the woods before sunrise, out of sight. Squires feed the mounted chargers from bags of oats to keep them silent and calm. Hushed whispers flit among the knights. A quick, strained laugh is followed by an echo. The cool, steel-on-steel grind announces a sword sliding from its scabbard. The sound reverses as it is replaced seconds later.

Chandon and his six officers walk their horses to the edge of the trees. Chandon glances upward and to his left at the castle five hundred feet above him, a mile distant, then across to the cart path and stream to his front. Finally, he turns in his saddle and looks to their rear, where the archers lie hidden beneath the boulders fifty feet above the tops of the oaks, within easy bow shot of the stream. He seems satisfied.

"Our moment has come, gentlemen. Remember, surprise is our best weapon. Make sure your troops hold stone-still and silent until I give the word. Muzzle the horses. Two Roberts, you anchor our flanks as usual. Garsis and John inside them, and Gaillard, you and Perducas with me in the center. No banners, they will only slow us down. Hold tight ranks between each platoon during the charge. When the Moors are in front of us and we know their full strength my squire will pass my signal by flag to the archers to loose their arrows. They will fire three, maybe four volleys before we reach the Moor line. We charge as one from the wood at full gallop until we are on them. Crush them quickly. Our aim is to annihilate this lead element before they realize what hit them, and before the main Moor force has time to respond. At my signal, we then turn and ride back up the valley and around the west end of the castle mount to join Rodrigo, who will be waiting in support. Garsis, you will hold the rearguard and protect the archers as they retire with us."

Gaillard asks, "Our wounded?"

"Gather those you can, but we must move fast or we risk getting trapped by the main Moor force. Leave the rest. We will capture a Moor officer or two today and then exchange prisoners."

"Understood."

"Good luck, my friends, and may God be with us this day."

The officers canter back into the oaks to their platoons, where final instructions are quietly passed. Encouraging words are offered, then repeated. Confidence floats breathlessly among the oaks. The horsemen draw up into ranks, two rows of gleaming, steel-encrusted heavy cavalry. Broadswords are pulled from their scabbards, killing gear checked and made ready. Squires slide back further into the woods. Arrows are nocked.

The woods are silent as midnight. Then the painful waiting commences.

# Ode

The gurgle of the floor fountain stretches skyward to the upper reaches of the honeycombed heavens, where it roams about, a child at play, bathing the space in a lovely aquatic murmur. The day is dying. The warm glow of the waning sun enters the slender windows high above and careens off a thousand prisms to create a dancing patchwork of orange and gold upon the white marble floor.

Two dozen men sit cross-legged on silk floor pillows. The men are silent, but the air has the expectant feel of a looming performance.

The slender fingers of the musician flex, then begin to brush and tease the strings of his guitar with the delicacy of a skilled lover, the vibrating melody joining with the liquid resonances to produce a rich and satisfying song.

The eyes of the audience close. Satisfied smiles sprout then blossom as heads begin to bend and sway to the soothing rhythm, newborn wheat moving under the gentle caress of a warm spring breeze.

A short while later, a young man rises from his pillow, turns and faces the gathering. He raises his upturned palms as if to beckon his muse, then closes his eyes, and with the exaggerated features reminiscent of a man blind from birth, begins the meted intonation of his poem.

*"The Pleiades*
*Spend the night in this place of rest,*
*And in the morning,*
*Rise wind-borne in the enchanted dome*
*That makes all we see in it seem small."*

The poet's rich baritone twines around the musician's improvised chords and together they dissolve into the aquatic landscape, producing a rich, uncanny harmony filled with promise, as if the marriage was intended from the beginning of time.

*"See the beauty that yearns to be here,*
*Tangible and near:*
*Orion stretches his wide, forgiving hand toward it;*

*The full moon of heaven*
*Draws near in secret conversation;*
*And the bright stars descend,*
*Wanting to be steadfast among its flowers,*
*To no longer circle the distant lands of the sky,*
*But be like those in its courtyards*
*Who came before them,*
*Among the servants that please him*
*With their presence..."*

At the back of the gathering a man leans discreetly to his left and whispers, "Zamrak is a master. The Alhambra has never seen his like, Sire."

Without opening his eyes, the Sultan's smile widens. "Yes, he has a rare gift."

*"...So do not see a castle,*
*For I surpass all that can be seen,*
*I make distant lands appear*
*And extend my hand,*
*Beckoning.*
*And do not see a garden,*
*For I am blessed with stars that scatter fragrances*
*That return once more and set the exiles free."*

The poet's last words are coaxed upward into the reaches of the sculpted dome, the echo stretching for several seconds before fading into oblivion. The poet sits. The musician continues to gently stroke his lover for several more minutes, then stops, allowing the strings to vibrate into silence. Only the aquatic murmur remains.

# Rivulet

Chandon sees the first Moor horsemen appear to his extreme right. Ten, then fifty. They walk in double file, eyes scanning, but as expected, their gazes are drawn upward to the castle when it comes into view. Several stretch out their arms and point. Large, bright blue triangular banners with unreadable gold script rest atop twelve-foot pikes carried by the first two riders. The Moor cavalrymen appear unarmored, or perhaps with chain mail under their long, flowing blue robes. On their left arms are the famed Moorish heart-shaped leather shields, and their heads are covered with thin metal helmets with draping boiled leather neck guards. Most have full beards. Their weaponry is light; broadswords, daggers, javelins, nothing more.

The Moor commander rides just left of the column, twenty paces behind the banners. A bright white turban wraps his head and neck, leaving only his tanned, mustached face visible. His fine, light brown wool robe hangs down to his calves, ending at expensive leather boots. His broadsword hangs by his side from a long colored leather sash around his shoulder, its tight crescent hilt a telltale Granadine stamp. Fine, expensive steel, a close cousin of the famed Damascus steel of the east. A red and white checkered cloth drapes the rump of his beautiful, solid-white mount. Two officers ride further back in the cavalry column, dressed like their commander, but with no checkered marker.

The Andalusian horses are small by European standards, fifteen, maybe sixteen hands, some with beautiful, light tan coats with bright blond manes and tails. Others are solid black, gray, chestnut or brown. The horses carry no substantive armor, only ornate, wide stirrups and decorative bridles, high-backed leather saddles with horns in the front.

Following the first fifty cavalry, infantry march in four columns, eighty strong, clothed in white robes with burgundy capes, turbaned tightly so that only their dark eyes show. Daggers are strapped to their left upper arms, their pikes held carefully vertical. Small crossbows hang from their belts. Their round red shields have a bold white hand painted on them. The feared Berber warriors from the Maghreb in North Africa.

The second set of fifty cavalry also contains two officers and is identical to the first set except that unusually large crossbows hang from their front saddle horns, stretching to their horse's knees. Chandon frowns, then narrows his eyes and studies. Chandon has never seen or heard of anything like it. A mild, slightly ominous sixth-sense raises the hairs on the back of his neck, but only for a second before his pounding heart flattens them.

And that is all. The formation moves forward, unaware. One-hundred eighty Moors, five officers. Chandon remains satisfied, confident of the inevitable outcome. He raises his blue kerchief and waves it in a circle around his head three times. He looks to his left, then to his right, to catch the eyes of his officers. He raises his mighty broadsword and screams, “Charge Bretons!”

The first volley of arrows flies true, dropping two dozen Moors and a dozen horses. The Granadine flag falls to the ground, the proud bannerman pierced through the shoulder, the steel broadhead buried deep in his chest. The horseman immediately in front of the lead Moor officer is struck through the neck with a hushed thrump and folds over on his horse. Momentary panic ensues while the lethal source is identified. The commander looks left along the arrow arch, sees the culprits above the trees. His eyes are instantly drawn lower as the three hundred foot wide line of horse flesh and gleaming knights barrel out of the oak woods at full gallop. He cups his mouth with both hands and screams something forward and then turns and screams it to the rear. The large heart-shields rise. The infantry fall to their knees behind their smaller shields.

The second volley takes down only four of the tardy Moors. Between the second and third volleys the Berber foot soldiers tighten ranks and face the charge, while the lead cavalry breaks into two groups, the latter half circling round to form ranks on either side of the infantry square. The stream is at their backs. The third volley drops only one Moor who foolishly gawks over his shield. The rear cavalry sprints forward to the front of the infantry square. Horse legs tighten straight, launching an instant cloud of dust. The knights unexpectedly slide from their saddles, reins in hand. As if by magical intonation, the horsemen speak and the horses drop to their knees and then collapse to their sides, backs facing the charge. The fourth volley only wounds three horses. Distant thunder rolls on a near cloudless day. The dismounted horsemen kneel, take up their massive crossbows behind their bedded Andalusian stallions, fit their bolts, then pick targets. The infantry behind the Moor crossbowmen raise their pikes into a porcupine.

Chandon's heavy cavalry is forty yards out now, all sod-flicking hooves and war whoops, clanking armor and brandished swords, terrifying in its awful momentum.

The Moor officer shouts his command, releasing their bolts in a single volley. Strangely, the crossbows are not aimed at the knights, but instead at the chests of the on-rushing chargers. As if on cue to some phantasm's choreography, dozens of stallions crumple to the ground in unison, knights sailing forward through the air like gilded dolls. The lucky ones come free of their stirrups, somersaulting painfully into the ensuing dust cloud. Those flying head-first break their necks as they hit the hard earth. Those locked in their stirrups to the pierced stallions get rolled upon and broken by two thousand pounds of horse flesh as the ugly metal-flesh contraptions twist and turn, contort and roll in a devilish, unnatural dance, until both are still.

The Moor crossbowmen place the end of their massive weapons in the dirt between their legs, push their feet into the front hooks, insert a curved lever, bend their knees, and with a quick straightening of the back, are finished. The next foot-long bolt is inserted and the bow raised once more to fire. Six seconds. The second volley is loosed by the time the charge reaches the Moor line, taking down several dozen more cavalrymen at point blank range.

The culled Breton units at the flanks engage the Moor cavalry in a crushing thrump of steel, followed by grunts, thuds, and maniacal neighs. The lightly-armored Moors are no match, and begin to fall to javelin and broadsword. In the center the Breton chargers easily jump over the bedded horses and bowmen, but suddenly face a steel porcupine. The pikes are not aimed at the armored knights, but at the horses, which stop with wide, panicked eyes, blades sinking into their unprotected necks. Some twist and scream, trying frantically to retreat. Others fall, pulling their knights earthward. Several riders make it past the front quills and into the underbelly of the unprotected infantry, to devastating effect. The small infantry crossbows only dent the plate armor and pin-cushion haunches. Upward sword thrusts do not reach their targets. The hard-swung Breton broadswords cleave limbs and split heads, a dozen white Berber robes instantly dyed bright crimson.

As the initial clash begins to subside, the Moor crossbowmen urge their horses up but do not remount, instead wading through the mayhem and shooting at will over their mount's rump at the flailing knights. Many of the infantry drop their pikes, break free of the tangled mass and begin to descend like wolves upon the dismounted Christians. Some of the Bretons lie still on the earth already. Others offer confused groans and struggle to rise under fifty pounds of gravity-burdened armor. Some have managed to rise already, and are searching frantically for their broadswords and maces. A dismounted cavalry is much less intimidating and far more vulnerable to an infantry assault.

The Berber daggers are drawn. The thin blades wiggle easily into the soft spot between the shoulder armor and the hauberk and on into the heart. If a knight has foolishly raised his visor to get a better view of his attackers, a dagger jabbed into the eye and driven into the brain is the preferred choice. In either case, a quick scream and the work is done.

The ground adjacent to the stream grows dark with fresh blood, slicked by some nightmarish crimson rain. The scene is littered with bodies. The sweet pungent scent of death grows thick in the air. Battle lines vaporize under the Moor and Christian free-for-all. If anyone had cared to look skyward, they would have seen the clutch of vultures circling in tight formation, staring intently earthward from a quarter mile up.

Robert Cheney has already dispatched four Moor horsemen on the left flank. Broadsword in his right hand, studded mace in his left, he slashes violently left then right then counters with his mace. He deflects a lance thrust so that it glances harmlessly off his chest plate, then turns and thrusts forward into the surprised face of the Moor, severing his windpipe. The man's dark eyes are still opened wide in surprise as he crumples forward into the dirt. Cheney urges his charger to the right, coming side by side with a Moor officer, who swings in a wide arc at Cheney's head, inches too short. Cheney kicks slightly forward and follows with a mace counter which clips the officer in the right temple. Blood and brain spray both knights. Cheney spreads his vengeance and has his way.

As he turns left to counter a pike thrust he is blinded by bright white pain as a heavy bolt violently buries itself into the back of his right shoulder. It pierces his backplate and shatters the right clavicle, steel broadpoint resting against the inside of his finely-engraved breastplate. His broadsword drops to the earth. He turns to accuse the coward who dares shoot him in the back. A Berber infantryman grabs his dead arm with both hands and yanks with all his weight. Instant, nauseating agony envelops the Breton. Two other Berbers join the game.

Cheney slides from his horse, landing with a metallic crush in the dust. His visor is still down after the fall but through the viewing slits he stares into the turbaned faces of three Berber warriors, his good arm pinned under him. "Damn you, coward infidels!" The Berber crouches as if to tend to the wounded knight. Cheney feels the biting point wiggle its way into his armpit, then gasps as he feels it slide between his ribs and into his chest, helpless to resist. His blue eyes widen in disbelieving shock, and then the world begins to grow dim, followed by a slow exhale.

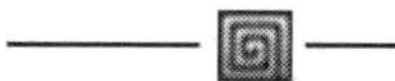

Chandon's awkward attempt at flight after the first volley of bolts leaves him bruised, breathless and dirt-crammed, but otherwise only stunned. He tests his joints and is satisfied. Rising, he turns back to see his cherished Ajax in death quivers. "Damn." Chandon's sword is point down in the earth four paces away, still swaying back and forth. One strong pull retrieves it. He makes his way to his dead charger and locates his mace, then turns to face the enemy. He surveys the mayhem. Maybe sixty of his mounted knights remain. "Bloody hell!" He immediately deduces the chain of events, knowing full well that his force risks annihilation and must fight for its life. He moves to the battle line.

The Moor crossbowman sees his approach, cocks his bow and hastily takes aim as the distance between the two men closes rapidly, but his hasty release causes the bolt to fly harmlessly past Chandon's head. The Moor crouches and is mid-cock as Chandon reaches him. The broadsword separates his turbaned head from his body just as he looks up and appreciates the peril of a poor aim. Chandon moves on, easily fending off several pike thrusts with his broadsword, then dispatching the bearers. A bolt from a small infantry crossbow hits him mid-chest with a sharp slap, denting the plate but not penetrating. He buries his mace into the skull of a kneeling crossbowman.

As the Moors become aware of Chandon's presence, and skill, the infantry back away to let him pass. They do not confront him directly, but instead gather into a group of four, then eight, then twelve, and slide behind to surround him. Daggers and pikes are made ready. Weighed down by his plate he knows he doesn't have the speed to slip away. He turns full circle and counts the wolves.

He bangs his sword hilt against his chest plate. "Where is your honor? Fight me! Fight me, cowards!" Only a menacing silence is returned, but the circle tightens.

Chandon turns to his left as a horseman thunders up, then readies himself to receive a javelin thrust. Instead, the Moor commander halts his mount just outside the circle of wolves and gracefully slides from his saddle, his broadsword drawn. The wolves part. The man utters a few short guttural words and waves his left hand dismissively. The Berber infantry back away, still in a circle, but larger now.

In thickly accented Castilian, the Moor says, “Infidel Christian knight. I, Prince Hasan al-Nisawi of Granada, challenge you.”

Chandon reaches up and unbuckles his helmet, tosses it to the side. He unlocks the four leather grips joining his chest and back plates and lets them fall to the ground. The armor on his shoulders and arms are next. Finally, he slips off his lobster gloves. “I accept your challenge, Prince al-Nisawi of Granada.”

Al-Nisawi reaches his hand out to the infantryman to his left and accepts a dagger, which he pitches to Chandon’s feet, then reaches under his robe and draws his own jeweled needle dagger with his left hand and steps forward confidently. Chandon drops his mace and picks up the dagger.

“Tell me your name, Christian, before you die.”

“I am William Chandon, sir, knight of Brittany. May the better man prevail.”

The battle is winding down, partly from sheer exhaustion, partly from the depleted ranks on both sides. The battlefield is a confusion of sound, bright metallic clangs, snorts from tired, angry horses, the growing chorus of moans from dying men, the sharp dinks as small bolts strike armor, piercing screams, ugly curses. The dust is thick, choking.

Two Breton knights see the death duel unfolding and urge their stallions forward to try and assist Chandon. One, then the other, are bolted to the earth, quick as a double lightning strike.

The Moor and the Christian both step forward two paces and ready themselves. Chandon’s broadsword is angled up and in across his body, dagger in his left hand, but gripped backward and pointed inward, flat to his arm. The Moor suddenly swings, level with the ground and with surprising speed and power, taking Chandon off guard. He deflects the brunt of the sword blow but it still grazes the thin plate covering his hip, producing a sharp, bright flash of pain. The Moor simultaneously whips his dagger, but Chandon is able to step backward with his right foot to avoid the thrust.

Al-Nisawi slashes again from the left but this time Chandon is ready. He turns and stabs forward at the Moor’s gut, but is himself blocked by a vertical parry. They circle slowly, silent, eyes locked, panting, looking for any opening. Thrust, parry; swing, parry; pivot; lunge, thrust; retreat. Back and forth they strike and dodge, thrust and counterthrust, charge and retreat, an entertaining lesson in swordsmanship if the stakes were not so high. The crisp ping of sword-against-sword rings out repeatedly. Four times the men engage then break apart, then six, then eight, then ten. Both knights are clearly tiring.

Oddly, Chandon allows his sword point to dip lazily toward the ground to his left, seeming to recklessly expose himself, perhaps from exhaustion. Within the same motion his left hand with back-pointed dagger cocks across his chest. Al-Nisawi sees the sword droop out of position and prepares to thrust.

Chandon steps forward and punches upward with the end of his sword hilt, catching his opponent squarely under the jaw. The Moor is stunned and staggers backward. Chandon steps forward to follow him, his dagger arm now uncoiling like a striking rattler, burying itself to the hilt in the Moor's left side. Al-Nisawi's eyes are incredulous. He takes a stutter step forward. Chandon's dagger withdraws, chased by hot spurts of blood. The Moor's sword begins to waffle, then drops to the ground. He releases his dagger. Al-Nisawi's eyes search Chandon's face in vain for an explanation as he now leans forward helplessly upon the Christian. The crimson rivulet plays out, stilling the dust. The Moor's knees buckle and he collapses into the dirt, dead.

Chandon kneels down and closes the Moor's eyes. "Rest, sir, you fought well."

The Berbers are uneasy, unsure what to do. Run? Charge? Quizzical, nervous glances are exchanged. Chandon rises and readies himself for battle, raising his bloody broadsword to the sky. The Berbers back away a half step.

An ox horn sounds on the horizon, its trill familiar. One, two, three blasts. Chandon turns to the northwest, scans the valley, and sees a dust storm maybe a half mile distant. He squints. Light cavalry, maybe a hundred strong. Mercifully, Aragonese banners. The horn sounds again in triplet, louder now.

As the battlefield becomes aware of this new chorus and turns to look, shouts ring out in Arabic and are passed down the line. The Moors begin to regroup, coagulate into small bands, then larger ones, then begin to limp southward, their cavalry protecting the rear-guard.

The Bretons disengage and allow the Moors to walk away. Swords and mace are lowered. Visors are first lifted and then helmets ripped off and dropped, revealing wet, matted hair and bright red faces. A deep weariness settles upon them, causing their shoulders to droop, eyes to tear up. Some turn and sleepwalk aimlessly around the body and horse strewn field, searching in vain for friends, bending down to lend a comforting word to the mortally wounded. They must pick their steps carefully to avoid the scores of dead and dying. At final count, ninety-seven Bretons and sixty-four Moors pass from this world on the fields of Jaén.

The stink is already settling low to the blood-drenched ground, almost visible in its hateful oppression. The vultures circle with growing impatience, now a dozen strong.

The sun sinks behind the distant crag, mercifully burying the awful carnage of the day. Shades of breathtaking pink spill magically halfway across the cirrus-canopied sky, nature's biting irony to all the unnatural death unleashed. Sight lines shorten and darkness slinks in, stilling the countryside. A cool, refreshing breeze blows in from the northeast. Just south of the castle, five hundred feet below, campfires become visible. Tens then hundreds dot the landscape for a half mile east to west. Faint outlines of Moor knights are visible to the trained eye, mirages almost, as they cook their meals and begin to settle in for the night.

The castle bustles now with hasty preparations for siege. Angry shouts ring out, commands are barked, soldiers jog from place to place, carts are hastily rolled back and forth with supplies, swords grate and scrape on a stone grinding wheel, golden sparks flying high and wide. Spears are racked by the dozen, quivers of arrows placed on the ramparts, cauldrons of tar lugged to the toothed towers above the metal-encrusted gates. Pitch fires are lit. Anxious horses shake their heads angrily as they are hobbled.

As evening deepens, Chandon is drawn to the quiet, pulled forth almost against his will. With a black felt cloak slung over his riding trousers and white shirt, he leaves by the west gate and makes his way to the end of the castle mount, as far away from the massive cross as he can get. His limp is noticeable, his movements tentative. The silence seems to steady him, breathing energy back into his weary bones. A flat boulder at the edge of the cliff calls his name, an excellent vantage point overlooking the fire-dotted valley. Chandon winces as he sits, then stares out into space.

It is darker now and the brilliant stars begin to peek tentatively through widening, slivered breaks in the clouds. Perseus slowly drifts into view high above. The great warrior stands tall and proud as he contemplates the scene, finally resting his eyes upon Chandon. The great warrior's face softens.

He lowers his bloody sword then lays down his hideous prize of asps. He reclines and settles into a cross-legged posture, chin resting in both palms, his downward gaze fixed upon the Breton. The great warrior is mesmerized by the strange sight set before him, the rich possibilities etching an amused expression into the lines of his bronzed face.

Moments pass. Chandon inhales a deep breath, holds it, then permits himself a long emptying exhale. Then another. A third. After five minutes, his head bows forward as if in prayer. His shoulders begin to shake, at first gently, then harder. Drops speckle the warm gray stone then fade. Chandon sniffs, rubs his sleeve across one eye and then the other. He whispers, "Forgive me, my friends. Forgive me." He takes a final deep breath, exhales his remorse, then gingerly rises, begins limping back to Castillo de Santa Catalina.

A hint of a smile eases onto Perseus's face. The cloud cover tightens and the great warrior vanishes.

## Translations

That same evening, forty miles to the south. She sits on a pillow at her low-slung desk, one leg tucked beneath her, the other outstretched, her olive-toned leg a perfect contrast to her flowing white cotton robe. Her left elbow rests on the wood, her finger absently twirling the chestnut hair that curls loosely in ringlets down to the small of her back. Before her lies a splayed, leather-bound translation of Rumi's poetry, the elegant Arabic cursive all swirls and dots and lines. Several candles and an ornate silver oil lamp light the pages.

Her right index finger betrays the object of her attention, all her energy focused on unlocking the riddle before her. She reads, then re-reads the poem, her finger sliding right to left across the page in lock-step with the Sufi poet. She licks her lips and then tests it aloud, softly intoning the gentle rhythms of the Arabic. She squints her emerald eyes, a portrait of concentration. She picks up her reed pen and methodically dips it into the ink pot, then scribbles on a piece of parchment.

Two commentaries also lie open. She checks the book to her right, absorbs for a moment, then returns to Rumi. She reads the poem once more, finger in tow, then absently lifts her head, tilts it slightly to the left, staring into space. Her face magically blossoms, pursed lips to half grin to white teeth, transforming her from attractive to beautiful to stunning. All in the span of three seconds; then gone. She returns to the page and its next waiting puzzle, supremely satisfied.

An hour later she looks up from her book and rubs the fatigue from her eyes. She rolls her head from side to side to loosen her stiff neck, Y's into a taut, feline stretch and yawns loudly. She looks over her shoulder. "Baba (*Father*), I am going down to the courtyard to enjoy the stars for a few moments."

Her father looks up from his book, struggles for a moment to remember where he is, absentmindedly nods his approval, then dives back into his treatise without a word, allowing himself to be happily swallowed whole by the vellum leviathan.

She exits the stairs to their suite, steps out into the courtyard, stopping in front of the shimmering black pool. She closes her eyes as she takes in a deep breath of the cool night air, holds it for a luxurious moment, then exhales. She tilts her head back to drink in the stars. The sky is alive with brilliant pulsing diamonds, the spill of milk brushed across the heavens from horizon to horizon. She smiles at the simplicity of the beauty cast above her. One by one she locates her friends and bids them cheerful welcome; Orion, Cassiopeia, Perseus, Hydra, Hercules, Gemini, Vega, Andromeda, Ursa Major then Minor.

She locates Polaris then looks to the northern horizon where Granada's army fights. Virgo shifts her stance. Confident she is unseen, she bends and lays down her sheaves of wheat. Virgo's expression is one of amusement, joined perhaps by a slight twinge of mischief, but as she continues to study the young woman a knowing smile eases onto her face, followed by a slight affirmative nod of her head.

As her quarry's eyes track back to the south, Virgo quickly grabs her sheaves and freezes into place, a statue of diamonds once more.

## Feathers

Two hours before sunrise Chandon jerks awake, startled. He swings his feet and sits up, cursing the biting pain in his left hip. His joints are stiff, leaden. Uncertain of what has him so uneasy, he draws in a deep breath, holds it, then listens. Nothing. He concentrates. Still nothing. But he can't shake the vague, unsettled feeling. Something isn't right. He tries to decide whether to lie back down.

Frustrated and tired, he sighs and reaches over to the oil lamp on the table next to his cot. The dim blue flame grows taller and yellows, the thin black soot line squiggling upward. The room brightens. He glances at his armor piled on the floor, still blood spattered. His broadsword and mace lean in the corner. A turbaned phantasm violently intrudes into his mind's eye. His head sags with the recollection, then he recovers and shakes the ghost away.

He cups his ears, inhales, and listens once more. Nothing. Then he hears it. A faint metallic ping. Then another. A third. Hushed voices, followed by an abrupt silence. An abbreviated shout, then rustling. He is instantly alert. Slippered feet pad down the hallway past his door. He barely hears the unintelligible whispers as they pass, but slowly, the awful recognition dawns – Moors are in the castle!

No time for armor. He jumps up, grabs his broadsword and mace, opens the door, steps into the hallway and looks left toward the keep. No one. Chandon turns right just as two white-turbaned Berbers, dark eyes flashing and daggers drawn, race round the corner and freeze, three feet in front of him. Before they slide completely to a stop Chandon's broadsword thrusts forward into the throat of one Berber, while simultaneously his mace swings wide, crushing the skull of the other. Both Africans crumple to the stone floor. Chandon waits, weapons ready, but no one else appears.

He turns and sprints towards the castle keep, twenty paces down the hallway. He slows as the tunnel caverns out, his eyes scanning the scene. To his left, sentries by the main entrance are scattered haphazardly on the ground, blood pooling. A cord of slaughtered knights are crumpled round the fireplace, shocked expressions still on their faces. They are flanked by fifteen, maybe twenty, Berbers holding leveled crossbows, half at mid-cock. To his right, ten paces away, Moor infantry are erupting from the stairs leading down to the dungeon. Their heart shields are up and their broadswords are ready for battle.

Chandon screams, "Moors in the castle! Moors in the castle!"

Eyes snap in his direction. A few seconds later a hammered alarm bell begins to sound in the courtyard. Shouts ring out and the garrison jumps to life. Dozens of feet scramble this way and that. White-eyed horses begin to neigh and rear. A second, then a third bell begins to clang. Santa Catalina awakens violently in the darkness to mayhem.

Chandon strides forward to the stairs hoping to plug the leak, broadsword and mace rising for the kill. His first broadsword cut strikes downward over the Moor's heart shield, catching the unlucky man between his helmet and shoulder, cleaving through the leather neck guard deep into his trunk, unleashing a geyser. The crush of the studded mace shatters the second Moor's shield and on the second swing catches a Moor full in the face, his features disappearing into red pulp. As Chandon raises his broadsword for his next kill a steel-tipped bolt strikes his left shoulder, snapping the collarbone and burying itself to its feathers. A second thrumps itself deep into the soft flesh of his left thigh. A blinding white light, then the world begins to spin as it grays, the noise of the fight first oddly muffled then mute. Chandon crashes backward, hitting his head on the stone floor, his broadsword and mace clattering.

An hour later it is over, just as the first rays of dawn are breaking over the castle mount. Scattered throughout the keep among the dead, Christian knights sit huddled in small groups, whispering furiously, Berber infantry guarding them with crossbows. Chandon lays where he fell by the dungeon stairs. His shirt and pants are blood drenched, but the pool six inches to either side of his thigh has mercifully not continued to widen, the artery narrowly missed.

A Moor entourage enters the keep from the courtyard. Heads swivel and gape. In the lead is a tall, tanned Moor, his striking blue turban framing his wide, dark brown mustache. He is middle-aged and leathery, battle hardened. He wears a full length white robe and fine leather riding boots. His Granadine broadsword hangs from a tooled leather sash. This man is imposing, almost certainly Nasrid royalty. He halts in the middle of the room, hands on his hips, absorbing the scene before him. He is clearly pleased.

Two Berbers drag Rodrigo forward, face down, and drop him in front of the Moor prince. His face is bruised, his nose broken.

Blood trickles from his scalp down his cheek. His legs are too wobbly to stand.

Rodrigo raises up on his arms and looks upward. "By what treachery have you captured my castle, Moor heathen?"

The prince offers a thin smile and then says in flawless Castilian, "Your castle?" He laughs. "Muslim sweat built this castle, Christian. You are an unwelcome guest. For two hundred years this castle was Granadine. When Fernando stole it from us, we laid our trap. Far under the keep, at the back of the dungeon, we sealed the entrance to the limestone caves that lead to the base of the castle mount. We were free to enter in the dead of night, to reclaim our birthright. The castle gates were breeched from the inside, Christian. Santa Catalina is no more, the garrison forfeit. Behold Muslim Jaén." He spreads his arms wide.

"I curse the day the prophet Muhammad was born. Damn him and damn you, Moor coward!"

The Moor's face darkens. With lightning speed he draws his broadsword, steps forward and before Rodrigo has a chance to blink, the two-handed swing cleaves the knight's head from his body. It rolls several feet, finally coming to a stop, his dead eyes still open, searching the ceiling for clues. Rodrigo's limp body slumps to the stone, blood spreading into a slick, widening circle.

"You must learn some manners, Christian. Blasphemy is a capital offense in Granada." He bends down, wipes the bloody broadsword on Rodrigo's shirt.

Chandon groans. He attempts to rise, then falls back flat, helpless.

The Granadine prince turns, walks to Chandon, looks down and narrows his eyes, resting his sword point on Chandon's chest. "Who are you, knight?"

Chandon senses his peril and focuses. "Sir William Chandon of Brittany, victor of Auray."

The Moor's eyes widen. "So... the great Chandon. I know of you." He studies the Christian. "Foolish to fight beside Enrique and Aragon. He will lose. My six hundred rode with Pedro to victory at Nájera, Chandon. You and your cavalry stood firm at the flank while the French and Castilian cowards ran. I did not expect to find you in Jaén."

The Moor considers Chandon in silence, then says, "I am Prince Farqad al-Bistami of Granada, Military Vice-Vizier to Sultan Muhammad, may Allah praise his name." He pauses. "It appears from the battlefield that my new tactics of horsed crossbowmen met with your approval, Chandon. I perfected it after Nájera." A grim smile eases onto the Moor's face.

A Moor knight draws close and whispers into the prince's ear. Al-Bistami locks onto Chandon, eyes smoldering, hate filled. "You killed my nephew, Christian."

Nephew? Chandon's haze clears. "Your nephew fought bravely, Prince."

Al-Bistami brushes the feathers on the end of the shoulder bolt with his sword point.

Chandon winces, then yelps. His eyes harden. "Your nephew challenged me. It was a fair fight by the code of chivalry. I prevailed. Do not dishonor his name or his valor."

Al-Bistami looks to his left for confirmation. A quick nod gives the answer. He returns his broadsword to its scabbard. "May Allah welcome my nephew's soul into paradise." Al-Bistami turns to his officers and says, "How long before Jaén is ours?"

"Within the hour, my Lord. Our troops are already at the city gates, which stand open."

"Good. Secure the city. Tomorrow we send two thousand cavalry to capture Baeza and Úbeda. Those two jewels will soon be returned to their rightful owners."

"What about the garrison, my Lord?"

"Any knight that wishes to stand ransom goes to the dungeon for safe keeping. Treat them well. Contact a representative of the *Order of Merced* to arrange the details. One thousand silver pieces per landed knight, two hundred for mercenaries. No bargaining. Knights and infantry without ransom, squires and attendants, go back to Granada." A rueful smile. "The Sultan needs slaves for his building projects. Execute any that resist or cannot make the journey. The horses are forfeit." He hesitates. "And saw down that cursed cross."

"What of Chandon, my Lord?"

Al-Bistami turns and considers Chandon. "Will he live?"

"He has lost much blood, my Lord, and the bolts will surely bring infection. Unlikely."

"Send for Salamun the Jew; he will know what to do."

"Yes, my Lord."

"Chandon will be sent to Granada as prisoner of war. No ransom. If we can keep him from dying he will be the first English knight to enter the Alhambra. A fine prize for our Sultan." The Moor turns and strides up the stairs and into the courtyard.

# Conclave

The Sultan's meeting with the Mexuar Council was more subdued than usual, his speech strictly informational about recent events within the kingdom, including a quick summary of their victory at Jaén. By design he treads carefully, steps around contentious doctrinal issues, steering clear of all legal matters of *Sharia law*[2], inevitable sources of controversy.

At the departure of the Sultan and his entourage of *viziers*, the meeting does not end, but instead the *imams* and *qadi* of the Mexuar Council engage in their predictable parsing of the Sultan's words, the discourse sustained and tense. At times during the conversation tempers flare as heated disagreements over the Sultan's choice of a particular word or a facet of a particular event step center-stage. Sometimes, less frequently, the room is unified, punctuated only by silent collective head nods and approving whispers. Always, however, there is an underlying tension in the room, as the Mexuar Council is divided between a fundamentalist Muslim Berber agenda and a more tolerant and liberal Nasrid Muslim agenda, an incessant and bitter tug-of-war between North African Berbers and the Arabs of al-Andalus.

As the drone mercifully begins to wane, the Mexuar Council, thirty-five in all, starts to drift out of the ancient, uncomfortably tight space to return to their mosques and offices around the palace complex and within the city of Granada. Fifteen minutes later all that remains are the empty floor pillows of the Council, arrayed in tight concentric circles by rank about the Grand Imam's station.

Soon only three men remain, each on different circles, heads bowed low as if in prayer. The room stills, sounds fade, then only silence.

After several minutes, two of the men rise from their pillows near the back of the room and make their way to the Council's inner circle, seat themselves in front of their senior and bow their heads once more. The silence stretches.

Without looking up, the senior Berber imam begins at a whisper that reaches no further than their intimate conclave. "The game is afoot, brothers. Our quest to recruit a member of the

2 A glossary of Muslim/Arabic terms is included in the back matter.

Sultan's Vizier Council to our cause is finally complete. We now have the means to bring about the Sultan's demise. The Alhambra will soon be ours."

The two others do not look up, but their smiles grow wide as they begin to nod their heads approvingly.

The man to the right of the senior imam says, "Excellent, Master. Who is the traitor?"

The senior imam remains silent as he considers the request. "One who is well-placed to do our bidding."

More silence.

"How will he betray the Sultan?"

The senior imam looks up, makes eye contact with the other two men. "All will be known in due time, brothers. Patience. For now we must wait as our plot is set in motion. Soon Granada will assume its rightful place as a part of the Marinid Empire, and the reign of the blasphemous Nasrid Arabs will be at an end. Praise be to Allah."

The two respond, "Praise be to Allah."

"Bless his Holy and Merciful Name."

"Bless his Holy and Merciful Name."

## Razor's Edge

Chandon awakens in a billowy cloud to hushed voices and the crisp, scraping sound of a blade being drawn across a whetstone, first one side then the other. The world is out of focus. His pupils take seconds and a firm command to sharpen. Despite his best effort he cannot raise his head from the pillow. He turns to the left, eyes now absorbing. White linen tent. The cloth inhales, then exhales, then stands limp as the wind blows. It repeats in the opposite order a moment later. A black cauldron simmers on a small fire in the corner, white vapors dancing playfully above it. The blade on the whetstone is impossible to ignore. Odd herbal smells fill the tent. He lowers his chin and looks down the length of his body, bone white and naked except for a small cotton loin cloth, sees the notch of the feathered bolt emerging from his thigh, remembers. He tries to touch his shoulder, but discovers that both arms are strapped down tight.

An old man comes into view. He approaches the cauldron, crushes a handful of leaves into it, mutters something, then stirs the pot. The man turns then walks to the side of the table where Chandon lays, intentionally standing in easy eye-shot so he can be seen. He wears a long, flowing blue robe. A shoulder length shock of white hair, a full white beard, kind, teary eyes. Wizardly.

The old man unexpectedly smiles and says in flawless Castilian, "I am Salamun, Royal Physician of the Granadine court. You, Young Knight, lie at death's gate. I am commanded to bring you back to the land of the living. You have lost much blood and your shoulder bone is broken. Thankfully cleanly. But these two bolts will kill you unless they are removed quickly and disinfected properly. I have bathed you and strapped you down tight so you cannot move. Now our work begins."

The old man turns and grabs a flask from the table, pours a measured amount into a beaker, then comes forward and lifts Chandon's head. "Drink this." Burning oily awfulness slides down Chandon's throat. He gags, but swallows, coughs, then groans. Salamun smiles. "Good. Spotted Corobane elixir. A poison. Sufficiently diluted, it will only paralyze your limbs and put you into a deep sleep for a day or two." Chandon's eyes widen with alarm. "Trust me, Young Knight. Before you stands a Jew who has lived a long and prosperous life as Royal Physician to the Sultan and his family." The wizard chuckles.

Salamun walks out of sight to a side table and then to the fire, now holding a surgical blade in his hand. He eases it over the flame, flipping it side to side. The wizard turns and comes close to Chandon, bends down, then whispers, "You will live, Young Knight, you will live." Three attendants, young boys, approach and stand ready to assist. One holds a stack of fresh linen towels, another a wooden tray with assorted medical instruments; clamps, saws, knives and threaded steel splinters. The third holds two jars of liquid, one light red, the other deep burnished gold.

Salamun's face grows fuzzy and the room dims. Weakly, Chandon says, "Thank you, Salamun. I place my life willingly into your hands." His eyelids flutter, then close.

Salamun smiles. "Let us begin the healing, boys, yes?" The Jew first drapes linens over the leg, then carefully dabs the gold liquid around the ugly wound. He grips the blade firmly, touches it to Chandon's skin, then slides it outward from the bolt, the flesh neatly parting. Chandon lies motionless, moaning in his poisoned sleep.

The two-wheeled cart rattles and shakes, pulled by a pack horse along the dusty road. The horse walks slowly, deliberately. A turbaned man rests in the saddle, reins loosely held in his left hand, his head down, daydreaming. The patient lies on pillows and is covered with a thin blanket. He is strapped down so he will not jostle about.

The caravan stretches back half a mile. First, blue Granadine banners, then a double line of cavalry, then a hundred pack horses loaded with food, gear and booty. Next come two dozen carts with the wounded, Berber infantry, then eighty riderless chargers roped together and herded. Immediately behind the testy stallions, the two hundred shackled prisoners sleepwalk, flanked on either side by mounted Moor knights. A double line of cavalry brings up the rear. The mass ambles southward. Granada.

One wheel of the errant cart rolls up onto a skull-sized stone, rises, hesitates, then abruptly drops, shaking the cart violently. The driver's head snaps up, startled. He whoas his mount, pivots in the saddle, sees the rock, then scans his luggage. Satisfied, he faces forward again and with two quick cheek sucks the horse begins to lumber ahead. Within a minute the man's head begins to sag again.

Chandon's eyes flutter open during the earthquake, struggle to focus. Disoriented, he rolls his head to the right. Nothing but endless olive groves. His eyelids begin to droop, then struggle open, then close for good as the cart moves on.

Chandon has been lifted out of the cart and brought to Salamun's tent on a stretcher and placed on a table. Miraculously, the patient has slept through the transfer. The young assistant holds the oil lamp close, lengthens the yellow flame. Salamun removes the blanket and begins his examination. He carefully cuts the shoulder bandage and folds it back. A felt brace wraps under both armpits and is cinched tight behind him, forcing his shoulders to arch backward to hold the collarbone in place.

The wizard studies the wound from several angles, then picks up a needle from the tray beside him and teases some of the sutures. He seems satisfied. "The bone has set well. The sutures are tight. Some swelling, but nothing serious. And the bleeding has finally stopped. Good." The wizard turns to his young assistant. "Disinfect the wound again and change his bandage."

He moves down and studies the leg. A dull, dark red-brown ring on the white linen cloth marks the entry wound. The Jew seems puzzled. He leans close and sniffs, causing his bushy white eyebrows furl, timed to his frown. He grasps the ankle and rolls the leg outward, examining the inside of Chandon's thigh. He motions for the lamp to be brought closer. A faint red streak runs from bandage to ankle. The wizard looks worried. He unwraps the bandage and stares intently at the ugly wound. The sutured flesh is painted angry red upon a pale white background. The wound is puffy and leaks thin reddish-yellow fluid. Salamun presses his finger around the wound, testing it. Yellow pus oozes between the sutures. He continues to examine the wound. He notes no darkness under the skin beyond the immediate wound, an encouraging sign. But the unnatural sweet smell, though faint, is unmistakable now.

The wizard sighs. "Infection has set in. I must have missed a piece of trouser driven in by the bolt. Alfonso, come, we must operate. Find Johan and Diego. Light the fire and prepare my surgical tools. Fill the cauldron. We must be quick if he is going to live. Strap him down tightly so he cannot move. I dare not risk more Corobane, so please bring the leather bite strap so he does not chew his tongue off." The old Jew reaches down and shakes Chandon awake.

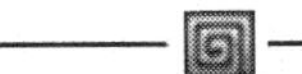

"Young Knight, you must drink this." Salamun eases his hand under Chandon's neck, lifts his head. Chandon's eyes are open but unfocused. He tentatively sips the warm herbal brew, testing it. He grimaces, then slurps a heavy dose. A third time, then a fourth. Salamun lowers Chandon's head back to the pillow and says, "Good. Good."

Chandon moans, his face hot with fever, his body sweat-drenched. He drifts back into fitful sleep.

"Alfonso, wake him every two hours and make sure he drinks this. No less than four sips. His leg bandage must be changed four times a day, and keep a cool wet cloth on his head during the night. If anything changes send for me at once."

"Yes, Master." The boy looks up and meets Salamun's eyes. "Will he live, Master?"

The old Jew carefully considers his answer. "Unclear." A pregnant silence passes. "Perhaps. The next two days will be critical."

The boy sits at the table in the corner of the tent under the dim hue cast by the oil-lamp, on watch until sunrise. He tries unsuccessfully to concentrate on the leather bound book that is splayed open, glancing up at the patient from time to time.

Chandon remains strapped down, a light sheet covering him. His thick blond hair is matted wet, and his cheeks are bright red. He jerks his head from side to side trying to escape some pursuer. He moans softly, then louder. He whimpers as if tormented. A moment later he mumbles something frantically. His fists tighten into balls, then he shouts, "Sosanna, no. Sosanna! NOOOO!" His eyes fly open, blind, his face filled with anguish. He lifts his head, tries to rise, then drops back, his eyes already closed. He whispers a phrase in some foreign language. A moment of peace and then the silence is broken, and it begins all over again.

The boy marks his page then closes the book, rises, sinks a linen cloth into the bucket of cool water, squeezes it, then wipes Chandon's face. He walks to the entrance, turns the flap and searches for the coming gray, then yawns.

A day later, mid-morning, the caravan is passed by a half mile long, double line of cavalry under blue banner, riding hard to the north, shrouded in a choking dust cloud. The rolling thunder barely registers to Chandon. His eyes flutter but do not open. He stirs, groans, but cannot break the plane of consciousness.

Shrill, rapid-fire whistles wake Chandon. Seductions march effortlessly up and down tonal scales, frantic to turn a feminine head. Lovesick birdsong. He opens his eyes. The fever has broken. He breathes in the cool morning air. Too weak to move, his head is pinned to the pillow. He searches for some piece of information to anchor himself.

The terrain has changed, the olive trees vanished. Earth tones have been replaced by lush greens. The caravan eases through the dense foliage, angling downward along the crease between two rolling hills. Squat, dark green trees are encased in five-starred white blossoms. Honey bees buzz about, flitting from flower to flower. The floral, citrusy perfume lies heavy on the air. Intoxicating. The cart ride is smoother now, more comfortable. Irrigation channels wind their way through the trees, the damp earth within betraying day-old floodwaters. The ground in the orchard is covered in thick, lush grass, a bovine paradise.

The cart emerges from the orchard into an open field, the scene widening dramatically. He sees pale-green spring wheat six inches tall stretching into the distance, then rows and rows of grape vines, followed by more orchards. Recognition slowly dawns. Chandon has heard of the famed *Vega de Granada*, the fruit, vegetable and bread basket of the Moor kingdom. The Vega is vast, the most fertile lands in Europe.

Clots of farmers are scattered about the fields, lazily pulling earth into irrigation dams, weeding with their spades, spreading manure, harvesting. As they become aware of the entourage, heads rise to gape. Some wave in welcome, then return to their work without an acknowledgment. At the eastern horizon, snow-capped mountains gaze down upon the verdant scene.

The cart path cuts through the northern edge of the Vega, angling southeastward toward Granada's Fajalauza Gate. As the caravan closes on the city walls, riders emerge, offer their welcome, then begin to chat with the lead officers. Commands are passed back. The Breton horses are herded off to waiting paddocks to be sorted and branded. They will soon understand Arabic.

Massive blue banners fly over the gate. Dozens of sentries stare down at the prisoners as they pass into the city. Two hundred pairs of anxious Christian eyes dart back and forth, tentative, unsure what to expect next. They whisper furiously to each other, shutter. Once inside, the train splits and begins to disperse in different directions, prisoners escorted down one street, Moor cavalry ambling down another, infantry a third. Four riders from the front column circle back to flank Chandon's cart, which alone takes a left fork.

The narrow street tunnels through shuttered, cream-colored, two-story stucco buildings. Windows overlook the street, their eaves lined with boxes crammed with red geraniums. Fancy curved ironwork covers the street level windows. Bougainvillea clings to the stucco, neon pinks billowing towards the roof line. Engraved iron plates mark the names of the rich merchants who live within.

The tunnel opens into a plaza, densely populated and bursting with activity. Market stalls rim the edges, joined by tethered goats, caged chickens, carts filled with vegetable displays. There is a public water source, a communal oven. Thin, light-colored smoke rises, dispersing into the gentle breeze. Heads turn to glimpse the cart's treasure, but seem disappointed and return to their busyness.

Chandon hears the unmistakable glee of children at play. Moving bright laughter, shouts, teasing. Six young boys become aware of the cart, approach warily from the back, curiosity getting the better of them. Chandon sees them now. They come close to the side of the cart, grow silent as they stare, then erupt in furious whispers, chased by giggles. Their game ends when they are shooed away by a knight sporting a gruff guttural scold.

The street enters another row of buildings then finally emerges at a stream. The horses clop over the wooden bridge, then once across, the street widens and splits. They take the left fork and begin winding their way uphill.

Chandon's eyes scan the high ridge above him as it comes into view. The land rises steeply just east of the stream. Heavily treed at the base, the top is bare. The fortress is impressive by any measure. Rectangular, white-washed stone defensive towers of different sizes and shapes rise at intervals along the thirty-foot high stone and brick walls that stretch around out of view. It finally occurs to Chandon. The Alhambra, the legendary fortress-palace of Granada, Royal Court of Muhammad V, Sultan of Granada, ruler of al-Andalus. A confused combination of fascination and dread sweeps over him.

Chandon lies paralyzed on his pillow, tracking the white walls at the southwestern end of the fortress as he rises up the slow paved incline. He wants to see the blossoming panorama of the city spreading out behind him. He tries unsuccessfully to roll his head to the left, finally gives up. Sentries stroll on the walls above him. The cart passes through a large, arched ceremonial stone gate and continues its upward trek. Chandon's anxiety builds.

After a short stretch, the road switches back sharply to the left, now bounded by walls, climbs some more, then opens into a courtyard in front of the Alhambra's Justice Gate, the main entry into the palace complex. He strains to look forward, winces at the pain in his shoulder, but can just see the formidable square tower overlooking the courtyard.

An unusual twenty-foot high, twelve-foot wide circular keyhole opening marks the entrance to the tower. Two sets of four elaborately dressed pikemen flank the giant keyhole, statue-like, their eyes tracking the cart's approach. A second smaller matching keyhole opening lies within the protected walls of the tower, gated shut by a studded iron-clad door.

Two dozen archers stare down on his approach. The cart rolls to a stop just outside the tower. The massive iron-clad door splits and creaks outward in slow motion. A dozen heavily-armed Moors emerge, then fan out to surround the cart. A palace officer silently inspects Chandon, then frowns. He turns and exchanges Arabic with the riders, then faces Chandon and says in accented Castilian, "Christian knight, your infidel eyes are not fit to behold the glorious Alhambra. You must be blinded." The Moor climbs up on the back of the cart, kneels down over the paralyzed knight.

Chandon's eyes whiten with panic as he tries in vain to recoil. The Moor pulls a length of black cloth from his sash and drapes it over the prisoner's head. Chandon can only offer a weary exhale in response. The Moor steps back off, turns and leads the cart into the tower. The four escorts turn back. The gate squeaks shut, followed by loud mechanical clanks of the braces and locks being fitted back into place behind him.

The play of horseshoes across smooth stone follows the cart as it turns hard right and angles up the incline. Muffled whispers echo from the stone walls into Chandon's darkness.

## The Floating Tower

The two ambassadors from the Marinid Royal Court in Fez stand alone in the Alhambra's Courtyard of the Mexuar, in the heart of the Comares Palace. Their eyes absorb the scene as they both slowly pivot in opposite directions, gathering impressions in the silence. Their forced solitude is calculated, meant to intimidate. They have been waiting twenty minutes already after being deposited by a courtier. The midday sun beats down upon their turbaned heads and beads of sweat dot their foreheads. The courtyard is absent of divans or pillows to recline upon, adding to their discomfort.

Before them, resting just above the floor in a recessed hexagonal cutout, is a circular, fluted white marble fountain five feet in diameter, a dramatic focal point in the polished-marble tiled room, magically bubbling life-giving water above its gleaming surface. Where does the water come from? Where does it go? Fountains are rare in Fez, the African desert stingy with its most precious resource. Such an opulent liquid display speaks at a primal level to a desert people's psyche.

The high walls of the palace mute nearly all sounds, insisting on tranquility. The soft bubbling of the fountain holds center stage, echoing pleasingly off the walls. Outside the palace, diffuse activity can just be discerned. Light hammering starts then stops then starts again, draped sporadically with sparse laughter, an occasional neigh. The air is fragrant. A heavy spicy aroma betrays myrtles somewhere close by, but the spice is intriguingly interlaced with an ethereal citrus hint.

The courtyard itself is compact, perhaps thirty-feet square, and open-roofed. Smooth, white-washed stucco walls on the eastern and western sides stretch two stories high, meeting the dark wood roof line which extends out over the edge of the courtyard. Dozens of tapestries hang to the floor, famed Granadine silk, decorated in extraordinary detail with arabesque shapes and patterns punctuated by beautiful cursive Arabic script. The cool silk tapestries, alternating in blue and white, then red and gold, produce a soothing visual effect. In the four corners of the courtyard stand chest-high Granadine ceramic vases, vertically winged and lavishly glazed, decorated with scenes of leaping gazelles. They are perfectly balanced to rest on their narrow circular bases. Spirea stems littered with white blooms emerge from the vases' throats, an exquisite statement of elegance.

On the north side of the courtyard a single step up leads to a carved stucco portico formed from a triplet of suspended Granadine horseshoe arches. Three doors lead into a darkened second room. Two small windows in the shaded room serve as a spectacular mirador, an impeccably placed viewing port that overlooks the expanse of the city. Bright-colored ceramic inlays, blues, greens, reds, and yellows, grace the low reaches of the walls, with intricate stucco carvings set above. The effect invites entry.

One ambassador says to the other, "Shall we enjoy the view?" His companion nods. They are about to pass through the central arch when the courtier emerges from the shadows. They are left wondering if the interruption was timed. It was.

"Excellencies, the Sultan is ready to receive you." He lifts his hand, palm up, indicating the opposite direction.

The two ambassadors follow the courtier, turn left, step upward, then left again, then right, upward once more, traversing the defensive maze, finally stepping through a doorway into another sun-sculpted enclosed courtyard. They halt, betraying their careful training, and stare, mouths agape.

"The Courtyard of the Myrtles, Excellencies."

This courtyard is unlike any these well-traveled Africans have ever seen. A rectangular pool of shimmering crystal-clear water lies before them, forty-feet wide by one-hundred-twenty feet long. This liquid opulence is staggering, confounding to the visitors. Before them is enough water to slake the thirst of a small desert city.

Dozens of fluorescent orange fish amble lazily in threes and fours, mouths ovaled into syncopating flares, a heated aquatic conversation caught mid-sentence. Sunken in so that their tops are at pool level is a hedge of precisely cropped spice-myrtle, running north-south on either side of the pool the full length of the courtyard. From each of the four corners of the courtyard rises a single orange tree in full blossom, white stars thick on the dark green canopy. The collusion of myrtle and orange birth the magical perfume wafting over the palace grounds.

As the ambassadors continue to marvel, the courtier holds his position, arms at his side, facing the pool, clearly a practiced posture for this location.

"Remarkable," both ambassadors utter simultaneously. The barest hint of a smile forms on the courtier's face.

The courtyard is ringed by a two-story building, white-walled with earth-toned trim, terra-cotta tiled ceramic roofing, keyhole doors puncturing the smooth lower walls at irregular intervals. Several lead upstairs. Small, latticed keyhole windows ring the second story on the north and south sides and running columned arches top the east building. There are matching circular marble fountains inset at each end of the massive pool, each spilling a trickle of water down a narrow trough and into the waiting ocean, barely rustling its mirror sheen. The dribbles produce an uncanny dream-like shimmer to the reflections of the buildings in the water.

The ambassadors pivot left to see mirror-images of the tall whitewashed stone tower, one rising skyward into the deep blue, the other pointing earthward, a gently undulating copy. Fascinating visual effect. The tower is square at its base, climbing to four stories to assert its will over the courtyard. This is the largest tower in the Alhambra by far.

After giving the ambassadors just enough time to be sufficiently awed, the courtier turns and indicates their goal. "The Hall of the Ambassadors, Excellencies. Please."

The façade in front of the tower contains a central keyhole doorway fifteen-feet tall and eight-feet wide, with three suspended arches in perfect symmetry to either side. Dense white stucco ornamentation raised above a colorful, polychrome background floats over the arches. Near the top, nestled among the arabesque carvings, they read an endless repetition of the famous Granadine motto, "The Only Victor is Allah," in elegant, sweeping Arabic calligraphy.

The pool edges to the entrance of the façade, only a finger-width lower than the marble floor leading into the palace, giving the uncanny sense that the tower magically floats on the cool, clear water.

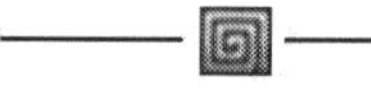

The courtier's words intrude on her solitude, breaking her concentration. She tenders a frustrated sigh, then, curiosity getting the better of her, she kneels, rests one hand on her desk and leans forward far enough to look down into the courtyard. Her chestnut curls touch the polished wood. She brings her face close to the screen, her brilliant emerald eyes scanning. To her right, the courtier and the two ambassadors are now approaching the entrance to the Hall of the Ambassadors. They wear fine yellow and white linen robes stenciled with gold lace, and crimson turbans. She instantly makes the connection - Marinid ambassadors from Fez. As the men disappear into the palace, she reclines back onto her pillow, considering. Satisfied, she executes an arched-back, double-armed stretch, bookended by a deep exhale. A mischievous half-cocked smile forms, lighting her Arabian beauty. Another moment of leisure, then she returns to her Sufi poetry.

Two palace guards flank the entrance to the tower. They are dressed in pure white robes, a single bright red sash tied about their waists. Ornate Granadine broadswords hang from leather straps around their shoulders and jeweled daggers are slipped under their sashes. They have dark mustaches but no beards, long dark hair, their expressions vacant but somehow menacing.

The ambassadors stop to remove their leather sandals in imitation of the courtier, their eyes twisting upward to steal an admiring glance of the carved stucco and intricately painted wooden ceiling above them. They then step through the central archway and into the tower.

As the two transition from the bright sunlight of the courtyard to the dim interior of the tower, their eyes struggle to adjust, producing a temporary blindness which scaffolds their unease. The courtier stops, another precise calculation. As their vision improves, their eyes are drawn to small, carved marble niches on either side of the palace entry way. Ornate carved stucco frames the niche openings, then spreads out into a seamless maze covering the walls of the hall.

Within each niche rests a flared translucent alabaster bowl eighteen inches in diameter, filled with water so precisely that the surface tension causes it to bulge over the top of the knife-edge rim. Seven iridescent bougainvillea blossoms float on its surface. A dipped finger would spill the flotilla. The diffuse, angled light of the room charges the parchment-thin alabaster with a faint pink hue. Bounding each niche is another burst of Arabic calligraphy.

The courtier steps forward into the main hall and stops again. The ambassadors follow, halting one step behind him. He indulges the visitors with a feast for their eyes, the miracle that awaits. It becomes obvious now that the four stories of the tower is in fact hollow, a six-hundred year culmination of Muslim mastery over the art of grandeur through careful combinations of architecture and ornamentation. This is the Alhambra's legendary Hall of the

Ambassadors, throne room of the Granadine Sultan. Their hearts begin to race.

Towering candelabras command the four corners of the hall, their hundreds of flickering yellow flames casting unexpected shadows, breathing life into the inanimate stucco, the carvings shimmering and dancing, playfully hinting at imprisoned secrets. Calligraphy leaps out from the walls, poems of praise and announcement ready for the worthy to absorb and contemplate. The hall seems conceived as an immense book of poetry, its hidden contents to be teased out rhyme by rhyme.

The smooth floor is covered with inlaid tiles of a single theme, intricate blues interlaced and woven around the golden Granadine dynastic shield, ad infinitum. Vivid blues, greens, yellows, and reds interlock to form the dado tilework linking the floors to the stucco carvings of the walls.

Arched windows are perched high above, five per side set in careful symmetry, They are latticed, permitting only a meek offering of diffuse light from above. Repeating scrolls of calligraphy run above and below the windows, circling the room.

The carved walls somehow direct the viewer upward into the tower's hidden dome, an enormous, square-mouthed wooden ceiling suspended in a single piece over the entire hall, recessing upwards toward a single point high above. Closer examination shows that the dome is an enormous marquetry, thousands of brightly painted, hand-carved cedarwood pieces, individually inlaid upon an ebony background. There are repetitions of seven different types of large starburst patterns draped across the glowing wooden sky, a faceted central red orb at the dome's apex marking the center of the universe. The Seven Heavens of Islam. Traversing diagonals hint at the Quran's Four Trees of Life. The ceiling is a stunning combination of religious symbolism and woodcraft.

The ambassadors' eyes trail back to earth, then forward into the three key-holed archways in front of them across the hall. Behind each arch is a small mirador above enormous backlit panels of inlaid stained glass, the small translucent tiles woven about a central starburst into a pixilated calculus of color. Yellows and greens at the top, blending to reds and blues and purples at the bottom. The color menagerie unleashes a rainbow across the floor all the way to the entrance steps, the illusory origin of the colors disorienting to the entering visitor. Another calculation.

In front of the central archway is a low-slung white divan atop a large, decorated crimson Persian rug. Despite their squints, the intense sparkle and shine of the colored glass blinds the ambassadors from this angle, making it impossible for them to discern more than a reclining human form. Several persons stand behind the divan, two sit on large pillows to the left of the couch, one to the right. The ambassadors's disorientation is intended, and perfectly executed.

After two full minutes of intimidating silence, in a loud voice of formal announcement, the courtier intones, "Honored ambassadors from the Marinid Royal Court in Fez." He pauses for effect, then begins discernibly louder, "His Royal Highness, Muhammad V, son of Yusef, ruler of al-Andalus, eighth Sultan of Granada, builder of the Alhambra, elder of the Nasrid clan, defender of the faith. May Allah bless and protect his reign." The echo frantically chases the incantation around the tower for an additional second, then gives up, the room again silent. Both of the courtier's arms rise, hands palm up, indicating the central archway. After a moment, he backs into the shadows and disappears.

The ambassadors move forward, their mouths parched.

## Our God

The cart stops again, Arabic is exchanged, then moves forward. Chandon's head rattles side to side as the cart's wooden wheels bite into the groves of the pavement, and the makeshift blindfold begins to slide from his face. First a hard right then a left as the road rises through the defensive tower maze. They pass through a second inner gate. The black cloth finally sags enough to grant him a cyclopsian window on the world.

The cart breaks into bright sun, constricting Chandon's pupil. The scene broadens, the fortress wall retreating as an open plaza lined by a collection of two-story, white-washed buildings comes into view. Beyond, to the north, a white tower rises, the tallest building in sight. A cadre of pikemen march to an Arabic cadence from an unseen officer near the wall to the left. Off-duty palace guards linger about in knots, casually talking. As the cart moves forward it is quickly outpaced by the rumors of its cargo. One by one the soldiers tiptoe and contort to glimpse the strange prize. The nudge of an elbow, a raised brow, a quick halt of words mid-sentence. Heads turn in unison, curious, as they mark the English knight's passage. Conversations soon resume, the tempo now more lively, flushed in gossip.

The cart circles to the right then passes through one then another high-arched ornamental gate into the building-lined *medina* of the Alhambra, the fortress unexpectedly transformed into a bustling town rife with commerce, chock-full of merchants, artisans and slaves busying about, the only hint of the fortress the distant tower-laden walls to the north and the south.

Despite his determination to absorb the alien surroundings, Chandon's energy wanes. His eyelid begins to droop, then closes, is willed back open, then closes for good. The gossipy murmurs chase him into a fitful sleep as the cart moves deeper into the medina.

A cool breeze taunts the limp white gauze tied loosely at the edges of the window beside Chandon's bed, tickling the curtain into the room, playfully retreating back into the courtyard, then moving forward again, an invisible game of tag. His eyes open, his much needed rest interrupted by a rhythmic sound he cannot immediately place. He sees that dawn approaches, the world outside his window just coming visible, but locked still in grays and muted tones.

A crisp, pearly tinkle announces a small fountain just out of view to the left. Beds of unknown flowers border the narrow path that bisects the courtyard outside his window, then right-angles in the center to east and west, forming a gravel cross in the peristyle garden. There are interspersed shrubs, several miniature palm trees, a single fragrant orange tree tucked into the far right corner. Wisteria tendrils strangle the support columns of the tiled roof portico circling the courtyard, the thick drape of grape clusters breathing their heady purple perfume into the room. There is no activity in the courtyard, the building is fast asleep.

Chandon focuses on the faint otherworldly soundscape. He listens. A man's nasal intonations dance around the room, the strung-together chorus alternating between lengthy, sustained notes and undulating rhythmic trills. The sound is expansive, then compact and more urgent, then expansive again. The intonation is purposeful, determined. The voice is distant, but penetrating, a defined presence within the courtyard. Definitely a song. But nothing like anything he has ever heard. The sustained notes are too lengthy, however, for easy identification of any demarcation of words. The lovely melody halts, hesitates just long enough to make Chandon wonder if it is over, then begins again with a new sequence of tonal undulations interwoven with sustained notes.

After several moments the song stops once more, followed by a pregnant hesitation, then begins anew, more urgently. The resonance of the singer's voice is pleasing, even to Chandon's uninitiated ears. Clearly an artist at work. But the song is tinged somehow with a faint melancholy rimming its contemplative tone. A lament perhaps? Or a remembrance? There is certainly a suggested message, but of what?

The performance ends, the last note lingering in the air for seconds, the reverberation binding together with the growing color of the quiet sunrise.

A short while later he drifts off, begins to dream of a long-forgotten world of bright sunshine and lush, emerald-green pastures. He gallops his childhood pony, Blue, fast as the wind. He smiles in his sleep, his arms twitching with the reins, his eyes dancing beneath closed lids.

Chandon's eyes open to the blue-robed wizard. "Good afternoon, Young Knight." The wizard offers a welcoming smile.

He searches for a name, then whispers, "Salamun."

"You have slept two full days since arriving at the Alhambra. Terrible fever after your surgery. You have tested my healing skills, Young Knight." The smile broadens. "How do you feel?"

"Very weak. My shoulder aches and my toes tingle."

"To be expected. Patience, Young Knight, patience. You are lucky to be alive."

"Where am I?"

"Ahhh... the Sultan's Royal Hospital, inside the medina of the Alhambra. A town within a fortress within a city. Never before has a Christian knight been treated here. You are a guest of Sultan Muhammad. He desires your healing and it shall be so. Your personal physician awaits your every call." Salamun offers a playful, exaggerated bow.

"How long since Jáen?"

Salamun purses his lips and scratches his head, thinking. "Six days since you were captured. No, seven."

"I remember almost nothing between then and now."

"Not uncommon, especially with fever."

The silence stretches, then Chandon says, "Thank you, Salamun, for saving my life."

The wizard beams. "Here, let us have a look at those wounds, Young Knight." He pulls down the blanket and with his scissors cuts the leg bandage off, begins to carefully poke around the wound. Angry red around the incisions, but the sutures look clean, flesh already rejoining flesh. No pus is visible, and the swelling has eased some. He tests the wound with his finger, gently pressing in several strategic places. Chandon flinches each time.

Next, he reaches down and tickles the bottom of Chandon's foot, the instant toe-curl betraying proper nerve function. "You will have a nice scar, Young Knight." The old Jew chuckles, pleased. "Your leg looks much better. You will walk again."

"Salumun?"

He looks up. "Yes, Young Knight?"

"You are a Jew. How is it that you live peacefully among the Moors, even favored at court? In both England and Brittany, Jews are forced to live..." He struggles for the right word, then says, "apart."

For the first time a serious expression settles onto Salamun's face, curls into a half-frown. "You mean in walled slums, yes? As outcasts. I have talked to Jews from all over Europe, Young Knight. So needless. Not so in Granada. In my own case, my family's roots worm deep into Granada's storied history. We trace our heritage, and my family name, to Samuel ibn Naghrela, Samuel HaNagid to Jews, a renowned scholar of Muslim Córdoba; writer, warrior, poet, statesman. Quite the man." The frown departs as suddenly as it came. "He became Grand Vizier to the Almoravid Sultan of Granada. Alas, that was over three hundred years ago."

Salamun muses in silence then shakes off his uncharacteristic seriousness and grins. "Of course, I also happen to be the best physician in all of al-Andalus, which helps me sustain my position at court." He chuckles then lapses back towards serious. "Under fundamentalist Almohad rule, life for Jews became more difficult and we did then what we Jews have always done, melt into the earth, disappear. But the Arab Nasrids are far more tolerant, enlightened even. A great many Jews now live in Granada. Some of us have free reign at court. And we worship in peace. Jews are valued for our knowledge, and our differences are respected.

"You see, we Jews are *dhimmi*, people of the book. Our Torah and Hebrew scriptures are sacred in Islam. As is your Bible. The Quran, the holy book of Muslims, insists that we be treated well; demands it in fact."

"Are there Christians in Granada?"

Salamun sighs. "Only slaves. It was not always so, Young Knight. Christians, too, are dhimmi. Alas, as reconquista has played out, a Christian presence here has become increasingly difficult. First they were only taxed, grudgingly allowed to stay provided they were discreet in their worship and did not try to convert Muslims.

Later, however, they were forcibly driven out, largely in response to Christian atrocities of *mudéjars*, Muslims living in conquered lands to the north. An eye for an eye. A sad state of affairs, yes? Still, there are opportunities, even for slaves. My three young assistants, Alfonso, Johan and Diego, were brought in childhood to Granada as Christian slaves. They are now learning the medical arts and have bright futures ahead of them. Fine boys."

Salamun begins to examine Chandon's shoulder. He works in silence as he removes the bandage, prods, runs his finger across the knot forming around the broken bone. He seems satisfied. "Your shoulder is healing well, and the bone is already knitting. We should be able to remove that brace in a few more days."

The comfortable silence lengthens.

"I heard a strange song this morning, Salamun. Perhaps in my dreams, though it seemed real."

"When?"

"At sunrise."

"Ahhh... you heard the *adhan*, the Muslim call to prayer. By Islamic law, all Muslims must pray five times each day. It is one of the five pillars of their faith. A *muezzin*, the caller, climbs a tower next to the mosque and sings in glory to our God to announce prayer time. It is lovely, yes? You will soon get used to it, and I dare say, come to enjoy the way it marks the day."

"Our God?"

"Yes, Young Knight, our God. The God of my people, the God of Abraham; and the God of your people, the God of Jesus; and Allah, the God of the Prophet Muhammad – one and the same. Yes, our God. Muslims hold Jesus in great esteem, you know, as they do the Jewish prophets. As I said, we are both dhimmi."

Chandon seems lost in thought. He whispers, "The song was beautiful."

The wizard's eyes twinkle. "There are many things you once knew, were certain of even, that will require careful reconsideration, Young Knight. Granada is a most unusual land."

Salamun is done. "Good. You are healing nicely, Young Knight. I will have Alfonso come by later and put fresh bandages on. But let the wounds breathe for a few hours first. You must drink my secret herbal brew to speed your healing. Four times a day, no less. Unpleasant, but effective. And you must eat to build your strength back. You will find Granada's foods a marvel. I will stop by to see you each day, but for now, rest and eat, eat and rest." He wags his finger playfully. "Within a few days I want you up and walking on that leg." He offers a parting smile.

"Thank you, Salamun."

An exaggerated bow, followed by a hearty chuckle, then he is gone.

## A Mince of Words

The two ambassadors are self-conscious as they cross the hall and the alcove comes into focus. The Sultan reclines on a wide, solid white divan, gold-embroidered silk pillows arrayed behind him. He is dressed in flowing colored silks and linens, no turban or crown. His nut brown hair is shoulder length, his mustache precisely trimmed, a cropped, sculpted beard. A handsome man, his Arab lineage is unmistakable. He is much younger than they would have guessed, perhaps in his late twenties. Behind the couch stand four Royal Bodyguards, solid red robes with a single golden sash, no turbans. They are imposing and heavily armed. Oddly, their faces are pale, clearly not Arab or African; two redheads, two blonds. Northern Europeans.

The Sultan's elite personal bodyguard are former Christian slaves groomed from childhood within the protective confines of the palace. Rare northern European Muslims, impervious to African or Arab infiltration, immune to the political wiles of the realm, their loyalty to the Royal Family is beyond question. They are the most feared warriors of the kingdom, known even to the Christian armies. A papal death warrant dogs their every step, the recantation of their Christian birthright beyond redemption to the purveyors of reconquista. As a result, there is no possible ransom for these men in battle; they fight to the death. Their vacant gazes are locked on the ambassadors as they track their movements, their hands resting on their broadsword hilts. Their apparent passivity is an illusion. They are ready to strike in a fraction of a second in response to a misplaced step, a sudden move, an insult.

To the right of the Sultan sits a much older man on a large white pillow. He is dressed in fine white robes, no turban, grayed hair and cropped beard. The Grand Vizier, supreme counselor to the Sultan. To the Grand Vizier's right is a much younger man, perhaps in his mid-thirties, dressed identically. Both Arab, both unarmed. To the left of the Sultan sits a third counselor, middle-aged, leathery, armed with a crescent-mooned Granadine broadsword and jeweled dagger. He wears tan robes, a blue turban, and is clearly a knight of the court.

The ambassadors stop five paces in front of the Sultan. They raise both forearms, palms up, bow as a single unit, then rise. The more senior ambassador speaks with a silky lilt, "Your Highness. We bring greetings from his Excellency Abu Faris Abd al-Aziz ibn Ali, son of Abu al-Hasan ibn Uthman, Sultan of the Marinid Empire. I trust you have received the Sultan's gift?"

"Indeed, Ambassadors. A fine dagger." The solid gold scabbard lies beside him on the couch. Expertly tooled with arabesque ornamentation, the scabbard is encrusted with rubies and emeralds and other precious stones and has a solid silver handle laced with a spider web of calligraphy. Exquisite; a work of art. "Please convey my thanks to the Sultan, and wish him well on the first anniversary of his reign." The Sultan indicates the two pillows in front of his couch. "Please." The ambassadors step forward and sit, folding their legs in front of them. They rest their cupped palms in their laps.

The Sultan lifts his hand to his right. "May I present my Grand Vizier, Lisan al-Din ibn al-Khatib; prolific author, poet, historian, philosopher, physician, and... occasional politician." The Sultan offers a wry smile. "Polymath of the realm, knower of all things knowable." His smile warms. The ambassadors nod in tandem in Ibn al-Khatib's direction.

Ibn al-Khatib is known from Fez to Baghdad, one of the most formidable intellects in the civilized world. "To his right is Ibn Zamrak, poet of the Royal Court and the Grand Vizier's protégé. He is now my personal secretary. Zamrak's many poems adorn the walls of the palace. And his recitals are sublime." Another double nod response. He lifts his hand to his left. "Prince Bashir al-Waziri, my Military Vizier." A final pair of nods complete the introductions.

"Your Highness, we must complement you on the grandeur of the Alhambra. Your courtyards whisper many wonders and your poetry is exquisite. The sacred water is a fitting tribute to the wealth and prosperity of your kingdom."

"I am pleased, Ambassadors, that you have enjoyed your visit. We are indeed blessed by Allah's great abundance. Perhaps on your next visit you will have time to see my latest and most spectacular creation, the Palace of the Lions."

Their eyes widen, followed by a few moments of silence before their business commences.

"Your Highness, the Sultan has learned of King Pedro of Castile's victory over Enrique of Trastámara at Nájera. We also understand that Granada has successfully invaded Aragon, reclaiming Jáen, Baeza and Údeba for the Muslim realm. The Sultan wanted us to convey his congratulations on your victory." The man holds for a response but receives none. He continues, "It seems that the balance of power in the Christian kingdoms is shifting." He hesitates before he continues, "Sultan al-Aziz desires to renew the alliance between the Marinid Empire and the Kingdom of Granada, so that we might join forces and together better serve the needs of Islam."

The Sultan considers the man's words. His face is expressionless. "You may tell Sultan al-Aziz that Granada would welcome a renewal of our alliance. I will have my Grand Vizier draw up the necessary documents."

The ambassadors are pleased.

"If I might, Your Highness?" The Sultan nods. "There was a disturbing...rumor...heard in Fez recently, that Granada sent troops to fight beside the Christians at Nájera." The ambassador slithers along. "I am certain this was no more than Christian propaganda, Your Highness... but the Sultan was curious to know if you had heard such a rumor?" His words trail off into silence.

The Sultan's eyes narrow. "The 'rumor' is accurate, Ambassador. I sent six hundred cavalry to support King Pedro. I was honoring our commitment to Castile as vassal state. King Pedro is a friend of Granada. His triumph over Aragon and its papal backers is essential to our sustained well-being."

The ambassador licks his lips. "But, Your Highness... Muslims fighting beside Christians? It is forbidden by Sharia law."

"I would not expect the political subtleties of al-Andalus to be immediately obvious to those in Fez. Loyalty, Ambassadors, plays a crucial role in ruling a kingdom in these changing times."

The silence stretches out, grows more tense.

"There was another rumor, Your Highness, that an English Christian knight, a certain Sir William Chandon, of Brittany, was captured at Jáen and brought to the Alhambra. The Sultan is curious as to why?"

The Sultan's expression hardens. "Funny how word travels so fast, Ambassadors. Already across the Strait of Gibraltar before even I hear of it." He lets them absorb the implications of his words. "I was told only yesterday of a Christian knight in the Alhambra. He was sent as booty by my commander after the victory at Jáen. Alas, grievously wounded. My physician tells me that he will not survive the week." The Sultan offers a tight-lipped smile.

"Ahhh... Sultan al-Aziz will be saddened to hear of the knight's perilous condition, Your Highness." The man pauses to lick his lips once more. "I am sure he would welcome the opportunity to send a fitting tribute to his funeral, if Your Highness would be so kind as to advise Fez of his passing."

The Sultan's expression turns steely, then grim. "With pleasure, Ambassadors." He hesitates, deliberately raising the tension in the room. "I am afraid that urgent matters of state await me. I wish you both safe journey. Pirates have been especially troublesome near Algeciras of late. Do take care."

The abrupt dismissal takes the ambassadors off guard. Their eyebrows betray their surprise, a six day journey terminated after ten minutes. They turn to each other to steal a quick glance, exchange silent words to discern a course of action. Both men rise, bow, back away ten paces, then turn and walk from the hall, the courtier mysteriously appearing at the entrance from some secret doorway to accompany them. The ambassadors step back into the sunlight and are gone.

No one has moved, the room suddenly much tenser. The Sultan waves his right hand in a circle to dismiss his bodyguards, who slip from the room. "Rumors, always rumors. Bashir, I want the source of these leaks found and dealt with once and for all. I cannot govern if Fez is aware of every move I make."

"Yes, Sire, it will be done."

He turns to his right with a frown. "Lisan al-Din, remind me why I would want a Christian knight in my palace?"

Al-Waziri offers, "Sire, I can ensure that the Christian does not recover from his wounds. A simple matter."

Ibn al-Khatib sighs. "Sire, Chandon is valuable to us. He is one of the most famous knights in Europe, known and respected by all. By fighting for Aragon, he represents one of Pedro's most dangerous enemies. By holding him here, he is effectively removed from the war, a taken pawn cast to the side. Pedro will be in our debt."

Ibn al-Khatib muses for a moment. "Chandon also affords us the opportunity to learn the ways and language of the English. Pedro is now allied with Edward the Black Prince of England, Sire. Prince al-Bistami tells me that without Edward, Pedro would not have won at Nájera. The English hate the Pope and will fight to keep France and the papal army out of Spain. Though they do not yet know it, the English are our allies.

"If we tread carefully we may yet be able to secure southern Aragon for ourselves when the fighting ends, expanding Granada northward, adding land, more ports. We can finally break the will of the Christian reconquista, Sire, perhaps forever. We have already reclaimed Jáen, Baeza and Úbeda. They must be held at all costs. Pedro thinks that we invaded Aragon to open a second front for Castile. Let him believe this. In actuality, however, it is only the first step in our own *jihad,* Sire, securing a future of hope for Granada and her peoples."

The Sultan absorbs this information. "I assume he does not speak Arabic?"

"No, Sire."

"Does he speak Castilian?"

"Yes, Sire. They say he is quite intelligent. Well-educated."

"Does he know anything of the faith?"

"No, Sire, only the standard Christian propaganda." The Sultan frowns. "Fez will be nervous as long as we hold Chandon, Sire, fearful that it will pull us closer to Pedro and away from them. They are not fools. They fear that Granada will somehow manage to inherit Aragon for itself when Pedro wins the Civil War, cementing a permanent Castilian-Granadine alliance. Chandon will be an excellent bargaining chip as we renew our ties with Fez."

"Bashir?"

A heavy sigh. "I agree, Sire. The infidel could be of some use to us. I would suggest we hold him in the Alcazaba's dungeon."

Ibn al-Khatib winces, then shakes his head. "I disagree, Sire. He should be treated as an honored guest."

Al-Waziri frowns, but remains silent.

"How serious are his wounds?"

"Salamun tells me that he will live, Sire. His recovery will be slow and he will limp, perhaps forever. He will not ride any time soon or wield a sword. The man is harmless, Sire. If he is to be of use to us, he must be treated well, not punished."

Several moments of silence ensue as the Sultan weighs his options. "I agree. The Christian is to be treated as an honored guest of the Alhambra. Lisan al-Din, I am putting you personally in charge of his education. He must learn Arabic and his ignorance of the faith must end. And he must learn to bathe." They laugh. "Teach him the ways of Granada and the mysteries of the Alhambra. We must civilize this Christian, Lisan al-Din. Once he knows us and trusts us, we will use him to further the glory of Granada. He is your new student, so teach him well. Bashir, have him guarded and watch him closely."

Ibn al-Khatib looks troubled. "But, Sire, that is impossible. You know that I am working day and night to finish my encyclopedia of the medical arts. It is needed desperately in the Royal Hospital, Sire."

An exasperated, "Lisan al-Din, why is it always books?" He shakes his head side to side, then raises a finger as an idea suggests itself. "You can enlist the assistance of that daughter of yours." He muses. "Yes, Layla can teach him Arabic, and she can learn English. She will enjoy that." A mischievous grin. "And, of course, Zamrak is at your service." The young man nods.

A resigned, "Certainly, Sire." He chases this with a sustained, weary sigh, knowing full well the battle in front of him. Surely the Sultan's intended motive.

"Bashir, perhaps when the Christian has recovered we can use him to learn more of English and French battlefield tactics. But first find the spy that delivers our secrets to Fez."

"It will be done, Sire."

## Heavenly Aromas

Chandon's eyes jerk open, his sixth sense cocked and ready. It dawns on him that he is unarmed, vulnerable. He remains perfectly still, feigning sleep, his heart pounding, as he listens for any betraying sound. He can hear only faint fountain whisper from the courtyard, but he clearly discerns a presence close by. He decides to act, rolling his head to the right and training his eyes on the courtyard.

A silhouette stands frozen just outside his window, the gauze obscuring all detail. A hand reaches forward, parting the curtain. A head pokes through, the black turban completely shielding the man's face, revealing only two smoldering, ebony eyes. A killer's eyes. In heavily-accented Castilian the man says, "Infidels are unworthy of the glorious Alhambra. Your life is forfeit, Christian. Heal, and then I will have my vengeance. I will slit your throat and bathe in your blood." Before Chandon can formulate a response, the man has vanished.

"I had an interesting experience this morning."

Salamun looks up from the wound dressing and smiles. "Oh?"

"A Moor stood outside my window and swore vengeance upon me. He said he would let me first heal and then he would slit my throat and bathe in my blood."

The wizard stops fussing with the bandage and locks onto Chandon's eyes, the concern obvious. "What did he look like?"

"Black turban covering everything but his eyes. Accented Castilian. He was not joking."

"I assumed that the fact that you are here by the Sultan's edict would offer enough protection, but it appears I was mistaken. Let me see what I can find out. In the meantime, I will have Prince al-Waziri post a bodyguard outside your room day and night. The guard will be clothed in a solid white robe, bright red sash."

"I would prefer a sword, or at least a dagger."

"Not possible, Young Knight, even if you could use one, which you cannot. We must be vigilant. But have no fear, the palace guard will protect you with his life."

Chandon frowns and looks away. "I am resting easier already."

By now Chandon anticipates the call to prayer, welcomes its beauty and artistry, and can even discern words tucked unseen into the chorus. His window curtain is somehow inadvertently left tied back wide today and he continues to drink in the courtyard garden as the day slowly dies, the pleasing sights and smells beckoning. Just after the muezzin finishes, Chandon sees the door open on the room opposite his across the courtyard. A Moor in a long white robe emerges with a small rolled carpet tucked under his arm. He steps out of sight to Chandon's left and then a moment later he hears several interruptions of the steady stream of sound issuing from the fountain. Washing.

The man comes back into view, face and hair and hands wet, looks up to orient his direction then spreads the mat on the paved floor. He stands erect, then raises his hands, palms out, begins to recite something to himself. He lowers his hands, cups them in front of him at his waist, then bends over and puts his palms on his knees, his murmuring steady, only a faint whisper at this distance. He stands erect once more, then lowers himself to the mat and bends over to touch his forehead and palms to the ground. Then he raises up on his knees, lips in constant motion, then prostrates himself again. Up on his knees once more, he whispers something to his right and then to his left. After a final short recitation he rises, rolls up his mat, then returns to his room. Muslim prayer. A fascinating contrast to all that Chandon knows of prayer.

Chandon spends most of the evening wrestling with the Salamun-seed planted deep in his psyche – one God, three religions. How does Christian then justify persecution of Jew or Muslim? How does Muslim justify persecution of Christian or Jew? Simply because their rituals and traditions, their styles of worship, differ? Each religion claiming primacy, two willing to fight to the death for it. What does our God think of that? He eventually tires of the one-sided debate and drifts into an unsettled sleep. Near morning he dreams of his estate in Brittany, of Sosanna.

The patient's dietary progression over the past week has moved from thin broths to vegetable soups to hearty meat soups, and at last his first true Granadine meal awaits. The building anticipation has been rich. The tray on the table beside Chandon's bed stuffs the small room with such a cacophony of heavenly aromas that a thick slice of air could fill his belly. A large loaf of freshly baked bread slathered with butter steams seductively. A lidded clay pot cradles baked spring lamb seasoned with salt, ground cumin, aniseed, chopped mint, parsley, and rosemary, then topped with *almori*, the ubiquitous savory-sweet sunbaked seasoning made of salt, honey, raisins, pine nuts, almonds, hazel nuts and flour.

There is a plate of sliced eggplant tossed with olive oil and salt, then grilled over an open flame; a bowl of steamed purple chard with green onions and tiny whole neon-pink radishes. Dessert is a golden-crusted pie made from tart cherries and apples, drizzled with honey. Finally, a plate of dried fruits; figs, halved apricots, raisins and dates. Such bounty is unknown to Europeans, even at court.

Diego says, "I hope you enjoy your feast, my Lord." The boy smiles.

"Young sir, you are my savior!" Diego blushes then grins.

The meal begins with the deliberate two-handed placement of the bread and butter on the small serving tray on Chandon's lap. The Christian's eyes widen, a groan of joy escaping as he chews. The loaf quickly disappears. He moves to the vegetables, foods Chandon has never seen or tasted, quizzically grunting his approval.

Afterwards, Diego, in mock ceremony, lifts the lid of the clay pot to Chandon's raised eyebrows and with a devilish grin begins to cut his meat. Chandon dives in with abandon, surfaces to sip the cool drink, pomegranate juice sweetened with honey. Chandon beams his approval. Finally, he devours the pie and all of the dried fruit. Chandon marvels at his good fortune throughout the meal, stops several times to roll his eyes, groan with delight.

"My God, I feel like a new man!" He burps loudly. "Yes, indeed, a new man." Diego is all smiles.

The palace guard standing just outside the door remains expressionless.

## Only Love Can Explain Love

9 June 1367. "I refuse, Baba!" Her hands are on her hips, her piercing emerald eyes furious. It is uncanny how sharp anger painted on the face of a beautiful woman inevitably makes her that much more alluring; if dangerous. "And you cannot force me to!"

Ibn al-Khatib sighs and shakes his head, weary of the fight. "Layla, Layla. As I said, this was not my idea; it was the Sultan's. And it was not offered as a choice." He swallows. "He is still upset at your refusal to join the Royal Harem, you know. That was no casual honor you scorned. Only the most beautiful, the most well-bred and worthy are chosen."

"I will not be a concubine, Baba, or a palace decoration, or even the Sultan's wife. You have educated me far too well for that, so blame yourself. Mama would never have agreed to putting me in a cage, and you know it. I will give myself to whom I choose, when I choose!"

Ibn al-Khatib's eyes well up. "Your Mama... she would have better answers for you." He dabs his eyes with his thumb and finger, then takes a deep breath, holds it. "You inherited her strong will, and her temper, that much is certain." He sighs again. "For the record, I do not disagree with you, Daughter. But your study of Ibn al-Arabi, Rumi, and all the other Sufi masters, puts you at risk. We are secure now because I am Grand Vizier, but the Berbers grow in strength, and their pressure on the Sultan for increased orthodoxy is relentless. There are those at court that whisper their disapproval of you, Layla, and by extension me, and it grows louder and bolder each day."

"The Africans do not concern me, Baba."

"They should. These are delicate times, Layla." He pauses to hone his words, then presses on. "Our Sultan has asked Zamrak to help us educate the English knight." He looks up at his daughter and says, "Zamrak loves you, you know."

Their eyes meet. Her face is bathed in exasperation. "Baba, that subject is closed. He is your protégé; he will not be my husband."

They slip into a strained silence. With a forced resolve, he says, "Nevertheless, we must each do our duty. The Sultan commands it. Cheer up, you only have to teach him Arabic and learn English. Zamrak and I will teach him Granadine culture and the secrets of the Alhambra. He is still in the Royal Hospital. He was seriously wounded, so it will take time before he is ready for any lessons."

"Good." She pouts. "I assume he has not learned to properly bathe?"

Ibn al-Khatib chuckles. "Alas, no, he smells. But rest assured that is first on the agenda; Salamun will see to it."

"What is his name?"

"Sir William Chandon of Brittany. You will call him Sir William." He offers a wry smile as his daughter's mouth opens for a barbed retort. He tamps it down with his hands, then laughs. "Call him Chandon. He is one of the most famous English knights, you know. Fluent in Castilian and French. Smart, well-educated, they say."

"We shall see. I assume he is old and gray?"

"Ahhh... Salamun says he is young and handsome." He smiles playfully. "You may just enjoy yourself."

She skewers her father with those blazing emeralds.

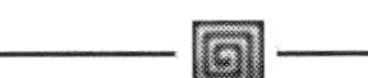

After evening prayer, the storm has mercifully passed, and the two bask in the quiet solitude of the library, as usual hard at work into the deepening night. He reclines on his divan, large writing desk balanced on his lap, books open and tossed about at odd angles in every bare spot within reach, in some places two deep. His ink pot rests precariously, large stains on the desk betraying his penchant for clumsiness. Mint tea sweetened with honey nestles on a thick book beside him, its lacy steam tendriling upward. His quill dances on the parchment as he plows through a translated Greek text on medicinal herbs, his eyes oscillating between book and parchment, a furious race against time.

She is at her window desk immersed in Rumi. The library has white-washed walls and dark trim, sparsely populated by European standards. Two low-slung desks for Layla and her father, twin divans, a small, four-legged inlaid storage cabinet, and several silk cushions scattered about on the floor for visitors. On two walls stand floor-to-ceiling book cases crammed and disorderly from overuse, a step stool lending reach when needed. A large map hangs on one wall and beside it a fine silk tapestry. Tapered candles adorn nearly every flat surface, skinny candelabras stretching high above each desk, wax carelessly dripped on the ceramic floor.

Ibn al-Khatib looks up from his notes, inviting the world back into focus. He glances over to his daughter and sets his quill down. "Tell me what you learned from our friend Rumi today."

She lifts her head then pivots, flashes that gorgeous smile. "Baba, I have been feasting on Master Rumi's *Masnavi*. What magical words!"

"Wonderful. Which book?"

"I am only in Book I. I have just finished *Only Love Can Explain Love*."

Her father's eyebrows lift, followed by a tentative, "And how did you find it?"

Several moments of careful formulation pass before she says, "Rumi seems to suggest that the love shared between man and woman can lead both to the source of all love, Allah, the lost Beloved of both male and female. Our African friends will have a field day." She smiles, then looks into space as she summons the Sufi's verse:

*"Whether love comes from earth or from heaven,*
*In the end it draws us to the Beloved."*

"I believe Rumi is correct, Baba," her confidence natural and unassuming. "The love of man for woman, and woman for man, can lead both into union with Allah. I like that thought. A new and very powerful idea."

"Indeed..." His eyes fill as he summons the image of his wife Danah's face.

"Master Rumi also says,

*"In speaking of Love, the intellect is impotent,*
*Like a donkey trapped in a bog;*
*Only love itself can explain Love,*
*Only Love can explain the destiny of lovers."*

She reflects on this a moment, still looking into space, then says, "Do not worry, Baba. When the time is right I will not turn my face away from love." She looks back at him, radiant.

"Layla, you are a most impressive young woman," his voice laden with emotion.

Silence follows, then a more serious, fatherly, tone. "I have been thinking, Layla." She looks at him, concerned now, as he continues to admire the floor. "Sufis say that it is impossible to learn the Sacred Way to the Beloved through reading alone. The Way must instead be experienced if it is to be truly understood.

For the record, Rumi agrees. Traditionally, this door is opened for the novice within a master-pupil relationship." He turns his eyes upon her. "You will be twenty next month. I believe it is time for you to study with a Sufi master, Layla. To find your own Way."

Instant eruption of excited little girl. She catches herself, straining for composure. "But, Baba, the dangers at court you spoke of..."

He exhales. "I am too old and too stubborn to bow to fundamentalist pressures. They need to read Rumi! Besides, there exists a long tradition of female Sufis. Perhaps you will be the next Rabia Basri!" He smiles as she blushes.

Her excitement returning, she says, "But, Baba, who would serve as my master?"

"I have already inquired with Mansur al-Mussib. We have known each other for many years. He is willing."

"But, Baba, he is the most famous Sufi Master in Granada. He must have many disciples already. I would only be a novice."

"Nevertheless, he said 'yes.' Some privilege comes, I suppose, with being Grand Vizier to the Sultan." He smiles at his daughter. "Mansur knows Rumi well. The translations you have been studying are his." His smile relaxes. "He reminded me, Layla, that his first goal will be to expose your weaknesses of character, that you might then better approach your own perfection. This will be your first step towards *tawhid*, mystical union with Allah. It is tawhid that Rumi refers to in what you quoted. It is what all Sufis seek. Do not expect the Way to be easy, Layla. His word will be your law."

"I understand, Baba. I will make you proud."

"You already make me proud, Daughter."

She rises from her cushion, rushes forward to smother him with a hug as he pretends to fend her off in mock annoyance. She holds his gray head in both hands and kisses his forehead. "I love you, Baba. May Allah bless your days."

"I love you too, Daughter."

"It is late and you are tired, Baba. I will have Aisha prepare your bed."

"You know I cannot sleep, Daughter. Besides, I must finish this book. The Greek herbs beckon!" He shoos her with both arms, a ritual they have repeated hundreds of times. "I have my tea, go! You need your beauty rest." The standard rejoinder. She playfully frowns, then grins, skips off to her sleeping quarters, his little girl once more. He watches her, content. He whispers, "Blessed are you, Allah, for bestowing the gift of my daughter.

May Layla find her Way to you, O Lord, by whatever path you think best."

He again conjures Danah's face to exchange gentle words of greeting and love, his eyes welling up as he relives ancient memories.

## Night

His day of reckoning at hand, Chandon is both excited and nervous.

The day before, Salamun informed him that the time had come to re-learn how to walk. "It will be painful, Young Knight, but the longer we wait the more likely you will end up with a permanent limp, and neither of us wants that, yes?"

Diego has changed his bandages, and Johan has dressed him in a long, loose-fitting white cotton robe, tied tight at his waist with a long sash. Alfonso leans a wooden crutch fitted to his height against the bed.

"My Lord, you will slip this under your right shoulder when the time comes. But use it only for balance. If you put too much weight on it you will re-injure your shoulder."

"I understand."

Salamun looks on, contemplating. "Be careful, Young Knight. If you fall we will be back to square one. Three more months in bed." He winks at Alfonso. "My young squires have refused to wait on you any more, you know, so you better get this right!" The three assistants grin in unison.

"I will be careful, Salamun." Chandon scowls playfully at the boys.

He is sitting up in bed, legs dangling off the side. He lifts the crutch in his right hand then arranges it so he can use it to lever himself up. He plants his right foot then slowly puts some weight on the good leg. He attempts to stand, dangling his bad leg above the floor. His leg muscles quiver. Erect, he eases his bad leg to the floor, winces on contact, then begins to ease some weight onto it.

"OWWWW!" He groans as he applies more weight to the leg, lips pursed, exhaling his pain. He is standing, though. He grimaces as he moves the crutch underneath his shoulder, then reaches over to caress his collarbone knot.

Salamun is across the room, the boys on three sides in case he wobbles. "Try and take a step."

He concentrates, leans on his crutch, then lifts his bad leg and slides it gingerly forward three inches. To move his good leg, he must now place all his weight on the bad leg.

He hisses through clenched teeth, "DAMN! That hurts! GRRRRR..." He moans with agony but completes the move. Once in command of his face, he exhales then smiles triumphantly. The four spectators clap their approval.

Two shaky steps later, Salamun barks, “Good. Good. CAREFUL! Better. Careful. Excellent! You will soon have the hang of this, Young Knight.”

Thirty minutes later he has moved across the room, turned and come back. Chandon is panting from the exertion, sweat dripping onto the floor.

Salamun nods his approval. “Enough for one day. You have done well, Young Knight.” He wags his finger. “Five round trips tomorrow. You will be strolling with a cane by Friday.” He hesitates, then suddenly serious, says, “Now, for some very important news.”

Chandon looks up, interested.

“Ready?”

Chandon raises his eyebrows.

“You stink!” The three boys erupt hysterically. The wizard doubles over with laughter, hands on his knees, unable to catch his breath.

Chandon blushes, missing the humor. “It has been some time since I have bathed, Salamun. As you well know, I have had a few minor distractions of late.”

The wizard sobers up. “Indeed, indeed. Yes, well, you are in for a treat. Muslims have perfected the art of bathing, you know. And nowhere is this done better than in the Alhambra. So you shall learn to bathe as a Muslim bathes. Trust me, Young Knight, you will be thanking me for your great fortune. Life will never be the same. Besides, it will also loosen your muscles and speed your healing. Come, squires, bring the stretcher, our Young Knight will enjoy the baths this morning!”

Chandon has been separated from his robe and loin cloth in the anteroom of the Muslim bath, the *hammam*, then carried by two muscular bath attendants into the warm room where he is lowered onto a stool on the marble floor.

A most unusual room. Columned horseshoe arches line the square room. The domed ceiling high overhead has a clutch of eight-pointed stars cut into it, roof openings that allow small filtered beams of daylight in through blood-red glass, lending the otherwise unlit room a eerie twilight hue. Salamun sits down on a stool across the room and watches, clearly amused. The light from above is diffuse enough that it is difficult to recognize Salamun a mere ten feet away, a subtle discreetness Chandon welcomes.

The temperature here is noticeably warmer than the anteroom, a mid-summer's day. He begins to perspire. The attendants retreat then return with two large pitchers of warm water that are poured over the patient, one after the other, the torrent completely soaking him. This is repeated. Chandon sputters as he wipes the water from his eyes, then slicks his hair back.

Salamun speaks Arabic to his mute attendants, and they pause to examine his leg and shoulder, aware now of his wounds and the special care required. The attendants commence scrubbing his body with soaped rough-textured mitts, beginning at his toes and ending at his neck, tender around his injuries. A soap-sud sculpture. The attendants are anything but gentle, kneading his muscles as they climb. While not especially modest, Chandon is unaccustomed to having his private parts scrubbed by another man. He looks up at Salamun with alarm, embarrassed.

Salamun laughs. "Relax, Young Knight, relax. Welcome to the Arab baths! Never fear, these bath attendants are sworn to secrecy on all matters of size." The wizard slaps his leg as he roars. Salamun begins performing his own washing, following a similar path. "When you are healed, you will do this yourself."

After they reach his neck, Chandon is rinsed, and then a special perfumed soap is applied to his hair and beard, lathered by hand until his head is shrouded in a thick white foam turban, then he is rinsed again thoroughly.

Chandon is now lifted and carried into the hot room, the steam knotted and thick. Condensation plops noisily from the ceiling, faux rain. He is set down on another bench at the edge of a heated cistern. The steam clasps the sunbeams mid-air, the dozen angled columns of light linking ceiling to floor. Salamun walks on thick-wood sandals to preserve his soles from the fires below, and again sits across from Chandon and basks in the heated steam. Salamun issues a loud, "Ahhh...paradise."

The two bath attendants dip their pitchers into the steaming cistern, then pour them over Chandon. The fiery water produces a gasp and a wince, but somehow the temperature is precisely balanced to be both temporarily painful yet also deliciously comfortable after only a moment of acclimation. His atrophied legs tingle and come alive, his shoulder ache evaporates. The soothing heat works its way deep into his muscles, healing all ills. The attendants repeat the process three more times. Chandon closes his eyes, content.

"Salamun, you may be on to something here." Chandon basks.

After about fifteen minutes, the attendants carry him into the next room, another dim, star-domed vault, but this one cool and comfortable, an early spring day. Salamun follows a pace behind. Pitchers of cool water are poured over Chandon, the profound contrast taking his breath away, then making perfect sense.

"The cool water will close your pores, Young Knight, a very important step in a hammam. If you were well, you would have the option of a massage now, a real treat. Soon." The wizard beams.

After about five minutes the attendants retrieve their patient, dry him off, restore a clean loin cloth, sash a new robe around him, then deposit him on a pillowed divan in the next room, similar in makeup and temperature, minus the water. Salamun sits on an adjacent divan. Both men are brought sweet mint tea to sip.

After a few moments of comfortable silence, Chandon says, "Salamun, how is it that such baths are unknown in England or France?"

"Ahhh...thermal baths like you just experienced are actually a Roman invention, Young Knight. Essential to civilized Roman life. For cleanliness, certainly, but also for socializing, politics, entertaining even. After the collapse of the empire the baths were associated by Christians with all things evil. Sadly, they were lost to history. The Arabs, however, were enamored with the baths. They adopted them wholeheartedly and brought them to the far corners of their kingdoms. Do not forget that Arabs are a desert people, Young Knight. Water holds a special significance for them, its life-giving nature burned deeply into their souls."

He continues, "Part of the importance of the baths in Arab culture also has to do with the role of ablution required in Muslim prayer, a ritual cleansing with water. *Ghusl* in Arabic. Before prayer a Muslim must at very minimum wash himself or herself; hands, hair, feet, face. This is called the minor ablution. *Wudu*. You will see a water source just for this purpose outside all mosques." Chandon nods his head.

"But Ghusl is a cleansing of the body and the soul. It is required by Muslim law after being in some general state of unworthiness. Fighting in a battle, for instance. One bathes to remove all stains, all barriers between the worshipper and Allah. Not unlike baptism for you Christians. Truthfully, the Arab baths are so pleasurable that most Muslims bathe daily regardless." He grins. "So do I. Very civilized, yes? There are four public baths in the Alhambra alone, dozens more that are private. This one is the biggest in the medina. The Royal Bath between the Comares

Palace and the Palace of the Lions is the finest in all of al-Andalus. Diplomacy is conducted there. Strategic planning, affairs of state."

"Have you ever bathed there?"

Salamun sighs. "Alas, no, I have never been invited. Some things remain off limits to Jews, even those favored at court." He smiles. "Perhaps someday we will go together, yes?"

Chandon nods, then turns pensive. "Salamun?"

"Yes, Young Knight."

"Are women allowed to bathe here?"

He chuckles. "Of course. Though not while men are here. In the public baths in the medina, men may bathe in the morning, women in the afternoon. It varies, but never together." He grins. "For obvious reasons."

As they both finish their tea in silence, the level of relaxation is palpable.

"Salamun?"

"Yes, Young Knight." The Jew looks up, smiles.

They lock eyes. "Thank you." The Jew nods, pleased. After an awkward hesitation, Chandon says, "Would it be possible to shave off this beard of mine? I normally keep myself clean-shaven."

"Ahhh...certainly." His hand moves instinctively to his own long gray beard. He raises his hand and the attendant draws close. The Jew whispers in his ear and the attendant responds with a curt nod.

"Consider it done. The barber will arrive momentarily. Do not worry, Young Knight, his blade is long and sharp, but he is very careful." The old Jew laughs and laughs.

Two days later, the pair traverses the courtyard of the hospital at a snail's pace, one with a crutch, limping hard, the other with arms clasped behind his back. They talk of all subjects, endlessly. Chandon's bodyguard follows a discreet distance behind, eyes scanning for trouble.

Chandon inquires about Salamun's family. The old Jew was married for thirty-two years. Sadly, his wife passed four years back from consumption. They had two children, a boy and a girl, both grown, with their own families now. His daughter is in Granada, the wife of a silversmith. His son is in Málaga, a rabbi, a source of obvious pride. He dotes on his five grandchildren.

The wizard returns the favor. "How about you, Young Knight? A handsome young man like you must have many beautiful women to choose from."

Suddenly serious, Chandon sighs, then says, "I was in love, once, Salamun, though never married." He falls silent. "A tragic story, I am afraid. I will tell you about it someday." He is clearly uncomfortable.

The old Jew is wise enough to know when to change the subject, and they move on to agriculture in the Vega, irrigation techniques, fertilizers, crop rotation. Chandon takes an active role in the running of his own farm in Brittany and thus has more than a casual interest in how Granada and its Vega manages to produce such abundance. He is continually shocked by the primitive nature of his own farming techniques, his ignorance.

During a comfortable moment of silence, Salamun says, "You are to have new teachers, Young Knight."

Chandon looks up. "You are teacher enough for me, Salamun." He smiles.

"Nevertheless, you will soon be under the favored tutelage of the Grand Vizier to our Sultan, Lisan al-Din ibn al-Khatib. A great man. He is learned and wise. We have known each other for many years. And also his protégé, Ibn Zamrak, the palace poet."

Chandon's eyebrows raise. "Indeed."

"Good men. You will like them."

He exhales his discomfort. "When?"

"In a few weeks. When you are sufficiently healed."

Salamun has an awkward expression on his face, as if he has more to say.

Chandon grins. "Yes, Wizard?"

"There is to be a third tutor. Ibn al-Khatib's daughter. She will teach you Arabic. You are to teach her English."

"Really? A woman?" Chandon gives the old Jew a dubious look.

"She is no ordinary woman, Young Knight. Bright as her father, educated by him. But I must warn you, she has...opinions...and a temper." He grins. "And then there is her beauty."

Chandon offers a quizzical look.

The wizard continues, "Most unusual green eyes. Huge, brilliant emeralds. They say she is the most beautiful woman in Granada."

Chandon grins. "And you, what do you say?"

Salamun offers only a coy smile. "She is beautiful, no doubt of that. But I am an old man, what do I know? All young women are beautiful to me!" He beams. "Not your typical Muslim female, that much is clear. I have known her since she was a baby. A princess of the court now, though not of royal blood. Controversial. Dangerous, some say. She is training to be a Sufi."

"A Sufi?"

"A Muslim mystic. The Sufi quest is to achieve union with our God while still on earth. Not unlike the goal of the Christian and Jewish mystics. Sufis are respected in the Nasrid court. An unusual path for a woman, but there is precedence, at least historically."

"Sounds like an interesting woman. What is her name?"

"Layla. 'Night' in Arabic."

Chandon tests it for heft. "Layla." Again, "Layla."

## Give and Take

20 June 1367. The diplomatic entourage arrives at last at the Guadalquivir River, the hundred yard wide expanse of deep green shaming Granada's Darro and Genil Rivers. It has been a five day journey and the Granadine ambassador, Tariq al-Harish, is accompanied by fifty heavily-armed cavalry, an effective deterrent to any ambitious bandits. Al-Harish shows his safe-passage documents to gain entry to the bridge and moves on into the city.

Sailing vessels in great variety, both Christian and Moor, are tethered to the docks lining the western edge of the river, the source of the city's wealth. Torre del Oro, the famed Tower of Gold, far off to the right proclaims days of Moor glory long passed. Ahead are Sevilla's city walls and beyond the Giralda, minaret of Sevilla's Great Mosque, now cathedral, unmistakable in its grandeur, the tallest feature by far in the city. The tops of the towers of a fortress can just be seen. Originally the Sultan's sumptuous palace, the Alcázar has since been recast Castilian.

Hostile leers dog the entourage's passing through the narrow city streets. Creative whispered insults then ugly shouts of disgust float on the wind for what seems like a lifetime. The Moors move on, ignoring the barrage, proud, but painfully aware of life's cruel irony; their people made this city great. Sevilla has been Christian for one hundred and twenty years, a fraction of its history.

They arrive at the palace gates at dusk, stable their horses then settle into the King's Inn. An audience is requested for the following morning.

Al-Harish is dressed in his finest silk robes of blue, white and gold; Granadine colors. He sports a diplomatic crest on both sleeves and a flowing white turban. With him are two attendants who wrestle a small wooden chest. After a short wait in the courtyard the three are ushered into the Hall of the Orange. Once inside, Al-Harish's first glimpse is disorienting. He appears to be standing in the Hall of the Ambassadors in Granada. Square floor plan, red, green and blue polychrome background highlighting the impossibly dense raised white stucco carvings, half-hemisphere dome marquetry ceiling high above. Impressive, but clearly borrowed, a lesser copy of the original. Sultan Muhammad has lent Pedro a cadre of his stucco, tile, and wood artisans to satisfy his Granada-lust. This Moorish ornament in Sevilla's Christian court was finished only last year, to a decidedly mixed reception by the Castilian nobility. Moor artisans are hard at work now on the King's personal bed chamber and private retreat within the palace. It is rumored to be splendid.

King Pedro sits on an ornate throne of inlaid ivory and shimmering gold. Surprisingly, Pedro is dressed in flowing Granadine silks. No turban, but he could easily pass for a Moor prince. As al-Harish enters, Pedro beams, rises and strides forward, offering a loud greeting. "Tariq! It has been too long! Too long, sir!"

Al-Harish raises both forearms, palms out, then bows. "Your Majesty, the pleasure is mine." The ambassador smiles. Pedro clasps him on both shoulders, clearly pleased to see the Moor.

"Come, let us catch up. Come, Tariq." An ornately carved, wooden X-shaped folding chair of Granadine design is brought for the ambassador. Pedro returns to his throne. Four counselors are present: Don Alfonso Tello and Don Juan Duque to his right, Don Ruy Mexia and Don Sancho Coronel to his left. All four are silent, heavy-lidded; sullen. Six palace guards line the wall behind the throne. "And how is my Sultan?"

Not even a pause at the insult. "In good health, Majesty. Sultan Muhammad sends his warmest regards from Granada."

Pedro is overeager, boyish. "You heard, no doubt, of my victory at Nájera? My triumph! That half-blooded scoundrel Enrique is on the run. He hides like a girl in Zaragoza!" The king howls with laughter.

"We have indeed, Majesty. All of Granada celebrates your victory. Majesty, I have brought a letter for you from Sultan Muhammad. May I present it?"

"You can do better than that, Tariq. Read it!"

Al-Harish bristles at the lack of protocol. He glances at the expressionless counselors.

"Go on, Tariq. My counselors are trustworthy." The king looks first left then right. "If only for today!" He roars with laughter. The counselors don't seem amused.

Al-Harish removes the scroll from his robe, breaks the Royal Seal and begins in a formal voice.

*"To King Pedro of Castile, on the tenth day of June 1367, from Muhammad, Sultan of Granada. May Allah's peace and blessing be upon you."*

The counselors frown in unison.

*"My very warm congratulations on your decisive victory over your half-brother at Nájera. I trust that my six hundred cavalry proved worthy in battle. As you will have received in my earlier communiqué of the tenth of April, I have invaded Aragon's southern border in an attempt to apply pressure to your enemy. I am pleased to inform you that Granada has captured Jáen, Úbeda, and Baeza. They belong to Aragon no more."*

This is not news to Pedro. He has known of these events for three weeks now. Pedro stops the ambassador by raising his right hand, "A moment please, Tariq." He leans towards the counselor to his right, whispers something. The counselor whispers back. Pedro frowns, then lowers his hand. "Please continue."

*"My forces have captured a number of Aragonese troops from the garrisons. They will no longer trouble you."*

"More Christian slaves," the counselor to Pedro's far left mutters, just loudly enough to be heard by all.
Al-Harish continues.

*"I have also sent with my ambassador two thousand gold dinars, payment against our agreed upon six thousand dinars annual tribute."*

Al-Harish motions to his two attendants, who step forward with the chest, lower it to the floor with a metallic thud three paces in front of Pedro. They open it, revealing a shimmering pot of gold. They run their fingers through the pile to excite the unmistakable jingle guaranteed to warm any king's heart. Pedro's expression remains unreadable. The attendants retreat and al-Harish begins again.

*"I trust that this gold will help retire your war debts. In addition, I am pleased to inform you that my troops have captured one of your most dangerous enemies, Sir William Chandon of Brittany."*

Pedro's eyes widen. He leans over and exchanges more whispers with the counselor.

*"Chandon has been denied ransom and is being held prisoner of war in the Alhambra. He will no longer oppose you. Finally, I trust that my artisans continue to serve you admirably in the construction of your private retreat and bed chamber. I have authorized another shipment of tilework and cedar to Sevilla. They should arrive shortly. I have also included a chest of the finest Granadine silks for your court. As always, Granada honors the treaty between our two great kingdoms and I renew my personal pledge to assist you in all ways for which I am able. May Allah's blessings and peace remain upon you."*

*Muhammad V*
*Sultan of Granada*

Al-Harish rolls the scroll and returns it to the pocket inside his robe. Pedro fingers his beard, frowning, as he considers the Sultan's words.

"I am pleased to hear of the Sultan's defeat of Aragonese forces and the occupation of the Castilian cities of Jáen, Úbeda and Baeza. I am sure that my subjects will be treated well. As for the Aragonese troops, the Sultan is free to dispose of them as he desires. I must tell you, however, Tariq, that no such communiqué was received informing me of the Sultan's planned invasion." He locks eyes with the Moor. "A serious oversight."

Al-Harish looks puzzled, then uncomfortable. "I assure you, Majesty, the message was sent by horsed courier."

"Nevertheless, it was not received."

"My sincere apologies, Majesty. I am at a loss. Perhaps he fell victim to border bandits. Upon my return to Granada, I will seek an explanation."

The silence stretches out uncomfortably. "Tariq, when does the Sultan plan to return my three jewels to their proper owner?" His face is a blank slate.

"Majesty, that is certainly the Sultan's intent." A careful pause, then, "Although...the Sultan believes that an Aragonese counterattack is imminent and therefore that his sustained occupation of the three cities would be prudent. At least for the time being."

Pedro shakes his head with disgust, offers a sarcastic, "Naturally." Frowns crease the faces of the king's counselors. "Please thank the Sultan for the two thousand dinars." He looks up. "I had hoped for much more. I am in the debt of Edward the Black Prince, as the Sultan well knows. Please tell the Sultan that I require complete payment of this year's tribute by August."

"I will inform the Sultan of your request, Majesty."

Pedro's face brightens. "As for Chandon, that is indeed welcome news. Were it not for Chandon, Enrique would now be safely in my dungeon, the war at an end. A pity. A formidable knight, that Breton. Please convey my thanks to the Sultan."

"Indeed I will, Majesty."

Pedro rises in dismissal, followed by his counselors and then al-Harish. "Thank you, Tariq. Please convey Castile's best wishes to my Sultan. You will feast with me this evening. I will have the court musicians play for us, and perhaps afterwards, some chess." He offers a warmer smile now.

"I would be delighted, Majesty." Al-Harish bows, then steps backward three paces, turns and departs.

Tense moments pass. Pedro begins to pace back and forth like a caged animal. His counselors remain mute, stand clear of the building tempest. Pedro erupts in a bellow, "Two thousand dinars! He captured three times that in Jáen alone! For God's sake, the man has paid me with my own gold! Damnation!" He turns to face his counselors. "Don Sancho, how much do we still owe Edward?"

"Ten thousand gold florins, Majesty. And the Majorcans one thousand."

"Damn Muhammad! He aims to play me. Feigns helping me so he can capture my lands and reap a profit. My friend the Moor!" The king snorts. "And the odds that Enrique will counterattack? Virtually nil, I should think." He raises his eyebrows, incredulous.

Don Alfonso answers, "I agree, Majesty. Enrique's sole aim will be to rebuild his army at Zaragoza and prepare to meet us again on the field. He has no means to project power southward."

Hands on his hips, Pedro shouts his frustration. "Damn that Moor!" After an exaggerated sigh he begins to calm down. "Well, at least Chandon is neatly tucked away."

"Majesty, it is unwise to refuse ransom to a knight of Chandon's stature. It is a clear violation of the rules of war. What if Aragon retaliates?"

A sinister grin. "There is the beauty of it, Don Alfonso. It is the Moors who are breaking the bonds of chivalry, not us." He considers his options a moment more, then says, "Enough of this. Find me some means to pay my debts, Lords of Sevilla, else I will be forced to raise your taxes. Again." The king strides out, noble eyes now darting nervously about the room.

# Blasphemer

Chandon continues to heal, the strolls and daily visits to the baths working wonders for his appearance and attitude. The Granadine feasts have allowed him to regain his natural weight and he again looks healthy and trim. A handsome man. Thankfully, he can finally dress himself. A sling cradles his left arm, but he can lift it out to stretch and strengthen his shoulder. His cane remains a constant companion but his limp lessens by the day.

Chandon has discovered, to his delight, that the hospital contains two indoor toilets, each discreetly tucked into a shielded alcove at each end of the courtyard. A four-inch by eighteen-inch bricked opening is set in the floor, flushed by a constant flow of cool water. A sitting stool is provided, together with a filled water basin in a wall niche for cleaning. Indoor plumbing is a marvel to the Christian, his only connection to indoor toilets the reek of a chamber pot.

Chandon's daily routine consists of a light breakfast of bread, cheese and fruit, early morning walks around the hospital courtyard under the watchful eyes of his bodyguard, a late morning bath, his feast, a strolling conversation followed by a light cold supper with Salamun, followed by more conversation, often stretching to sunset. He is a prisoner still, but only in name. He walks and walks. He converses non-stop with Salamun, a knowledge reservoir he taps at will. He enjoys an organic, solar sleep cycle, rising and setting with the sun.

With his new found energy he has grown weary of the hospital confines, and Salamun mercifully has granted his request to begin exploring the medina by himself, provided his bodyguard accompanies him. Today will be his first foray abroad and his excitement is already building.

Chandon opens the door to his room and steps out into the cool morning air. The mélange of aromas is captivating; wisteria, spice-myrtle, rose, orange, and dozens of unknown flowers teaming up to offer a heady, penetrating perfume. He is surprised to see that his bodyguard is absent; a first. He has heard nothing, but this disappearance triggers his sixth sense, raising an instant alarm. His eyes flick around the courtyard searching for any hint of danger, but all is calm, no one in sight. He wishes once more for at least a dagger to defend himself. He weighs his options.

Wait for my bodyguard? Leave the hospital unguarded? Shout for help? He smiles ruefully. Never. He frowns, decision made, and begins to limp towards the main door of the hospital.

The bright sun is just topping the mountain-backed roof line as he exits, the Upper Royal Road of the medina rising gently to his left. The baths are fifty yards downslope. He steps out and turns left, following the knotted throng, maybe two-thirds women. Safety in numbers. The road is fifteen-feet wide and paved with small white stones, thousands upon thousands anchored to the surface. A six-inch wide line of small black stones is cemented vertically into the paving, bisecting the street. At twenty-foot intervals intricate patterns in black stone emerge, black on white murals entertaining the feet.

Buildings rise on both sides of the street to two, occasionally three, stories, white-washed stucco with dark wood trim, thick wooden doors, small windows on the upper floors. Flowers spill down from window boxes, pinks, reds and blues forming ornate tapestries against the creamy stucco. Tiled roofs whose gutters are sunk into the ground at the edges of the street. The faint sound of rushing water implausibly leaks from beneath the white and black paving. Side streets only wide enough for two to walk shoulder-to-shoulder dart off at odd angles between buildings, forming the dense maze of the medina.

Forty yards further and the street forks, the expanse between broadening into a small plaza. Chandon stops and absorbs. The buildings around both sides have open fronts, merchant wares neatly arranged on tables. In the center of the plaza is a fountain surrounded by stone benches for lounging. Neat flower beds. The smell of baking bread is heavenly, causing his stomach to grumble its demands. Two cypresses tower behind the buildings at the top of the plaza. Carts laden with wares litter the scene; fruits and vegetables, leather goods, meat sellers with tethered goats and boxed chickens. A cobbler, several fabric merchants, a blacksmith. A pleasant tangle of goods. Chandon's fellow travelers fan out and begin to shop. Rising above the buildings to the right is the fortress wall, guards standing at ease at fifty-foot intervals, staring outward.

Chandon decides on the left fork, begins admiring the produce. This is a wealthy town, that much is obvious from the impressive diversity of goods. Merchants look up without registering his presence. As he passes, however, they look up again, begin to whisper. The pattern repeats itself as he circles the plaza. The large number of people scattered about is comforting, and Chandon begins to relax.

Unseen by his quarry, the turbaned Berber trails, twenty paces behind, blending in seamlessly with the townspeople. The Berber leisurely strolls, keeping a safe distance between them, stopping from time to time to admire wares. He chats with a fruit merchant, buys some dried apple, then moves on. Chandon dawdles, killing time, making his way around the plaza.

The muezzin begins the noon call to prayer. Chandon looks in the direction of the sound but cannot see the caller. He admires the richly decorated summons, notices that a number of men are emerging from buildings, beginning to make their way down the street. Many of the women shoppers follow. Several merchants begin to spread prayer mats in their stalls. Curious, Chandon begins to make his way back down the street, following the crowd, but he can't quite keep pace. The Berber examines some leather goods as Chandon passes, then turns and trails him, once more matching pace.

The gathering crowd gains strength as it moves. The Royal Hospital appears on his right, then the hammam. Now in uncharted waters, a large two-story square building emerges to Chandon's right. The courtyard in front is dotted with orange trees, red and white striped Moorish horseshoe arches outlining the three building entrances. Beside each doorway an armed palace guard presents a living statue, eyes glued to the ground. A slender three-story tower rises on the opposite side of the building. Chandon sees the prayer caller as he sings anew his summons to the faithful.

Outside the building there is a scalloped fountain. Those that pass stop, dip their hands into the water, rinse their forearms and face. Those without turbans run wet hands through their hair, lips moving in silence. The queue about the fountain builds then slowly dissipates as the cleansed move on into the building, removing their shoes at the door, lining them in neat rows.

Chandon enters the courtyard, stops to contemplate his options. A prayer service in the mosque is clearly about to begin, the street emptying rapidly. He pauses momentarily, then reaches down to untie his waist sash, wraps it around his head in a poor attempt at a turban so that his hair and face are hidden. He leans his cane against an orange tree, moves forward to the fountain, then imitating the worshippers, bathes himself, moves to the left entrance, removes his shoes, and with his eyes downcast, steps into the mosque.

The Berber watches. A sinister smile forms on the man's face. He moves to the fountain, washes, then steps into the mosque behind Chandon.

The mosque is lit by large silver lanterns, but as Chandon's eyes adjust he beholds a sea of red and white striped double arches supported by tall marble columns, defining a perfect symmetry within the square building, the view from any angle or location identical. Architectural harmony.

Worshippers move into the building, turn to the right, filling the carpeted space right to left. As they reach their spot, they kneel down. He sees in the far left corner a roped off area where head-scarved women kneel. Chandon follows the crowd, finds a discreet place next to a column and kneels.

He sees the elaborately decorated niche in the eastern wall in front of him. Salamun has spoken about a mosque's *mihrab*, precisely oriented towards the Muslim holy city of Mecca, to the east. It is a window to paradise, a prayer funnel, a pathway to Allah. The building is now maybe two-thirds full. A bearded man in black robes and a crimson turban emerges, flanked by two attendants, then moves to the mihrab, remains standing. The imam, spiritual leader of the mosque.

The room stills, the faithful kneeling reverently. The imam begins to sing, his rhythmic chant filling the space. He stops. The room repeats a phrase with a unified voice. They stop. The next choral dialog begins. Two rows back, the Berber stands and shouts, "Infidel! Infidel! A Christian is among us! Blasphemer!" He points accusingly at Chandon. Mouths open, aghast, the crowd instantly vertical. Angry words rise in volume, then livid shouts. Fists are raised and pumped.

The Berber screams with anonymity, one among a crowd, "Kill the infidel! Kill the blasphemer!" A hand yanks Chandon's sash off his head, his blond hair and clean shaven face a vivid proclamation of his guilt. Chandon tries to stand but is brutally knocked down. Several grab his feet, begin to drag him from the building. Others pull his robe off, his ghostly flesh evidence enough for a verdict. A yank on his bad leg elicits a cry of agony. Mercifully they do not re-break his shoulder. Naked now except for his loin cloth Chandon is violently pulled out beside the fountain and surrounded by a wave of seething rage. Shouts of "Death to the blasphemer!" leap into a chorus.

The crowd begins to part as the three mosque guards move forward, stare down Chandon, now bleeding from his mouth. An Arabic torrent erupts from one guard, clearly accusatory but unintelligible to the Breton. Silence is obviously not the right response. The guard steps forward and slaps Chandon. The guard repeats himself, louder now, more insistent. Chandon raises both hands, palms out, "I meant no harm, I meant no harm. I was only trying to learn your ways." Not good enough. The guards push the crowd back, roughly force Chandon into a kneeling position, then one draws his long Granadine broadsword. Chandon searches frantically for a solution. He raises his hands palms outward once more, yells, "I meant no harm! I meant no harm!" It seems clear that they mean to have his head. The guard grips his sword for a two-handed beheading, then steps forward.

Chandon hears a familiar voice shouting unintelligible Arabic just outside the circle.

"In the name of the Sultan, halt! Anyone who harms the Christian must answer to Sultan Muhammad!" The man repeats the line. The executioner looks suddenly unsure of himself, but does not sheath his broadsword. The blue wizard pushes through the crowd, faces down the guards.

"I am Salamun, Royal Physician to Sultan Muhammad! This Christian is in my care and must not be harmed! By our Sultan's decree, I demand that you release him!"

The imam emerges from the crowd. Salamun recognizes the man. Imam Abd al-Malik, a Berber. A furious word duel commences. Reluctantly, as if not satisfied, the imam flicks his wrist and the guard stands down, sheathes his broadsword. The crowd begins to slowly file back into the mosque, muttering angrily as they leave.

Chandon is visibly shaken. He has never seen an angry Salamun. "Fool! Think, Young Knight, think! Blasphemy is a capital crime to Moors. Another minute and you would have been executed." The old Jew tries to calm himself. "Are you hurt?"

A steadying breath. "No. My leg is killing me, but I will survive."

"What were you thinking?"

"I was attempting to attend a Muslim prayer service." Lame grin.

Salamun rolls his eyes. "And where is your bodyguard? We had a deal, Young Knight."

"I do not know. He was gone when I woke. I felt it was safer to be in the medina among people. It was a bad decision to enter the mosque. I meant no harm, Salamun, please forgive me."

Salamun's face relaxes. "You are forgiven. You were lucky I was delayed in coming to the hammam today."

"What did you tell him?"

"Who I was and that they would have to deal with the Sultan if they took your head. We were lucky, Young Knight. Jews do not carry much weight at court, and the imam was reluctant to let me have my way, especially in front of the crowd. The imam is a Berber, no friend of the Sultan. Testing his resolve was not smart. I will have to answer to the Sultan for this." He sighs. "Johan was supposed to check on you this morning. I assume he never came?"

"No."

A worried look comes over the wizard's face.

"Twice now you have saved my life, Salamun." He smiles weakly.

"Let us try and make it the last, Young Knight." He gives in and returns the smile. "Come, let us get you back to the Royal Hospital before the prayer service ends and a riot begins anew. We need to find out what happened to your guard. And Johan. I do not like the sound of this." They begin to move back up the street, Chandon's limp noticeably worse.

Backed into a shadow just inside the entrance to the mosque the Berber's black eyes burn with hate as he tracks their retreat.

# Murmurs

"Luis, bring my chess set, let us play. And have Garcia light some candles." The Sultan reclines on a blue and gold pillowed divan in the Hall of the Abencerrages within the Palace of the Lions. He sips sweet mint tea as he reads *ghazals*, love poems. The sun has just set behind the hill across the Darro valley, the brilliant reds and pinks spilling into the windows near the top of the octagonal domed tower then fading to rich purples and blues as they settle to the floor.

The Palace of the Lions is the private domain of the Sultan and the Royal Harem, and he has personally overseen its design and construction. The Hall of the Abencerrages is a favorite space within the palace and he uses it as his bed chamber. The floor is paved in unblemished white marble, the lower walls decorated with brightly colored tilework, then raised ornate cream stucco on a polychrome background rising above towards the sky, the swirls and patterns of the dense Arabesque punctuated with Quranic calligraphy.

Unlike in the Hall of the Ambassadors in the Comares Palace, the octagonal domed cupola three stories up is a dense honeycomb formed from thousands of individual molded stucco pieces of various prismatic triangular constructions; *mocárabes*. The mocárabes coalesce into an elaborate eight-pointed star, the heavens, resting upon the cubic hall below, the earth, inviting the visitor's gaze upwards to the divine. The mocárabes are designed to produce an illusion of celestial movement as the sun tracks the sky, no two seconds of the day producing the same view from below. The calculus of the ceiling produces a meditative sculpture on the nature of time, the separation of heaven and earth, Allah and man.

The dome has a marvelous way with sound, the thousands of honeycombed cells combining to lift and tilt, contort and amplify soft whispers. A marble floor fountain five feet in diameter gurgles pleasingly from its single vertical jet. A hole at the base of the fountain leads water into a narrow channel that flows down two steps and out into the courtyard, the faint echoes of rushing water magnified by the high reaches of the hall to bathe the entire room in soothing aquatic murmurs. The fountain basin has curious blood red stains splashed about, lending an eerie red sheen to the gently rippling water under the late afternoon light.

On either side of the hall are recessed columned alcoves four feet deep, a step higher than the hall, the left of which upon entry is the Sultan's bed chamber. The bed chamber is curtained for privacy, carpeted with fine Persian rugs, the thick down-stuffed mattress and pillows placed directly on the rugs then topped by silk sheets and crushed-felt blankets. During the summer, the windows at the top of the tower are opened, the air flow through the doorway and over the mountain water chimneyed upward, providing natural cooling. The hall has tall, thick wooden doors rich in carved arabesque designs, but except during winter, they remain open for ventilation and instead blue felt curtains cover the entry, a gap left at the top to permit a breeze.

The slave slips a hand through to part the curtains, slowly enters a single step, then bows. He carries a lit taper that he carefully lifts to the candelabra to coax back the fading light. He makes his way to each of the four corners of the hall, illumination rising in meted increments.

"Thank you, Garcia," in Arabic. "I can see again."

"You are welcome, Sire." Garcia extinguishes the flame, bows once more, then slips out.

Luis returns carrying a large wooden chess set, the board inlaid with black and white marble squares, which he places on a short table resting on a Persian rug next to the fountain. He begins to remove the carved ivory pieces from their box and set them in proper rank. The chess set is a gift from King Pedro of Castile, complete with Christian-themed pieces, a constant amusement to the Sultan. It remains his favorite. He rises, comes forward and sits cross-legged on his silk floor pillow. "Tell me, Luis, are you ready to be beaten today?"

The slave smiles. "Sire, there must be a first time for all things." The Sultan chuckles as he pushes his white pawn forward two spaces. Luis mirrors the move. A knight gallops out to the left. Luis's pawn slides forward one space, loosing his queen. The battle begins. Luis, despite his youth, is the more gifted player, a fact the Sultan prefers since it betters his own game. On a good day, their duels often last an hour or more.

The two remain focused on the killing ground, silent. A half hour later a servant enters bearing two alabaster cups of sweet mint tea. The Sultan nods, tests his tea with a sip, then casually slaughters a knight with his bishop. Triumphant smile. Luis considers the brash move only briefly, then slides his rook forward six spaces. "Check." The Sultan's smile fades. And so it continues. Twenty more minutes and it is over, Luis, his rook, one knight, one bishop, and four pawns imprisoning the vanquished king on his lonely black square. “Checkmate, Sire.”

The Sultan exhales. “Mmmm... A good match, Luis.”

“Indeed, Sire, a very good match.” He gathers then boxes the pieces, then stands.

As he turns to leave, the Sultan says, “Luis, I have need of companionship tonight. Please ask Qasim to come for my request. And have Garcia extinguish the candles. Leave the oil lamps lit.”

“Certainly, Sire. Have a good evening. Tomorrow your fortunes may change, Sire, and grant you a victory.” They both smile.

A whisper. “Sire. You desire my services?”

“You may enter, Qasim.” The Head Eunuch of the Royal Harem passes through the curtains, bows before the Sultan.

“Your wish is my command, Sire.” He bows once more. Qasim’s effeminacy is striking. He is small boned, his face a portrait in girlish features, painted nails, lacy henna embroidery on his hands, heavy purple eye shadow, clothes one would normally expect on a princess. Ample evidence of his emasculation before puberty. The eunuch’s movements are precise, measured but graceful. He has been groomed for this role from childhood, and being head of the Royal Harem is a privileged position at court. Qasim oversees the Sultan’s three wives, their five young children, the four Royal Concubines, and manages their living quarters in the second story suites spanning the entire north end of the Palace of the Lions. He is also responsible for ensuring that female meddling in state affairs is held to a minimum, often his most serious daily challenge. Eunuchs are the only males allowed inside the Royal Harem, and Qasim has a staff of six, together with a dozen female servants.

“Qasim, I desire a companion this evening.” The Sultan conjures, then savors, his favorite image of Layla. He follows it with a wistful sigh. Forbidden fruit.

Qasim indulges the Sultan’s obvious preoccupation with silence. Then, “Certainly, Sire. Should I summon one of your wives?”

“No. There was a Christian girl captured at Úbeda. Striking green eyes.”

“Yes, Sire. We call her the green-eyed princess of Aragon. Lovely. A fine addition to the Royal Concubines.” The eunuch pauses awkwardly. “Sire, if I may?”

“Please, Qasim, speak freely.”

"Sire, your wives pine for you. It has been weeks since you have taken any of them into your bed chamber. They will be...jealous...if you select a slave over them."

The Sultan frowns as he considers the eunuch's words. "I have a desire for green eyes, Qasim. I will send for each of my wives later in the week."

"Certainly, Sire, I understand. I shall return with the green-eyed princess shortly."

"Please send Hasan with my evening clothes. And have my bedding prepared."

"Of course, Sire." Qasim bows, then glides from the room.

Qasim turns right just beyond the curtain and nods to the two Royal Bodyguards who stand watch outside the entrance to the Royal Harem. He opens the tall wooden door with his key, passes through, relocks it, then turns right and climbs the narrow stairs to the second floor. He unlocks another door guarded by an armed Royal Eunuch, enters a small vestibule from which long hallways emerge to either side. He turns right, opens a door, then moves into the suites of the Royal Wives which ring the compact courtyard of the harem. The children have already been put to bed, a eunuch busy reading bedtime stories. Tonight, Aladdin and his magic lamp, a favorite tale from the *Arabian Nights*. Faint, sporadic giggles can be discerned as the eunuch's muffled voice raises and lowers dramatically.

The three Royal Wives lounge on floor pillows around a low table on a plush carpet in the small, open-skied, torch-lit courtyard. They range in age from nineteen to twenty-five, all achingly beautiful. The latter, the Head Wife, the Sultana, is four years younger than the Sultan. The wives are joined by two eunuchs and the five play a board game. They sip hot mint tea, the array of sweets arranged on a silver platter untouched. The game is only an excuse for their favorite diversions, court gossip, the rigors of child rearing, defects in character of this or that servant, a scathing critique of the various concubines. The usual.

Tonight, the obvious is center stage – which wife does the Sultan most desire? Dice are rolled, pieces moved, bawdy laughter rings out as a favorite target is considered then promptly gutted. A female musician plucks a guitar in the far corner, humming in step to the rhythm, providing a soothing backdrop which cannot quite mask the subtle undercurrent of tension that floats lazily over the courtyard.

"Madams." Qasim bows.

All three women turn and look up, expectant, eager to find favor. “Well, Qasim?” says the Head Wife.

His awkward pause betrays the answer and the smiles of the women fall.

Eyes to the ground, the eunuch begins. “Madams, I am afraid the Sultan desires a concubine this evening.” He looks up. “He has assured me, however, that he will call upon each of you by week’s end.”

Hurt looks are first exchanged, then venom begins to seep into their voices.

“Which one?”

“That is of no consequence, Madam,” knowing full well that the truth will be ferreted out by morning. Gossip seems to float on the breeze within the Royal Harem, the secrets impossible to bottle and cork. The anticipated fury of angry whispers commences as soon as Qasim leaves.

The eunuch frowns as he exits the courtyard, then sighs, knowing that tomorrow will bring a special challenge if harmony is to be restored to the harem. The thought exhausts him. He heads back down the hallway, passes into the entrance vestibule, then unlocks the door leading down the other hallway into the rooms of the Royal Concubines. After several steps he enters an antechamber. He whispers to the eunuch on duty, who nods. Qasim opens a side door, knocks softly, then both step into the small room.

“My Lady.” Both eunuchs bow. They dismiss the female servant before continuing. “You have found great favor today, my Lady. The Sultan desires your companionship this evening.”

The stare is vacant, resigned, a portrait of sadness. She whispers, “I see.”

“My Lady, you are new to the Royal Harem. I can assure you that if all goes well tonight great things will come of this. The Sultan is a kind man. Handsome. You will find him most agreeable.” She stares back, her face blank. “Ali will help you dress.” Qasim turns to the other eunuch. “Make sure to apply the Royal Perfume.” A curt nod is returned.

The four two-inch tall bright yellow flames rising from each of the standing oil lamps swerve and spurt in the upward breeze, the joyful dancing quartets coaxing the raised stucco ornamentation to life, that they might join the revelry. A soothing dusky glow envelops the hall, competes with dark liquid hues along the walls and columns that struggle skyward to join the eight-pointed honeycombed star, the shadows progressively lengthening as the muted light rises heavenward. The carefully designed and nuanced lighting is a perfect complement to the gentle sounds of flowing water.

A whispered, "Sire?"

"You may enter, Qasim."

The eunuch enters, bows to the Sultan, who reclines on his divan. "Sire, your wish is my command." Qasim turns and raises his open palm towards the curtain. "Behold, the green-eyed princess of Aragon." The girl steps through the curtain and into the hall, then stands perfectly still, expressionless, staring at the floor.

"Thank you, Qasim." The eunuch bows again, then leaves.

Several moments of silence pass. She is a angelic statue. He says, in flawless Castilian, "Please come stand by the lamp so that I may see you." He rises from the divan.

She moves forward into the light, eyes locked to the floor. Her long, curly raven hair hangs down to the middle of her back. She wears a full length, pure white silk gown loosely tied around her waist, an exquisite contrast to her dark complexion and curls, sheer within a hair of being not quite opaque. He breathes in a wisp of a wonderful musky, citrusy scent, carefully applied in strategic places to enhance her allure. He admires her for a moment, then reaches out and lifts her chin so he can see her face. Stunning green eyes stare back, eyes he has seen before. The dancing flames reflect off her irises, causing the deep green to sparkle gold. A beautiful young woman. His heart begins to pound. Her face remains blank.

"Tell me your name."

After a moment, she whispers, "Auria, Sire."

"Auria. A lovely name. Where are you from, Auria?"

"Aragon, Sire. I was born in Zaragoza."

"How did you end up in Úbeda?"

"My father was stationed there, Sire. My father was the garrison commander." She hesitates, then says defiantly, "Don Álvar Dias de Haro. Sire."

"Was?"

"My father is dead, Sire." Her lower lip quivers. "Killed in the battle two months back."

The Sultan sighs. "I see. I am sorry to hear that. How old are you, Auria?"

"Seventeen, Sire." Her vacant stare melts into the floor.

The silence stretches to a minute, then two, as he considers. Decision made, the Sultan reaches forward with both hands and unties her silk gown, reaches up and pushes it back from her shoulders so that it slides to the floor. She stiffens, then remains motionless. A charged moment passes, tension rising as he savors the generous curves of her body.

He licks his lips. “Have you ever been with a man, Auria?”

The strained silence lengthens, then a soft, sad, “No, Sire.”

His eyes widen. The barest hint of a smile forms, his heart beginning to race now. “Come, Auria. Do not be afraid. You will find me a skilled and gentle lover.” He reaches for her hand, leads her into his bed chamber, her green eyes clinging desperately to the cool marble floor. He closes the curtains behind them.

For a short while, lazy sounds of water loiter alone in the room, fluid ripples and undulations playfully echoing upward and into the heavens. Soon, however, the aquatic murmurs begin to contort and curve to wrap themselves gently around soft sounds of pleasure, punctuated here and there by sharper masculine groans of discovery that begin to quicken the air with urgency.

## Lessons

She exits the south entrance of the Comares Palace into the mid-morning sun, steps onto the white-stoned Lower Royal Road, turns right, walks for fifty paces, turns right again, then marches through the arches of the Court of the Machuca. Her pace is purposeful, quick.

It is already warm, a presage of the looming swelter of Granada's summer. She climbs the stairs leading to the protected walkway atop the outer fortress wall which links the palace complex with the Alcazaba, garrison of the Alhambra. In truth the walkway is an emergency escape route for the Sultan and the Royal Family, but it is the shortest route to the city. The Alcazaba is a fortress within a fortress, the oldest structure by far in the Alhambra, perched on the western end of the hilltop complex.

Two paces behind in lock-step is her lady-in-waiting, Aisha, a dozen years her senior. Both women are dressed for travel through the city in *hijab*, literally 'curtained' from view, wearing baggy, shoulder-to-toe, flowing light gray linen robes with long sleeves and matching gray cloaks. Dark gray scarves obscure their pinned-up hair. No skin beyond their faces and hands is in view, all traces of femininity concealed from wandering eyes.

As she reaches the top of the wall, Layla turns and looks back to the east over the roof-line of the medina. She blocks the sun's glare with her cupped palm and focuses on the majestic Sierra Nevada rising high in the distance. She flashes that smile. She loves the mountains, admires their defiance of the coming heat as they sport year-round snow cover. She pauses to track a quintet of chimney sweeps cutting and slashing at impossible speeds above the Courtyard of the Myrtles in a dangerous game of chase.

The two women turn and begin to walk west along the wall. After thirty paces they tunnel through the Tower of the Galinas and move on. They looks down on the stall-lined gully to their left, the bustle of the Alcazaba's morning market now in full swing, conversations a low background buzz. Delicious smells of baked bread, spices, roasted nuts, and grilled meats waft skyward.

Layla lifts her eyes to the view directly in front of her. The two large square towers of the Alcazaba stretch high above, guards sprinkled about on their ramparts. A taller third tower rises even higher a hundred yards behind, the tallest point in the city, topped by large flags sporting the unmistakable blue, white and gold of Granada.

She looks to her right, to the north, over the outer wall. The expansive view of the city spread below her is impressive, and she stops for a moment to admire the scene. Across the Darro valley lies the dense, white-washed maze of the Albayzín. This is the oldest part of the city, filled to the brim almost overnight by Moors desperately fleeing Jáen after the conquest by King Fernando in 1246. One hundred twenty years later it is a complicated tangle of merchant stalls, markets of every kind, artisan workshops, storehouses, mosques, baths, conservatories, and hundreds of homes for Granada's middle class. The buildings line the narrow, high-walled, twisting streets that hug the slope, all seemingly jumbled together without rhyme or reason. The conspicuous *carmen* houses that dot the scene stand out from the crowd. Expansive, multi-storied private homes with inner peristyle courtyard gardens and fountains, the domain of the Granadine upper class; silk merchants, traders, judges, nobility, court functionaries not blessed with living quarters within the Alhambra.

The Albayzín rises from the river back up the steep hill opposite them, hemmed in finally by Granada's outer defensive wall a mile distant and at the same elevation as the Alhambra. To the south and west the alternating multi-hued green patches of the Vega stretch to the horizon, where it is ringed in by low mountains.

Just before the pair reach the Alcazaba, they exit the wall to the left and descend the stairs, emerging on the far western edge of the market. They turn right, walk past the guards into the narrow paved ravine nestled between the outer wall of the Alhambra and the high inner wall of the Acazaba. Fifty yards more and they arrive at the tower containing the Alcazaba's Arm's Gate, the Alhambra entry point closest to the center of the Albayzín. The two zigzag through the gate's defensive bends and pass through a tall iron gate, emerging into the open air outside the wall. An angry equine snort startles them, followed by a muted whinny, then a closer nicker, betraying the stable hidden within the walls. The wide paved road in front of them switches back a half-dozen times as it tames the steep slope to the river. After a moment's pause to catch their breath, they set off at a brisk pace downhill towards their goal in the Albayzín.

The two women arrive at the Darro. With a span of only fifteen feet, the Darro is more of a mountain stream than an actual river, but it is nonetheless the life's blood of the Alhambra and Granada. The four bridge guards leer at the women as they approach, searching for any offering of feminine glint. Disappointed, the men exchange a playful smile between themselves, followed by a crude whisper of admonishment for female stealth as the two pass. Undeterred, the women cross over the arched brick bridge in silence, eyes fixed to the ground, then enter the jumble of the Albayzín. Sensing hidden treasures, the guards bend to track the women's movements.

The pair turns to the right and walk along the river for fifty yards and then head left, uphill into the maze. Ten minutes and two backtracks later, hearts pounding from the climb, they find their destination, the *madrasa*, Quranic school of the Albayzín.

Layla composes herself, then knocks on the thick wooden door and waits. After a lengthy delay, she hears the rough metallic clanks of door hardware, then the door swings partially open, revealing a young man her age. Long, pure white robe, white skull cap, wispy dark beard. His expression is unfriendly. He stands in a manner to simultaneously observe the intruders while blocking their entry.

An impatient, "Yes?" is formally issued.

"I am here to see Master al-Mussib."

The young man's eyes widen. "This madrasa is for the education of men. Women are NOT permitted." He stands rigid, clearly not intending to move. An acrid scent of unwelcome seeps from his pores.

Expressionless, but more forcefully, she says, "Nevertheless, Master al-Mussib is expecting me."

He eyes her in silence. "And you are?"

"Layla al-Khatib, daughter of the Grand Vizier to Sultan Muhammad." This has the desired effect and now the young man seems unsure of himself.

After a lengthy pause as he weighs his options, he says, "A moment." He backs up, closes the door, then bolts it for effect. Layla and Aisha turn to look at one another. A single raised eyebrow then a hint of a devilish grin forms on Layla's face. Aisha giggles into her palm, tries to compose herself.

A full ten minutes later, the door hardware again begins to move and finally the door opens wide. A bearded, middle-aged man in deep blue robes and white turban emerges, flanked by the original sentry, now frowning, and two companions. The older man smiles and bows.

"My Lady, the Albayzín madrasa is honored by your presence. Please forgive my student. At times he can be...overzealous. I am Yusef al-Nur, a teacher at the madrasa. Welcome." Palm up, he beckons them inside.

"Thank you for your hospitality, Master al-Nur. It is a great pleasure to be here. My lady-in-waiting, Aisha." He bows again and then both women step inside the madrasa. Layla offers a smug, mocking smirk to the young sentry as she passes.

The madrasa is a converted two-story carmen house. Classrooms ring the large, sun-bathed peristyle courtyard garden. Wisteria vines climb the corner columns, but the faded purple blossoms are already beginning to drop. A lone orange tree shades the bubbling water in the white marble fountain at the center of the garden. Pink and yellow roses between the spice-myrtle hedges that quarter the courtyard sport blossoms still rolled tight. The layout of the second floor of the carmen mirrors the ground floor and contains the living quarters of the teachers and select pupils with special promise that also board at the madrasa. Most are day students.

Layla can hear the muffled sound of lessons being conducted in several of the rooms. She trains her ears. A teacher recites a passage interpreting a deed of the Prophet Muhammad, a familiar *hadith*. The recitation stops then the class repeats the words. The teacher moves on to another hadith and the students follow. She can see into the classroom across the courtyard. Five young men sit on pillows around the master, who speaks, pauses to consult the open book in his hand, then speaks again. He ends with a question as he looks from student to student. A hand is raised tentatively in response, then another. The student's mouth opens to loose some wisdom, but she cannot discern what he says. The master chuckles then nods to the second student, who tries for a better answer.

To her left a half-dozen young men her age sit on the grass at the edge of the courtyard, reading. As she and Aisha follow Master al-Nur across the courtyard the young men's heads begin to rise, one by one, until all lock their gazes for a collective gawk. Several frown, others whisper. She feels intensely self-conscious and averts her eyes.

On the other side of the courtyard they enter a narrow hallway that tunnels through the building, leads through another door, then opens into a second smaller enclosed courtyard, similarly decorated, but in miniature. No sign of students. The space is silent except for the soothing gurgle of the fountain. Tranquil. They turn right and circle the courtyard under the portico, finally reaching their destination at the western eave. Al-Nur indicates two pillows placed together beside the door leading into a windowless room. As if they were expected. The pillow closest to the garden is in the full sun, the other further back and completely shaded.

"Please," indicating the pillows. "This is the Sufi madrasa, a paragon of silence and peace. Master al-Mussib will be with you momententarily." He bows, then turns and leaves. The two women find each other's eyes for mutual encouragement. Weak, anxious smiles are exchanged. Layla chooses the sun-drenched perch to spare Aisha from the swelter. They sit in silence, cross-legged, spines rigid, hands cupped in their laps, and wait.

An hour and fifteen minutes later, they are still on their pillows, spines bent low, heads wilting. A bead of sweat drips from Layla's nose to the black stone, forming a neat dark circle. She reaches up with a sleeve and mops her face... for the fourth time. She frowns. From time to time she feels her bile involuntarily rise at the sustained delay. She swallows to squelch her rising anger and tries hard to relax.

The door creaks open a sliver, then stops. She sits up straight, attentive. After a moment the door swings wide and out limps a crippled old man leaning heavily on a wooden cane. He wears a deep blue robe and a white turban, his long gray beard stretching to his stomach. He takes in the scene, smiling broadly, chuckles, then bows.

"I am Mansur al-Mussib. I am pleased to make your acquaintance, Layla."

Disarmed by the familiarity, she struggles to rise, but too quickly. Her joints are stiff and she becomes flustered in the process of unkinking. She blushes scarlet as she blurts out, "It is a great honor to meet you Master al-Mussib." She bows awkwardly. His smile is warm, grandfatherly. Midnight eyes set deep over droopy bags; intense, but somehow kind. The Sufi master of Granada.

He turns to his right, "Aisha, we will be some time. Please relax. A student will bring you a glass of water and some fruit." He begins to limp back into the darkened room. He motions her forward with an inward curled palm, "Come, my dear, come." Layla steps into the dim light, the cool air a welcomed change.

"Could you close the door behind you, please, Layla?" She does, heart pounding now.

In the corner of the room a standing oil lamp hovers over a short couch. A bookcase filled with volumes stands beside the couch and a semicircle of floor pillows surrounding a larger central pillow on a fine wool rug marks the center of the room. It is clear that he was alone in the room for the entire time she spent in the furnace; doing what, she can only guess. She involuntarily frowns.

He creaks his way onto his floor pillow, a lesson in arthritic agony, exhales the pain when finally cross-legged, beard just touching the floor. She reclines on one of six pillows that semicircle around his, bright and attentive, her uncomfortable dampness beginning to thankfully ease. He smiles at her but remains silent. He lowers his stare to the floor then closes his eyes. After an awkward moment she shrugs and does the same. They both remain perfectly still. Ten minutes. Then twenty. Thirty. Finally, his eyes open and he lifts his head. She senses the movement and does the same, meeting his eyes.

He says, "Layla, you have passed three important tests." He pauses. "Can you tell me what they were?" He waits, expectantly, his dark eyes boring into her.

She begins to squirm with uncharacteristic doubt. "Tests, Master al-Mussib? I am confused."

"Test one: You offered the better pillow to your servant, revealing your good heart and good character. Test two: You endured the long wait in the discomfort of the sun, even though there was no apparent logical reason requiring you to do so. Test three: You were able to sit in silence, patiently, even though no reason for its demands was made known."

She looks puzzled, smiles weakly. "Thank you, Master." She hesitates, then asks, "And if I had failed a test, Master?"

He smiles. "You would not be sitting where you are. "Congratulations."

She bows her head. "Thank you, Master. I am grateful."

"I know your father well, Layla. He has told me many things about you." He nods his head. "Many things." An uneasiness settles upon her. "Lisan al-Din and I were both students of Master Muhammad ibn Marzuq. In Fez, while the Sultan was in exile. Your father, though my junior, used that great mind of his to help me digest Master Ibn al-Arabi, the great Andalusi Sufi. We spent many long evenings sipping mint tea and pouring over the man's difficult words, teasing out many truths. We have been friends ever since. Lisan al-Din could have been a great Sufi teacher himself, you know. He was offered such a role at the madrasa in Fez. Alas, he chose a different path. It was he who arranged for the Sultan to invite me to Granada to form a Sufi madrasa."

He locks his penetrating eyes on her. "I also knew your mother, Layla. Danah was a fine, caring woman; deeply spiritual. Your father adored her. She was headstrong and had quite a temper!" He chuckles with the recollection. "A beautiful woman. Same remarkable eyes. You remind me greatly of her, Layla." That grandfatherly smile.

Her eyes widen with this new knowledge, then to her intense chagrin, well up. A single tear streaks each cheek, dropping onto her robe. She quickly erases the evidence.

"Thank you, Master." She hesitates. "I miss my mother."

"Mmmm... Forced separation from our beloved is the soul's fate, Layla, the essential reality of what it means to be human, to be alive. The Sufi Way is to discover the path home. We seek an experience a reunion with our Beloved, Allah, while still on this earth. Tawhid." He pauses. "Only love can light the way to Love, Layla. You must renounce the empty temptations of the world. You must relearn what you think you know. And we must melt your hardened heart, Layla." Her eyes drift to her lap.

"Yes, my dear, we must melt that hardened heart. Even though there is great risk in doing so. You will feel unsure of yourself, vulnerable, afraid of what you may find within. But the soft, compassionate heart lights the Way to the Beloved. You must beg Allah for a new heart, Layla. You need a heart that sees, hears, tastes and smells. A heart that can be consumed with love for another."

Her gaze rises, then a weak, "Yes, Master."

"Layla, the Way is no easy journey. Very few of the many Sufi seekers ever attain tawhid. It requires great sacrifice, great discipline, and of course Allah's Grace. You must make a complete surrender of your heart and soul to whatever Allah may require. Are you ready for this, Layla?"

A slightly more confident, "I am, Master."

"The one rule of the madrasa is that you must trust your Master with all your being. You must honor his every command, even when you may not understand his motives. Can you do this, Layla?"

"I can, Master."

He grins, then slaps his knee. "Good. Then we are ready to begin your training."

She straightens her back, eager for her first assignment. More Rumi? Perhaps Ibn al-Arabi? The possibilities seem endless, and intensely exciting.

"As you may know, Sultan Muhammad, may Allah bless his soul, founded the Maristan Hospital in the Albayzín, the first of its kind in al-Andalus. It is not far from here, actually. The Maristan serves the mentally infirm of the city, the lame, the deformed. Those cast out and homeless. Your first assignment is to be a servant to the staff at the Maristan Hospital. You will come to know their patients, tend to them in any way required."

Her mouth drops open, aghast, as her eyes widen. Her indignant tone is spontaneous. "But Master al-Mussib!" She blushes at her own impertinence.

He raises a finger. "Layla, the rule of the madrasa." She drops her eyes to the floor. "Do not worry. I have spoken with your father, everything has been arranged."

She wilts, the intense disappointment sinking into her bones. "For how long, Master?"

"That is for you to determine, Layla."

She looks up, eyebrows arched. "How, Master?"

"Trust me, Layla, you will know." He nods his head as he grins. "You already know."

Her gaze returns to the floor again. The old man is clearly amused. The silence stretches. "In addition, Layla, you will begin formal training in Sufi meditation practice. First, you must learn to breathe as a Sufi breathes. You will enter the Sufi rule of silence. No books are allowed." He pauses for effect. "For now."

Her shoulders go limp as she weighs the implications. All she can manage is a resigned, "Yes, Master." More silence. She looks up, "Master al-Mussib?"

They lock eyes. "Yes, Layla?"

"Am I your only female student?"

His smile broadens. "Yes, Layla."

She searches for the right word. "Will that present...difficulties...for you?"

He chuckles. "Oh, most definitely, Layla. Not only are you a member of the Royal Court, but you are a most beautiful young woman. Even I, a half-blind, crippled old man, can tell that. Your reputation is known to many, even the young men of the madrasa." He beams as she blushes. "And of course the Berbers do not approve of the education of females. I pity their ignorance."

"Will your students accept me as a Sufi disciple?"

"Student first, then disciple."

"But will they accept me?"

"Does it matter, Layla?"

She weighs this, then proudly says, "No. But it would pain me to complicate your life."

"Do not worry about me, Layla. All of my students complicate my life! Your journey is all that should concern you now. Dress modestly while at the madrasa and the hospital; spare the young men." He chuckles. "Dedicate yourself to your service and your meditation. My disciples will come to know you by your sincerity, your commitment to the Way, the manner in which you live your journey. When they do, they will respect you, Layla, and accept you."

As last she flashes that smile. "Thank you, Master, for this opportunity. I will not disappoint you."

"I know you will not, Layla. If I had any doubts I would not have accepted you as a student." He beams. "Come, it is nearly time for noon prayer. You and Aisha will join us." He commences his slow-motion, painful rise.

## Implications

The seven men, naked except for their beards, emerge one by one from the crimson-hued, starry mist of the warm room of the Royal Baths, nestled conveniently between the Comares Palace and the Palace of the Lions. They walk into the plush waiting towels lifted high in welcome by their eunuch bath attendants. The men dry themselves then arm their way into long cotton robes, tie their sashes, and slide into the cool anteroom, refreshed and ready to begin the business of the day. A plucked guitar whispers its complicated melody from the second story balcony overlooking the scene, mingling with the soft bubbling splash of the floor fountain.

The Sultan reclines onto his divan as the six sit on precisely placed, rank-ordered pillows that semicircle him. In attendance are Ibn al-Khatib, Grand Vizier, and Prince Bashir al-Waziri, Military Vizier, to either side of the Sultan; Prince Farqad al-Bistami, Military Vice-Vizier, recent conqueror of Jáen, Baeza, and Úbeda, seated beside al-Waziri; then Tariq al-Harish, Royal Ambassador to Castile and Ahmad al-Mubarak, Royal Ambassador to the Marinid Empire, to Ibn al-Khatib's right. Prince Jalil al-Ghudari, Master of the Royal Treasury, completes the circle. The Vizier Council. The room remains silent, expectant. Two of the Sultan's Royal Bodyguards stand just inside the entrance to the anteroom, a matching pair planted just outside the locked door. After the men are seated, two eunuchs arrive on cue. One distributes mint tea counterclockwise while the other follows just behind with a small platter of dried dates and figs.

The Sultan raises a finger and the head eunuch approaches, leans close to hear his whisper. "That is all, Idris. Please complement the musician and your staff. Tell my guards they may wait outside. I will ring if I need you."

A demure, "Certainly, Sire." The eunuch bows and withdraws. A moment later the music evaporates, the muted liquid gurgle of the fountain the only sound remaining. The silence stretches out.

"Gentlemen. There is much to talk about." The chosen order of discussion within the bath-councils is never haphazard, a reflection of the Sultan's present anxieties and preoccupations. His decision on sequence made, he begins, turning first to the al-Harish, the Royal Ambassador to Castile. "Welcome back to Granada, Tariq. What of Pedro and Sevilla?"

"An...interesting...visit, Sire." Grins circle the room. "Pedro was his usual boisterous self, the nobles predictably venomous." The grins are exchanged for smiles. "Pedro's chess game has improved." He pauses for effect. "Very slightly." The Sultan chuckles. "As expected, Sire, Castile was already aware of our capture of Jáen, Baeza and Úbeda. As you anticipated, Pedro demanded to know when we will return the cities. I communicated your intent as instructed. He clearly believes we will not relinquish them anytime soon, Sire. The reality, of course. Pedro is nothing if not astute.

"It was a surprise to me, however, Sire, to learn that our courier never delivered your communiqué indicating our initial intent to invade Aragon. Not politic. I have inquired at length. It seems our courier never reached Sevilla, Sire. In fact, his whereabouts remain unknown." He hesitates. "I suspect foul play, though it is unclear from what direction. Aragon? Our enemies in Sevilla?" He hesitates. "The Marinids?" The ambassador to the Marinids turns to examine al-Harish, eyebrows raised, but remains silent. "We have never had any trouble sending unarmed letter couriers into Castile, Sire. After all, he had papers guaranteeing safe passage. In retrospect, it was my mistake not to have provided him an armed escort. My apologies, Sire." A curt nod from the Sultan indicates his acceptance.

Al-Bistami, Military Vice-Vizier, offers, "Sire, it is highly unlikely that Chandon and the Breton cavalry suddenly appeared at Jáen by chance. The Aragonese garrisons at Baeza and Úbeda were also stronger than we anticipated, recently reinforced. I suspect that Aragon was informed of our move in advance. By whom remains unclear. Certainly not by Sevilla."

The Sultan frowns then turns back to al-Harish. "Go on."

"Your goodwill deposit of two thousand dinars against our annual tribute was met with scorn, Sire. Pedro was clearly upset that it was not more. We have no credible information as to the exact amount he owes Edward the Black Prince for his services at Nájera, but my sources suggest that it is probably in the range of ten thousand florins, perhaps twelve. He demanded that we pay our entire year's tribute by August, Sire. Typical Castilian arrogance. I would suggest that we drag out our additional payments well into the fall. As a matter of principle we cannot agree to such outrageous demands."

The Sultan strokes his cropped beard as he considers, then turns to al-Ghudari, Master of the Royal Treasury. "Jalil, what was the total booty captured in Jáen, Baeza and Úbeda?"

"Eight thousand dinars, Sire. An exceptionally generous take." A satisfied smile, followed by a nod of appreciation to al-Bistami, who returns the favor.

"And the Royal Treasury?"

"At present, just over twenty-eight thousand dinars, Sire. But the taxes on the silk merchants are not due until next month. With our large sale to Baghdad in March taxes should be up substantially from last year."

"Good." The silence drags out as he thinks, then abruptly he turns to Ibn al-Khatib. "Lisan al-Din, would it be shrewd of us to offer to loan Pedro the money he needs to pay Edward? Bashir seems to think that Pedro cannot win against Enrique unless he has Edward by his side. I suspect that the Black Prince will not fight for free." Grins circle the room again.

"An interesting idea, Sire. It would certainly put Pedro firmly in our debt. As I have said, it is very much in Granada's best interests that Castile triumph in this civil war. If Enrique wins, you may rest assured that Aragon's papal backers will insist upon a swift call to re-engage reconquista." He stops to consider further, then says, "I suspect, however, that Castile's nobles will vehemently oppose any loan from Granada, Sire. They fear being beholden to Muslims."

"And what guarantee would we have of repayment? Suppose Pedro still loses the war," al-Ghudari adds.

Al-Harish counters, "Lisan al-Din, I am not so sure the nobles would oppose such a loan, especially knowing they will be taxed to provide Pedro's needed cash if no other means is found."

Ibn al-Khatib responds, "I agree that the Castilian nobles will look beyond their own coffers for the money. The question is where? Perhaps Pedro will promise Edward land if they are victorious."

Al-Harish offers, "Allowing England a foothold in Castile would be a desperate and dangerous move for Pedro. England is ambitious. Once Edward is through the door, Castile might soon be speaking English."

"The English possess a formidable army," al-Bistami adds.

Ibn al-Khatib continues, "Agreed, but times may soon become desperate for Pedro if Castile's treasury is indeed dry. Perhaps Pedro could be approached secretly with the idea of a loan. Bypass the nobles." Ibn al-Khatib turns to face the Sultan. "Sire, with your permission, I would like to consider your idea a bit further so that I may ferret out all of the possible implications." It will soon become a chess problem for the Grand Vizier.

The Sultan nods to Ibn al-Khatib and turns back to al-Harish. "Tariq, please go on."

"Sire, Pedro's remodeling of his palace to match your Granadine style nears completion. Impressive, but clearly inferior to the glory of the Alhambra. Our masons have even managed to incorporate our motto, 'The only victor is Allah,' into the stucco work in a few discreet places. It is a good thing the Castilian nobles do not read Arabic." They all laugh. "The fact that we have captured Chandon and made him a prisoner of war appeared to be unknown to Pedro or the nobles, Sire. Pedro was obviously pleased. A shrewd move by Prince Farqad."

The Sultan considers this for a moment, then frowns. "Shrewd, yes, but not without risk. We hold a famous knight without ransom. Dangerous. Lisan al-Din, what of Chandon?"

"He is recovering, Sire. Up and walking now, albeit with a cane. Salamun tells me he expects Chandon to make a full recovery, perhaps by the fall." Ibn al-Khatib's look becomes one of amusement. "He is bathing now." More grins, except from the Sultan, who seems annoyed.

"This incident at the mosque..." The Sultan angrily shakes his head side to side. "As you all know, our tensions with the Mexuar Council run deep enough already without stirring up additional trouble. The Berbers make up almost one third of the Council now. I cannot believe that Salamun and Imam Abd al-Malik crossed swords over Chandon. The outcry was swift and predictably vocal. And aimed at me. This, I do not need, Lisan al-Din, Chandon or no Chandon. Is that clear?"

"Yes, Sire. An unfortunate event." He muses. "I remain concerned, however, about the manner in which this confrontation transpired."

"Explain."

"The palace guard that was assigned to protect Chandon was found murdered, Sire. Chandon came out of his room in the hospital and found his bodyguard mysteriously absent. He logically sought the safety of the crowd in the medina. The murderer could not have been far. My guess is that the assassin was also somehow involved in provoking the events at the mosque."

The Sultan looks to al-Waziri, Military Vizier. "Bashir? You have been too quiet. Speak."

"Lisan al-Din is correct, Sire. Very puzzling. Troubling, in fact. The guard was later found in a storeroom within the hospital. He had been stabbed with a dagger. Up under the ribs and into his heart. I knew this man well, Sire. A veteran. He would not have been lax in his security. It should have been impossible to surprise him, to have gotten close enough for a dagger thrust. I can only conclude that he was murdered by someone he knew very well. And trusted."

"Ahhh...our conspiracy rears its head once more. The leaker of our state secrets also wants Chandon dead. Why?"

"Unclear, Sire." Al-Waziri pauses. "We found Salamun's young assistant with the guard. The boy's throat was slit. Tragic."

"I see." The Sultan sighs. "Lisan al-Din, please convey my sincere condolences to Salamun. I know he is like a father to those boys." Ibn al-Khatib nods to the floor. "Bashir, as I have said before, we must get to the bottom of this. Find your leak and you will find your murderer."

"I understand, Sire."

Ibn al-Khatib looks up, turns to the Sultan and says, "Sire, I think it would be wise to move Chandon into the Comares Palace, at least temporarily. He can be placed under tighter watch there. The guest room in the south wing is presently vacant."

The Sultan nods. "Agreed. See to it, Bashir. No more surprises. And use my Royal Bodyguards." The Sultan seems pensive. "Lisan al-Din, have you and Zamrak begun Chandon's education yet?"

"Next week, Sire."

"Good. For Chandon to be useful he must develop a strong sympathy for Granada. A proper education is the key. Please see to it personally, Lisan al-Din. Layla is still to teach him Arabic and learn English?"

Ibn al-Khatib hesitates. "Indeed, Sire. But given recent events, I will rest much easier if those lessons take place within the safe confines of the Comares Palace."

The Sultan nods his agreement, then says, "I have heard that she has begun studies with the Mansur al-Mussib in the Albayzín madrasa. Risky, Lisan al-Din, very risky. The Berber hounds on the Mexuar Council are watching. Any misstep and they will pounce. On me, not her. Am I clear?"

"Yes, Sire. You have perhaps heard, Sire, that Master al-Mussib has her serving in your new Maristan Hospital? An excellent learning experience for my daughter."

"I had not heard, no." He considers a moment further, then says, "Good. Please be careful, Lisan al-Din. I cannot have her kicking a hornet's nest."

"Of course, Sire. I will ensure that her Sufi education remains uneventful."

Al-Bistami redirects the conversation. "Sire, it was rumored in Jáen that Chandon and Edward the Black Prince, though close friends from childhood, are now bitter enemies. Perhaps we might leverage this?"

"Interesting. Do we know what severed the relationship?"

"No, Sire. Clearly, Brittany has sided with France and not England in the war, no doubt a betrayal in Edward's eyes. But the rift seems deeper than that."

"I see. Find out what you can, Farqad, and how we might use this to our advantage."

"I will, Sire."

Silence settles in. The Sultan takes a deep breath, holds it, then exhales. Court business exhausts him. He would much rather be designing new buildings and gardens. He turns to al-Mubarak, Royal Ambassador to the Marinid Empire. "Ahmad, tell me about the latest rumblings in Fez."

"Fez remains unsettled, Sire. With the coming to power of the new Marinid Sultan, some level of calm has returned. But the rush is now on to see who can bend the Sultan's ear, control him. As you know, Sire, the Marinid Grand Vizier continues to exert a strong and...questionable...influence at court." A wisp of a smile forms on Ibn al-Khatib's face at the gentle dig.

"Tell me about the Sultan."

"A Berber, Sire. Young. He just turned eighteen. By intent, actually, so he will be that much more dependent on his viziers for governance.

"The present Marinid Grand Vizier, Wadih al-Rida, though Berber, is somewhat more moderate in his politics and religion, Sire. Educated in Baghdad, with Sufi training. In my view, he could be useful to Granada, Sire. With his friendship would come the Sultan's ear. As you know, the Marinids seek a renewed alliance between Fez and Granada, stronger ties between our kingdoms. They view our friendship as potential leverage with the powers of the East. Granada garners a respect in Baghdad which they covet, but will not soon enjoy. They also desperately need our trade, Sire. They want for grain especially. I suspect that we can use these needs to our advantage."

The Sultan holds up a finger to stop the conversation. "They may desire an alliance, Ahmad, but the Marinid ambassadors were impertinent. They are ignorant of our political realities, and arrogant. I have no use for intolerant Berbers that try and dictate what Granada should and should not do."

"Indeed, Sire. It is more than obvious that the Marinids would love to absorb Granada, not befriend it. I suspect that al-Rida will have more influence in official dealings between Fez and Granada moving forward. He should be more moderate. Hopefully."

"Good. Lisan al-Din, what is the status of the new treaty with Fez?"

"I am working on a draft, Sire, and have instructed the Royal Calligrapher to begin assembling a fitting design for the formal document."

"Good. Make sure we demand our fair share, Lisan al-Din. What I most desire is an agreement from Fez that they will support us with troops should the Christians ever choose again to invade the kingdom. Please continue, Ahmad."

"There is a strong resentment in Fez of the close relationship between Granada and Castile, Sire. Our alliance with Castile is viewed as a threat. Your sustained relationship with Pedro is seen as a destabilizing influence to the Maghreb."

Ibn al-Khatib interrupts, "Are you aware of any direct contact between Fez and Aragon."

Ahmad turns to his left. "No. But it should be watched carefully."

"I agree," adds al-Waziri. "Aragon surely is re-arming for their next confrontation with Pedro. It would be good to know precisely whom their backers will be. Hopefully not Berber."

The Sultan frowns. "Ahmad, is there any hint at all of a Marinid spy in our court that is whispering state secrets into the southerly winds?"

"None, Sire. But I will put out feelers among my contacts in Fez."

"Please do. But be discreet." The Sultan drifts back into silence as he thinks. After a moment he interjects, "In addition to my issues with the Berber imams on the Mexuar Council, I am beginning to hear disturbing rumors of emboldened Berber officers in the garrisons of Málaga and Almería. Rising tensions between the Berber infantry and my Granadine regulars is a distraction we must avoid. Bashir, I think it is time we made some changes to the organization of our armies. We will disperse the all-Berber units, absorb them back into the regular infantry units, and place the Berber officers under the direct command of the regular officers. Ones you trust."

"I have heard similar rumors, Sire. That would be prudent. Diffuse these tensions before they can spread, become emboldened. I will see to it."

"Good. Anything else, gentlemen?"

Al-Ghudari, Master of the Royal Treasury, raises a finger. The Sultan nods. "Sire, we have been approached by a Christian trade delegation from the Republic of Genoa. They desire a trade agreement with us. For silks, ceramics and steel."

"Ironic, is it not, that the Christians want our goods, but will not leave us in peace to practice our religion." The Sultan sighs. "Lisan al-Din?"

"The Genoese are the richest merchants on the Mediterranean, Sire. They own the best ships, and they have significant influence within the papacy. That may be of use to us. A trade agreement would be lucrative, Sire. There is no source of fine silks equal to those of Granada within the Genoese trading sphere."

The Sultan nods. "Agreed. Silk and ceramics only, no steel. I do not want my troops ever fending off Granadine blades."

The Sultan's eyebrows lift as he tracks from person to person. "Anything else?" The room remains silent. The Sultan reaches for a small bell, jingles the head eunuch to attention.

State matters put to rest, the Sultan's mood visibly brightens. He intends to spend the rest of his day indulging himself with his pet designs for the on-going remodeling of the Generalife, his country palace a quarter mile north of the Alhambra.

## Living Poem

Chandon's eyes blink open at the muffled sound. He turns his head to the small, double-arched, jalousie window and sees that the sun has been up at least an hour, maybe more. He frowns, annoyed at having overslept. Even after three days he hasn't yet acclimated to the dim morning light of his new quarters.

His second floor room on the south side of the Courtyard of the Myrtles within the Comares Palace is compact but comfortable. White walls, embroidered silk hangings, a large crimson wool rug covering almost the entire floor. A single divan, a bookcase and writing desk, three small oil lamps and a candelabra, two floor pillows, a standing clothes cabinet angled into the corner. Spare but fine furnishings. The second soft knock at the door finally registers. He is fully alert now.

He hears a muted, "Young Knight?"

Chandon clears his throat, then says, "Yes, Salamun."

"Are you awake?" A chuckle from beyond the door.

"I am now, Salamun." Chandon smiles to himself as the chuckling grows louder. "Give me a moment to dress, Wizard." He tosses back the linen sheet, rolls over, then rises from the plush floor mattress and stretches. He is warming to the idea of sleeping on the floor. Quite comfortable. He pulls on blue cotton pants over his loincloth, then arms into a loose white shirt that stretches to his upper thighs. He ties a blue sash around his stomach then slips into his suede shoes. He takes a sip of water from the glass on the bookcase and bends to the small basin beside it. He dips his hands into the cool water, splashes his face. He runs his wet fingers through his hair then dries himself with a towel. He moves to the door. His limp has lessened but is still noticeable. The cane has vanished.

He unlatches both door locks then opens it to the beaming Jew, who steps forward, clasps both of his shoulders, shaking him as he says, "A fine summer day, Young Knight! Why are you sleeping it away?"

Chandon can't help but smile. "Good morning, Salamun. Forgive me. A wizard kept me up too late telling me strange stories. I could not find a way to shut him up." Salamun laughs. "You are early today."

"Indeed. A servant will bring us breakfast. We can eat while we talk. You are to meet one of your new tutors. Your formal education begins today!" He beams.

"I see. Which one?"

"Yusuf ibn Zamrak, the court poet. He prefers just Zamrak."

As the two exit the room, Chandon glances at his new bodyguards, one to either side of his door. An odd sight. The two are of northern European descent, a fact that is somewhat unsettling. Each wears a long red robe, gold sash. Cropped beards, no turbans. Heavily armed. Their vacant expressions are glued to the floor, but their demeanor exudes lethality.

Salamun has told him that they are members of the Sultan's personal staff, his Royal Bodyguard, former Christian slaves groomed for this role from early childhood. Chandon merits two pairs, one accompanies him from sunrise to sunset, the other stands night watch. Round the clock protection.

The knights of the Royal Bodyguard are the most feared in the kingdom. His simple test yesterday showed that these two do not understand Castilian. Thankfully, one of his evening guards does.

The two descend the narrow stairs and embrace the bright sunlight and fresh morning air. Chandon surveys the tower rising to his left, then his gaze returns to admire the mirrored water. The white-washed buildings dance lazily on the pool. Goldfish drift about in groups. The scene is very tranquil.

It strikes Chandon once again just how remarkably different this Muslim palace is compared to the stark stone behemoths of power that define both English and Breton courts. The Comares Palace is compact and elegant, a model of carefully planned harmony, studied peacefulness bookended by understated opulence. He has seen nothing comparable to it anywhere. His expansive stone castle in Brittany is embarrassingly crude by comparison. The subtle spicy fragrance of the myrtle hedge tickles his nostrils, the sunken green ring nestled between the water's undulating reflections and the polished white marble an elegant architectural statement.

The two stand in silence for several moments until Chandon asks, "So when do I get to explore the palace on my own?"

"You will begin to unlock its secrets today, Young Knight. With your tutor." The old Jew looks up. "Behave yourself and you may soon get some freedom to explore by yourself." The wizard grins.

"My guards are not particularly friendly. I must be important to warrant four of my very own."

Salamun shrugs as he chuckles. "For some strange reason the Sultan is determined to keep you alive, Young Knight."

Chandon grins. "Where are we meeting Zamrak?"

"Here. He should arrive momentarily." Salamun indicates the street-side entrance to the courtyard to their right. "You will find his Castilian flawless. He is also fluent in Hebrew, Greek, and Persian. He composes his poetry in Arabic. Obviously." Chandon nods.

They turn to their right as they hear footsteps. A man enters the southeastern corner of the courtyard at a leisurely pace. Plain white robe, no turban, cropped beard. Tanned and of obvious Arabic ancestry; handsome. Chandon guesses the man is his elder, but he carries an air of youthful exuberance.

As the Arab approaches, he offers in flawless Hebrew, "Master Salamun, I trust that God's Grace smiles upon you this fine day?"

The Jew beams then responds in Hebrew, "Master Zamrak, God's Grace smiles upon me every day. I trust the muses continue to bless your poetry." A quick smile from Zamrak. Salamun switches to Castilian, indicates Chandon with an upturned palm, "Master Zamrak, may I introduce your new pupil, Sir William Chandon of Brittany."

Chandon bows. "I am pleased to meet you, Master Zamrak."

The poet returns the favor, smiles, then says, "Please. Salamun is a master, I am only Zamrak." Salamun chuckles.

"A pleasure, Zamrak. Please call me Chandon." The poet nods.

Salamun turns to Chandon. "Young Knight, I leave you in capable hands. We will share our meal this evening, then perhaps a stroll around the pool, yes?" Chandon smiles, watches the Jew depart.

Zamrak steps forward, lays his hand affectionately on Chandon's shoulder. "So, Chandon, I am instructed by the Sultan to introduce you to the many glories of the Alhambra and the great culture of Granada. The finer points of life." He smiles. "Any question that I can answer I would be happy to, so just ask. Shall we begin?"

"A pleasure, Zamrak."

"Come." They turn left and begin to walk side by side toward the tower. "Tell me about yourself."

Chandon lifts his eyebrows. "Let me see. I was born in Radbourne Hall, Derbyshire, in England."

"Ahhh...England. Very good. When were you born?"

Chandon is taken off-guard by the poet's directness, but he is a fan of candor. He continues, "1339. I am twenty-eight. And you?"

"1339. Let me see." Zamrak stops and looks skyward for a moment, then says, "That is 739 by the Islamic calendar." Chandon appears puzzled. Zamrak notes this then smiles, "Ahhh...your first lesson, Chandon. Muslims keep their own calendar. A lunar calendar. It begins on Friday, 16 July, in the year 622 by your Julian calendar, the day that the Prophet Muhammad fled Mecca for Medina, may Allah bless his name. Today is the fourteenth day of the month of *Shawwal*, in the year 768." He pauses to let Chandon absorb this. "I was born in 733, 1333 to you. I am thirty-four." A coy grin. "But I am very young at heart." Zamrak laughs loudly, then says, "Please continue."

"A Muslim calendar. Interesting." They begin to walk again. "My family owned a farm. But I am not of noble birth. I had the great fortune to be selected for education by the friars of Saint Andrews' Church in Radbourne."

Zamrak halts once more as he interrupts, "Ahhh...Good. I, too, am of humble birth. My father was a blacksmith in the Albayzín of Granada, and I was educated at the madrasa there. I had the great fortune to be selected by Grand Vizier Ibn al-Khatib for special training. When Sultan Muhammad returned from Fez to reclaim the throne in Granada, I was selected to become Master Ibn al-Khatib's protégé. Later, I was made personal secretary to the Sultan, where I have had the great blessing to indulge our mutual love of poetry. The Sultan has been busy refining the magical décor of the Alhambra, as you shall soon see. Please go on."

"Later I was sent to the court of King Edward III, where I received training in the military arts." Zamrak nods. "With his son, Edward the Black Prince. I was groomed to help England win the war with France. Three years ago I led the army of Jean de Monfort of Brittany to victory over the House of Blois at the Battle of Auray, in France. To England's great pleasure. I was awarded Breton noble status, Viscount of Saint-Sauveur. I now live on my estate in Brittany." He frowns. "Or at least I used to."

"I see. Yet you fought against Pedro of Castile at Nájera, who was supported by Edward and the English. Why?" Again, the refreshing candor.

"Jean de Monfort pledged his allegiance to King Charles V of France, not England. As my patron went, so I followed."

"Indeed. I understand." Zamrak turns pensive. They begin to walk again. Zamrak raises his palm indicating the passage into the wall to their left. They enter, turn left, go down some steps, then turn right, down more steps, emerging into the compact elegance of Courtyard of the Mexuar. Zamrak stops and opens his arms. "Behold the Courtyard of the Mexuar, formal entrance to the Comares Palace. This is where foreign ambassadors and visiting dignitaries are received before entering the palace proper to meet the Sultan. As you can see, it is crafted to impress."

Chandon attempts pronunciation. "Courtyard of the Mesh-you-are."

Zamrak smiles. "Excellent." They step down and approach the white marble floor fountain. "Water plays a pivotal role in Muslim architecture, Chandon. And in our religion; even our psyche. As you can imagine, to a desert people, water is life, precious beyond belief. The Prophet Muhammad was born, lived and died in the desert. Naturally, water figures prominently throughout the Quran, as a symbol of paradise, for ritual cleansing. Water is life-giving, and also a statement of wealth and power." He indicates the fountain. "The pleasant echo of the bubbling water reminds the visitor of our heritage. And of course it makes them wonder how the water magically appears in the middle of the floor in a palace!" He chuckles. "More on that later. Think of the fountain as understated opulence with strong symbolic overtones."

Chandon considers this, then says, "The sheer size of the pool in the Courtyard of the Myrtles conveys not only Granada's opulence, but also serves as a reminder of its power and influence."

Zamrak raises his eyebrows, then beams. "Good, Chandon, good!" Zamrak again reaches for Chandon's shoulder, turns him around to face the two story façade.

Chandon stares in amazement, then shakes his head in disbelief. Zamrak seems pleased by the reaction. Rising above the colored dado tilework is a sea of intricately-carved raised creamy stucco on a lavishly colored polychrome background. He has seen nothing like it in any palace in England or Brittany. Positively alien. But beautiful.

"Sultan Muhammad completed this three years back. A brilliant rework of the original façade, I dare say. I had a hand in the design of its ornamentation." He points to the Arabic calligraphy bounding the windows. "Behold, a poem of mine frozen for eternity."

*"I am a crown and my doors a parting of the ways: in me the West leads to the East. Sultan Muhammad has entrusted me to open the way to the victory that has been foretold and I await his coming just as the horizon ushers in the dawn. May Allah adorn his works with the same beauty that resides in his nature."*

"My poetic tribute to the Sultan. But also a subtle snub of Baghdad, capital of eastern Islam. The West, Granada, is superior to the East, Baghdad. And a riddle besides. Two doors, each required for completion of the artistic symmetry of the façade. But only one leads to the sumptuous palace. The right door is a dead end. A metaphor for life." He beams. "Clever, yes?"

Zamrak is obviously proud of his accomplishment. "Look there." He guides Chandon's eyes to the top of the left window. "See the cursive 'Y', the two vertical strokes to its left, followed by the two sweeping horizontals? Remember, Arabic is read right to left." He indicates with his finger as he recites, "'There is no victor but Allah.' The Nasrid motto. The words are the Sultan's, but the design of the calligraphy is mine. You will find the Nasrid motto seven hundred and seventy-seven times within the Alhambra. Seven is a number of special significance in the Quran; the seven heavens, the seven sins, the seven days of the week."

"Impressive. European palaces are decorated with paintings and murals, but there are none here."

"In Islam, Chandon, representation of the human form or its likeness in public structures is strictly forbidden. It is considered idolatry. You will see no paintings or portraits or tapestries of humans or animals anywhere in the Alhambra. It would be an insult to Allah, a kind of blasphemy. Instead, calligraphy is considered Islam's highest art form. When the Angel Gabriel began to reveal the Quran to the Prophet Muhammad, Allah 'taught by the pen, taught man what he did not know.' Allah literally wrote his truth with a quill. In Arabic of course. For over seven hundred years we have refined the calligraphic form of Arabic to its highest expression. What you see before you."

He indicates his own composition. Again, the obvious pride. "The Alhambra, greatest of the world's Muslim palaces, is adorned throughout with my calligraphy and poems. The carved stucco lends it permanence. The palace is a living poem. The tilework and stucco creations are designed to delight the beholder, to be a feast for the eyes. They form a complex tapestry, a backdrop for the poetry, certainly, but also their endless repeating patterns lead the viewer to contemplation of the infinite, Allah. There are many levels of meaning, layer upon layer. Think of the entire Alhambra as a puzzle to be savored."

"Fascinating. My castle, though known throughout Brittany for its splendor, feels crude by comparison." Zamrak shrugs, then smiles. He again touches Chandon's shoulder to turn him, leads him onward.

"Come, I will show you the Hall of the Mexuar where the imams and judges of the Mexuar Council meet to pass sentence on court cases, decide matters of Quranic interpretation, and meet with the Sultan. It is one of the oldest rooms in the Alhambra. And then I will show you the fabulous Mexuar Oratory, private prayer chapel of the Mexuar Council, with its own mihrab, a gateway to Mecca, to Allah. One of the best views of Granada. Come, you will enjoy this." Chandon smiles, eager to learn more.

She rests on her knees upon her prayer mat, back straight, in Sufi meditation practice, *muraqaba.* As Master al-Mussib has instructed, her palms rest in her lap, upturned and cupped together forming a triangle, ready to receive Allah's blessings. Her untamed chestnut curls cradle her face, then spill over her shoulders in disarray. Her head is bowed, eyes closed, her face a study in resting beauty. She focuses only on her breathing, the sacred breath of life. She intones "Allah" three times within her mind, then attempts to move the word from her head to her heart. She has been told by her Master, repeatedly, that she must learn 'to see the world through the eyes of your heart.'

She begins to track her breath as a casual observer, slowing down her breathing, deepening it. Inhale, then exhale. In, then out. In, then out. She mentally whispers, 'Calming, smiling; precious moment, wonderful moment; Allah, tawhid; Allah, tawhid,' synchronized to the rhythm of her breathing. She eases into the comfortable repetition. And so muraqaba begins.

The first twenty minutes are easy, but as has been true all week, the last ten minutes of her morning practice become a kind of torture, her thoughts taking on a life of their own, flitting wildly about as if commanded by playful *genies*. Snow-capped mountains, the route to the madrasa, an observation Aisha made yesterday, what she ate two nights ago. Suddenly she becomes aware that she is thinking of a line from Rumi.

She forces herself back to her breath. Battle lines drawn, she becomes aware a minute later that she has been thinking of a move she made on the chess board during her victory over her father last week. Back once more to her breath. In, then out. In, then out. Allah, tawhid. Allah, tawhid.

The faint sound of voices worms into her consciousness. Her wandering mind seems to relish any excuse to desert the discipline, predictably embracing the distraction like a long lost friend. A moment later she becomes aware that her breath is nowhere in sight, and frustrated, she sighs, thinking, 'surely that was thirty minutes.' She offers a quick prayer of thanksgiving, then opens her eyes.

There are two voices in the Courtyard of the Myrtles. Her jalousie window allows the sound to drift in on the breeze. One voice she recognizes as Zamrak, prompting a quick frown. The other voice she cannot place. She cups her ears and listens. She can just discern the words. Zamrak is speaking about the history of the Alhambra. His companion interrupts, asks about Sultan Muhammad's exile. Zamrak answers, then continues his narration.

Curiosity getting the better of her, she uncurls, rises, then fists clinched, stretches luxuriously into a Y and exhales. She twists her neck first left then right, raises both outstretched hands up into the air as far as she can, tiptoes. She then walks over, leans in over her desk, pressing her face to the finely meshed jalousie to scan the courtyard.

Below, to her right, Zamrak and the man walk slowly away from her towards the Hall of the Ambassadors. They are inside the myrtle hedge, Zamrak closest to the pool. The man is several inches taller than the poet, his muscular frame impossible to hide with a loose robe. Shoulder length, wavy, dirty-blond hair. She notes the slight limp, weighs the options for an instant, then comes to the only logical conclusion. Chandon. She focuses more intently now, curious.

Zamrak stops and points to the Hall of the Ambassadors, then begins a discourse on the governing principle of Islamic architecture, which insists upon hiding magical interiors beneath plain exteriors, the manufacture of surprise on entry a cherished and calculated effect, a metaphor for the duality of the body and the soul. Chandon nods his head, interested. The Englishman asks another question which she cannot quite make out. Zamrak stretches his hands with animation to amplify his point, then talks excitedly about the recent delicious shock of visiting ambassadors from Africa as they entered the courtyard. Both men laugh. They begin to walk on.

She pulls a word from Chandon's next query, "wives." Zamrak stops and begins to speak of Muslim marriage customs. Chandon listens, absorbing, then responds with, "I can imagine, yes." He chuckles. She hears Chandon use the word "harem" in his next question, followed by Zamrak's discourse on the Royal Harem. She frowns once more.

They begin to walk again. Chandon poses yet another question. He is speaking softly and to her dismay she again cannot quite discern his words. Zamrak abruptly stops, turns to face Chandon, looking much more serious, flustered even. Zamrak lowers his voice and she cannot catch his response. Chandon speaks again. Undecipherable. She hears Zamrak plainly say, "Actually, she and her father live right over there." He turns and points directly at her and Chandon pivots to follow his finger.

Layla instinctively dives for cover. The candlestick crashes to the desk and the clutch of reed pens go flying, the pens bouncing then rolling to the far corners of the room. Her heart is pounding. As she recovers her composure, a smile eases onto her face as she realizes that it would be impossible for either man to see her standing behind the jalousie. She giggles hysterically into her palm.

Aisha steps into the far end of the room, offers a concerned, "Layla?"

Layla composes herself. "I am sorry to alarm you, Aisha. I managed to trip over my own feet. I am fine. I will reset my desk."

Aisha seems skeptical but retreats, tendering a frowning double-glance as she leaves.

Satisfied that Aisha is gone, Layla returns to the window, presses her face close. The two are now at the far end of the pool, standing just outside the entrance to the Hall of the Ambassadors, Chandon on the left. As they step up into the anteroom, Zamrak stops and points out a feature on the ceiling, attaching an explanation.

As Chandon turns and raises his head to look, Layla finally steals a glimpse of the face of the English knight. Clean shaven, virtually unheard of for Muslim males. Much younger than she imagined, perhaps only five or six years her senior. Her emerald eyes absorb his features, searching in vain for deeper insight into exactly what kind of man this is, if the terrible rumors can possibly be true. She smirks with the sudden recognition that the man is strikingly handsome. Chandon nods at Zamrak, then the two turn and walk on into the Hall. Layla lingers at the window, pensive. The barest hint of a smile forms, then is chased away by a commanding frown.

"Explain Muslim marriage practices to me. I understand, for instance, that a Muslim man can take many wives. Is this true?"

"Mmmm...a common concern of Christians. It is indeed written in the Quran that a Muslim man may take up to four wives. But if he chooses to do this he is also commanded to treat each wife equally well, and with the utmost respect. In fact, the Prophet

Muhammad had many wives. But his motivation was noble. After his first wife died he often married widows of Muslim warriors killed in battle so that they were not forced to live a life alone. Sometimes he married to solidify political alliances." He shrugs. "Or so the story goes. One of his last wives, Aisha, he married for love.

"In point of fact, most men in Granada have only one wife. The exceptions tend to be confined to the leadership of the various tribal clans, where inheritance is a key concern and male children are required. The Sultan, for instance, as head of the Nasrids, has three wives. Still, you can imagine that maintaining peace in a household with more than one wife presents its own unique set of...challenges."

"I can imagine, yes." He chuckles. "Tell me about the harem?"

"Ahhh...always of interest to foreigners." He smiles. "In Arabic, harem means 'forbidden.' The Royal Harem is located in the Palace of the Lions." He points to his right. "Just on the other side of this building. It contains the Sultan's wives and children, and also the Royal Concubines. It is off limits to all men, under pain of death. Only eunuchs are allowed inside the Royal Harem."

Chandon grimaces, shakes his head, "I see. Tell me about Layla." Zamrak halts and turns to face the Englishman. To Chandon's surprise, Zamrak appears agitated. Chandon seems to have touched a sensitive nerve. He lifts his eyebrows in surprise.

After composing himself, Zamrak responds, "I know Layla very well. She is the most beautiful maiden in all of Granada." He searches for the right words, then says, "She has a fine mind. A mind of her own." Then, more forcefully, "But she is stubborn. A tempest." He shakes her out of his head.

Chandon says, "I am told she is to teach me Arabic."

Zamrak's gaze bores into Chandon, searching his face for some sign. Satisfied, he proceeds, "Indeed. I would tread carefully if I were you." He frowns again.

Zamrak's intentions crystallize for Chandon. Evidently, unrequited love. He makes a mental note to ask Salamun for more detail but decides for now to steer clear of the whole subject.

"Actually, she and her father live right over there." He turns and points to the second story window at the far northeastern corner of the courtyard. Chandon pivots to look. Directly across the courtyard from his own room. The two turn and begin to walk in silence towards the Hall of the Ambassadors.

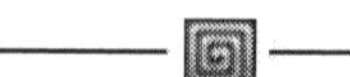

Chandon's sleep has been restless of late, but this night is worse. He tosses and turns as his mind races through all that he has absorbed. Three sessions now with Zamrak, but so much more to learn. He finds himself simultaneously attracted and troubled by this profoundly alien culture. Just as Salamun said he would. He tosses back his thin sheet in frustration, reaches over and lights the lamp. He decides on a stroll about the courtyard to still his conflicted mind. He dresses then unbolts and opens the door, then says to his bodyguards, "I cannot sleep. May I have permission to walk about the pool for a short while and enjoy the moon?"

The guard to his left considers for a moment, then responds in accented Castilian, "We will accompany you." Chandon shrugs and makes his way down the stairs into the courtyard.

Thin, filtered lamplight leaks from the jalousie window in front of him. Layla's room. She is up late. No other window in sight besides his own is lit. The full moon illuminates the palace with a magical iridescence. The white-washed buildings seem to come alive, dance playfully in the midnight-black water. Zamrak told him yesterday, only half-jokingly, that the entire palace complex was designed specifically to be viewed by moonlight. The evening is warm and still. Tranquil. The familiar heady spice of the myrtles quiets his mind. The faint sweetness of orange blossom eases in, chased by a pleasant hint of wood smoke. Not even a whisper of sound beyond the delicate fountain trickle.

His guards station themselves at the base of the stairs. Their bodies freeze into pillars, but their alert eyes continue to scan the courtyard. This setting is safe. A dozen guards stand just outside the palace entrance and sentries are posted at all major doorways between buildings.

Chandon breathes in the night air to still his thoughts. He inhales deeply, then releases it. He turns to his right and begins to circle the shimmering ebony rectangle in slow motion, hands folded behind his back, his favorite contemplative posture. He lets his thoughts wander, tries to relax. He stops and looks up to his right at the full moon to admire its brilliance, smiles at the jovial face returning his gaze. He says, "A good evening to you, sir." He nods, then rejoins his stroll, drifts into thought about all he has learned, the many contrasts to life in Brittany.

On the north side of the courtyard he again stops and enjoys the moon's lame attempt to dance a jig in the dark water. He grins. As he rounds the west end of the pool he gazes up at the dim window light once more, considers all the rumors he has heard about her, then mutters to himself, “Should be interesting.” He chuckles.

Just as his eyes are about to return to the pool he sees a faint shadow ease in front of the window. A hint of a human form is all there is, nothing to betray an identity. Still, he knows instinctively it is her. He stops and stares, mesmerized.

Finished with her tea and her careful sneak of a quick, forbidden communion with Rumi, she realizes that it has grown late. She has outlasted her father for once, unusual for him. A flicker of worry crosses her brow, then evaporates. She rises from her divan and stretches. An odd tingling of her sixth sense insists upon her attention and she looks about the room, puzzled. It is as if she has heard a faint sound she can't quite place. Dissatisfied, she steps to the window and leans close, scanning the courtyard.

After a moment she locates the stationary figure. There is ample moonlight to tell that it is him. And that he is looking directly up at her. She swallows hard, suddenly aware that the room is backlit and he can see her shadow. Unlike before, however, she feels no need to hide and instead remains perfectly still. After a pregnant moment of locked gazes, his arm suddenly sweeps in front of him as his leg kicks back, and he performs an exaggerated deep bow of submission. A grin tickles the corners of her mouth, then fans out into a full smile to frame her beauty. He begins to walk onward. She tracks him a moment longer, then turns and prepares for bed.

Perseus tunnels his hands around his eyes to shield the tedious moonlight. A thin smile eases onto the great warrior’s face, then begins to widen. He raises a hand to grab Virgo’s attention, but sees that she is far ahead of him, beckoning already for a word. A short while later a night of interesting dreams gets flung earthward.

## Whispers

It is an hour past midnight and the Alhambra is fast asleep, the grounds hushed, peaceful. The new moon's inky veil obscures prying eyes. The night is cloudless, the wind still as death, the twinkling starshine breathtaking. The windows in the palace towers are dark. Crisp fountain-tinkle can be heard from several directions. An owl plays his somber nocturne somewhere close by. A faint ghost on the outer wall stands watch, ambles slowly to the east, pauses to stare down upon the drowsy Albayzín for several minutes, then turns and begins to retrace his steps, a circuit he will follow a hundred times more before sunrise.

The Partal Gardens abut the east end of the Palace of the Lions, bounded to the north by the outer fortress wall and to the south by a short barrier wall that overlooks the Lower Royal Road. The Partal is a lush garden paradise intended for the enjoyment of the privileged at court.

The Tower of the Ladies rises above the large rectangular reflecting pool on the north side of the gardens, the centerpiece of the sixty-year-old palace, precursor to both the Comares and Lion Palaces. Unlike with the Comares Palace, the impressive pool is given free rein here. Loosed, it opens directly into the lush gardens, beckoning the visitor.

Palm trees and skinny cypresses whisper tales of desert memories. Billowing magnolias, oaks and chestnuts dot the terraced landscape, providing welcomed shade. Small, impeccably placed water features are tucked neatly into corners, their soft whisper steady, contemplative.

The large, terraced garden is parsed into dozens of compact, irregularly shaped myrtle-ringed beds divided by stone paths and short runs of stairs. The floral menagerie includes oranges and pomegranates, plums, fabulously fragrant red and yellow and white roses, spiraled boxwood mazes, spirea, acanthus, stretching hot-pink bougainvillea, geraniums, cestrum, arbored purple wisteria, fiery cockscomb, jasmine, pink tamarisk, candytuft, marigold, ethereal gardenia, scented yellow water lily.

Bubbling fountains betray pools hidden from sight behind hedges. Small waterfalls are buried within the canopied green of aquatic moss draped precariously upon their cascades. An infinity of moving water links pool to pool, flowing eagerly down carved troughs set within the short staircases. Soft gurgles and sprinkles and drips and splatters. The Islamic garden, a living, liquid art form, Quranic paradise brought to Earth.

Tonight, however, the envious moon exacts its revenge on Partal pride, forcing a humbling opacity upon the brilliant floral display.

Thirty feet east of the Tower of the Ladies, hugging the fortress wall, is the compact but exquisite Partal Oratory, the Sultan's private garden mosque. The natural southeastern turn in the outer wall at this location allows the mihrab sunken into the center of the oratory's eastern wall to align with Mecca, as if the entire hilltop was oriented precisely for just this purpose. Muted lamplight seeps from the jalousie windows. Faint whispers betray a human presence within.

Two watchmen robed in concealing black stand just outside the oratory entrance, invisible, flanking the closed door. The interior evokes the Hall of the Ambassadors in the Comares Palace, only in miniature. Ornate stucco walls are splashed with an arabesque infinity, then tilework dado, wooden coffered ceiling, Quranic calligraphy. Tall silver lamps stand in each corner, their flames turned low to avoid attracting attention.

Inside, ten individuals are seated on a tight circular arrangement of pillows. Each wears a long black robe. Black turbans which drape down upon their shoulders are pulled around their faces and pinned, leaving only their eyes exposed. Complete anonymity. Several pairs lean in towards each other, whispering; others remain silent. On the floor beside the person seated in front of the mihrab rests a large leather-bound book. Beside it sits a lit tapered reading candle in an carved ivory holder.

In the center of the circle, upon a square of red silk, rests a shimmering orb upon a wooden stand. The polished brass sphere is ten inches in diameter and has several thin bands of silver wrapping its circumference at odd angles. A dense web of markings cover the entire surface; lines of longitude and latitude, engraved numbers and symbols, gradations, Arabic calligraphy. A scientific instrument of some sort.

The person in front of the mihrab clears his throat. "Brothers, let us pray the *dhikr*, the remembrance, the invocation of the Beloved. Together let us recite the ninety-nine names of Allah." The leader first sings the name in Arabic. A brief pause follows, then the nine together recite the attribute.

*"Ar-Rahman - The Compassionate.*
*Ar-Rahim - The Merciful.*

*Al-Malik - The Sovereign Lord, Our King.*
*Al-Quddus - The Holy, the Pure, the Perfect..."*

And so it goes until all ninety-nine names are intoned. The dhikr ends with the leader softly singing,

*"We Praise the Greatest Name of God, Allah.*
*A...a...alla...h*
*A...alla...h*
*A...a...a...alla...h*
*Al...lah*
*Allah."*

The reverberation of the dhikr's ending note lingers for a moment, then trails into silence. Each person folds his legs beneath him into a meditation posture, flattens his open-fingered right palm to the ground. The left hand is then balled, thumb fitted into the curved index finger and rested in the lap. As the muraqaba begins, the room congeals into stillness, not a wisp of sound to be heard.

After twenty minutes, the leader reaches down and picks up the book and opens it to a marked page, lifts the taper close, then reads, "As is written in the *Rasail Ikhwan al-Safa*, the *Epistles of the Brethren of Purity*,"

*"Turn, brother, from the sleep of negligence and the slumber of ignorance."*

The speaker begins to recite their strange creed. He speaks a single line, then halts; the others repeat the line together. He then moves to the next line, the others follow, and so on, a rhythmic back and forth cadence.

*"We are the Ikhwan al-Safa, the Brethren of Purity.*
*We are the guardians of truth.*
*We are the defenders of inquiry.*
*We are the protectors of sacred knowledge.*
*We are purveyors of the natural sciences.*
*We are the hidden imams.*
*We are the sleepers in the cave.*
*May Allah bless his humble servants.*
*May Allah guide our thoughts and our actions.*
*Praise his holy name."*

Silence, then he begins a chant, solo. "As proclaimed in the Epistles,"

*"Know that among us there are Sultans, princes, ministers, administrators, tax collectors, treasurers, officers, chamberlains, servants of kings, soldiers.*

*We are defenders of culture, persons of piety and virtue.*

*Brothers, we are many, yet we are one.*

*We seek perfection:*
*Arab in ancestry and Islamic in faith,*
*a Babylonian in education,*
*a Hebrew in astuteness,*
*a disciple of Jesus in conduct,*
*with the piety of a Syrian monk,*
*a Greek in the natural sciences,*
*an Indian in the interpretation of mysteries,*
*and above all,*
*a Sufi in our spiritual quest."*

The recite-repeat-recite-repeat cadence begins anew.

*"We are the Ikhwan al-Safa, the Brethren of Purity.*
*We are the guardians of truth..."*

The leader sets the taper down then closes the book, lays it on the floor. He lifts his palm towards the metal sphere. "Brothers, before you is a revolutionary astronomical instrument, a recent gift of our brothers at the Maragheh Observatory in Persia. The instrument has been ruled blasphemous by the small-minded fundamentalists in Baghdad. This object was smuggled at great risk through Babylon, Egypt, and the Maghreb. The Granadine Brethren of Purity now stand guard over it. We will defend it with our lives. It is called a "spherical astrolabe," and it was invented and perfected by the followers of our brother, the Persian astronomer Nasir al-Din al-Tusi, may Allah rest his soul."

The speaker leans forward and lifts the metal sphere from its stand with both hands, his arms sagging under its considerable weight. He passes it to his left. Heads slowly nod, eyes grow large, fingers caress the sphere, point to this or that feature. Several appreciative whispers are offered as the instrument rounds the gathering.

"Unlike the standard flat-disk astrolabe many of us are familiar with, this machine has a complex set of internal gears, allowing it to rotate about its axes, providing a far more precise calculation of the bearer's local latitude given the local time, and vice versa. As you know, brothers, astrolabes are critical for determining *Qibla* and *Salah*, the direction to Mecca and the times for prayer. But they also find use in adjusting our calendar, determining the location of the planets, predicting the position of the Sun and the Moon, setting horoscopes, and so forth. Perhaps most importantly, brothers, the astrolabe, in a suitably modified form, can be used by mariners to determine their position at sea and hence enable them to follow trade routes. While calculations with disk astrolabes are sufficient for navigation within the Mediterranean Sea between Syria and al-Andalus, this new spherical machine presents revolutionary possibilities." The shrouded faces are now glued expectantly to the leader.

"As you know, brothers, the great western ocean beyond Gibraltar lies unexplored. Even the most fearless mariners, Muslim or Christian, dare not attempt a cross-ocean journey. The astronomer's in Maragheh have proved that our Earth is round, that we inhabit a rotating sphere. They have demonstrated this, brothers, using mathematics and have even estimated the distance required to circle the world. The journey is many thousands of miles. Disk astrolabes are not sufficiently precise to permit such a journey over open water. The spherical astrolabe, however, possesses that precision. The Persian astronomers have rejected Ptolemy's model of the universe and replaced it with their own creation. The mathematics that governs their new system has been used to produce the calculations of the spherical astrolabe." He pauses expectantly. "Imagine, brothers. Sail into the unknown of the setting sun and arrive finally in Persia. Think of the lands to be discovered along the way. Imagine the undiscovered countries to be claimed for Islam. For al-Andalus." Excited nods and furious whispers erupt.

"Brothers, we are guardians of the truth, the defenders of inquiry, of exploration. It is imperative that the spherical astrolabe never find its way into the hands of the Christians. They must remain ignorant of its true nature and its potential, else they will use it against us. We must also guard its secrets from the closed-minded among the faithful who shun the many contributions of Muslim astronomers as blasphemous. Let us recite our creed, brothers, as a pledge to defend this scientific instrument of inquiry and the truth it embodies." The ten men join their voices into a soft chorus.

*"We are the Ikhwan al-Safa, the Brethren of Purity.*
*We are the guardians of truth ..."*

The ten rise in silence, their meeting ended. Pillows are tucked into bins, the oratory lamps extinguished, and the group files one by one from the oratory door and into the camouflage of the inky garden maze. The black-robed wraiths disperse in different directions. Four walk back into the palace complex, one of whom carries the shrouded orb. Three exit onto the Lower Royal Road that leads up the hill and into the medina, two head towards the Alcazaba, and three leave the Alhambra through the Arm's Gate for the long walk back down into the Albayzín. Within five minutes, all evidence of their gathering has vanished, safely tucked away until the next new moon.

## Impossible Angles

She is again dressed in hijab, her gait surprisingly quick given her stature. Aisha, three steps behind, struggles to keep up. The two avert their eyes from those they pass, ignore the now-familiar leers and catcalls of the bridge guards, cross the Darro and enter the Albayzín. Instead of turning right to the madrasa, however, they turn left, walk for one hundred paces, then cross the street and head uphill into the narrow, high-walled alley.

The two march in silence, Layla absorbed in replaying her conversation with her father from the previous evening. The Maristan Hospital, Sultan Muhammad's gift to the city, safe haven for the deformed, the mentally ill. Men, women and babies. The poorest of the poor, ill omens to their families, unwelcome even within the homes that birthed them. With no place to go, these outcasts would otherwise die on the streets or fall prey to animals outside the city walls, the standard fate for pariahs. The Maristan Hospital, in serving Granada's disadvantaged, is the first of its kind in al-Andalus. The layout and organization of the Maristan is loosely modeled after the Hospital of Bimaristan Nuri in Damascus.

In her father's customary manner, a lecture on the medical arts absorbed much of their evening, prompted, as usual, by her single question: 'Baba, what do you know of the Maristan Hospital?' She smiles with fond recollection at his predictability. As always, she indulged him, eager to learn from his encyclopedic mastery of all subjects.

He reminded her first that fourteenth century Muslim medicine is the most advanced in the civilized world, due in large measure to the acquisition and translation into Arabic of the vast medical knowledge of the ancient Greeks: Hippocrates, Galen, Aristotle, and many others. The pioneers of Muslim medicine built upon this Greek bedrock, thanks first to the efforts in the east of the Persian Ibn Sina (known as Avicenna) in the eleventh century, then extended in the west under the great twelfth-century intellectual flowering of Córdoba, courtesy of Ibn Rushd (known as Averroes) and Maimonides (Moses ben-Maimon to his fellow Jews). During its heyday, Córdoba alone had fifty hospitals for the treatment of all manner of ills.

Layla learned that the seminal gifts of al-Andalus to the world's medical arts are many and varied. The roots of modern surgery rest here: the design of surgical instruments; the use of narcotics for anesthesia; employing alcohol for the sterilization of instruments and wounds; the use of catgut for stitches; the development of retraction tools; the honing of surgical technique using animals; the use of postmortem autopsy as a learning and teaching vehicle; the mandate of post-operative hygiene; preemptive treatment for loss of blood and shock. The list is endless. A Granadine knight injured in battle by crossbow or lance thrust is far more likely to survive his wounds than a Christian knight.

The logical progression of Muslim medicine from perfection of the mechanics of surgery to the more subtle and perplexing afflictions of infectious disease is a topic of great contemporary interest given the horrific onslaught of the Great Plague in 1348-1350, which eviscerated much of Europe, eventually finding its way to Granada and the Albayzín. As might be expected, Ibn al-Khatib had his own ideas on the subject and reminded his daughter that he wrote a treatise on the plague, promoting the still controversial notion that the horrific disease spreads by contagion, direct person to person contact, not by breathing fouled air. His advice for containment of the plague, employed with much success in Granada in 1349, mandated the physical removal of the stricken from family living quarters. The city was largely spared.

Predictably, her father ended his lecture by trotting out well-thumbed copies of Avicenna's *Canon of Medicine,* Maimonides' *Medical Principles,* and Averroes' *Colligent* for her to peruse and discover for herself. Without a hint of ego he casually adds that his own medical encyclopedia currently under construction will supplant these classics and become the new touchstone of the medical arts for centuries to come. She grins as she walks.

Only fifty yards up the hill they turn right and finally arrive at the entrance to the Maristan Hospital. Layla stops, wary of what she will find inside. The exterior of the building is unassuming. Two-storied, whitewashed, twin horsehoe keyholed windows ring the exterior, a low-angled terra-cotta tile roof, a large wooden door. An Arabic inscription beside the entrance reads,

*"Maristan Hospital – Gift of Sultan Muhammad V to the Peoples of Granada, May Allah Praise His Name. May our city's outcasts find refuge and peace within these walls. There is no victor but Allah."*

She pauses to catch her breath, steady her nerves. She has never been in a hospital, of any kind. She remains unconvinced that there is any value in this type of Sufi training. She takes a deep breath then exhales, resigned to obey Master al-Mussib's command. She steps forward and raps the heavy metal knocker three times, wondering what this strange new world will bring.

The two women are led by an attendant through the anteroom and into the room of the Maristan's Chief Administrator, Majahid al-Khayyat, a tanned, short, bald and pudgy, middle-aged man of obvious Arab ancestry. He exudes the demeanor of a favorite uncle. As al-Khayyat rises from his low-slung desk, the attendant introduces the two.

"My Lord, this is Layla al-Khatib, daughter of the Sultan's Grand Vizier and a student of Master al-Mussib. Her lady-in-waiting, Aisha. They have come to assist the Maristan staff."

Al-Khayyat comes forward, beaming, and clasps Layla's shoulders, shaking her with unexpected familiarity. It is impossible for the two women not to grin.

"Yes, yes, yes, I have been expecting you two. Welcome, dear ladies, welcome! I am so glad you have come. The Maristan only has a permanent staff of ten. Our volunteers are the life's blood of our work. Master al-Mussib's students are our angels. I am most grateful for your willingness to help, Layla." He is all smiles and nods.

Layla responds, "I am honored, sir, to serve. While I am inexperienced in such work, I am a quick learner and no stranger to labor. Aisha is available to help with laundry or cleaning or whatever else might be needed."

He beams, "Good, good, good." Smiles and nods. "Layla, you will find your service here unlike anything you could ever imagine. Here we are the hands of the Prophet, may Allah bless his name." His smile fades. "The mentally ill, the broken, outcasts left to die, all are welcome here, Muslim, Christian and Jew. We ask no questions, demand no answers. Within six months of opening we had taken in seventy-five men, women, and children. We bathe them, clothe them, feed them, and tend their wounds." He stops and locks onto her eyes. "We love them." His smile returns. "First, Layla, they will break your heart and make you cry. But then they will make you smile, laugh even! You will see. There is much joy within these walls, my dear, even amid the obvious suffering. All our patients require is love and attention, attention and love. Just like us, yes?" He stands smiling, hands on his hips.

After a moment he purses his lips then furls his eyebrows, concentrating. He relaxes and smiles again, turns to the attendant with raised index finger, "Domingo, send for Constancia. I think Layla should start in the baby ward. And introduce Aisha to the laundry staff." His grin just doesn't fade. Layla is amused, wonders what sustains his irrepressible affability and charm.

"My Lady." She offers a slight bow. "I am Constancia, head nurse of the baby ward. We are delighted to have you here." The middle-aged Castilian woman has an easy, self-assured manner. Her calm, unassuming nature puts Layla at ease. Tall for a woman, kind almond eyes. Her gray-laced, dark brown hair is woven up into a bun. Motherly. Layla instantly likes her.

"I am honored, Constancia." She returns the bow. "Please call me Layla."

"Come, Layla, let me show you the baby ward." Layla turns and smiles her goodbye to Aisha. Aisha offers a weak, uncertain look topped by raised eyebrows. Constancia and Layla turn and begin to walk towards the door leading into the next room.

"We will first pass through the women's ward. The baby ward is on the other side. The men's ward lies across the courtyard. That is where the other students of Master al-Mussib serve." Layla follows Constancia's left palm out the window, sees a large open courtyard with a central pool. Several people mill about. As Constancia opens the door, the two move inside the large room two paces, then stop. Constancia means to give Layla time to adjust before moving forward.

A biting, acrid smell of stale urine immediately strikes Layla, causing her to grimace. Then an aggressive fecal whiff assaults her, chased by the pungent remnants of spent menstrual blood. Layla's heart begins to pound. She tries to steady herself and concentrate instead on the scene in front of her. The room is perhaps fifteen feet wide by forty feet long; bed mats, folded back for daytime use as sitting pillows, line either side of the central walkway. Maybe two dozen women are scattered about, most sitting, several standing; one looks dreamily out the window.

Three nurses in gray robes dart about to this or that person. One nurse sits, reading to a young girl. Another to her right is changing the diaper on an old woman. Layla's eyes recoil in shock from the pruney naked body. As the residents gradually become aware of their visitor, they begin to rise and shuffle toward her, zombie like. Layla takes a deep breath, tries to steady herself. Constancia reaches out and squeezes Layla's arm, injecting calm.

Constancia speaks with a voice of surprising authority. "Ladies of the Maristan, I want to introduce you to our new nurse, Layla. She has come to say hello. Please make her feel welcome." The residents range in age from young girls to shriveled old women. Their ancestry crosses all boundaries; Berber, Arab, Castilian, Jew. All are dressed in thin, cotton robes, hair down. Many have obvious physical deformities, a misplaced feature here, a wrong-angled joint there, a cleft lip, a useless arm, a dragged foot. She sees the unmistakable vacant stare of the mentally deformed. Several wear paranoid, darting eyes. Curiously, though, all have bright, beaming smiles plastered upon their faces. Several grunt with glee as they approach.

One young girl waves her arms in circles, laughing hysterically. As the ragtag group edges forward to encircle Layla, several raise their hands, begin to stroke her. Their smiles only widen, followed by excited peals of laughter. A girl her own age reaches up and with her fingers traces the lines of Layla's face over and over again, squealing with delight. Completely surrounded, Layla has to will herself to remain still. Finally, with as strong a voice as she can muster, she says, "I am pleased to meet you, ladies." Despite her best attempt, she only manages a weak, uncertain smile.

Constancia giggles, then says, "Ladies, that is enough for now. You will have a chance to play with Layla later." She reaches out and guides Layla through the throng and on towards the baby ward.

"The ladies can be a little overwhelming the first time you meet them. It was the same for me. You did just fine, Layla, just fine."

Constancia closes the door behind her and indicates with her sweeping palm. "The Maristan baby ward. At present we have eight babies, all under the age of four. They have been left on our doorstep, the parents anonymous. We have named each of them, of course." She smiles, then reaches out to inject more calm. "Are you ready, Layla?"

"I think so." Her heart is racing.

The room is perhaps half the size of the lady's ward. A dozen wooden cradles ring the outer walls of the room. A nurse is bent over a cradle to their left, changing a diaper. The middle-aged woman looks up and smiles. The urine-fecal-blood mélange lingers for a moment, then is thankfully muted. The room is silent except for the nurse who coos to quiet her baby. The two make their way to the first cradle to their right.

"This is Hasan, Layla. He is two." The baby boy's head is perhaps three times its normal size, the enormous skull compressing his features into a squashed doll's face. His mouth opens and closes, opens and closes, a fish out of water, his teeth yellowed and pointed, fang like.

As quick gasp, then Layla's mouth opens in shock and a soft "Oh my..." slips out. The boy's head is too heavy for him to turn, but his bright blue eyes roll to the left to track his visitors. After a moment a hint of a smile begins to tickle the corners of his mouth, growing wider with excitement. He begins to make a soft gurgling noise.

Constancia chimes in, "Hasan loves to laugh. He is a good boy." She reaches down and rubs her finger across his cheek. The smile widens and the gurgling grows. Constancia looks up for Layla's reaction. Her lower lip is quivering. Her eyelids offer a vain attempt to stem the flash flood, but the dam abruptly fails, allowing two tears to course down her cheeks. Constancia reaches for her arm, steadies her. "It is fine to cry, Layla. We all do." She offers a kind smile, then another arm squeeze.

Layla wipes her face, sniffs, then takes a deep breath. "Forgive me. I am better now."

Constancia answers, "There is nothing to forgive, Layla. Tears are a gift."

As they move to the next cradle, Layla's anxiety builds, her heart pounding. "This is Maryam. She is about six months old." Layla looks down upon a sleeping baby girl covered by a thin sheet. Her face is angelic, perfect. Normal. She suckles in her sleep. Thin, wispy dark hair. A beautiful baby girl. "Maryam was left on our doorstep just two month's back." Constancia reaches down and lifts the sheet. Layla leans forward and peers in. The baby's arms and torso appear normal, but her hip joints are all wrong, the left leg bent outward at an impossible angle, the right rotated in its socket by ninety degrees. Her right leg is only a quarter of the size of her left leg, and her right foot has no toes. Constancia lowers the sheet.

"Maryam will never walk, obviously, but she is otherwise healthy." Layla leans over and reaches down to stoke the baby girl's hair. Tears plop onto the sheet one after the other as her shoulders quiver. Constancia gives her time and space, then reaches for her, guiding her to the next cradle. "Come, Layla. Come."

A baby boy, perhaps three years old, sits up in his cradle at their approach. He has a diaper on but is otherwise naked. His arms dance in the air to his giggles at seeing Constancia. He squeals with glee, causing the two women to laugh.

"This is Nafi, our first." Constancia beams. "My favorite." She reaches down into the cradle and pulls up the boy. "Ohhhh, you are getting so heavy, Nafi. How is my beautiful baby boy today?" As Constancia rotates toward her, Layla focuses on the boy's cleft lip and palate, his split upper lip and upper jaw opening an ugly, wide hole in his mouth, teeth all askew.

Nafi is all smiles as he strains forward with both arms towards Layla. Constancia grins and hands him over without asking permission. Layla has no experience with babies, but with a surprised smile awkwardly accepts the boy into her arms. He leans back to take in her face, reaches up and touches her cheek, then beams. He swings both arms around her neck and squeezes her tight. The tears begin to roll once more, but this time Layla wears a radiant smile. She hugs the boy tightly, smothers him. Constancia looks on, satisfied.

After they have completed the circuit, Constancia says, "You will work with me today, Layla. I will teach you to bathe the babies, to change them, feed them, and cloth them. It is hard work, but you will do just fine. Within a day you will be at ease working on your own. You will see."

It has been an emotionally draining morning, but Layla is a little more confident now. "Thank you, Constancia, for your kindness." The mentor and her student exchange a warm smile.

Aisha tries to engage her in conversation on the steep uphill trek back to the Alhambra, but Layla remains pensive, offering only one word answers. She is reluctant to attempt to describe what she has just experienced. Aisha stares, having never before seen Layla at a loss for words. Eventually she gives up, and they walk on in silence. Layla feels the intense need to be alone, to absorb what she has seen and felt. She intuitively senses that her life has just changed in a profound way.

Ibn al-Khatib is much later than normal. He climbs the narrow stairs, several books and his calligraphy case under his arm, then enters their suite just past sunset, the late hour imposed by the demand for his finishing touches on the overall design and precise wording of the Marinid Treaty he has been fussing over. He shakes his head side to side, wondering where the day has gone. He has been looking forward to an evening working on his medical treatise. Alas, it will be a late start. The manuscript is perhaps three-quarters complete now, his restless excitement to finish the project growing with each passing day.

Layla would normally hear his footfall and rush to greet him with a hug and a kiss at the door. Oddly, she is absent today. He deposits his things on the table in the anteroom, removes his cloak, hangs it, then walks into their living room, curious.

"Layla?" He stops, the sight in front of him something he has never before witnessed. His daughter lies on her divan, curled into a fetal position, head resting on a pillow, book folded across her hip, sound asleep. He lifts his eyebrows but does not say a word. Curious, he steps forward and lifts the volume, rotates it so he can see the spine. Maimonides' *Medical Principles.* He smiles, opens it to her place, thumbs two pages back. The chapter is entitled, "On the Deformities of the Human Body." He instantly makes the connection. Today was her first day at the Maristan. He chastises himself for having forgotten.

He closes the volume and lays it down, then steps forward and kneels, leans close to study his daughter's face, something he never gets to do from this distance any more. Dense chestnut curls are sprayed about, her face completely at peace, a study in resting beauty. He is drawn back to her childhood, memories filling the space between them, his adorable little girl now a beautiful woman.

After a moment he whispers, "Danah, you would be so proud of Layla. You would be so proud of our little girl." A smile emanating from deep within his heart joins the welling up of his eyes. He rises, steps into her bedroom, returns with a blanket. He drapes it over her, tucking it neatly around her feet. She does not stir. He steps across the room and raises the lamp flame beside his divan, grabs a volume off the tall stack with one hand, his writing kit with the other, then sits down and scoots back. He eagerly opens the book, then begins his long evening of play.

Within two weeks, Layla has settled into her daily routine. She rises in the pre-dawn darkness and dresses. After sunrise prayer comes thirty minutes of meditation, then selections from the Quran and various commentaries and a quick breakfast. Next comes the ordeal of donning hijab, then the trek with Aisha to the Maristan, not to return until the afternoon. A refreshing visit to the Royal Baths follows, a sweet moment of relaxation, then back to her suite for memorization of various hadith assigned by Master al-Mussib until her father returns for dinner. Sunset prayer, then calligraphy practice in the evening, Master al-Mussib's latest inexplicable mandate, followed by more meditation. Early to bed. She has been so tired by the evening that she has slept like a baby, for the first time in years. She is content, happy.

Her mornings at the Maristan are spent in the baby ward, work she has come to adore. Maryam is her favorite. After noon prayer and a light lunch, she helps out in the lady's ward. Today she is drying and clothing the ladies as they emerge from the make-shift bath located in the room adjacent to their ward. Each resident emerges dripping and sputtering, shoulders arched high, arms tucked by their sides, hands modestly crossed in front of them in the universal posture of the just-bathed.

Layla greets them with a smile and words of encouragement, leads them by the hand to the corner of the bath, then sits them down on a stool. She next takes a large fluffy towel, first dries their head then wraps it around their shoulders. Next, she gently brushes out their hair, an act which elicits either contented smiles or soft groans of joy, sometimes both. The obvious delight imparted by the grooming brings a bright smile to Layla's face. The simple pleasures of life.

When finished, she removes the towel and begins to work her way down their bodies, first drying their arms, then shoulders, armpits, then breasts, torso, groin, legs, and finally their feet. When complete, she helps the ladies stand up, turns them around and dries their backside and any places she missed. She pins a loin cloth on them and picks up a fresh yellow robe and wraps it around their body, sashes it, then escorts them by hand back into the ward. On to the next resident.

She has gotten over the shock of their naked bodies, their deformities now invisible. In truth, she has come to enjoy the process, particularly for the joy it seems to bring to the women. She has always taken her daily bath for granted, never given the luxury more than a passing thought. No longer.

She turns and sees her next charge exit the bath, the drenched nurse directing the resident to Layla. An old woman, her first. Ancient and emaciated. Castilian. She has white stringy hair, creviced wrinkles, loose folds of pruny skin. A puff of wind would knock her down. Her withered breasts sag to her belly button. She sports no obvious deformity. Layla smiles.

"Come, my Lady, let us get you dried and dressed," then she leads her to the stool. The old woman's hair is brittle and knotted.

Layla takes her time to ensure she doesn't hurt her. The woman is silent, closes her eyes and smiles, rich with content. When finished, Layla begins to dry her off, gingerly working her way down her body, finally kneeling in front of her, concentrating on drying the old woman's gnarled feet.

For some unknown reason, Layla is drawn to the old woman's face, stops what she is doing and looks up. Otherworldly, intense gray eyes bore into her, the old woman's face radiant with its loving smile.

The woman whispers, "Peace be with you, Isa (*Jesus*) ibn Maryam (*son of Mary*)." Layla's eyes brim with tears, her chest constricts. She has an inexplicable sense that her heart swells within her chest, melts, then pours forth from her body. A profound feeling of love, of peace, sweeps around her, fills the room. She beams through her tears, feeling profoundly linked with this stranger in some deep, mystical way.

Layla whispers, "I love you, too, sister. Peace be with you." The two sustain their locked gaze a moment longer, then the old woman breaks eye-contact and looks out into space, the spell broken. Layla hesitates, unsure of what just happened, then looks back down at her gnarled feet, finishes drying them, helps the old woman rise, then clothes her. Layla turns her, places her hands on both shoulders and searches the old woman's eyes once more for confirmation that she didn't imagine what just happened. In vain. Only a vacant stare is returned. As Layla leads her back into the ward, the old woman grunts, clucks her tongue, mutters some gibberish.

"Describe for me again exactly what you felt as she said those words." Layla sits on her pillow in front of Master al-Mussib, head down, staring at the floor.

She searches but comes up empty. "Words do not do justice to the feeling, Master." She hesitates. "I felt as if my heart swelled, then melted and love poured forth from my body, linking me to this woman in some way I cannot name. We were one person. There was a union of our souls."

"Mmmm..." He looks carefully at his student, then smiles. "It was joyful?"

"Oh, Master, profoundly joyful! The greatest peace I have ever felt. But then it was gone, and afterwards I wondered if I had imagined it all."

"No, Layla, you did not imagine it. You have been given a great gift by Allah, Layla, a great gift. It was a glimpse, if only momentary, of the tawhid that we Sufis seek. Union with Allah. Annihilation of ourselves within Allah's infinite love. Love links our souls together, Layla, links each of us with our Creator. You experienced this holy joining." He muses. "I must be candid, Layla. This experience has come to you far earlier in your journey, your path, than I have ever before seen. Even for myself. But Allah knows best the time and the place to reveal himself." He thinks for a moment, then says, "You are student no longer, Layla. You are a disciple of the Sufi Way."

She looks up, radiant. "Master, I doubted your wisdom in sending me to the Maristan. I see now that it was the greatest gift you could have given me."

He demurs. "Layla, Layla, that Allah has given you. Allah, not me. I am but a humble servant of the Truth."

She nods, beams, then says, "Master, I am puzzled by the words the woman used. 'Peace be with you, Isa ibn Maryam.' Why would she call me Isa?"

"As Ibn al-Arabi, our great Andalusi Sufi philosopher, tells us, Isa is the 'seal of universal holiness,' the suffering servant of Allah. It is told in the Christian scriptures that before he died, Isa washed the feet of his disciples. To remind them that their role is to serve the needy, care for the outcasts, love the poor. Isa washed his disciple's feet as a sign of love and peace, just as you did. It makes perfect sense, Layla. As a Christian she would know that story. You were Isa to her, Layla. Yes, Isa."

Her father has invited her to his office in the Hall of the Kings within the Palace of the Lions to join him for noon prayer, a light lunch, then a chess match. She smiles at the thought, excited.

She steps from the stairwell, chess set tucked under her arm, and stops, letting her eyes adjust. The courtyard is empty. She looks up and scans the blue sky. A beautiful day. She breathes in the fresh air, holds it, then exhales. Her eyes track to the water. As if commanded, the dense school of iridescent orange fish rise to the surface, mouthing their ovaled greetings in perfect syncopation. She smiles and bows.

She pivots right and begins the short trek at her usual brisk pace. After twenty yards, she turns hard right to enter the corridor leading into the Palace of the Lions and collides at full stride with a wall of crimson. She gasps her surprise on impact, the chess set tumbling to the ground, pieces scattering everywhere. She backs up a step and tries to compose herself. As recognition dawns her heart begins to race.

"Imam Abd al-Malik. Forgive me. I should have been paying more attention to where I was going." She attempts an apologetic smile but does not quite get there. She falls silent.

The Berber's face is stone cold, expressionless, but his ebony eyes are alive, dangerous. She lowers her gaze, but she can feel his eyes move over her body; no hijab, exposed hair. She feels intensely self-conscious. His frown deepens as the tense silence ticks off. He whispers so that only she can hear, in a tone dripping with contempt, "Shameful. You bring dishonor to yourself, woman, and to your father, and to the Alhambra, and to Islam." He shakes his head with disgust.

As his words unroll her blood begins to boil, her furious emerald eyes boldly meeting his, offering a silent challenge. She stands firm but wisely does not speak.

He steps to the side, then edges past her, the quick snap of the Queen's neck under his boot announcing the casualty. She stands where she is for several moments trying to calm herself, willing the tears from her eyes. She bends down and gathers the pieces, then resumes her walk to the Hall of the Kings, much slower now under her heavy burden.

# Constructs

The three clergy are seated on ornate inlaid chairs on a raised platform at the far end of the darkened oak-paneled room. Six guards stand behind them in a semicircle. The vestments of the priests to the left and right mark them as bishops; their purple *cassocks* reach from shoulder to ankle, covered by white *rochet* garments to the waist and purple *mozzetta* capes. Purple, the ancient signature of royalty and privilege. Gold rings, *miter* hats, and large gold pectoral crosses hang from their necks to mid-chest.

The man in the center, on a larger throne-like chair, is a cardinal. He wears a bright scarlet cassock with matching *ferraiolo* cape, and an even more ornate, jeweled pectoral cross. Scarlet symbolizes a cardinal's willingness to die in defense of the Pope. Three old men. All are well fed, but the cardinal is especially rotund, awash in jowls and rolls of flesh.

The papal attendant leads the entourage into the room, deposits them about ten feet in front of the clergy, then stops and turns, raises his palm to the man standing to his left, and commences in Latin.

"Excellencies, may I present Sir Ernaud de Florenssan, papal liaison of His Highness King Charles of France; Don Gonzalo Ruiz Girón, ambassador of Aragon; Don Alfonso Méndez de Guzmán, aide-de-camp to Enrique of Trastámara; Antonio de Castrocario, ambassador of Genoa." Each man bows as his name is called.

"Gentlemen, may I present His Holiness's *Papal Legate*, Excellencies Bishop de Hulhac and Bishop de Fonte, *Apostolic Nuncios*; and the Most Reverend Cardinal Coysset, *Legatus a Latere*, who possesses full plenipotentiary powers of His Holiness, Pope Urban V."

Close-fitted, unreadable expressions drape the faces of all three clergy, but their eyes are alive as they bore into their visitors, probing for motives in this unlikely gathering. There is a tick of a nod from each nuncio as they are announced, but Cardinal Coysset remains motionless, sullen. The scent of arrogance rises from his scarlet *biretta* hiding the shock of white hair.

When the introductions have ended the visitors approach one at a time, first bow to the two bishops, then kneel in front of the Cardinal, kiss the extended ruby-studded gold ring on his thick, stubby finger, then step back and sit on a short stool, leaving them two feet lower than the clergy. By intent.

When the ceremonial declaration of Papal allegiance is complete, a gruff, "Leave us," is issued from Cardinal Coysset in concert with a flick of his pudgy wrist. The guards behind the clergy, the papal attendant, and the two pike-bearing door guards bow and file from the room, the last closing the thick oak door behind them with a crisp snap. The silence stretches out just to the point of discomfort.

Cardinal Coysset begins in a soft, raspy voice, "His Holiness, Pope Urban, would have enjoyed meeting with you, gentlemen. Unfortunately he is in the Italian Papal States at this time. He seeks a means for the safe...return...of the Avignon Papacy to Rome." A thinly veiled edge of contempt slithers along side his words. "In the Pope's absence, I possess full plenipotentiary powers in all matters of state." He offers the ambassadors a self-satisfied smile. His head pivots thirty degrees to his left as he switches to French. "Ernaud, it is good to see you again. I trust King Charles is well?"

"Indeed, Excellency, quite well. He sends his best regards, together with three casks of the Bordeaux wine Your Excellency so admires. From the Graves. The 1360 vintage. Best in a decade I am told." Cardinal Coysset nods his approval.

More silence. "To what does Avignon owe the pleasure of such a diverse set of distinguished visitors? I presume you have come to worship in His Holiness's new cathedral?" A thin, contemptuous grin.

After a slight hesitation the French liaison responds. "Excellency, I am sure you have heard that Pedro of Castile's forces defeated Enrique of Trastámara at Nájera in April. A complete rout. Enrique lost over seven thousand troops. Another five thousand were wounded, perhaps half of whom will eventually die. Enrique's broken army retreated to Zaragoza in Aragon for refitting.

"In short, Excellency, Nájera was a disaster; for Enrique, for Aragon, for France...for the Papacy. The only positive outcome was that several hundred of the Free Companies were annihilated. As you know well, Excellency, those mercenary scum are a great scourge upon France. They pillage and extort at will. The Free Companies will fight for anyone with gold, friend or enemy of the Papacy. The worst kind of mercenary. They are a plague on all, Excellency. King Charles paid them handsomely to fight beside the Enrique and the Aragonese. They are able troops, merciless. But King Charles' aim was to rid them from French soil, to safeguard Avignon, Excellency. They have now returned. For the moment they remain in Toulouse. For the moment."

"I see." The Cardinal strokes the cleft in his chin, absorbing the implications. He has been at the mercy of the Free Companies before, knows their ways. Just last year they arrived unannounced at the gates of Avignon and boldly extorted gold from His Holiness in exchange for not sacking the Papal Palace. Filthy heathen.

"Perhaps more importantly, Excellency, Edward the Black Prince of England joined forces with Pedro at Nájera. As did the infidel Moors of Granada." The cardinal frowns. "England was responsible for Pedro's victory. France cannot allow England a foothold in Iberia, Excellency." His tone sharpens. "We will not." He hesitates to settle his voice, then says, "England is no friend of the Papacy, Excellency. Pedro thumbs his nose at His Holiness. He persecutes the clergy in Castile, adopts the manner and dress of the infidel Moors. It is scandalous, Excellency. Scandalous."

Cardinal Coysset nods his agreement. "What would King Charles ask of the Pope, Ernaud?"

"His support, Excellency. Financial backing to rebuild Enrique's army. King Charles does not possess enough gold to re-hire the Free Companies to fight for Enrique and Aragon. But they must be removed from France, Excellency, before they choose to leave Toulouse and begin their pillage anew, as they surely will when they exhaust their gold." The Frenchman stiffens his back and raises his chin. "We also seek a Papal Blessing, Excellency."

The cardinals eyes widen. "Indeed... Why a Papal Blessing?"

"Excellency, we can use this revitalized Aragonese army to not only defeat Pedro and the English but to lead a crusade to push the infidel Moors out of Europe once and for all, conquer the Kingdom of Granada. The Moors fight beside Pedro, Excellency. They have unlawfully captured Aragonese lands. They make slaves of the Christians they subdue, Excellency. They rape our women, force His Holiness' flock to either convert or be executed. And they harbor the Jews, Excellency, place them in charge of Christian slaves. The Moors even allow the Jews to desecrate the Holy Eucharist. It is intolerable, Excellency."

Cardinal Coysset rasps, "Renew reconquista..." All three clergy nod their heads. "We could finish what Pope Alexander began and Fernando of Castile so tragically failed to complete. An interesting idea, Ernaud, very interesting. Go on."

"Certainly, Excellency. A Papal Blessing is required; indulgences for any Christians killed in battle against the infidels. Perhaps the Papal Standard to fly beside our colors into battle.

That is all we would require for reconquista, Excellency. First we defeat Pedro and the English, then we turn south to Granada. The Free Companies would jump at the chance to fight the Moors. Think of the riches. When the conquest is complete, Granada will be ceded to the Free Companies, Excellency. They will live off the fat of that cursed land, never to re-enter France."

Cardinal Coysset pivots his head to the right. "Don Gonzalo, would Aragon support giving a conquered Granada to the Free Companies?"

"We would, Excellency. Aragon and Castile will be finally joined, an impregnable barrier that would seal the Free Companies forever inside Granada."

"And what financial backing would Aragon require from the Pope to refit Enrique's army for battle?"

"Excellency, we estimate that we will need a total of twenty-one thousand gold francs. Aragon has raised five thousand. King Charles has already offered six thousand. The Republic of Genoa has offered three thousand. This leaves seven thousand francs, Excellency."

The cardinal turns to face the Genoese ambassador, eyebrows raised. "And what interests do our friends from the Republic of Genoa have in Iberia?"

Antonio de Castrocario clears his throat. "Excellency, as you know, Genoa is a close trading partner of Aragon. It is in our financial interests to see them triumph over Castile." The man hesitates, clearly uncomfortable. "But there is more at stake, Excellency." Cardinal Coysset eyes narrow as he smiles, pleased at ferreting out additional information. "Genoa has recently entered into a limited trade arrangement with the Kingdom of Granada for silks and ceramics." Cardinal Coysset's smile drops abruptly into a frown, but de Castocario pushes on. "Excellency, we have recently learned of some very interesting...rumors... coming out of Málaga."

"Well?" The cardinal has limited patience for Genoese ambitions.

"Excellency, it seems that a new scientific instrument has been invented in Persia. By Muslim astronomers." The Cardinal's frown deepens. "A magical calculating apparatus of some sort. One that supposedly allows mariners to calculate trade routes with far greater precision over long voyages than is presently possible."

"So?"

"Excellency, the best fleet in the Mediterranean sails under Genoese colors. If we possessed such a navigational tool of the requisite precision, we could finally attempt a crossing of the unexplored Western Ocean, find a western trade route to the Indies, the Spice Islands. And we could do this before the English, Excellency, before the infidel Moors. Excellency, an alliance of Genoa, Aragon, France, and the Papacy could rule the Western Ocean. England's power would wane. The Holy Roman Empire would be forced to bow to our demands. Imagine the lands to the west that we would discover, Excellency. Think of the potential converts to the faith."

Cardinal Coysset traces his cleft with his index finger. "How certain are you of the instrument's existence?"

"At present it remains only a rumor, Excellency. But from trusted sources."

"Where do these...rumors...say the machine resides?"

The ambassador hesitates. "In the Alhambra Palace in Granada, Excellency."

"Ahhh...now I see." A smug grin. "Reconquista, but with a handsome prize for those who press it." He muses. "Claim the western lands for Christendom..."

"Indeed, Excellency."

The conversation lapses into deathly stillness as Cardinal Coysset considers the proposition. Decision made, he begins, "For His Holiness' support, his financial backing, a Papal Blessing for crusade, the Papal Standard, and indulgences for any that are killed in reconquista, His Holiness would require one-third of the booty secured from the conquest of all lands within the Kingdom of Granada. All mosques must be converted to churches or be put to the torch. Jews and Moors must convert or be expelled. The Pope will also require a formal charter for absorbing any discovered western lands into Christendom, should we happen to possess Antonio's magical instrument. This charter will require a quarter of the profits from all future trade to, from and within this New World." The smug grin returns. "To be used to support the needs of an expanding Christendom...obviously." The man looks positively ravenous, his cheeks flushing with dreams of gold. "Ernaud?"

The French liaison's eyes widen, followed by a sigh, then a resigned, "Agreed, Excellency."

"Don Gonzalo?"

A pregnant pause, then, "Agreed, Excellency."

The cardinal continues, "Don Alfonso, will Enrique agree to this arrangement?"

No hesitation. "He will, Excellency."

"Antonio. One more thing is required of Genoa."

A weary, "Yes, Excellency?"

"His Holiness will insist upon Genoa's diplomatic aid in securing a safe haven for the Papacy in Rome."

"That I can guarantee, Excellency."

"Good. It is settled, then." He turns to his right. "Bishop de Hulhac will draw up the necessary documents. The cardinal extends his arm at a downward angle in dismissal. One by one the visitors rise, come forward, kneel and kiss his ring. When decorum is satisfied, the cardinal gathers his flesh, his scarlet flush matching his cassock under the strain of rising. He offers a satisfied smile to his guests. "In the meantime, let us adjourn to my apartments. We shall all sample King Charles' fine vintage, and drink to His Holiness' health, to the success of reconquista. And then we shall feast."

# Honor

The leopard paces, claws exposed, emeralds burning bright. "I do not have time for this, Baba!" She stops and turns to plead her case once more. "Or the desire. Or the patience. I cannot give up my duties at the Maristan. I will not! They are too important. I explained what happened last week, Baba, what Master al-Mussib said."

"Yes, yes, I know. And I understand. But Layla, this is not negotiable. It is only for an hour and only three days a week. You will still have time to reach the Maristan by late morning. Stay an hour later if you like."

She fumes, hands now on her hips, head tilted slightly to the side, eyes wide and furious, a combat posture he knows well. Inherited from her mother. "Ahhh! I refuse to waste my time!"

His temper flares, hardening his features. "Young Lady, let me remind you of your role at court and your duties as daughter of the Grand Vizier. Our Sultan feels that we must learn English, and educate Chandon, so we can bring him around to our cause. It may well be important for Granada's future. The Sultan only reluctantly agreed to allow you to become a disciple of Master al-Mussib, very reluctantly, and in spite of the clamor of the Africans on the Mexuar Council. He puts himself at considerable risk by allowing it. He did so because of me, not you. Your assistance with educating Chandon was part of that deal. You will not renege."

She sighs. The fires begin to die down as she realizes she has pushed him too hard. A resigned, "Where?"

"Here in the Comares Palace, just outside in the courtyard. Much safer, given all that has transpired around him. His guards will be present. Aisha can chaperone from a discreet distance."

"When?"

"At nine. Salamun will introduce you." His expression relaxes back to playful. "And behave yourself." He smiles to himself as he looks away to avoid her glare. She re-loads for a biting retort, but catches herself just in time, instead furling her eyebrows, frowning in silence.

Two large pillows are set at the northwest corner of the Courtyard of the Myrtles, the short table set beside them topped by two volumes, a writing kit, sheets of paper, a pitcher of water and two small tumblers. Salamun and Chandon stand close by, cross-armed, chatting. His two bodyguards remain at the base of the stairway leading to his room, eyes alert, but at a discreet distance. Only a few cirrus clouds rest high in the sky. It is a quiet morning, the air is still. The sun has yet to rise over the edge of the palace roof line, but hints of the swelter to come are already obvious.

Chandon wears blue cotton pants with gold stenciling down the legs, a matching blue shirt, and suede slippers. He visited the hammam early this morning, and now is squeaky clean and groomed.

"How old is she?"

"Mmmm, let me see... She just turned twenty. Old to still be unmarried." Salamun looks up to catch Chandon's eyes, then grins. "She was a baby when the Black Death struck Granada. Spring of 1349. A terrible time. I worked with her father to help save the city. Hundreds died, but far fewer than in most places. Her father's radical idea of quarantine of the sick was effective but highly unpopular. The sick and the dying were forced to leave their homes, evacuate to a camp outside the city walls. Most that left never returned. Burned on oak pyres at sunset. You could see the sad glow from the Alhambra each night. But the city was largely spared as a result."

"I see. We were not so lucky in England." He muses. "Twenty. And she is going to educate me?" He rolls his eyes. "This should be interesting."

Salamun chuckles. "Behave yourself, Young Knight, else she may have your head! Trust me, she is far more dangerous than your would-be assassin." His laugh is jolly. Chandon raises his eyebrows and opens his mouth in mock fear, then smiles. The old Jew grins mischievously. "And be careful she does not capture your heart. You have been warned!" Chandon's smile fades.

They both hear footsteps on the stairs at the far end of the courtyard, turn, unfold their arms, stand up straight. She steps out, followed by her lady-in-waiting, turns and registers their presence, then begins to walk towards them.

Chandon sifts her as she approaches. She is shorter than he would have guessed. Small boned. Her stride is fluid, confident. She wears a full-length, loose-fitting, white cotton robe, a burgundy belt tied around her waist. Two thin burgundy stripes start at her shoulder and run down the baggy sleeve to her wrist. Dark leather sandals. A white silk scarf with gold embroidery is loosely draped over her pinned-up hair, spilling onto her shoulders.

He can see the unruly chestnut curls lurking behind her ears, straining for freedom. Her attempt to sequester her hair has the exact opposite effect of that intended. The tease of chestnut adds magnificently to her allure. He is instantly curious. She is ten paces out when she flashes that smile and daggers him through the chest. His heart begins to race. It is uncanny how her smile frames her face, flaming her beauty as if lit by a thousand candles. There has been only one other woman who ever unnerved him with her looks. Now two. She has his undivided attention.

Her eyes are glued to Salamun, however, not him. She opens in flawless Castilian, "Salamun, how wonderful to see you! I trust you are well?" She warmly embraces the old Jew, who is all smiles. He basks in her affection.

"Layla! It is always a delight to see you, my dear. I am well, yes, very well, thank you. My you look lovely today! Alas, a girl no more!"

She beams. "Salamun, you are always so kind." She turns and says, "You remember Aisha."

"Of course, of course." He bows. "My Lady." Aisha returns the bow with a grin.

He studies her eyes. Such an unusual brilliant emerald green. He has never seen anything quite like it. The white and gold of the scarf offers a wonderful contrast to her olive-toned features. She is clearly of Arab lineage. One of the desert beauties of legend.

Salamun lifts his palm to his right. "Layla, may I introduce William Chandon of Brittany."

She turns her eyes to him. He bows, hoping she will remember the moonlit night. "My Lady. It is an honor to meet you." His voice is strong and deep, resonant. A voice used to command. He offers his most charming smile.

As she studies him she appreciates that her impression from a distance was true to the mark. Very handsome. Chiseled features, but intriguingly boyish. Dirty blond hair, brown eyebrows. His clean-shaven face is...unusual...but she must concede, pleasing. A small, half-moon scar decorates his forehead above his left eye. His nose has been broken. Twice? Penetrating, dark brown eyes. He is a big man, a head taller than her, but his frame is taut and angular. He looks the part of a famous knight.

She offers only a slight acknowledging bow in return, remaining expressionless, serious. "The pleasure is mine, sir." Her voice is soft and silky, but somehow imbued with confidence and verve.

After a protracted moment, Salamun clasps his hands together and grins. "Well then...we will leave you two to your lessons, yes?" The wizard chuckles, amused. "Shall we, Aisha?" The two stand in silence, turn and watch Salamun and Aisha depart. At the end of the courtyard Aisha stops at the entrance to their suite, fusses with something just inside the stairwell, then emerges, places a pillow on the marble beside the door, reclines, opens her book, then leans back against the wall, the ever-discreet chaperone.

The air is dense, too weighty to breathe comfortably. The silence stretches out awkwardly. He sighs, deciding to act. "So...shall we sit, My Lady?" He indicates the pillows.

"Certainly." They each settle in to face one another. "Please call me Layla."

"Wonderful. Good to meet you, Layla. My friends call me Chandon." His smile is warm, infectious. "I am grateful, Layla, that you are so willing to take the time to instruct me in Arabic. A fascinating language. I am deeply appreciative."

She thinks, 'If only you knew.' She nods but remains stone-faced. The moment stretches out before she offers a slightly too curt, "What languages do you speak, Chandon?"

He relaxes a little. "Well, English is my native tongue, of course. I am fluent in French and Castilian. And Breton dialect. A little Latin. And you?"

"I speak and write several dialects of Arabic. I am fluent in Hebrew and Castilian. I do speak a little French and some Persian."

That awkward silence. "I understand that you were severely injured. I trust your wounds are healing."

"Thank you for asking. Yes, I am feeling much better. I still have a limp, but I am determined that it will only be temporary. Salamun is not so sure." He muses. "I owe my life to Salamun, several times over. He possesses knowledge of the medical arts that are far beyond what is known in Brittany or England."

"Indeed. He and my father have spent many years perfecting that knowledge. Salamun has been my personal physician since I was a baby. He also attends to the Sultan and the Royal Family." An affectionate smile. "He is a kind and gentle man. My father is working on a new medical encyclopedia. Salamun is his constant foil for his new ideas."

"I see. I am supposed to meet your father next week for more lessons on the history and culture of Granada. So far, my only teacher has been Salamun. And now Zamrak." She frowns but instantly erases it. He notes her response, a confirmation of Salamun's story of Zamrak's unrequited love.

"Yes, there is much to be learned about Granada. It is far different than England, or Brittany. Far different even from Persia or Egypt."

"Indeed, that much is already obvious to me. Your food alone is a miracle!" He has a warm, boisterous laugh, which coaxes a hint of a grin from her. "And what a discovery the baths have been. How marvelous to be clean!" She actually smiles.

More silence. Her tone turns more serious. "How was it that you came to be wounded and captured?"

He frowns. "We were betrayed at Castillo de Santa Catalina, in Jaén. The Moors...the Sultan's troops...snuck into the castle in the dead of night to surprise us. I took two bolts defending the keep, in my shoulder and thigh. Their treachery was an affront to the rules of war. To honor."

She furls her eyebrows and frowns. "Rules of war?... honor?... how ironic." She shakes her head side to side, exasperated. "That castle was built by my people, not yours, to thwart a Christian invasion. The Sultan was simply recapturing that which belonged to Granada."

"I lost many fine men at Jaén, Layla, many friends. Their families are broken, fatherless."

"As did Granada. You are a Christian knight. You have killed many of my people." She looks down and says to her lap, "Including my cousin."

"Your cousin?"

"Prince Hasan al-Nisawi. My cousin."

Chandon sighs. "I see. You must have an uncle named al-Bistami."

"My mother's elder brother."

A deeper sigh. "Prince al-Nisawi challenged me to a duel in the middle of battle. It was a fair fight, as all would attest who witnessed it. I prevailed. His was an honorable death."

Despite her best attempt to suppress it, her bile rises. Her heart begins to pound, boiling her blood. She raises her voice to match stride.

"Chandon, how can there be honor in death? You knights truly baffle me. Christian, Muslim, you are all the same." Her face now wears the mark of contempt. "You hide the horror of war beneath a thin veil of 'honor' to give yourselves courage and shield your fears. To preserve your childish pride. To justify the havoc you unleash upon our world." Her expression is withering. "Honor? HONOR? There is nothing honorable about war! Or your stupid duels. War is terrible. Men die. Families suffocate in their grief, then starve. War destroys, it never builds. How will we ever find room for peace if war is seen as honorable? HOW?!" She struggles for some composure, looks away to steady herself, takes a deep breath. His eyes have been glued to his lap through the latter half of her tirade.

Aisha glances up at her lady's rising voice, concerned. She shakes her head and exhales wearily, returns to her book.

The silence lays tense upon the courtyard. He begins speaking to his lap. "Today I may be a prisoner. But I was raised a gentleman, and educated. I was trained as a knight and sharpened for battle. I was groomed for command. As you say, I have killed many good men, French, English, Castilian...and Moor. And though I have always fought by the rules of war...honorably...I have never enjoyed it, Layla. Ever. You cannot see a good man die and not feel a small death in your own heart. You take a life, even if it is someone trying desperately to kill you, and you subtract a part of yourself from the world. Forever. I am not proud of what I have done. My heart is heavy with the burden. Heavy..." His voice begins quavering with 'my heart'. He stops to compose himself. "Despite what you may think, Layla, I yearn for a time of peace, too. My heart is sick with death, sick." He takes a deep breath, angry with himself for letting his emotions steal his voice.

She is genuinely moved. She has never seen such honesty...or emotion...from a knight. Ever. She chastises herself again for letting her temper slip out.

They sit in tense silence for several minutes, Chandon still staring down, Layla now scanning the sky, each wondering who will make the next move.

She unfurls a white flag. "Perhaps we should talk about Arabic and English?"

He looks up, smiles weakly. "I think that is an excellent idea." The mood brightens.

"So...Arabic is a complicated language, so we will start simply, with a few basic words. Certain pronunciations will sound strange to you. They will prove difficult to form with your mouth. It just takes practice. There are many dialects of Arabic, but we will focus on Andalusi Arabic. Spoken only. Writing is much more challenging."

He rests his hands on his knees, eager to put their confrontation behind him. "Good. Speak some Arabic to me." He wants an excuse to study her face.

She purses her lips and looks skyward for a moment as she considers, then begins, "I am sorry that I offended you. I let my temper get the better of me. Again." She grins.

"Interesting. What did you say?"

She hesitates. "That I am pleased to be able to teach you Arabic." She grins again. "Speak some English for me."

"Mmmm... Let me see." His expression turns mischievous. "You are the most beautiful woman I have ever met. And you have a ferocious temper." He smiles.

She raises her eyebrows. "Well?"

"I said you have beautiful emerald eyes." He fixes his gaze on her.

She blushes, looks down. Her response is barely audible. "Thank you." The silence stretches. She swallows hard, decision made. "I am sorry I angered you, Chandon. I meant no offense. Sometimes my...opinions...just seem to slip out on their own. Forgive me."

"No offense taken, Layla. I wish all women had such strong opinions. The world would be a better place. Let us put all of that behind us, shall we?"

"Agreed." Their eyes remain locked on each other for a few seconds longer than necessary.

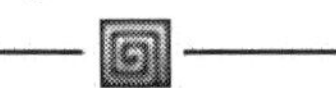

An hour later he says in Castilian, "Repeat after me." Then in English, "One. Two. Three. Four. Five." She follows, sporting a strong accent. Back to Castilian. "Good. You are counting now. Numbers one through five. Again." He repeats the numbers, she follows, her pronunciation crispening as she goes. One more time and she has it. She smiles, pleased with herself.

Chandon says, "Good. Now I will teach you how to introduce yourself at court." She grins. She is clearly enjoying herself. He says, "My name is Layla. Behold, I am the most beautiful woman in all of Granada." He stops, coaxes her, she follows. He laughs loud.

A skeptical grin. "What is so funny?"

"Nothing. You are doing great. You have a natural gift for language, Layla. Ready?" She nods, eager. "One day soon I will show Chandon my lovely chestnut curls." She repeats the phrase.

He laughs again, and says, "This is fun!" She offers a coy grin now, sensing the game afoot.

She says, "My turn." His smile fades, his face a portrait of concentration. "This is how you will introduce yourself when you meet the Sultan." A playful grin. She switches to Arabic. "My name is Chandon, and I am the first Christian knight ever to learn how to properly bathe." She coaxes him forward. He launches in, hopelessly butchering every word as he goes. He ends with a lame, puppy dog smile. She bursts out laughing at his ineptness, her beauty flaming up and taking his breath away. An odd feeling fans out from his chest to his toes, taking him off guard. The feeling requires a moment to catalog. When he manages to place it, he offers a content sigh.

After another lively half-hour of back and forth Arabic-English banter, they finally stop, laughed out. They study each other in silence for a moment longer. Both are smiling. "I really must be going, I have work to do."

"Ahhh...your Sufi training beckons."

She tilts her head in genuine surprise. "Yes, my Sufi training. How did you know that?"

"A great wizard told me. You are training to be a Sufi, a Muslim mystic." He pauses. "Very impressive. What do your studies entail?"

She hesitates, debates whether she is ready to let this stranger enter her sacred space. She chooses. "I am serving at the Maristan Hospital in the Albayzín, the Muslim quarter of Granada. The Maristan takes in the outcasts of the city to feed and clothe them, take care of them. Men, women and babies, some with awful deformities. It has been difficult work, but a great blessing for me. I have had several...profound...experiences there. I also practice various Sufi meditation forms. I study the Quran, of course, and pray a great deal." They both chuckle. "I even practice calligraphy. I meet with my Sufi Master at the madrasa, the Quranic school, three days a week for guidance."

"Perhaps someday soon I could join you in your work at the hospital. I would like that."

She rewards him with that radiant smile, then stands. He follows suit, offers a deep bow, which is returned, then she pivots and goes to gather Aisha, climb the stairs to change into hijab and prepare for her trek to the Maristan.

He remains still, arms folded, drinking her in as she walks away then disappears up the stairs. He whispers, "Interesting, very interesting." He beams, then turns and ambles back to his room, arms folded behind his back, face glued to the ground as he replays segments of the last hour. He shakes his head in wonder, continues to smile to himself.

She walks at her normal brisk pace, and Aisha struggles to keep up. Halfway to the Albayzín, Aisha blurts out, "The Christian knight is very handsome."

Layla slows, returns a quizzical glance. "Mmmm...you think so?"

"I do." A moment more of silence, then, "He could not keep his eyes off you."

She stops, looks more intently at Aisha, eyebrows now raised in mock query. But she can't prevent the grin from spreading across her face. "Well, it was his first time to speak Arabic. He had to pay careful attention to his teacher." Her grin twists devilish.

"Layla, I have seen that look before, but never once at the madrasa." They both laugh.

Later that evening, Layla sits crouched over her desk, reed pen in hand, practicing her calligraphy forms. She is not sure of the precise point of these exercises but indulges her Master's whims nonetheless, convinced that he has a worthy purpose in mind. It is tedious, tiring work. Letters and letters, then more letters, a strain to the eyes, even with extra lamps brought close.

Her father reclines on his divan, buried in his books. He comes up for air and after he wills his thoughts away from the text remembers the morning's battle. He looks up.

"You never told me how your time with Chandon went. Hopefully not a disaster?"

Her hand freezes in place on the paper, but she does not move, remains turned away from him, face glued to her desk.

"It was...interesting." She hesitates as she considers her next words. She swallows hard, committed. "I have decided that the process will be more efficient if we meet daily instead of three days a week. There is much to learn. English is not simple like Castilian. And you know how challenging Arabic can be for Europeans."

He furls his eyebrows. He turns and stares intently at the back of his daughter's head, puzzled. "I see." As he shakes his head side to side with disbelief, a mischievous grin eases onto his face. "Whatever you think best, Daughter."

At dinner that evening, Chandon is pensive, not his usual talkative self. Salamun sits across from him, attempts some light banter to loosen him up, to no avail. The wizard sighs, placing his hands flat on the table, eyes wide. "And so...?"

Chandon looks up from his plate. "And so...what?"

The wizard chuckles. "And so...how did it go this morning?"

"Ahhh...this morning." He searches for the right words. "It was...interesting," then returns to his food.

Salamun scolds with his finger. "Oh, Young Knight, I told you to be careful. I even warned you! Now you have gone and let her capture your heart." The old Jew beams. "Ahhh...young love! I remember it well, very well, indeed!"

Chandon looks up again. "Let us not be hasty, wizard. I am a Christian; she is a Muslim." He muses then shakes his head as he stares into space. "Still, I felt things today that I have not felt since..." His words trail off. "She is exquisite, Salamun." He frowns. "Opinionated." Salamun laughs loud. "We have decided to meet daily for our lessons."

The old Jew lifts his eyebrows in mock horror. "My, my, have we now? Life has grown very interesting, even for an old man. I am going to enjoy this. Yes, I am going to enjoy this very much." His laugh is infectious. Chandon's mood lightens and he chuckles, shakes his head in disbelief.

# Spurts

15 September 1367. It is late in the evening, deep in the maze of the medina. Families have long since settled in for the night, and the streets are empty. The Berber is pressed deep into a doorway along the narrow alley, hiding from the thin light cast by the lamp glow from the windows high above. He stands motionless, his smoldering ebony eyes dancing anxiously left then right then back again. He wears a stained, thin gray linen robe, a crimson cape, worn-out sandals. His white turban is smudged with dirt. It covers his greasy hair, drapes around his shoulders, then flows down his back. His bearded face is haggard from lack of sleep.

He hears footsteps down the alley to his left. He tenses, holds his breath and listens, then presses himself further back into the shadows. It seems impossible that it takes so long for the visitor to come into view. His heart is pounding. Sweat beads cling to his forehead, gorge themselves on the humid night air, then trickle into his eyes, stinging.

After an eternity the man comes into view. Black robe and cape, hood pulled forward and down over his head, obscuring his face. The man stops ten paces into the alley. He looks to his left, then to his right, starts again. The man stops once more directly in front of the Berber's hideout, pivots to his right. The Berber edges out of the shadows just enough be seen, then retreats into the darkness. The man nods once, then turns back to look down the alley. Alone. He edges forward into the doorway out of sight, stands a foot from the Berber so they can converse in whispers.

The man studies the Berber's face in silence, letting his eyes adjust. In Maghrebi dialect, he whispers, "You look nervous, unwell. And you smell." He exhales his disgust, then continues. "You have failed me, Matar. I removed the guard and silenced the boy so you could finish your work with ease."

The Berber whispers furiously, "Master, the Christian was more cunning than I guessed. When he saw the guard was gone he left the hospital and walked into the medina. Too many people were about. When he entered the mosque during noon prayer it seemed like a good opportunity to have others complete the job for us. If the old Jew had not happened along, the Christian would be dead now."

"And yet he lives, Matar."

The Berber hesitates. “Yes, he lives…for now.”

“He is tucked safely in the Comares Palace, Matar, protected by the Sultan’s Royal Bodyguards. Unreachable, even for you. We must now look for other opportunities.”

“Yes, Master.”

“Your presence within the Alhambra is now known, Matar. There is suspicion of foul play, a planted spy. They do not know your name or your relation to me. Yet.”

“They will never know, Master. I will disappear into the city. They have no means to track me there.”

“Matar, I am afraid I cannot take that risk.”

The eight-inch long, needle-pointed dagger rips forward, lightning quick, entering the Berber’s abdomen just below his ribs, the thin blade angled upward. Wide-eyed surprise is instantly written on the bearded face, his mouth flying open in shock. The Berber doubles over and tiptoes, trying in vain to move away from the pain. He attempts to mouth a word of accusation but can only gasp inward as the point slices deeper. The attacker holds the point of the dagger in place then places his hand on the Berber’s back for leverage, jabs the dagger in even further, piercing his heart, the work now complete.

As the blade is withdrawn the visitor steps back to let the Berber drop to his knees, eyes wide with terror. Shocked silence. The rhythmic spurts of hot blood slide into the dust of the doorway, the circumference of the dark circle quickly widening. He pitches face forward into the slippery mud, dead, his upturned, raven-clawed hand still twitching.

The robed man leans down and casually wipes his blade on the filthy gray robe, slips the dagger back into its sleek jeweled sheath, turns, then steps out into the alley. He looks both ways. Satisfied, he begins his slow walk back out of the medina.

The Sultan and Ibn al-Khatib sit in silence on plush silk pillows, their forearms locked to their knees. Each man concentrates on the ornate Christian chess set arrayed on the low, inlaid table between them. They are midway through the death-match, Ibn al-Khatib trying to be sporting, discreetly attempting to draw out the inevitable. Al-Waziri sits to the Sultan’s right, observing their moves. He seems preoccupied, pensive.

After fifteen more minutes, Ibn al-Khatib announces, “Checkmate, Sire.” The Sultan studies the board for a moment longer in disbelief, unsure how disaster struck without more forewarning. He sighs his capitulation. "The predictable end, Lisan al-Din. Still, a good match."

"Indeed, Sire, a good match."

The two men wait in silence for the Sultan's true reason for calling them both to the Palace of the Lions. "I gathered you both this morning because I want your opinions...on our Marinid conspiracy."

Both men turn in unison to study the Sultan.

"The facts are these. One: My communiqué detailing our intent to invade Aragon was intercepted before it reached Pedro, putting me at a serious diplomatic disadvantage with Castile. Two: The Aragonese received this same information, allowing them to reinforce Jaén, Úbeda, and Baeza before we attacked. Three: Fez clearly knew all of this, including the fact that Chandon had been captured and brought to the Alhambra after our victory at Jaén. Four: Someone has tried to assassinate Chandon." He shakes his head with disgust. "Gentlemen, the Marinids are receiving privileged information from my court. Some of this information was known only to my Vizier Council. My conclusion? One of my viziers is a Marinid spy."

He looks first to Ibn al-Khatib, then to Prince al-Waziri. "We three have been together since my childhood, long before the first day of my reign. We lived in exile together for three painful years. We returned from Fez in triumph together, a triumph made possible only with Pedro's support. You are my most trusted confidantes, and I trust you both with my life. I cannot say the same, however, of my other viziers." He stops, letting them absorb the information. "I am interested in your opinions."

They sit in silence for several moments. Ibn al-Khatib begins. "Sire, your facts are accurate and in my opinion your conclusion is correct. The Marinids have ample motive. They clearly lust after Granada's wealth and power. They would like nothing more than to absorb us into their empire, turn Granada into a Berber fiefdom. Our strong alliance with Pedro threatens that ambition. By backing Enrique and Aragon, providing them with our state secrets, they hope to strengthen Castile's only serious rival. Sire, Aragon is backed by France and the Papacy. If they defeat Castile they will naturally turn south in an attempt to reclaim Granada for Christendom. A renewal of reconquista. We would be forced to invite the Marinids to send troops to reinforce us. We will soon have a treaty in place to do just that, Sire. Perhaps the Marinids would use that golden opportunity to betray us and lay claim Granada for themselves."

The Sultan responds, "Lisan al-Din, the treaty states that they would send troops to support Granada only if we request them. And in any case those troops would be under my direct control."

"Indeed, Sire, but suppose we have no choice and we require a Berber army to survive a protracted war with Aragon. Remember our history, Sire. The Almoravids. Córdoba invited them in as allies against the Christians. They refused to leave when the fighting was done and quickly conquered the Taifa Kingdoms. We feel the bite of that desperate move even now, three hundred years later." The Sultan strokes his chin as he considers the possibility.

Al-Waziri chimes in. "I agree with Lisan al-Din, Sire. In addition, holding Chandon here without ransom strengthens our ties to Pedro and Castile. It also aids the English, the sworn enemies of France and the Papacy, and by extension Aragon. I have learned that Chandon has a price on his head in England, Sire. I am sure that Edward the Black Prince would love nothing more than to claim Chandon as a prize. Perhaps arranged by Pedro to help cement an English-Castilian alliance. Brittany is vulnerable to English attack with Chandon in an English dungeon.

"The Marinids would have only two options. Help Chandon escape in order to gain favor with Aragon, which is highly unlikely. Or the more obvious choice, simply murder him. Remove an important pawn from the board before he can be moved to advantage. And the killing of a famous Christian knight by the Moors would give Aragon a thinly veiled reason to invade Granada, provided the Marinids make his death look like it came at the Sultan's request. Which of course would not be difficult to do."

The Sultan nods. "I see. That makes sense. Bashir, who, then, is our spy? Is it Farqad? Tariq? Ahmad? Jalil? Perhaps someone from the Mexuar Council? Who?"

"Unclear, Sire."

"Lisan al-Din?"

"It is not obvious to me, Sire." He hesitates. "Still, Ahmad is the ambassador to the Marinids, and he is of Berber ancestry. He would have the easiest and most direct means to secretly pass information to them."

The Sultan replies, "Yes, but he has been absent from court for much of this."

Ibn al-Khatib says, "True. The Mexuar Council is one-third Berber. Perhaps it would be prudent to have Bashir watch the Berbers on the Council...and Ahmad. For anything suspicious."

"Bashir?"

"I agree, Sire. It can be done discreetly."

"Good, do so. Any news on Chandon's would-be assassin?"

"Not yet, Sire. But we are presently following some leads. Several people at the mosque reported seeing a Berber they did not recognize. One claims to have seen him again in the medina two days ago. He will not elude us for long."

"Good, keep me posted."

"Certainly, Sire."

"He must be found, Bashir, and taken alive so that we can extract some useful information."

"Agreed, Sire."

"Good day, gentlemen."

The two viziers rise, bow, then turn and depart.

It is an hour before midnight, in the Partal Gardens. The moon is waning crescent, just enough of a vertical sliver to cast a ghostly hue upon the humid night. A welcomed breeze blows in from the north. The sky is dotted with top-lit, giant cotton balls tracking by at a decent clip, producing an uncanny timed sequence of midnight black to dim moonlight to midnight black, at precise half-minute intervals.

The man strolls through the empty gardens. He stops and admires the heady scent of a rose blossom, then moves on. In the periods of dim moonlight it is clear that he wears the heavy gold-embroidered crimson robe of the Mexuar Council, a scholar and interpreter of Sharia, the vast body of Islamic law.

He turns onto a pea gravel path, walks east away from the palace. To his left are flower beds, to his right a head-high, sculpted cypress hedge that lines the walkway. Every thirty feet the hedge indents to form a keyhole-shaped privacy niche containing two small stone benches facing a small bubbling fountain. As the man passes the third niche he stops and listens. He looks to his rear then slides into the niche. A man in a black robe and cape, hood pulled forward and down over his head, obscuring his face, sits on the left bench. The crimson robed figure seats himself on the opposite bench. The two remain silent, listening carefully for any sounds that do not belong to the garden paradise.

The man in the crimson robe says, "Tell me of Matar."

The manner in which the aquatic murmur of the fountain tendrils itself around his voice makes it clear that the water feature was designed to prevent eavesdropping.

"Alas, Matar has passed from this world, taking all of his secrets with him."

"A pity, but necessary. If only he had succeeded with the Christian infidel our plans would be moving to completion."

"Yes. An unfortunate turn of events."

"Do you have another plan in mind?"

"Chandon is now living in an upstairs room within the Comares Palace. He enjoys the company of the Sultan's Royal Bodyguards. He is impregnable to direct attack." Silence. "I believe, however, that he may have other, more subtle, vulnerabilities. At the moment, no one is tasting his food. A foolish oversight. I am attempting to find a secure means to have a poison delivered to sweeten his meal."

"Ahhh...Good. Someone we can trust, obviously."

"Yes. But even so, after their deed is done they will join Matar. It will take some time before I am ready to move. I must be sure."

"And what of your plan to assassinate the Sultan?"

"Progressing. The Sultan has one unfortunate weakness. Beautiful women."

"Mmmm...Ibn al-Khatib's blasphemous daughter?"

"Exactly. The Sultan pines for her. Her refusal to join the Royal Harem played nicely into our hands. The Sultan has a new favorite play-thing, chosen because she looks like Layla, green eyes and all. A Christian slave from Aragon. Shameful. She will be his undoing."

"How?"

"I will dress the green-eyed slave as Layla, use her as bait." A sinister smile eases onto his face. "It seems our Layla will have a change of heart and come to her senses. She will request to see the Sultan in private to make amends for her rejection of his...affections. Because Layla is unmarried and not a part of the Royal Harem, he will be forced to remain utterly discreet. He will leave his bodyguards and come to her alone in the dead of night. The green-eyed slave will be waiting for him. As will I. When he gets close enough to realize it is not Layla, it will be too late."

"Excellent. When?"

"Patience, the timing must be perfect."

"What about Ibn al-Khatib?"

"I will visit his suite as soon as my work with the Sultan is complete. Sad to say, the Grand Vizier will die protecting his daughter's honor. I will enjoy her body...then I will slit the devil's throat."

The crimson-robed man offers a thin smile. "You possess the cunning to make an excellent Sultan."

"And you an excellent Grand Vizier. Granada will soon join its rightful place as part of the Marinid Empire. Very soon."

The Sultan, Ibn al-Khatib, and Zamrak sit on pillows in the eastern portico of the Palace of the Lions, sipping mint tea. They have been discussing Zamrak's plans for some new poetry to celebrate the Sultan's recent renovations to the Generalife. A classical ghazal, an Arabic love poem, has been decided upon.

A servant leads al-Waziri into the courtyard, indicates the Sultan. The trio's conversation ceases and they watch in silence as the Military Vizier approaches, bows. "Sire, we have found the Berber assassin."

The Sultan nods. "Good, Bashir, very good. And what information about our conspiracy has he offered us?"

The vizier hesitates, then says, "Sire, the Berber was found dead in the medina this morning, stabbed through the heart with a dagger. Identical to the wound on Chandon's guard. No doubt made by the same individual."

The Sultan frowns. "I see."

Al-Waziri grasps for a positive. "At least Chandon should be safer now that this assassin has been removed."

Ibn al-Khatib counters, "Let us not forget that whoever killed the Berber remains at court. He is clearly a capable assassin himself. I do not like the sound of this, Sire. The true conspirator is attempting to hide his tracks, remove anyone with knowledge of his true identity. I suspect the threat has grown, not lessened." He muses for a moment in silence. "Sire, I think it would be prudent for you to leave the palace and retire to the Generalife. At least for a few weeks."

The Sultan responds, "Not possible. The remodeling will last at least another month, Lisan al-Din, and I do not want to interrupt the work. As it is I have missed my summer sojourn. Besides, I think it sends a dangerous message. The Sultan does not flee the Alhambra because it cannot be made safe for him."

Al-Waziri turns to the Sultan. "Sire, I will redouble my efforts. We will leave no stone unturned. The murderer must have left a trace of his identity, somewhere. Rest assured, we will find him."

The Sultan sighs. "See to it, Bashir. And double the guards at all of the entrances to both the Comares Palace and the Palace of the Lions. Knowing that an assassin wanders about the Alhambra is not sweetening my dreams."

A somber al-Waziri nods curtly, then bows and departs.

## Shivers

Chandon opens the door to his room and descends gingerly down the narrow stairs, stepping out into the morning light. It will be another hot day. Thin, broken clouds. He inhales a deep, satisfying breath, happy to be free of his room. His bodyguards mark their normal posts, stiff as statues to the left and right of the stairwell entry, eyes roaming the courtyard. To the trained eye, these men are killing machines.

They ignore him. As usual. As an experiment, he turns to his right, says, “Sabah al-khayr.” *Good morning.*

Both guards turn their heads to study Chandon. Their stern expressions remain fixed, but the guard to his right mumbles, “Sabah al-khayr.”

Chandon decides to press his luck. Salamun has been teaching him new phrases each evening, correcting his many miscues, insisting on incessant practice to bury his heavy accent. He tries, “Ahtaaju an atadarraba ala al Arabia.” *I need to practice my Arabic.* The guard who spoke returns a blank stare. Did he understand me? He decides to try something simpler. “Ma esmouk?” *What is your name?*

The guard considers the request, then, “Esmee Musa.” *My name is Musa.*

The other guard unexpectedly joins in. “Esmee Yazdan.” *My name is Yazdan.*

Chandon celebrates his conquest. “Esmee Chandon!” He thumps his chest as he responds, but his smile is not returned. He mentally rehearses his next phrase before voicing it, trying to retrieve the proper pronunciation, something Layla constantly chides him about. “Motasharefon bema refatek.” *Good to meet you.*

Both guards nod. “Naam.” *Yes.* They turn their heads back outward to the courtyard, ignore him once more.

Satisfied, Chandon looks across the courtyard, sees Aisha, then looks to his left to the far corner of the courtyard and confirms that Layla has beaten him out this morning. She sits on her pillow, head already in a book. He smiles, begins limping towards her. The two bodyguards turn to each other, roll their eyes. When he is about ten paces away she senses his presence, looks up, closes her book, and flashes that smile. He confidently opens with, “Sabah al-khayr.” *Good morning.*

She tilts her head and relaxes into a grin, clearly amused. She answers in English, “Good morning.” No accent.

He then says, “Kaifa haloka?” *How are you?*

“Just fine, thank you for asking.”

He stops in front of her, squints his eyes, purses his lips, concentrating. “Eshtaqto elaiki katheeran.” *I missed you so much.* He gauges her expression to see if he was understood.

She looks down to hide her blush, then forces herself to look back up and into his eyes, holding his steady gaze. She whispers in English, “And I you.” The air tingles for a moment until the spell is broken. She switches to Castilian, “I thought we would practice English and Arabic phrases for a while and afterwards perhaps I can teach you some chess. Everyone at court plays chess.”

He grins. “Wonderful. I have always wanted to learn chess.” He eases down onto his pillow, straightens his back and drops his hands to his knees, his standard drilling posture. They focus on phrases for the dinner table, culinary vocabulary.

They have pulled their pillows to the low table between them. He memorizes her face as she sets the chess pieces on the board.

“At court we prefer to play with Christian chess sets, an irony we enjoy immensely. This one was a gift to my father from King Pedro of Castile.” She touches each piece as she names it. “The king. His queen.” She looks up with a devilish grin. “Clearly the most powerful piece. This is the bishop.” She pauses. “The knight. Alas, not very powerful.” She laughs. He is beaming. “The castle. And of course the king's pawns.” He pays careful attention as she gives a brief lesson in the allowable moves of each piece.

“What is the most powerful piece on an Arabic chess board?”

“The Grand Vizier, of course.”

“Your father.”

“My father.” She grins.

“Ready?” She is a gifted player, evenly matched with her father. Since he is a novice she intends to play loose and easy, allowing him to learn.

“Ready.” He places his elbows on the table, rests his chin atop his two fists, concentrates on the board.

She pushes her king’s pawn out two spaces. He considers a moment, then mirrors her. She pushes her king’s bishop three squares out on the diagonal. He moves his king’s knight forward and to the left. She brings her queen out three squares. He moves his queen’s pawn forward one square, loosing his queen’s bishop.

She senses something and looks up to study his face, but he stares at the chess board, ignoring her. She looks back down and then moves her queen's knight's pawn forward one square. He pushes his queen's pawn forward one square.

Without thinking she takes his pawn with her king's pawn. He instantly takes the pawn with his knight. Without hesitation, she takes his knight with her queen. He takes her queen. She looks up, shocked at her carelessness, frowns. His eyes remain glued to the board. Her mouth twists into that beautiful devilish grin. "Never played chess before, sir?"

A sheepish grin. "Only once or twice. A lucky move."

Suddenly at a disadvantage, she becomes a picture of feminine determination, studies every move now, visualizing the many possibilities before and after each decision. The game draws out for twenty-five more minutes, an even exchange of pieces. She eventually snares his queen, but as the game plays down to a knight, a castle, and four pawns each, it becomes clear that they have fought to a draw. She is impressed. She says, "Sir, I offer you a draw."

He bows his head in agreement. "My Lady, I would be delighted to accept your kind offer." They each tip their king.

"You are skilled, sir."

"As are you, my Lady."

"Where did you learn to play chess?"

"The good friars at Saint Andrews' Church in Radbourne. They considered it an essential part of a first-rate education." She grins.

"Where is Radbourne?"

"In Derbyshire. England. I was born in Radbourne. Lovely country, much greener than here. Pastures, hills, streams and small mountains. Lush." He pauses, then says, "You would like it." She smiles.

"How far from London?"

"About three days by horse. North."

"How long has it been since you were there?"

He thinks for a moment. "Nearly ten years now. Sad to say, I am no longer welcome in England."

"Are your parents still there?"

"No. My parents are both dead, God rest their souls. I do have a sister there still. She is married to a cobbler. Two children. They live in a village outside Radbourne." He hesitates, then says, "My family is of humble origin, Layla."

"Yet you are a famous knight."

"I was lucky to have been noticed by relatives of King Edward who summer on an estate outside of Radbourne. I was invited to court...for more education."

"Ahhh...the arts of war."

"Yes, the arts of war. And chess." They both smile.

"Tell me about Brittany."

"Brittany is beautiful. Rolling green hills, plush oak and hickory forests, chock-full with game. Lovely trout-filled brooks, miles and miles of fertile farmland. After my victory at the Battle of Auray three years back, I was awarded noble status by Jean de Monfort. I am now Viscount of Saint-Sauveur." He rolls his hand and dips his head in mock ceremony. She laughs. "My castle and estate are in central Brittany, a day's hard ride from the coast. I have a large farm and many woodland acres; a fine estate. I am richly blessed."

She considers her next words carefully. She looks to her lap, then back up and says, "Yet you never married."

He inhales, holds it, then exhales, serious now. He looks down, then answers, "No, I never married."

She senses a ghost in the nuances of his voice. Her voice settles to nearly a whisper. "But you were in love."

Silence.

"Yes, I was in love."

She remains quiet, giving him room to elaborate. Instead he looks up, tone brightening. "Tell me about you. You were born in Granada, raised at court."

"Yes, I grew up at court. My father was Grand Vizier to Sultan Yusef, Sultan Muhammad's father. Sultan Yusef built the Comares Palace. A good man. Sadly, he was assassinated by a black African slave as he prayed in the Great Mosque. My father was Muhammad's tutor when he was a boy. Eventually my father helped arrange for Muhammad to be appointed Sultan by the Mexuar Council. Alas, only five years later he was deposed by his half-brother, Ismail, in a coup orchestrated by their mother."

"His own mother?"

"Yes. It was a time rife with court intrigue."

"And you and your father were forced into exile, to Fez, in Africa."

She frowns. "Yes. The barren desert. Baba and I spent three long years in Fez. Sad, terrible years." She hesitates, then speaks to her lap. "My mother died that first year, unexpectedly. Some unusual African fever. She was well one day, deathly ill the next. Three days later she was gone."

Silence.

"Salamun was not with us. He was forced to remain in Granada during our exile, confined to the Jewish quarter. My father was powerless against the fever. After she passed, he retreated into his grief, and his books." She hesitates. "I was left to fend for myself, to try and understand. I was only twelve." Her voice begins to quaver on these last words. As she looks up, a single tear streaks down both cheeks.

"I am so sorry, Layla. I, too, have known the pain of unexpected loss. It stays buried deep within our hearts, then comes calling when we least expect it."

She takes a deep breath, blows, then wipes her eyes. She is amazed that she is this willing to be vulnerable in front of him. She makes a mental note to ponder this further. "Yes. Fortunately Aisha came to care for me."

"Your lady-in-waiting."

"Yes, but also my friend. Aisha is my surrogate mother, you see."

"When did you come back to Granada?"

"Five years ago, courtesy of King Pedro of Castile. By then Muhammad's half-brother Ismail had been murdered by his cousin, another Muhammad, this one a hashish addict. The cousin was hateful and abusive, a terrible man. Upon Muhammad's return his cousin fled to Sevilla for sanctuary, together with all of the leaders at court that supported him, forty-one all told. Pedro executed every one of them. He dealt personally with the Sultan.

"Yes, Salamun told me about that. He said that Pedro had the Sultan's head delivered to the Alhambra."

She grimaces. "He did. A welcoming gift for us. Perhaps also a reminder to Muhammad. King Pedro has since been known as 'Pedro the Cruel.' But the kingdom has been peaceful and prosperous ever since, and closely allied with Castile. Pedro's palace in Sevilla is decorated like the Alhambra, you know. He evens dresses as a Granadine prince, and speaks Arabic. Sultan Muhammad is popular with our people. The Palace of the Lions was finished last year and the Comares Palace extensively remodeled. The Alhambra and the city of Granada have been reinvigorated. The Vega thrives once more. All of our cities and border towns have been re-fortified and their garrisons strengthened. The silk trade brings great wealth to the kingdom now. It sustains us."

"Tell me about the tensions between Fez and the Sultan."

"The Marinid Empire, whose capital is Fez, is dominated by Muslims of Berber origin. Desert peoples of North Africa. The

Marinids are a particular clan of Berbers. We, my family, the Sultan, most of his nobles, are of Arab ancestry. The Nasrid clan. We trace our roots back to Damascus and the Umayyads. The Berbers are a proud people, but war-like. Fine horsemen, formidable in battle. They consider themselves the rightful rulers of the West. All of the West. With few exceptions, they champion a more radical vision of Islam, an Islam of *jihad*. Jihad literally means 'struggle' or 'conquest'.

"Ironically, the Berbers favor a jihad against both the Arabs of al-Andalus and Christendom. And the Jews of course. The earliest Berbers in al-Andalus, first the Almoravids and after them the Almohads, precipitated the tensions with the Christian kingdoms three hundred years ago. They turned peaceful co-existence between Muslims and Christians into conflict, and ultimately war. The Jews were caught in between.

"The Berbers are much less tolerant of scientific and philosophical knowledge, of inquiry. They do not invite questions, nor will they tolerate them. They are more literal in their interpretation of the Quran and severe in their administration of Sharia, the canon of Islamic law." A weary sigh, then she continues. "The Berbers believe they are defenders of the faith. There are Berbers at court in Granada, and many on the Mexuar Council. Even within the high ranks of the military. Always they push the Sultan to bend closer to their view of...the truth. The Sultan is young, but wise. He resists the Berbers at every turn, insists on tolerance within the kingdom. He listens to my father's counsel."

"I am told the Sultan is my age."

She lifts her eyebrows. "I see. Twenty-eight." She considers decorum for a moment before she says, "I am twenty." She pauses for effect. "But very wise for my age." They both laugh.

A coy grin. "I am told the Sultan collects the most beautiful and desirable women within his harem."

Her eyes grow hard, her face stern. "The harem is no more than a prison, Chandon, where women are valued only for their looks and their bodies, not their minds."

He realizes it is time to change the subject. "How is it that while living in Fez among the Berbers you were able to become so well educated?"

"I was forbidden by the Berbers to attend Quranic school, the madrasa. The Berbers feel that a woman belongs sequestered in her home, unseen, never to be heard from." She shakes her head side to side as she purses her lips. "Instead, my father taught me. In hindsight it was the best thing that could have happened to me. My father had access to all of the latest books. He introduced me to many new ideas, many people. Even the Sufi masters. He has always encouraged me to think for myself and make my own decisions. Once we returned to Granada it was easy for me to continue my education. I learned to teach myself." Her expression softens.

Chandon continues, "I find the role of women in Granadine society...different. From what Salamun tells me, Muslim women seem to have no legal rights to speak of. A husband may divorce his wife, then possess their children as he sees fit; or confine her to his home as if she were his property." She nods. "And Salamun told me a woman may not appear to testify in law court against a man, or if she does, her voice counts less than that of the man she accuses. Puzzling."

She frowns. "What you say is true, Chandon. Still, there are many examples of Andalusi women of great education and influence, especially during the Golden Age of the Umayyad Caliphate. In Córdoba." She turns wistful. "I often imagine what it would have been like to live then. To freely walk the grounds of the Madinat al-Zahra, the Sultan's magical palace-city. Madinat al-Zahra was said to be a hundred times more lavish than the Alhambra, if you can imagine that. Sometimes I dream of that Golden Age, feel its call. I sometimes think my heart was born there..." She shakes off the spell. "Baba has told me that our most ancient relatives lived in Córdoba. Centuries ago. Are things different for women in Brittany?"

"To some extent, yes. Young women of the court can attend school, though only if they come from wealth and their father deems it important. They do enjoy more rights concerning marriage, and also in the law courts. It is much the same in England. Clearly, though, abuses abound."

"I see. I am told by my father that the Berbers on the Mexuar Council disapprove of my studies at the Sufi madrasa. It seems that the presence of any female, even one educated and training to be a Sufi...distracts the male students." She grimaces. "Ridiculous. When I visit the madrasa or the Maristan Hospital, I cannot walk alone and I am forced to dress in hijab, in a hot, baggy wool robe, hidden from the world."

"Now that is a real shame." He grins and after a moment, she relents and grins as well.

A comfortable silence stretches out. Chandon says, "We have been meeting for two weeks now, my Lady, and while I have learned much Arabic, and you much English, I have yet to behold the glory of your beautiful chestnut hair. I can think of nothing else." He beams.

She blushes, but meets his gaze, then a coy grin. "I am sorry, sir, but it is forbidden for a knight to behold his lady's treasure." She flashes that smile. He laughs loud.

Ibn al-Khatib comes down the stairs, exits into the bright sunshine, stopping while his eyes adjust. He looks to his immediate right. "Good morning, Aisha."

"Good morning, My Lord."

He looks across the courtyard, sees the bodyguards, frowns. A sound he has not heard in ages intrudes. His daughter's bright laugh. He turns, amazed, and looks to the end of the courtyard, sees the two of them sitting on their pillows. The Christian is making a funny face as he struggles with pronunciation. She laughs again. Ibn al-Khatib shakes his head in disbelief, then smiles, drawn back to her childhood a lifetime ago, the happy years in Granada...before the Great Exile. Just the three of them. A time with laughter and love. Curious now, he turns and walks towards the two.

Chandon is the first to see him approaching, and he erases the grin from his face and hastily rises. Layla looks puzzled, then tracks his eyes over her left shoulder, becomes instantly serious, and also rises. Both pivot to face the Grand Vizier.

Ibn al-Khatib opens with, "Sabah al-khayr." *Good morning.*

Chandon and Layla simultaneously respond, "Sabah al-khayr." Chandon bows.

The Grand Vizier turns to face Chandon. "Kaifa haloka." *How are you?*

Chandon looks puzzled. "Ana asef, la afham. Aed men fadlek?" *I'm sorry, I do not understand. Can you say it again?*

More slowly, Ibn al-Khatib repeats, "Kaifa haloka."

This registers. "Ana bekhair, shokran." *I am fine, thanks.*

Ibn al-Khatib smiles, nods, then turns to his daughter. "Can you translate into English for me. 'I am pleased to finally meet you.'" She does.

Chandon formulates his pronunciation. "Motasharefon bema refatek." *Good to meet you.*

Ibn al-Khatib nods his approval, "Jayed." *Good.*

An awkward moment of silence follows, then Ibn al-Khatib switches to Castilian. "Thank you for the gift you have given me this morning."

Chandon looks confused. "Gift, sir?"

"The gift of my daughter's laughter. I believe you are the first man to ever make her laugh."

Layla blushes, examines her sandals. Chandon smiles, then responds, "You are most welcome, sir. As you are aware, your daughter is uniquely gifted." He chuckles. "As skilled at chess as anyone I have ever faced. And she excels with language. She has learned more English in three days than I have managed of Arabic in three weeks. No doubt she is a fine reflection of her father and mother." He mentally kicks himself. "God rest her soul."

"Her mother especially." After a moment of pensive silence Ibn al-Khatib says, "I must excuse myself, the Sultan awaits. I believe I am to give you a tour of the Palace of the Lions soon. I look forward to talking more."

"The pleasure will be mine, sir."

Ibn al-Khatib exits through the door behind them.

The two lock eyes as he departs, faces all serious and stern. After a protracted moment, a hint of a grin begins to slink onto his face, widens. It proves contagious. They both burst out laughing, doubled over with their hysteria.

They sit on their pillows facing the cool water, the soothing fountain trickle all that can be heard. She has a large leather bound volume spread open in her lap, several pages bookmarked with small sheets of paper. She speaks with her hands in a manner he finds adorable. The more animated her explanations become the faster her hands fly, trying desperately to keep up. His legs are crossed, forearms on his knees. He listens intently, nods repeatedly as he stares into the depths of the water. He smiles, turns and looks at her long and hard. She stops, forces her hands to settle into her lap, grins.

"I will read a stanza of Rumi. First in Arabic so that you can discern the lovely rhythms of the poem. Last night I spent some time attempting to translate two of them into Castilian. I will then share my translation. Ready?"

He nods, amused.

Her index finger drifts to the page as she finds her place. "Let us try this one first." She clears her throat, then begins, the gentle Arabic lilt rolling out musically. She stops, then carefully considers the piece of folded paper with her translation. She brings the words alive line by line, with a short pause between the couplets.

*"Out of myself, but wanting to go*

*Beyond that, wanting to see*

*In your eyes, not power, but to*
*Kiss the ground with the dawn*

*Breeze for company, wearing white*
*Pilgrim cloth. I have a certain*

*Knowing. Now I want sight."*

She looks up. "Of course, perfect translation into Castilian is impossible. Rather than try it word for word, which leaves the whole thing dead, I attempted instead to convey the deeper meaning behind the words. Of course, you then lose some of the lovely meter and rhyme." He nods his understanding. She continues, "Besides, Rumi wrote in Persian, which does not directly translate into Arabic either. So I am taking liberties." She grins.

Chandon says, "Very interesting words. Read it once more." She does. "Wonderful. Tell me about Rumi."

"Mmmm...well, his full name was Jalal al-Din Muhammad Rumi. Rumi for short. He lived in northern Persia and died about a hundred years ago. Master al-Mussib says he is one of the greatest of all the Sufi masters. These poems are from a volume of poetry called *Masnavi-I Manavi*, which means, literally, 'Rhyming Couplets of Profound Spiritual Meaning.'

"The *Masnavi* consists of six volumes. The poems deal with many topics, some embedded within parables or stories, but ultimately they peer deeply into the human condition, our souls. He names both our failings and our triumphs, celebrates the universal desire of the earthly beloved, man and woman, to reunite with our lost eternal Beloved, Allah. Supposedly, all of the poems were composed spontaneously during his ecstatic union with Allah. Tawhid. It is the ultimate union that every Sufi seeks, an annihilation of self, an absorption into the pure love of Allah.

"Every Sufi. Even you?"

A tick of her head. "Yes."

He grins. "I thought you said Master al-Mussib told you not to read during your training."

That devilish grin. "Well, he...suggested...I not read at the beginning of my training. But, he has told me since that a little Sufi poetry is fine...from time to time." She grin widens. "But only in small doses."

He teases, "If you say so... Choose another."

She leaps forward a dozen pages to her marker, settles on her spot. She seems uncharacteristically self-conscious, tentative. She takes a deep breath then intones the flowing Arabic rhythms. He picks up several words, but not much meaning. Without looking up she concentrates for a few silent moments on her folded paper, then begins in Castilian.

*"Face that lights my face, you spin*
*Intelligence into these particles*

*I am. Your wind shivers my tree.*
*My mouth tastes sweet with your name*

*In it. You make my dance daring enough*
*To finish. No more timidity! Let*

*Fruit fall and wind turn my roots up*
*In the air, done with patient waiting."*

She stops, eyes glued to the book. After a protracted moment, she raises her gaze, turns to her right. His grin is gone. His brown eyes are alive, burn into her. He whispers, "It is a feeling I share, Layla."

# Realities

The grim, crimson-cloaked messenger from the Mexuar Council hastens to the gate leading from the palace complex into the Alcazaba. The color of his robe betrays his station, but even so, the guards stop him to examine his papers before allowing him to pass into the Alhambra's garrison.

He turns the corner and enters the massive tower of the castle keep, the oldest building in the entire Alhambra, its brick foundations chocked with thousand year old Roman mortar. He winds his way up the stairs, exiting onto the expansive Arms Square within the central fortress grounds, two stories higher now than where he entered. The Arms Square contains the officer billet, the armory, the granary, the kitchens, water-flushed latrines, and the ever-present hammam.

The messenger turns, spots his target, then erases the thirty paces separating the door to the keep and the small guard house. He is shown inside, where he presents the official document from the Mexuar Council to the officer on duty. The man reads it once, looks up to eye the messenger, then reads it again. He frowns, then sighs, motions for his adjutant, whispers instructions.

The adjutant exits, steps behind the building to what appears to be a five-foot wide hole in the courtyard. Two guards stand to either side. Narrow stone stairs rim the giant well, spiraling downward from the surface four turns, then stopping, the next step empty space. Twenty feet below the truncated stair lies the Alcazaba's dungeon. The adjutant whispers to one of the guards, who retrieves a rope ladder from the guard house, walks down the stairs and secures it to two large metal hooks on the wall. He drops the rope into the darkness, then climbs back out. The adjutant walks down the stairs as far as he can go, then stops, leans forward to peer into the dimly lit cavern. Several guards mill about below. Small, iron-barred cages line the walls. The adjutant carefully steps onto the rope ladder and begins his descent.

Fifteen minutes later, the adjutant returns, enters the guard house, then whispers to the officer, who returns a curt nod. The officer lifts his palm, inviting the messenger to walk with him outside. "Please." They step into the sunlight.

Before them are two men in filthy rags, flanked by the two guards. The prisoner's heads are bowed in submission, their faces unshaven, hair greasy and matted. They stink. Their faces exude an unhealthy pallor, their bloodshot eyes ghost-like from time spent in the dank, subterranean dwelling. Aragonese knights captured at Jaén. Terror is painted upon their faces.

After making a cursory examination of the prisoners, his disgust more than apparent, the messenger turns and speaks to the officer, who calls a guard over, gives an order. The guard pulls out two lengths of rope and begins to tie each man's hands behind his back. The prisoners wince as the knots are tightened. Satisfied, the messenger beckons, then sets off, trailed by the prisoners then the two guards. The Christians start and stop, wobble and stutter, as they relearn how to walk.

Chandon and Salamun exit the Comares Palace into the foot traffic of the Lower Royal Road. It is a humid, sweltering afternoon. Chandon's arm pits are already damp, his forehead beaded. They turn right, to the west, his bodyguards trailing five paces behind, hands glued to their sword hilts, eyes scanning. They have advised against leaving the safety of the palace, but Salamun was insistent, and al-Waziri reluctantly agreed. The time has arrived for Chandon to see more of the Alhambra. Only during the daylight hours, however, and only under close guard.

The knight and the wizard stroll, side by side, zinging Arabic phrases back and forth in their favorite cat and mouse game. Salamun asks a question. Chandon then answers as fast as he can. Salamun corrects his pronunciation, or if bad enough mocks him first, then corrects him. They laugh often. After a few exchanges they switch roles.

Chandon's Arabic is improving rapidly, his vocabulary growing by leaps and bounds. His limp is barely noticeable now, a fact that continues to amaze Salamun. The Breton has asked for and received iron weights to strengthen his arms and legs. Each morning and evening he stretches, then works his muscles hard. His morning visits to the hammam are followed by a half hour of full body massage. He is regaining his former strength and agility. He repeatedly asks for a sword, or at least a dagger, which is consistently refused.

After fifty paces they pass the arched entrance to the Court of the Machuca on their right. Chandon does a double glance, then stops. A large crowd has gathered inside the courtyard, just beyond the large sculpted marble fountain. He switches to Castilian and asks Salamun, "What is going on?"

"I am not sure, Young Knight. This is the Court of the Machuca. Where the *qadi*, the Islamic judges on the Mexuar

Council, issue pronouncements, *fatwa*, on matters of religious law and scriptural interpretation. This is also where they pass judgment in court cases."

Salamun turns to the bodyguards, speaks a quick burst of Arabic. The bodyguards frown in unison, then nod. Salamun says, "Come, we will explore." The four pass through the arches, walk past the fountain, then join the crowd of perhaps fifty facing the single story building that spans the north end of the courtyard.

Salamun whispers, "The chambers of the Mexuar law court. It must be a ruling by the qadi in a criminal case." They ease into the crowd, work their way to the front where they can see. Chandon's bodyguards are on high alert, their faces menacing. As they pass, the Royal Bodyguard's unmistakable robes and their weapons register their station, and the four are given wide berth. Several in the crowd point at Chandon, whisper to those around them.

The two filthy prisoners, hands tied behind their backs, are led out of the building by the two guards, precipitating a fevered drone in the crowd.

Chandon whispers to Salamun. "Aragonese knights. In pretty bad shape." He studies them. "I recognize these men, Salamun. They were a part of the garrison of Castillo de Santa Catalina. In Jaén." The guards stop the prisoners ten paces in front of the crowd, indicate that they should turn and face the building. More insistently, Chandon says, "What is going on, Salamun?"

"Unclear, Young Knight. Perhaps they were accused of some crime and have appeared in court to answer the charges."

A hush comes over the crowd as four guards dressed in Mexuar cloaks exit the main building, followed by three qadi of the Mexuar Council, all crimson and gold. Behind them is a black-skinned giant dressed in pristine white. Perhaps six and a half feet tall, the African is an imposing presence. His arms are sleeveless, the muscles of his forearms and biceps bulge as if pumped with air. A simple gold band is tied around his head. At his waist is strapped a jeweled Moorish sword scabbard, curved, not straight like a broadsword. The three qadi stop. One of them steps forward, unrolls a scroll and prepares to read.

Chandon whispers, "Interpret for me." Salamun nods.

The qadi begins in a practiced voice, "People of Granada, the Mexuar Council has heard the case of the two Christian infidels before you. They both stand accused of sedition, attempting to incite a riot in the prison ward of the city. A capital crime. During capture, the two blasphemed the Prophet Muhammad. Also a capital crime." The reader pauses for effect, intentionally stoking the tension. "The case has been heard by the Mexuar Council. The ruling of the court is that the two infidels are guilty of sedition and blasphemy and are thereby condemned to death. The will of Allah be done."

The reader motions. The guard pushes one prisoner forward, turns him around to face the crowd, forces him to kneel, then steps back. The reader turns and makes eye contact with the executioner, who nods, comes forward and stands at the side of the kneeling man.

Chandon turns to Salamun, whispers furiously, "There must be something we can do."

Salamun shakes his head. "Nothing."

Chandon's hands ball into fists, his jaw muscles clinched tight.

The African draws the thin, curved blade from its scabbard with a metallic hiss. The kneeling knight begins to whimper, mutter to himself. The African spreads his legs for stability, grips the curved sword with both hands, raises the blade above his head, then turns and looks to the reader.

The air tenses as the reader lets a moment pass to heighten the drama. He nods and the blade moves downward in an arc, too fast to be seen. All that can be heard is a gentle whoosh as the head drops to the ground, eyes still open, rolls forward a few feet then stops. The crowd's gasped reaction is delayed, not erupting until the head hits the dirt. In slow motion the headless body pitches forward, the shock of bright blood pulsing into the dust for what seems impossibly long. The man's feet attempt a convulsive dance, then mercifully the body stills. The crowd quiets. The African takes out a cloth, meticulously wipes his blade, then backs up two steps, making room for the next prisoner.

Chandon again turns to Salamun. "We must DO something, Salamun! Help me. PLEASE!"

Salamun is insistent now. "I understand your pain, Young Knight, but there is NOTHING to be done here. This man cannot be saved."

Chandon pivots, takes his best shot in Arabic, "Yazdan, help me stop this!"

Yazdan frowns, then whispers, "That is not possible. The Mexuar Council has ruled, and their decision is final."

Chandon turns back to face the carnage, sees that the second prisoner is now kneeling. A biting fecal reek hangs heavy in the humid air. As the African raises the curved blade above his head, the prisoner makes eye contact with Chandon. His lower lip quivers as he mouths, "Help me." Chandon raises up on the balls of his feet, arms taut by his side, fists bouncing against his thighs. Yazdan reaches forward and rests his hand on Chandon's shoulder.

"There is nothing to be done. Stand still."

The prisoner mouths his silent plea once more as a pale yellow pool gathers in the indention made by his left knee. Chandon is looking into the knight's eyes when the blade severs his neck. Chandon winces at the contact, his head drooping as his shoulders sag.

After a moment, Chandon turns and begins to walk back to the street. Yazdan raises a hand to stop him, intending to offer a kind word. Chandon refuses to make eye contact, pushes past him. The bodyguards shrug to each other, then turn and follow. Salamun trails behind the three, head bowed, frowning.

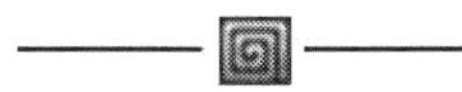

Salamun, Diego and Alfonso have joined Chandon in his room for the midday feast. Now that he is sequestered in the palace, Chandon rarely sees the boys, who have their many duties at the Royal Hospital to tend to. He misses their company and wants to make this a special occasion. Salamun is a willing co-conspirator. A servant has brought in a small, low-slung table, set it, then three servants from the Royal Kitchens have come with their feast, spreading it out before them. When the servants depart, the four wash their hands and settle into their cushions, the boys wide-eyed and eager. Chandon and Salamun share satisfied smiles.

The Breton still marvels at the bounties of the Granadine Vega, shakes his head in wonder as he surveys the table: two large loaves of freshly baked bread; a crock of butter; two whole venison loins, seasoned with salt and fresh rosemary then grilled over coals, sliced thick and topped with sautéed wild mushrooms; saffron-tinted rice, with roasted garlic and pine nuts; boiled beets, sliced and tossed with sautéed sweet pearl onions and wilted spinach; the boys' favorite, cherry cobbler, the steaming, foot-wide golden crust drizzled with almond honey; a plate of dried fruits and nuts; mulled, honey-sweetened pomegranate juice with cut lemons. The aroma filling the room is almost dense enough to see, beyond divine. All four lapse into a stupor of anticipation.

Chandon breaks the silence. "Boys, should we dig in?" Giant grins and exaggerated nods answer him. He lifts the platter of venison and passes it to his left to Diego, then helps himself to the rice. The food circles the table and they commence, eating in silence, the only sounds groans of goodness and delight.

Plates are emptied then refilled. Eventually all the food disappears, except for the cobbler which sits atop its throne in the center of the table. Chandon dings his glass with his fork for their attention.

"Diego was the first to introduce me to the Granadine feast and in his honor he shall have the first bite of our cherry cobbler." Salamun beams.

"Thank you, my Lord." The boy offers an exaggerated bow. They all laugh.

"You are most welcome, young sir. Alfonso, do not worry, you shall be next. However, I have noticed that the white wizard is growing too large for his robes, so you two shall have his share!" All four burst into laughter.

Chandon dishes up a quarter of the cobbler into a bowl and passes it to Diego, whose eyes grow enormous. With his spoon Diego takes a large bite, groans, then takes another, a third. He comes up for air, beams as continues to chew. Salamun and Chandon laugh.

"Well?"

"Wonderful, my Lord, just wonderful!"

Chandon begins dishing up the next bowl of cobbler. Just as he finishes and sets it in front of Alfonso, Salamun says, "Diego?" Concern edges into his voice. "Diego?"

Chandon turns. Diego's face has flushed bright red, his mouth repeatedly opening and closing as if he can't breathe. His eyes are white with terror.

Both men leap up. Salamun forces open his mouth, searches for a cherry pit at the back of his throat. Nothing. Diego's flush has faded now, and he is turning pale. Salamun pulls him from the table and lays him on the floor. His breathing is labored.

Salamun becomes frantic with his awful recognition, "Alfonso, put your spoon down. NOW!" The boy complies. "Did you eat any of the cobbler? DID YOU?!"

Alfonso whimpers, "No, my Lord, no."

"Alfonso, run to the hospital and fetch my medical bag. The one in the cabinet, NOT the one beside my desk. Understood?" The boy nods. "As quick as you can run, boy. GO!" Alfonso scrambles out of the room, taking two steps at a time down the stairs.

"Chandon, Diego has been poisoned. Alert the guards."

Chandon runs from the room, leaps down the stairs, startling Yazdan and Musa, who are quizzically watching Alfonso run out of the palace entrance and onto the street.

"Yazdan, Musa, Diego has been poisoned!" Only blank stares. Chandon switches to Arabic. "Diego has been...has been...has been...BLOODY HELL!" Finally, he locates the word. "POISONED!" The two bodyguards exchange an alarmed look, then their instincts and training take over.

Yazdan drops into his command voice. "Musa, guard the stairwell with your life. I will alert the Royal Bodyguard." He draws his dagger, flips it, then stretches it towards Chandon. The Breton extends his hand. The bodyguard slaps the dagger hilt-first into his waiting palm. "Go back up to the room, Chandon, and bolt the door. Kill anyone who attempts to enter the room. Do you understand me?" Chandon nods. "NOW!"

Chandon counters, "But Alfonso is bringing medicine."

Musa says, "I will tell you when he arrives. GO! NOW!"

Musa draws his sword and dagger, steps just inside the stairwell out of bow shot and cocks into a defensive killing posture.

Yazdan draws his sword then turns and runs around the pool and darts into the passage way leading to the Palace of the Lions. A moment later, an alarm bell sounds. A second, then a third. Within two minutes the Courtyard of the Myrtles is awash in red-robed Royal Bodyguard, swords and daggers drawn. Orders are barked, all entrances and exits sealed.

Chandon kneels beside the boy, stroking his hair. The boy's face is pale blue now. His eyes are closed, his breathing is shallow. "Will he live?"

Salamun sighs, looks up at his friend, tears in his eyes. "No." The wizard breaks into a truncated sob, chokes it back, sniffs loudly. "Devil's Slipper. It induces numbness of the face and throat, then paralysis of the breathing muscles. The antidote must be delivered within three minutes if the victim is to have a chance. It will take Alfonso ten to bring my kit. It is a preferred choice for...assassins." He hisses the word. "Properly prepared, it is odorless and tasteless, quick acting."

"Assassins..." Anger surrounds the awful recognition, the weight of the world bearing down upon his shoulders. "Me." His anger is replaced with disgust. "They were after me." Chandon's head sinks to his chest.

Salamun puts his hand on his shoulder. Through his tears, Salamun whispers, "It was not your fault, Young Knight. No one could have known, no one."

A moment later, a think raspy gasp, then the boy's breathing stops, and he is still. Salamun checks his pulse then pulls the blanket over his face. He and Chandon continue to kneel, hands covering their faces, the shoulders of both men shaking.

Al-Waziri stands talking with Yazdan in the central courtyard of the Palace of the Lions. He turns and tracks the Sultan's entourage, notes the dozen Royal Bodyguard that encircle him. An approaching storm.

The Sultan is red-faced and livid. "Well, Bashir? SPEAK!"

Al-Waziri answers, "Sire, the boy is dead. Salamun and his two assistants were eating with Chandon in his room. There was poison in the cherry cobbler. Salamun thinks it was Devil's Slipper. Intended for Chandon, Sire. He was lucky. Yazdan, tell the Sultan exactly what happened." The guard fills in the details.

The Sultan shakes his head with disgust. "No taste tester? NONE? The Master of the Royal Kitchens will answer for this with his head!"

Al-Waziri looks up, "He already has, Sire."

"What do you mean?"

"We found him in the pantry. Daggered through the heart. Just like the others."

The Sultan fumes as he weighs his options. "I am leaving for the Generalife. This afternoon." He angrily shakes his head. "Hopefully I can find some safety there." Al-Waziri nods. The Sultan turns to the head of the Royal Bodyguard. "Zyad, dismiss the carpenters and masons and secure the grounds. And prepare my stallion." He stands thinking. "The Royal Harem will stay where they are but triple their guard. And contact my personal staff, tell them to prepare for the move. I want them in the Generalife by evening. Is that clear?"

"Perfectly, Sire. Consider it done." He nods his acknowledgment and departs.

The Sultan turns back to face al-Waziri. "And Bashir? If my Military Vizier values his title, he better bring safety back to my palace. TODAY! An assassin roams my court. STILL! This is INSUFFERABLE!" The Sultan turns and storms out.

Al-Waziri offers, "I understand, Sire. I will see to it," but the Sultan is already out of ear shot. He swallows hard then goes to round up the troops he will need for a thorough room-by-room search of the entire palace complex.

It has been a week since they last met. Diego's funeral was held two days ago in the Jewish quarter of the city just south of the Alhambra. The boy was interred in Salamun's family tomb, beside Johan. A wrenching day for everyone.

They sit on their pillows facing the water, silent. There is a thin hint of fall in the air, a welcome contrast to the unusually hot and persistent summer. The morning is crisp, pleasant, not a cloud in the sky.

Chandon is quiet, pensive. His chin touches his chest. She studies him.

"I am so sorry about Diego." A long pause as she carefully picks her words. "I have missed you so."

He looks up. "Thank you, Layla. I have missed you, too. More than you know." He shakes his head side to side, then lowers it to speak to his lap again. "I am not sure what has gotten into me." His voice begins to quaver as he says, "I am so weary of all the death." He struggles for control, tries to shake it off. Her eyes well up. "I witnessed the beheading of two Aragonese knights at the Court of the Machuca a week and a half ago. I recognized them from Jaén. I had spoken to one of them before the battle there. As he was about to be executed, he begged me for help. Begged. I could do nothing. Nothing. We locked eyes as his head was taken." A tear drops onto her robe. "First Johan, now Diego. Such sweet, innocent boys. Salamun's pride and joy. Gone. Both murdered by someone trying to murder me. My heart is heavy, Layla. I am drowning in guilt."

Another tear drops onto her robe. He lifts his head and looks at her, his eyes brimming. "I lost ninety-seven of my men on the plains of Jaén, Layla. Ninety-seven. Victims of my overconfidence. My arrogance. All but one of my officers is dead. Robert Cheney, Garsis du Chastel, Robert Briquet, and Gaillard Viguier, Perducas d'Albret. They were good friends, Layla. Gone. Who knows what will happen to their families?" His head sags, "So much death...so much."

She wipes her eyes then reaches over and touches his shoulder. "Come, Chandon, let us begin our lessons. We must focus on life."

He tries to shake the melancholy from his head. He wipes his eyes, offers her a weak smile. "You are right, of course. We must focus on life. I will try."

# Alliances

The courtier ushers the visitor into the Hall of the Orange in the Royal Court in Sevilla, halting ten paces before King Pedro. The visitor is indulged for a moment to absorb, admire. The man studies the intricate stucco wall patterns hovering over of the bright polychrome background, then raises his eyes to take in the half-dome marquetry ceiling, finally training his eyes upon the king, whose face is set into a thin smile. Examiner examined.

Pedro sits on his ornate inlaid throne, dressed in his improbable Granadine silk finery. The visitor's left eyebrow arches. Pedro's smile stretches. Two pairs of counselors mark their normal positions flanking the king. Six palace guards line the wall behind, eyes discretely on the floor. The visitor has clearly not been here before and cannot completely mask his surprise at what he sees. Pedro the Moor? He has been warned, of course, but is always suspicious of rumors, preferring to decide for himself. He is skeptical no longer. Pedro allows the silence ample room to breathe, just to the point of discomfort.

The courtier lifts his palm, intones in a practiced voice, "Majesty, Lord John Templeton, Ambassador to England." The visitor bows.

"Lord Templeton, welcome to Sevilla. Please give my condolences to the family of Lord Sampson, God rest his soul."

"The pleasure is mine, Majesty. Yes, Lord Sampson's passing was a loss to us all. I will convey your condolences, Majesty, thank you. King Edward sends his warmest regards." He pauses for effect. "As does Edward the Black Prince." Pedro's thin smile returns.

"Good, good. Yes, it has been too long since the Black Prince and I have talked. He is well, I trust?"

"Very well, Majesty, thank you. He and his army are presently in Aquitaine."

"Ahhh...I had assumed he had returned to Wallingford Castle to be with Princess Joan."

"No, Majesty." After a protracted moment, he says, "Majesty, if I might be candid?"

"By all means, Lord Templeton."

"Majesty, the Black Prince's army is billeted in Aquitaine because he cannot afford to transport them back to England. As you will recall, the Black Prince is owed ten thousand gold florins for his support at Nájera. It has been five months, Majesty. The troops have grown predictably restless. They miss their families. Edward cannot return to England and leave his army in Aquitaine." Now an awkward hesitation. "I have been instructed to inquire about the status of the payment, Majesty."

Pedro frowns. "Yes, yes, I am well aware of what I owe the Black Prince, Lord Templeton. You perhaps know that I deeded substantial lands and titles to Edward. In addition to the florins."

"Indeed, Majesty. And the Black Prince is grateful, of course. Unfortunately, those lands lie inside Aragon, Majesty, of little use to the Black Prince while Enrique remains at large."

"Indeed. That is precisely why I require the Black Prince's continued support, so that both of us might profit. I must vanquish my bastard brother once and for all. Together, we crushed Enrique at Nájera. Only by sheer luck did he manage to escape us. I am readying my forces to invade Aragon. I am prepared to increase my promise of lands and titles to Edward for his continued support.

"What new lands and titles, Majesty?"

"The Black Prince shall have Zaragoza itself. The city, with all of its wealth, and the lands around it to a distance of fifty miles. Zaragoza is where we shall strike first. We will wipe Aragon off the map. Stab the heart and the body dies." Lord Templeton is silent. Pedro continues, "In addition, the Lordship of Biscay. In Castile." Pedro smiles.

Lord Templeton sighs. "Majesty, those are generous offerings, but how is the Black Prince expected to feed and billet his army without gold? He borrowed money to supply his army for the Nájera campaign...against your promise of ten thousand florins. His creditors howl to be paid. They will extend no more credit until they see gold."

"I understand. Tell the Black Prince that I have one thousand gold florins ready now, as down payment, and will have another three thousand next month. I will send the one thousand with you today...a good will offering. When we defeat Enrique, I will double the remaining six thousand. Twelve thousand, in addition to the new lands. The balance to be paid AFTER we defeat Enrique." Pedro crosses his arms, suggesting that this is his final offer.

"I see." Templeton considers an appropriate response, but instead exhales, letting it fade. "I will convey your offer to the Black Prince, Majesty." He hesitates. "One more thing, Majesty. The Black Prince has heard...rumors...that William Chandon of Brittany was captured by the Moors after Nájera." He scrutinizes Pedro for any clue. Seeing none, he pushes forward. "If it were possible for Chandon to be delivered to the Black Prince, alive, to stand trial for treason in England, it would be looked upon most favorably."

Pedro nods but remains silent. Lord Templeton bows, steps back three steps, then turns and departs.

The room remains quiet, tense. Pedro waves his guards out and the five sit in silence, pondering.

"Gentlemen? I am interested in your impressions. Candor please."

Don Sancho clears his throat. "Much as we expected, Majesty. The Black Prince is insolvent. Like us. It is not obvious to me that he will be able to secure enough loans to field an army for a new campaign against Enrique. Zaragoza is a fine prize, to be sure, but it cannot be claimed without victory, and victory takes gold. Deeding Zaragoza to England gives them a substantial foothold in Iberia. Dangerous, in my view. The Jewish lenders he will be forced to use will see our promise of Zaragoza as very high risk. They will demand an exorbitant interest rate to match that risk. As would I." He hesitates and encountering no resistance, continues. "Offering Biscay was unwise in my view, Majesty. Any land in northern Castile, especially those near Aquitaine, is easily claimed by the Black Prince without giving us the support we require."

"Mmmm...a calculated gamble. I felt I had to offer ripe fruit to whet his appetite. I must have the Black Prince by my side when I meet Enrique in battle. I MUST! Besides, it seems like Biscay is always a single step away from rebellion. Let Edward tame them."

Don Alfonso chimes in, "Majesty, a thousand florins will only be enough to satisfy the interest on the Black Prince's loans; it will not touch the principal. I suspect he will howl as loudly as his debtors when he learns how little we have sent."

"We will send three thousand more shortly."

"Provided Granada pays its tribute on time, Majesty. They conveniently ignored your request for full payment of the additional four-thousand dinars by August. A decision which, frankly, does not surprise me. It is certainly in character for the Moors, if annoying."

"We will come back to Granada in a moment. Don Ruy?"

"I was intrigued, Majesty, by the inquiry regarding Chandon. Most interesting. From what I have learned from my sources, it seems Edward and Chandon were close friends from childhood. The Black Prince evidently arranged Chandon's command of Jean de Montfort's army. Chandon's victory at Auray is his claim to fame. Edward feels strongly that Chandon is in his debt. Hard to argue. So when Chandon sided with de Montfort on the side of King Charles, Edward took it as a betrayal. A personal betrayal. As we all know, despite outward appearances, the Black Prince has something of a mean streak when suitably offended." They all chuckle. "It would seem that he would like nothing more than to see Chandon hang for treason. Delivering Chandon to Edward would help our cause, Majesty. The question is, how do we convince the Sultan to give him up?"

"Good question. Muhammad surely suspects that Chandon is valuable to us, else he would not bother to deny him ransom and sequester him. No doubt he will try and strike some sort of bargain to gain advantage. As usual. Don Juan, share with the others the overture from the letter we just received from our friend the Sultan."

"Certainly, Majesty." He clears his throat. "It seems Granada is prepared to offer Castile a loan. Five thousand dinars. On top of its annual tribute." Don Juan hesitates to let their surprised expressions clear.

"At what interest rate?"

"Ahhh...ready? Zero. It seems it is forbidden for Muslims to charge interest." More surprised expressions, then a flurry of murmurs.

"Majesty, you know that this is impossible. Accept money from the Moors to fight Christians? We would all be excommunicated!"

The king face hardens as he metes out his words. "Don Alfonso, correct me if I am wrong, but I am the King of Castile, not the Pope." Don Alfonso nods his acknowledgement, backs down.

Don Lorenzo deflects the tension by asking, "And in return, they would like what exactly?"

"It seems that the Moors would like to hold on to Jaén, Baeza, and Úbeda after all." Rueful smile.

Pedro's face reddens as his voice begins to rise, "As PROTECTION against Aragonese INVASION! DAMN MUHAMMAD! Those are MY CITIES!"

Don Ruy adds his calming voice. "We all agree, Majesty. Still, Granada possesses them, not us. Consider for a moment. Five thousand dinars would be enough for a...modest...refit of our army. Granted, it would not help satisfy what we owe the Black Prince, but that would be an important step forward for us in preparation for war with Enrique and Aragon. And victory."

Don Alfonso can't resist revisiting the obvious. "And risk excommunication, Don Ruy?"

Don Sancho chimes in, "I agree. The Pope is looking for any excuse to punish Castile. Why give him the ammunition he needs?"

"Gentlemen, let us not be naïve. The Pope is not neutral in this war. It is more than obvious that he supports Enrique and Aragon as a means to depose King Pedro and strengthen papal control in Castile. I have heard rumors that the Pope is backing them with a Papal Blessing. And papal gold." After letting them absorb this, he continues. "Gentlemen, we risk excommunication only if the Pope becomes aware that the transfer of the gold was in fact a loan." He turns to Pedro, "Majesty, first we insist on secrecy of the gold transfer from Granada to Sevilla. Second, in our treasury records, we label the gold as additional tribute from Granada. They are simply returning to us the Castilian gold they captured at Jaén; gold that is rightfully ours. Once it is in Sevilla, we will re-melt it into florins and stamp it Castilian." He pauses for effect, then intones, "There...was...no...loan." He beams his triumph.

Silence settles in as the others ponder the implications. Pedro rests his chin on his fist, scowling.

Emboldened by the silence, Don Ruy pushes on, "In addition, we demand Chandon as a part of the transaction. Perhaps even Moor cavalry, as at Nájera. By all accounts they were invaluable to us."

Pedro begins to nod his head. "Refit our army for war. Seal our agreement with Edward using Chandon as payment. I like it." He looks from counselor to counselor as he nods his head with increasing vigor, "I LIKE IT!"

"After we defeat Enrique and Aragon, Majesty, we repay the Black Prince and discreetly return Granada's gold. No one will ever know. Perhaps after we repay the loan, we will be presented with a...compelling...need to then recapture our three lost cities. Only as a means to secure Granada's border and protect them from the English in Zaragoza, of course." They all smile.

## Strangle Hold

Chandon sits on a stool in the men's ward, content. Three male nurses busy about the forty residents, the six madrasa students assisting them. Bathing, changing, clothing, cleaning, feeding. Chandon holds the bowl of warm porridge in his palm, loads his spoon half full then turns to the teenager sitting across from him. As Chandon opens his mouth wide, Hamid mimics him, his enormous pink tongue extending in anticipation. Chandon offers an exaggerated "Yuummmm..." as he moves the spoon closer, producing a lopsided grin on Hamid's face. Porridge safely tucked home, Chandon wipes the excess from the boy's lips, then says, "Good man," and begins again.

Hamid has no obvious physical deformity. His large almond eyes are vacant, however, refusing to focus on what lies in front of him, preferring instead to wander about the room. As the fifth spoonful nears its destination Hamid unexpectedly finds then locks his eyes onto Chandon. The spoon halts mid-flight. Chandon smiles.

"A good morning to you, sir." Hamid smiles then grunts with glee. A short moment later the spell is broken, all recognition gone, the boy's eyes freely roaming the room once more.

This is Chandon's second week at the Maristan. Layla insisted it would do his spirits good. She was right, as usual. He has not felt this peace-filled and alive in years. The five of them walk each morning to the Albayzín; Chandon, Yazdan, Musa, Layla and Aisha. Yazdan and Musa stand sentry outside the hospital entrance. No weapons are allowed within this sanctuary, and they refuse to remove them. Chandon helps out where needed within the men's ward. It is tiring work, but satisfying, unlike anything he has ever done, and a constant source of animated conversation as he and Layla trade stories of their experiences on the way there and back, first in Arabic, then in English. Impatience typically takes over midway through, and they switch to Castilian to race each other.

When he finishes feeding Hamid, he goes and changes into a plain cotton robe, picks up a towel and ventures to the end of the ward to retrieve Jabir, who is in for a special treat today. Jabir is a young boy, perhaps eight, born with no arms or legs. While his eyes are bright with intelligence and he has a quick smile, Jabir has never spoken a word.

"Good morning, young sir!" The boy turns his head to the source of the sound and beams. "I have a special treat for you today, Jabir." Chandon grins and raises his eyebrows with exaggerated expectation, inducing a giggle. "We, young sir, are going for a swim in the courtyard pool." Jabir grins. Several of the most severely handicapped boys who cannot walk are occasionally lifted and taken to the courtyard pool to "swim." The luxurious expanse of the shimmering pool is unusual, even in a palace. Measuring fifteen yards by thirty yards, the pool is a Courtyard of the Myrtles in miniature, another gift of the Sultan. A carved marble lion fountain is perched atop a pedestal at the pool's center. Water jets from the open roar, arching to the water below, amazing to all who see it.

Chandon cradles the boy in his arms as he leaves the building and heads for the water. His eyes track to the open windows of the lady's ward in front of him, hoping to steal a glimpse of Layla. Seeing nothing, he turns to his far left, the baby's ward. He smiles as he sees her standing beside the open window. She is holding a baby but is angled away from him. He returns to the task at hand.

Chandon first orients the boy so he can see the fountain and then begins to step down the stairs leading into the water.

"Ready, Jabir? The water will feel a bit cold at first but we will take it slow and easy until you get used to it." Water now up to his groin, Chandon lowers the boy until his back touches the shimmering surface. Jabir inhales sharply with surprise, then beams. Chandon lowers him further into the water, allowing the boy to float on top of his outstretched arms. Jabir giggles as Chandon smiles. Soon Chandon begins to play games, tossing Jabir up into the air, catching him just as he reaches the water, allowing a splash but preventing the boy from going under. Jabir's wide-eyed glee is contagious, and soon they are both laughing.

After a few moments Chandon kneels down on the bottom of the pool, allowing Jabir to float on his arms as they both relax and enjoy the delicious contrast between the warmth of the sunshine and the cool caress of the water. It is an unusually warm fall day. Chandon looks up then closes his eyes, allowing the sun to warm his face. A short while later, Chandon opens his eyes and looks down to check on Jabir, who he sees is staring intently up at him. The boy's mouth opens, then closes. His mouth opens again, followed by a gurgling sound. This happens once more, only this time, Chandon is shocked to see that Jabir is struggling to form a word.

Chandon leans closer to the boy. "Yes, Jabir? Did you say something, young sir?" This time he hears an unmistakable, "May-ya." *Water.*

"Yes, Jabir, may-ya. May-ya!" He lifts the boy up and hugs him tight to his chest. Chandon walks out of the pool and dries them both off, then goes to find Juan, the head nurse, to tell him the wonderful news.

The two stand side by side on the north wall of the Alhambra just opposite the Court of the Machuca at sunset, staring down on the Albayzín. The burnt orange glow deepens gloriously in hue as it nestles in behind the distant mountain rim at the far edge of the Vega, splashing the wispy clouds above them with bright pinks and lavish violets.

She points down into the city. He cranes his neck to follow her finger. A short burst of explanation follows, then her arm rotates twenty degrees and she begins again. He nods, asks a question, and her hands dance in response. Yazdan and Musa stand twenty paces to the west, one scanning inward, one outward. Aisha sits, reading.

After the city tour the two settle into a relaxed silence as they observe the day's pink-purple sigh and indulge in people-watching. The streets are beginning to empty, families settling into their homes for the night. The swallows have come out to play.

He continues to stare down into the city. "You were right about the Maristan, Layla. It was just what I needed to break free of my demons."

She pivots her head to catch his eye and smiles. "Yes. You are good with the boys. It seems to come very natural to you."

"It has all been very surprising to me, especially how much I enjoy it. I have never done anything like this. As a young man I did help the friars distribute food to the poor, but nothing like this. Somehow I find it...life giving. I do so little for these boys, yet I feel so good doing it." He searches for the right words. "It is humbling work, but very gratifying. I have nothing to offer them except a kind word, a smile. My presence." He stops, shakes his head. "The one thing I do know is that it makes me happy." He turns to face her, "Is that strange?"

"Not at all. I feel exactly the same way. I bring so little, yet receive so much. I cannot imagine my life without my babies and the women." She grows more serious as she studies the city. "Having grown up at court, I lived a life of privilege and luxury. I was never exposed to suffering. The deformed, the mentally ill, they were quietly removed, never to be heard from again. When Master al-Mussib insisted that the Maristan was where my Sufi training was to begin, I was profoundly disappointed, angry even." She looks up. "I am not proud of that. But I recognize now the wisdom of Master al-Mussib's request. This was exactly what I needed. I will never forget my first day; the sights, the sounds, the smells. My tears. I was not sure I had the strength to endure such work. And yet, after a few days, I discovered a part of me I never knew existed. As you say, it is humbling work, yet strangely life-giving. That is why I cherish it so. I focus my energy on others, not on myself. I love these women and children."

He smiles. "Yes, I can see that, Layla. Your compassion and your dedication are inspiring. Thank you for inviting me to join you." She returns his smile.

A comfortable silence stretches out as the dusk begins to roll in, graying the scene. Together, they survey the dimming horizon, now faded to a deep crimson-purple. She weighs her thoughts, then, decision made, leans close to him, their shoulders just touching, and begins just above a whisper. "I had a profound spiritual experience in the Maristan, while bathing an old Castilian woman. She called me 'Isa ibn Maryam'. Jesus, son of Mary. A deep spiritual connection grew between us. My heart swelled with love for her, connected the two of us together in some mysterious way, as if we were one. Sisters, but far deeper than blood relatives. Intense joy and love flooded over me." She pauses as she relives the experience. "Our souls were linked. Only for a moment, and then it was gone. I have never experienced anything like it. Master al-Mussib told me later that it was a direct encounter with Allah. My compassion, ignited by service to the lowly, invited Allah to come close, to stand beside me, announce himself to me. To bless an unworthy servant."

He absorbs her words, then offers, "Tawhid."

She nods. "Tawhid."

"I am happy for you, Layla. The Sufi Way is opening for you."

"Yes. I am unworthy, but I am blessed."

"God's Grace."

She smiles. "Yes, God's Grace."

The dark is settling in now and they can barely see one another. The fall chill begins to tiptoe in. The muezzin's melodic echoes begin to drift in from the *minaret*. They listen for a moment to the mesmerizing chant. She shivers and says, "We should be heading back to court; it is time for prayer."

During the early afternoon she stands by the open window of the lady's ward, catching her breath. She has bathed and dressed twelve women already. Eight more to go. The cool breeze in her face is refreshing. She inhales the crisp air, holds it, exhales. She tilts her head to catch the warm autumn rays full on, closes her eyes, basking in the peacefulness. The incontrovertible truth of the sudden realization takes her by surprise: she has never been happier.

She hears a commotion across the courtyard, opens her eyes. Chandon. He is dressed in a white robe, carrying a young boy with no right leg. She recalls him telling her about the boy two days back, a Castilian slave named Pero. Chandon is whispering to the boy, who giggles then laughs loud. She cannot help but smile.

They are headed to the pool, but at an oblique angle to her. She enjoys being able to study him unobserved. Chandon cradles the boy with an endearing, natural tenderness, rocks him in his arms. More whispers, then they both laugh loud. Her smile widens. As he steps down into the pool the boy's eyes grow wide with fear. Chandon slows, whispers a consolation, then lowers the boy into the cool water, whispering encouragement the whole time. After a brief gasp, the boy's fears melt and he grins. Chandon beams.

The barest wisp of an idea congeals deep in the recesses of her mind, lingers there long enough to coalesce, then rises into her consciousness, asserting itself and catching her full attention. He will be a good father. She searches for the origin of the thought, then gives up, puzzled. She continues to watch him, mesmerized. The two are playing now, tossing, splashing, giggling.

A moment later a grin eases back onto her face, widens to a full smile as she teases out the lurking idea, hones it to a point for fuller appreciation. 'He is a good man. Intelligent, but playful. He loves to laugh, but is sensitive and compassionate, interested in everything. He was molded by war, but is aware of war's cruel seductions; and weary of the abuses it has unleashed upon him. He longs for peace. He is kind and caring, and has a good heart.' She pauses then nods her head. 'Yes, he will be a good father.' She sighs contentedly. 'So unlike any man I have ever known.'

Her joy begins to swell with this recognition, and oddly, her heart begins to race. She is aware that something profound has shifted, changed forever, but is not quite sure what. She continues to watch him for a moment longer, makes a mental note to re-examine these feelings in the quiet of her room. Constancia's call breaks the spell. She returns to the bath to resume her work.

She has saved the best for last. Having changed and fed four babies this morning she moves at last to Maryam's cradle. She leans over and peers in. The baby girl lies on her back, still, but her enormous brown eyes track to Layla's face. As Layla leans close a beautiful smile slowly spreads across the baby's face. Maryam coos as her tiny arms begin to twitch and her fingers flex.

Layla melts as she scoops the infant up, bringing her to within six inches of her face. "And how is my beautiful princess this morning?" The baby coos. Layla hugs her tight to her chest. "Let us change that diaper, Maryam." Layla sets her down in the cradle then begins to unwrap the cloth. "Wet, wet, wet." She cleans her then lifts her bottom to slide another cloth beneath, folds it then pins it in place. Layla doesn't even notice the odd angles of the baby's legs now. She cocoons Maryam in a thin cotton blanket as Constancia has taught her, lifts her back up and into her arms, squeezes her tight once more. "Are you hungry?" Layla reaches down for the bottle of goat's milk and begins to feed her.

She walks over to the window and searches the courtyard for Chandon, but he is nowhere to be seen. As she feeds the baby her hips begin to sway, her primal mothering instinct miraculously engaged. She begins to hum an ancient song she cannot recall learning, a tune sung to her by her own mother, to her mother by her grandmother, to her grandmother by her great grandmother; a testament to the great circle of life.

These past weeks, Layla has found herself imagining what it would be like to be a mother. Having been given the opportunity to hold a baby and care for it, she finds that mothering comes quite naturally to her. The experience has been joyful, something she would never have guessed. She smiles to herself at the amazing discoveries of these past few months.

She has finished her duties in the baby's ward and is headed to the lady's ward to help with the bathing, an hour before noon prayer. She says her usual goodbyes to the other nurses then exits into the hallway, closes the door behind her. Halfway down the empty hall she opens the closet door on the right where the bath towels are kept and steps to the back of the room, lifts a large stack in her arms. As she turns around to leave, a man steps out from behind the door. She screeches her surprise, dropping the towels.

She composes herself then opens with a level voice, "Men are not allowed on this side of the hospital. What are you doing here?" Silence. The man wears the white robes of a madrasa student, but he has the end of his turban wrapped around his face, masking his identity. His ebony eyes smolder. He reaches up and begins to unwind the cloth, slowly revealing his face.

As recognition dawns, her heart begins to pound. The student at the madrasa door. After that first tense encounter he has never stopped scowling at her whenever they have crossed paths. It has been worse lately. He steps from his hiding place into the doorway, blocking her exit. It dawns on her that no one else is in the hallway between the two wards. Her mind begins to race through her options. She decides to try once again to intimidate him.

With her firmest voice she says, "I remind you that men are not permitted on this side of the Maristan. You must leave. Now!" More silence. "I am Layla al-Khatib, the daughter of the Grand Vizier to Sultan Muhammad, and a disciple of Sufi Master al-Mussib. I demand that you step aside!"

Menacingly, he says, "I know who you are, devil. You are the female blasphemer who corrupts the holy confines of the madrasa with your temptress ways. You are in a position to demand nothing." With lightning speed, his hand snaps forward, grabs the tucked gray headscarf of her hijab, yanks it violently, producing an explosion of chestnut curls.

Instantly livid, her face radiates fury. She hisses dangerously, "HOW DARE YOU TOUCH ME!" She seethes. "I will see you in the dungeon by nightfall!" Her right hand whips forward, slapping him across the cheek, the echo reverberating for a full second in the close space. He winces, the palm print already reddening, considers momentarily, then rears back and punches her full force in the face, catching her squarely on her upper left cheek bone, his ring opening an ugly gash a quarter of an inch below her eye. She recoils, dazed. She then stumbles forward, woozy, trying to comprehend what just happened. A rivulet of blood begins to race down her cheek onto her robe, her purpling eye already swelling shut.

He steps forward. "I will teach you, devil, that the proper place of a woman is underneath a man. I will shut you up once and for all. You are no Sufi, devil. There is only one way to deal with temptress female blasphemers." One more step forward then he pulls her against him. She is still woozy but is slowly recovering her senses. As she wakens to his erection against her stomach, panic sets in. She struggles, but he pulls her tighter against him, a rabbit in an anaconda's coils. She frantically tries to strike him again, but he successfully grabs her wrist this time mid-swing, wrenches it violently to an unnatural angle, causing her to yelp with pain. He slaps her hard on her bloody cheek.

She screams at the top of her lungs, "CHANDON!"

He slugs her again to shut her up, knocking her senseless, then clamps a hand over her mouth to silence her as he begins to pull her to the floor.

---

As he races down the hallway past the open door he catches a peripheral glimpse of two outstretched bare legs. He brakes violently, turns and is inside the room. A white robed figure, back to the door, kneels over her. His left hand covers her bloody mouth, pinning her head down. Her eyes are closed. With his right hand he has forced her gray robe up to her belly and is roughly parting her bare thighs.

His years of battle training trigger every primal instinct he possesses, all thinking gone now, brain no longer in command of muscles, blood boiling over with deadly violence. He reaches down and grabs the man's right shoulder, turning him while his balled fist swings a wide arc. The young man's face drops into surprise just as Chandon's fist catches him square under the jaw, snapping his head back, flattening him to the floor.

The man shakes off the blow, attempts to rise. Chandon steps forward and begins to demolish her attacker's face; crushing of the right sinus, splintering of the nose bone, fracturing of the jaw, on and on. The attackers face is bloodied, then mangled, then his features begin to dissolve into pulpy mush. The man crumples on his back to the floor, unable to raise his hands to fend off the blows. Chandon stands over him, his face not his own, fists covered in blood, triumphant. He kicks the attacker in the groin then eases down to the floor with the elegance of a long-practiced dance step.

Chandon's right hand stretches out and grips the man's windpipe, begins to squeeze. The attacker's eyes flash open with terror, realizing that his fate is upon him. Face beet red, both hands spring back to life as they try in vain to loosen the death grip as his legs begin to kick and squirm, but he cannot break the grip.

From somewhere deep within the recesses of his brain, Chandon hears his name.

"Chandon, Chandon, do not kill him." His instincts firmly in command he seems confused on the origin of the words. He shakes his head to clear the distraction, continues to crush the man's throat.

"William. William!" He feels a hand touch his back, then shake him. "William. William! Enough, please. Do not kill him. Please!"

His grip loosens, the attacker gasping and heaving for air. Chandon remembers now, tries to calm the hot blood coursing through his veins, gain some control. She has dragged herself to him. He turns to her just as she collapses back the floor, unconscious. He is instantly beside her. He pulls her robe down, pushes her hair away from her bloodied face. Her left eye is purple, swollen shut, the deep gash just beneath it showing a hint of bone.

"Layla? Layla!" He strokes her cheek, but she does not respond. He stands, walks to the open window, cups his hands to his mouth, yells in his loudest voice. "YAZDAN! MUSA! QUICKLY!"

Yazdan and Musa arrive breathless at the closet door, swords drawn, eyes darting about. Constancia arrives a moment later. Then Majahid al-Khayyat, then Aisha, finally Juan and two other male nurses.

Chandon steps into the hallway, his command voice engaged. "Layla has been attacked. She is badly injured. Yazdan. Run to the palace and find Salamun. Alert him that I am on my way with her. We will meet him in the Comares Palace at her suite." He turns to the other bodyguard. "Musa. Secure this scum and see that he is brought to the palace. Alive." The two bodyguards look at each other, trying to decide what to do. Chandon does not equivocate, locks his eyes on Yazdan, raises his voice, "Yazdan. GO! NOW!" The guard nods to Chandon, sheathes his sword, turns and runs down the hallway. Musa steps into the room to examine the prostrate prisoner.

Constancia kneels beside Layla, examining her. "Chandon, this cut below her eye is deep. You need to being her to Salamun quickly or she may lose it. Please hurry." Aisha sobs hysterically.

Al-Khayyat paces back and forth in the hallway, shaking his head side to side as he stares at the floor, "Oh my, oh my. How could this happen? Oh dear. Poor Layla. Oh my, oh my."

Chandon kneels beside her again, slides his arms underneath her and lifts her up. She hangs limp. He turns and begins to race-walk down the hallway towards the hospital entrance, the jumble of chestnut curls waterfalling to his knees. His face is tense now with purpose as he begins the long climb back to the Alhambra, Aisha behind him five paces, struggling to keep up as she continues to sob.

Chandon sits on the edge of Layla's divan in the Grand Vizier's suite. He stands up, paces for a moment, sits back down. A moment later he is back up pacing, an endless progression of restlessness that has already lasted over an hour. Ibn al-Khatib sits on the edge of his own divan, hunched over, face to the floor, hand shielding his eyes, silent. Aisha sniffles from the stool in the corner.

The door opens and a stone-faced Salamun emerges. All three rise and surround him, faces folded into question marks.

He attempts a smile, but doesn't quite get there. "She is resting comfortably. Our girl has been badly beaten. She was not violated. Layla is young and strong. She will fully recover...given a little time. Her right wrist is broken, but cleanly. I have set the bone. I was very concerned about her left eye, but it appears to be undamaged. Swollen shut, but best I can tell, intact. She is a lucky girl. We will have to watch it closely when the swelling lessens. I have sutured the ugly gash and treated it for infection, bandaged her up. She will have a nice scar." He offers a weary sigh. "Mostly, she needs rest, much rest."

Chandon blurts out, "May I see her?"

Salamun shakes his head. "No, Young Knight. I have given her an elixir to ease the pain and put her into a deep sleep. She should hopefully sleep for a day or two. Give her time." Salamun turns to Ibn al-Khatib. "Lisan al-Din, I will stop by every few hours to check on her. Have Aisha stay by her side and call for me at once if she awakens."

Ibn al-Khatib nods. "Thank you, Salamun."

Salamun lifts his medical kit, pats Ibn al-Khatib tenderly on the shoulder and says, "Do not worry, old friend, Layla will be fine." He heads back to the hospital.

The room is silent. Aisha walks into Layla's bedroom and shuts the door, leaving Chandon and Ibn al-Khatib standing together. Ibn al-Khatib eyes are brimming with tears as he turns to meet Chandon's gaze. He clearly wants to say something, but as his mouth opens to speak, his lower lip quivers and he stops. He tries once more with the same failed result. On the third try, he whispers, "Chandon. I am grateful. Thank you." Chandon remains silent, but nods his acknowledgment, then turns and leaves.

On the morning of the third day since the attack, Chandon leans against the wall, waiting for her. He stands up straight as he hears footsteps in the stairwell then walks forward to meet her. As Aisha steps out Chandon bows and says, "Good morning, Aisha."

"Good morning, my Lord."

"Where are you going?"

"To the Royal Kitchens, my Lord, for some tea and bread."

An awkward expression is painted on his face. He gets his courage up, leans in and whispers, "Aisha. I MUST see Layla. Please."

Aisha's face is pained with indecision. "My Lord, she is still sleeping."

"Aisha, please. I will not disturb her. But I MUST see her. Please!"

She turns and motions him forward, leads him up the stairs. "Come."

Across the courtyard, Yazdan and Musa turn to each other, exchange knowing glances, remain where they are.

Aisha has told him that he may have until she gets back from the Royal Kitchens. Ten minutes, no more. He sits on a pillow on the left side of her floor mattress, studying her. She sleeps on her back, head propped up on a pillow and turned to her right, facing him, covers pulled up and over her shoulders. Her blanket over her chest rises and falls with her breathing. Her hair has been braided, the long chestnut coil resting above her left shoulder. Her left eye and cheek remain bandaged. Her face is a study in shades of black, blue and purple. His eyes well up.

He reaches forward and touches her forehead. Warm, but not hot. He cups the top of her head with his palm to feel the sponge of her hair. He then begins to stroke her cheek with the back of his fingers. A single tear winds down his cheek. He withdraws his hand and looks down as he wipes the tear, then turns back to her. Her right eye is open, watching him. A single tear plops to her pillow.

He smiles and says, "Layla."

She attempts a smile but winces instead. She whispers, "William." She licks her lips, swallows hard. "You saved me."

His eyes brim. "I will never again let anyone or anything harm you, Layla, ever. I promise."

She whispers, “My William.”

Their faces relax into serious expressions, remain locked on each other, content. Her eyelid begins to droop, flutters, then shuts, is willed back open halfway, then shuts for good. He sighs, reaches again to stroke her cheek. “My Layla. My sweet Layla.”

# Desert Palms

3 December 1367. Chandon and Ibn al-Khatib step through the passage leading from the Courtyard of the Myrtles into the Palace of the Lions. Their movements are scrutinized by the Royal Bodyguards stationed in pairs on either end of the tunnel linking the two palaces. Ibn al-Khatib ignores them, but Chandon offers a curt nod as they pass. Already Ibn al-Khatib's hands begin to dance and flit as he launches into his elaborate explanations of the palace. Chandon smiles as he appreciates the origin of Layla's adorable hand puppets. Her father's daughter.

"The Sultan began work on the Palace of the Lions in the fall of 1362, just after the end of our exile. It was finished just last year. He was personally involved in its design and even helped in its construction." He offers an amused chuckle. "Muhammad has always loved to work with his hands, even as a boy. The Palace of the Lions is considered the finest example of Muslim architecture in all of al-Andalus and perhaps the world. Like much within the Alhambra it is layered with hidden meanings and symbolism."

They step down into the covered corridor at the western end of the courtyard, turn right then left, step into the small pavilion and stop. A matching pavilion lies across on the other side of the rectangular courtyard. Ibn al-Khatib is silent, allowing Chandon to absorb the scene and gather impressions. The courtyard is empty except for sentries statued at strategic locations. The morning is cool and crisp, pleasant, the cloudless sky a brilliant azure.

Dozens of carved marble columns ring the courtyard. Each six-foot high column is topped with a cubic capital carved with varying arabesque motifs over Granadine blue, and supports an elaborate pilaster, which in turn holds up lintels upon which the second story of the palace breathlessly balances. The spandrels between the columns are purely decorative, a delicate plaster curtain. Chandon looks up. The polychrome coffered ceiling of the pavilion is a perfect recessed hemisphere. He looks down and then along the walls. His eyes have been trained now to spot the hidden Arabic script within the densely carved stucco wall ornamentation, and he notes that he is again surrounded by thousands of words. A living poem.

"Amazing."

Ibn al-Khatib is pleased. "In Islam, Chandon, the walled garden plays a central role. The garden is an image of paradise, *al-Jannah* in the Quran, a word which means both 'garden' and 'secret place.' Traditionally, al-Jannah has four rivers, represented here by the six-inch wide troughs that begin at interior fountains within each of the palace halls and then course down several steps to the central courtyard fountain. The four rivers of paradise mark the four directions of the compass. The Islamic garden is first and foremost a sanctuary, a place to rest the heart, mind and soul; a paragon of harmony. But it is also a place of worship, where man meets Allah in paradise."

Ibn al-Khatib directs Chandon back out of the pavilion, and he has Chandon kneel at the corner of the courtyard.

"The columns represent the palm trees surrounding a hidden oasis in the desert. Do you see it?" Chandon nods. "Notice from this angle how the courtyard becomes a dense forest, surrounded by the Sultan's tents. It is meant to evoke our ancestry, our desert roots. The courtyard is open above to allow the moon and the stars to assert their will each night, to transport the viewer to the night sky in Damascus. There is no finer scene in the Alhambra than the Palace of the Lions by full moon."

"How many columns are there?"

"One hundred and twenty four, each placed in perfect symmetry."

"Remarkable."

Chandon stares at the central fountain. A circle of sculpted marble lions dominate the center of the courtyard. Their paws rest on an elevated circle of pure white marble. On the lions' backs rests a large circular marble basin containing a bubbling fountain. Out of the mouth of each lion a thin jet of water emerges, then collects in a circular trough in the pedestal. The four rivers of paradise flow atop narrow marble aqueducts, depositing their liquid treasure into the circular trough, where it disappears. Below the level of the four aqueducts and the lions lie four quadrants of rich garden dirt. Dwarf lemon, orange and pomegranate trees dot the garden, rising up only a few feet above the level of the rivers, interspersed with precisely groomed shrubs. Bougainvillea vines cling to corner columns, then fan out on the second story.

"Tell me about the lions."

"Ahhh... Palace of the Lions. The twelve lions were carved to represent the power of Granada, of al-Andalus, but the number twelve itself is very special. You see, Chandon, twelve is the first "abundant number" in mathematics, a number whose factors sum to more than itself. One plus two plus three plus four plus six equals sixteen, which is more than twelve. Unique, yes?" Chandon nods his understanding. "Twelve-fold motifs are the most commonly used patterns in the Alhambra. But apart from ornamentation with a mathematical basis, twelve's are everywhere. The twelve signs of the zodiac, the twelve months of the lunar year, the twelve tribes of Israel, the twelve sons of Jacob, the twelve imams of Islam." He looks up and grins, "The twelve disciples of Jesus." Chandon smiles. "Come." They walk back to the pavilion and follow the western river ten paces out to the circle of lions.

Chandon strokes the face of the marble beast. He sees now that each lion has subtle differences, leonine personality. He dips his finger into the water arcing from the roar. "Exquisite."

Ibn al-Khatib smiles. "I designed the fountain's plumbing. Quite a feat of engineering."

"I have spent considerable time trying to understand how the various fountains and water features are so effortlessly powered within the Alhambra." Chandon raises his eyebrows quizzically. "To no avail."

Ibn al-Khatib glows with boyish exuberance. His hands begin chattering. "The Darro River. Six miles north of the city, as the Darro winds its way out of the Sierra Nevada, we tap the river, divert water into an aqueduct, channel it into the Royal Waterway, then finally store it in three large reservoirs just outside the palace walls at an elevation well above the palace. The Royal Waterway enters the city at the east end of the Alhambra and the water has sufficient force to then drive all of the fountains within the grounds. Dozens. And of course it also services the many latrines. The spent water of the Darro leaves the palace and courses down the hill through an underground tunnel, rejoining the Genil River below the city."

"I have never seen anything like it."

"That is because it is unique, the first of its kind. Come, let me show you the palace halls." They walk due south along the narrow aqueduct ten paces to the columned portico. Ibn al-Khatib raises his palm, indicating the building in front of them. "The Hall of the Abencerrajes. The Sultan's bed chamber and private living quarters. It contains the entrance to the Royal Harem."

They turn around to face the courtyard. "Across from us is the Hall of the Two Sisters, to my eye, the finest building within the Alhambra. It is used for special social gatherings, celebrations, poetry recitals and musical concerts. It overlooks the Courtyard of the Lindaraja, which contains a lovely interior garden space and a spectacular fountain. The Sultan's private domain. It is enjoyed by the Royal Harem, the Sultan's visiting relatives, other special guests. Several of the viziers have suites overlooking the garden."

He turns to his right, points. "The Hall of the Kings. The Sultan often meets there with his Vizier Council, and sometimes with imams and qadi from the Mexuar Council. State business, banquets, that sort of thing."

Chandon muses. "For all of its remarkable splendor, the Palace of the Lions is never seen by the people of Granada, is it? Or even by visiting foreign dignitaries."

Ibn al-Khatib grins. "No. The Arab psyche cherishes hidden splendor, Chandon. Seclusion has primacy here. It is resonant with the concept of al-Jannah, a secret place, a sanctuary. You will observe that theme consistently throughout the Alhambra. Plain, undecorated exteriors hide the sudden surprise of exquisite interiors. A delicious contrast and a cherished art form, actually. We Arabs love compact spaces that exude refinement of artistry and splendor, but are tucked away, hidden from the casual observer."

"It is much more subtle than any European palace. Our palaces are big and bold, designed to project power and wealth. Crude by Granadine standards."

Ibn al-Khatib nods, "Yes. A very different idea altogether. Come, let me show you the ceiling of the Hall of the Two Sisters. Very unique, an unusual meld of mathematics and architecture. You will enjoy it." He is obviously relishing Chandon's company.

An hour later, the two emerge from the Hall of the Two Sisters and stop at the entrance. Ibn al-Khatib's palms stretch wide, measuring some phantom object. Chandon shakes his head. Next, Ibn al-Khatib takes his pointed index finger, joins it to his other palm at a right angle and rocks it back and forth indicating some construction principle. His hands relax to his sides then begin their circular dance steps once more. Chandon smiles, asks another question.

"By the way, the Sultan has indicated he would like to meet you today. He should be in the Hall of the Kings by now I think."

"Salamun told me that the Sultan had left the Alhambra for a nearby summer palace."

"Indeed. The Generalife, the Sultan's summer residence. It is close by, just a quick gallop across the ravine to the north." He indicates the direction. "He has been gone for many weeks now." He hesitates. "Since the poisoning."

Chandon's expression darkens. "Yes, the poisoning."

Ibn al-Khatib sighs. "As you can infer, Chandon, an unidentified assassin is likely still present within the Alhambra. He poses a danger to you, certainly, but also to the Sultan. The Military Vizier, Prince Bashir al-Waziri, is in pursuit, but after the poisoning, the Sultan felt that relocating temporarily to the Generalife made sense. I agreed. Isolated and much easier to guard. The Generalife is intended only for a summer retreat. It is too cold and windy for the winter. So the hope is that the Sultan's stay will not be overly long. He comes back to the palace once a week to meet with his viziers and sign documents."

"I see."

"Come, let us see if he is here."

Chandon nods, begins a mental rehearsal of his Arabic.

As the two step inside the Hall of the Kings, Ibn al-Khatib politely pauses to allow Chandon to study the design. The hall runs across the entire western end of the courtyard and is divided into five separate areas, three of which are large chambers illuminated through the porticos surrounding the courtyard. In between are shaded chambers. As Chandon stares first to his right and then to his left, he takes in the elaborate pointed arches between the rooms, the now-familiar dense stucco wall carvings covering every surface. The alternating light and dark of the chambers is somehow soothing to the eye.

They turn to the right, cross the shaded chamber, enter the lit chamber, turn left, then stop. A lone white divan and six floor pillows lie atop a large red Persian rug at the back of the room. The Sultan reclines on the divan. Zamrak sits on a pillow, reed quill in hand, furiously scribbling on a piece of paper. Zamrak stops, lifts the paper, reads aloud in Arabic. Chandon makes out a few words but only a sketch of meaning. The Sultan nods, says "Good, Zamrak, good. Much better." Two bodyguards stand behind the Sultan, glued to the wall, motionless, eyes on the floor. As the two approach, the Sultan and Zamrak simultaneously look up.

The Sultan examines Chandon closely, then smiles warmly and says, "Sabah al-khayr." *Good morning.*

Ibn al-Khatib nods his greeting, but Chandon responds, "Sabah al-khayr."

The smile widens, then a rapid-fire, "Kaifa haloka." *How are you?*

"Ana bekhair, shokran." *I am fine, thanks.*

The Sultan nods, then switches to flawless Castilian. "Your pronunciation is very good, your accent quite passable." He surveys Chandon for a moment more, curious. "I am pleased to finally meet you, Chandon. I have heard many good things."

Chandon bows. "The pleasure is mine, Sire."

Ibn al-Khatib offers, "I have been showing Chandon the Palace of the Lions, Sire." The Sultan nods approvingly.

"Exquisite, Sire. The finest palace I have ever seen."

The Sultan returns a satisfied smile. "I wanted to express my thanks for your...valiant defense...of Lisan al-Din's daughter. We are all grateful."

Zamrak looks down to hide his frown.

"Thank you, Sire." He searches for the right words. "Layla is a special young woman." Ibn al-Khatib turns to study Chandon's face.

The Sultan laughs. "Of that we are all in agreement." Zamrak's face remains glued to his lap. "Lisan al-Din, I trust Layla is healing?"

"Yes, Sire, she is up and moving again, praise Allah. Her face is still bruised, but she can see clearly from her injured eye. She will be fine. Salamun says her wrist is knitting well, and the splint can come off in a few more days."

"Good, good." The Sultan turns back to Chandon. "Rest assured that her attacker will be dealt with appropriately. She has nothing more to fear from him." Chandon nods. "Is there anything I can do to make your stay with us more comfortable, Chandon? Anything." He stretches out his up-turned palms.

Chandon's eyebrows lift. He purses his lips as he thinks. "Well, Sire, I would enjoy having some books to read. Books on Andalusi history and culture, science and medicine, agriculture. Even religion. While my spoken Arabic is improving, it would have to be in Castilian, I am afraid. Or perhaps Latin."

The Sultan nods. "Certainly. Lisan al-Din is our man of letters." He turns to Ibn al-Khatib. "Can you provide these to Chandon?"

"With pleasure, Sire. I have several recent translations that should serve nicely."

"Excellent. What else?"

Chandon hesitates. "Well, Sire, I believe it would be...prudent...for me to begin honing my sword skills. It has been seven months now since I have held a sword, and I am very rusty.

My wounds have healed enough to begin training again, and I would like get back into shape." The Sultan is surprised, but Chandon presses on. "A wooden sword is all I would require, Sire. Yazdan and Musa would make excellent sparring partners. We could confine our exercises to the Courtyard of the Myrtles."

The Sultan strokes his chin, pensive. "Done. A wooden sword. To be used only within the confines of the palace. And only with Yazdan and Musa."

"I understand, Sire. I am grateful." Chandon bows.

The Sultan seems satisfied. It seems clear he does not plan to offer anything else. He turns back to Zamrak, "Shall we finish our poem?"

Zamrak looks up from his lap, his face expressionless. "Indeed, Sire."

"Lisan al-Din, I will see you this afternoon. I have several things I would like to discuss before I meet with the rest of the viziers."

"Certainly, Sire." They back away three steps, turn and depart.

As they circle the courtyard, Ibn al-Khatib says, "I have one more thing I would like to show you this morning."

"Of course."

They pass through the guarded entrance to the palace located on the southeastern end of the courtyard, step into the high-walled narrow passage that leads out fifteen paces to join the Lower Royal Road. Ibn al-Khatib stops. The Grand Vizier turns to face Chandon. "I have an unusual request. I would like you to close your eyes and let me lead you to the street."

Chandon returns a quizzical expression, but says, "Certainly, sir." He shuts his eyes.

Ibn al-Khatib directs Chandon forward. After fifteen paces they stop at the edge of the Lower Royal Road.

"Now open your eyes."

An attendant steps forward along the stone street, leading a horse by the reins, and stops in front of Chandon. The sixteen-hand stallion arches his powerful neck into a downward, open 'C', his pride of place unmistakable. Instinctively, Chandon assesses the animal. Lovely dark, dappled gray on a light gray background, producing an uncanny blue sheen to his coat. Thick, flowing, wavy dark gray mane, ebony legs below the knee. His billowing, wavy light gray tail stretches almost to the ground, swishing back and forth anxiously. The pale gray face transitions to a charcoal mouth. His midnight black orbs focus squarely on Chandon, sizing him up. Chandon chuckles at the bravado. Not a bashful animal. Intelligent. Thick short neck, strong round rump; a coiled spring. Clearly a war horse, fast. Chandon smiles, nods his head approvingly. The stallion's ears are perked high and twitch independently at odd angles like nervous tics.

When the stallion has seen enough, he snorts, stamps his right front hoof, then whinnies. The attendant tenses the reins to make sure he doesn't rear, sucks his cheeks to calm the beast. Chandon laughs loud.

"One of my favorites. An Andalusian. Fast as the wind, full of spirit." Ibn al-Khatib pauses for effect. "He is yours now, Chandon. A gift."

Chandon turns to face Ibn al-Khatib, open-mouthed, dumbfounded. "Are you sure, sir?"

"I am positive. He is yours now."

"He is a fine animal, and I will treasure him. Thank you, sir, thank you."

"You are most welcome. My horses are stabled just outside the palace. We will keep him there." Ibn al-Khatib considers his words, then says, "Perhaps when Layla is fully recovered, the two of you might enjoy riding together."

"I would like that very much, sir. Let me guess, she is an accomplished rider."

Ibn al-Khatib nods, grins. "She grew up riding unbroken Berber ponies in Fez. Trust me, she knows how to handle a horse."

Chandon laughs. "No doubt." Chandon steps forward, pats the stallion's head, traces his palm down his rippled shoulder, along his dappled gray flank to his steel rump. He pivots and returns the stallion's hard stare. "You remind me of my first horse, sir. I shall call you Blue."

Just after noon prayer the Sultan and Ibn al-Khatib sit on pillows in the Hall of the Kings eating a light lunch of bread, cheese and fruit.

The Sultan seems pensive. "I have been trying to decide what to do with Layla's attacker."

Ibn al-Khatib sighs. "The young man's name is Tahir al-Shashi, Sire. Twenty-two. A boy, really. He has been at the madrasa for a little over two years."

"A student of al-Mussib?"

"No, al-Nur. Evidently al-Nur has had trouble with him before. Overzealous, and especially belligerent towards females. A loner.

I have learned that he is of Berber ancestry, which fits. No one saw this coming, Sire. Still, in retrospect, warning signs were present. The teachers at the madrasa are mortified. I have assured them that no retribution will be forthcoming. In exchange, they have vowed to cleanse the madrasa of any questionable students." The Sultan nods his approval. "Al-Mussib made the trek up to the Alhambra the afternoon of the attack to check on Layla. Given his health, no small feat. He feels terrible."

Silence.

"My inclination, Lisan al-Din, is to execute him. I need to send a message that such blatant acts will not be tolerated."

Ibn al-Khatib grimaces. "Execution of a citizen of the city requires a full trial by the Mexuar Council, Sire. He has relatives on the Council; an uncle I believe. Despite the boy's obvious guilt I suspect that the uncle would make any trial difficult for us. While we could no doubt carry the day, it could cost us significant political capital."

"Yes. Still..."

"In addition, Sire, Layla has expressed a strong desire that he not be harmed. Any more than he already has. Chandon beat him to within an inch of his life. He will never recover his looks."

"Yes, so I am told. Appropriate retribution for what he attempted." The Sultan muses. "I hear that Chandon appears to have taken an...interest...in Layla's well-being." The two lock eyes. "You should be aware, Lisan al-Din, that the Mexuar Council is starting to whisper. The usual African mischief I am afraid. Be careful, Lisan al-Din, for all of our sakes."

"Chandon is a good man, Sire. Honorable."

"No doubt. He seems to be warming to Granada. And his Arabic is improving. These are good things. But do not forget, Lisan al-Din, that Chandon is a pawn to be played, only a pawn."

"I understand, Sire." Ibn al-Khatib chews the inside of his cheek.

The Sultan returns to the subject at hand. "What would you suggest I do with the student?"

"Exile him, Sire. Send him back to Fez. He must have relatives there. Under penalty of death should he ever return to al-Andalus. Politically expedient and no is trial required."

"Mmmm...seems lenient for his crime."

"Then amputate his left hand. After all, he attempted to steal my daughter's purity. It will serve as a vivid reminder that he will never forget. He is a thief."

The Sultan nods. "Yes... Good. I like that. I will speak to Farqad. We will give him time to recover, then I will pass judgment, discreetly exile him from the Kingdom. Minus a hand."

"Agreed, Sire. A wise decision."

As Ibn al-Khatib circles the courtyard to return to his suite, his hands are clasped behind his back, eyes glued to the ground, weighing the import of the Sultan's words. Zamrak steps from behind the half-opened door of the Hall of the Two Sisters just as he passes. "Master al-Khatib, do you have a moment?"

Ibn al-Khatib awakens at the sound. Confused by the intrusion, he looks to his right, sees his former pupil in the shadows.

"Zamrak." He turns, steps up into the doorway and passes inside the hall. "How are you?"

A weak "Fine..." limps out of the younger man's mouth.

"I enjoyed the Garden Ode. Impressive, as always. For the Generalife?"

"Indeed. It is almost complete. It will adorn the Courtyard of the Water Garden. I am preparing a special stucco panel for it."

"Good, good, I look forward to seeing it. And you are enjoying your new role as the Sultan's private secretary?"

"Yes, though it does take time away from my poetry."

Ibn al-Khatib nods. The silence stretches. Ibn al-Khatib waits expectantly, eyebrows arched. Zamrak finally gets it out, "And how is Layla?"

Ibn al-Khatib studies him. "She is fine, Zamrak, healing. Thank you for asking."

Zamrak kneads his palms, seems very unsettled.

"Is something wrong, Zamrak?"

Silence.

He blurts out, "Master, I hear rumors. Disturbing rumors."

Ibn al-Khatib frowns. "Rumors, Zamrak?"

More hand wringing. "That Chandon is trying to win Layla's heart. And that she returns his affections." He looks up. "You promised Layla to me. To me."

Ibn al-Khatib billows bright red with uncharacteristic anger, and hisses, "I never promised Layla to anyone. Ever. She is my daughter; she will decide whom she marries. Is that clear?"

"I love her. I have loved her for years. You know that. I would be a good husband for her."

Ibn al-Khatib's fire calms in the presence of the man's obvious agony. "Yes, I know that. Zamrak, who can know a woman's heart? She is free to receive love and return love as her heart commands her. That is not for me to decide."

"But he is a Christian. How can you give your consent to that?"

Ibn al-Khatib's bile rises once more. "First of all, there is nothing to give my consent to. They enjoy each other's company. She teaches him Arabic, he teaches her English. No more." He chooses his words carefully. "But even if there was more, I value my daughter's happiness above all things. And I trust her judgment. Chandon is a good man. He is honorable. You have spent time with him; you know this to be true."

A tortured look crosses the younger man's face, chased by a resigned sigh. "I know nothing for certain any more, nothing." He hangs his head, shakes it side to side. "Nothing."

It is well past midnight when he arrives. He is dressed in plain clothes, his turban arranged to mask his face. His two bodyguards, one in front and one behind, scan in wide arcs for any hint of danger. Their rhythmic breath fog betrays the change in weather. The three approach the Palace of the Lions from inside the Partal Gardens, on the east side of the palace complex, step onto the Lower Royal Road, then exit to the right.

They pause at the entrance tucked between the Comares Palace and the Palace of the Lions for a final survey. Satisfied, one of the bodyguards steps forward, whispers to the closest of the sentries, and the three slip through the door, leaving no trace. Once inside, they turn right, keeping to the protected edge of the courtyard, out of sight, then immediately angle left, and after twenty paces, arrive at the Hall of the Abencerrages. The moonlit, ghostly-white lions track their movements in silence through the marble forest, the only sound a pearly tinkle issuing from each of the twelve beasts.

The two sentries acknowledge the entourage, then step aside. The turbaned man approaches and knocks on the tall wooden door. One tap, a pause, then two quick taps, a pause, then one more. The metal bolt slides and the door cracks open, allowing the man to slip through. The door immediately closes, and the bolt is pushed back into place and latched.

Silence.

The man unravels his turban, turns to face the person standing to his left. "Qasim, it good to see you, my friend."

"Sire, it is so good to have you back in the palace. We have missed you." The eunuch nods deferentially. "I received your note this morning, Sire. Everything has been arranged, with the utmost discretion."

"Thank you, Qasim."

"Your wish is my command, Sire." The eunuch bows, then retreats up the stairs into the Royal Harem. The Sultan removes his wool outer robe, drops it to the floor, moves to the thick curtain covering the door, parts it with his left hand and steps into the hall.

The tall yellow flames rising from the standing oil lamps produce a pleasing glow. The central fountain tickles the room with its aquatic murmurs. Deep, red-orange goodness emanates from four large braziers that vigorously pump heat into the room, bathing the space in a comfortable, summer-like warmth.

She stands beside the lamp nearest his bed chamber, facing him. Her hair is down in all its raven glory, and she is dressed in the white silk gown he loves. She locks her eyes onto his, smiles invitingly. He returns the smile, but does not speak. He steps over to her and stops a foot away, breathes in her musky, citrus scent. Around her neck is a thick gold and ruby necklace. A large gold and emerald ring graces the middle finger of her left hand. Two delicate mother of pearl and gold haircombs pull her tresses from her face.

"I have missed you, Auria."

"And I you, Sire."

He reaches forward and pushes her silk gown off her shoulders, letting it slide to the floor. He admires her body for a long moment, then reaches up with his right index finger, traces a curve down the side of her full breast. She shivers, her nipples hardening. He circles around behind her. He reaches up with his left hand to move her raven curls, exposing the nape of her neck. Her dark down V's towards her shoulders. He leans forward, and without touching her, breathes warm, moist air lightly upon her neck, then her ear. She shivers again and her lips part, her breath quickening. After an exquisite pause, he touches his tongue to the base of her neck, draws an upward curve, and at the same time reaches around with his right hand to cup her breast, gently squeezing her nipple. A light groan escapes as her knees bend involuntarily. He steps around to face her once more, now only a few inches separating them. She is breathing rapidly, trembling. A charged moment passes, the delicious tension in the hall almost unbearable.

He leans forward and kisses her. "My Auria. So beautiful. I have missed those emerald eyes, my princess. Come, let us enjoy the evening." She lifts her jeweled hand to meet his. He parts the curtain to his bed chamber, and they both slip inside.

# Threshold

Chandon wakes with a start. He cannot place the origin of his unease, but he is instantly alert nonetheless. He reaches for his wooden sword, sits up, listens. Nothing. An eerie, oppressive hush has settled on the palace. He rubs the sleep from his eyes, steps to the window. Huge snowflakes dangle limply in the air, take forever to feather to the ground. Snowfall in Granada? The air is still, the courtyard dark as a tomb. He scans with his peripheral vision for any activity. Only a thin covering of white on the myrtle hedges. He can't infer the time, but it feels late. No guards, no lights, the palace fast asleep.

Fully awake, he decides to go enjoy the rare snow. He dresses warmly, throws on a heavy cloak, then steps to the door, taps three times, unbolts the latch and steps into the dim lamp-lit hallway. His two bodyguards recline on floor pillows, backs against the wall, blankets pulled tight over their shoulders.

Chandon says, "Alonso, Nasr, it is snowing out. I am going to walk the courtyard for a little while."

The two begin to uncoil, attempt to rise. Alonso yawns. "What time is it?"

"Very late. Please, stay where you are and rest. The palace is fast asleep and I have my sword." Chandon smiles to reassure them.

The two guards exchange glances. They have seen Chandon spar with Yazdan and Musa, know that he can defend himself. "Call for us if you see or hear anything unusual."

"I will."

The two pull their covers tighter against the cold, and within a minute their heads begin to sag.

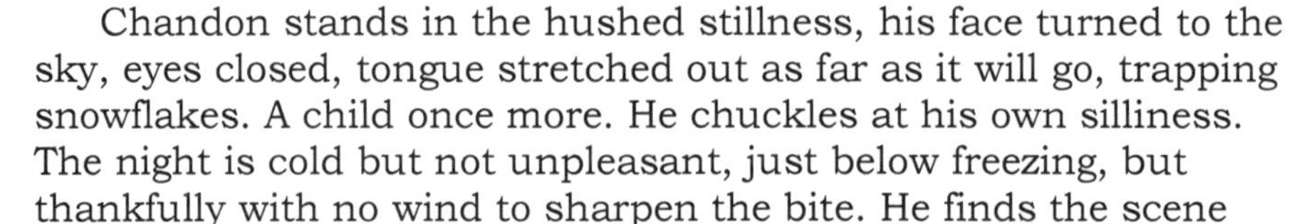

Chandon stands in the hushed stillness, his face turned to the sky, eyes closed, tongue stretched out as far as it will go, trapping snowflakes. A child once more. He chuckles at his own silliness. The night is cold but not unpleasant, just below freezing, but thankfully with no wind to sharpen the bite. He finds the scene comforting somehow, a reminder of days past. His mind wanders back to Brittany.

He checks Layla's window for signs of life but finds only darkness. His arms settle in behind him, and he begins to circle the pool, thinking through the books Ibn al-Khatib has lent him. So far he has devoured three; one on agriculture, one on medicine, and one on the history of the Arabs that he has finished this evening. Next up is religion. He is fascinated by the culture and its many achievements. So much more advanced in many ways than his own, but also laden with many contradictions.

He enjoys his time with Ibn al-Khatib, and their meetings have become more frequent in the past weeks. The Grand Vizier is a remarkable treasure-trove of knowledge. And a source of insight into his daughter. Chandon tries to extract information about her he has long puzzled over. He strives for discreetness in any question that brushes against her. Unsuccessfully, to Ibn al-Khatib's amusement.

Chandon has seen Layla only three times since the attack. Over a month and a half has passed. His visits have been very brief, in her library, and except for the one time, always with either Aisha or her father present. Awkward and compressed; frustrating. He pines for her company, can think of nothing else when not reading or dueling with Yazdan and Musa. All Salamun can think to do is tell him to be patient. And tease him.

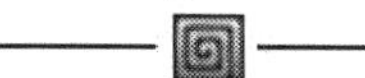

Her long lashes flutter wildly as the terror unfolds, her emeralds flitting back and forth behind closed lids as she struggles to escape. She groans, kicks her leg. Her head twitches, first left then right. Her mouth and eyes fly open as she gasps, followed by a slow, weary exhale. Nightmare. Again. She groans with the vividness of the images as the dividing line between reality and dream thankfully seeps in and widens. She knows where this dream will end if unchecked.

Afraid that the nightmare will resume where it was paused if she closes her eyes and tries to sleep, she gingerly eases herself up in bed, turns and rests her feet to the floor, stands, then walks to the window. Her mouth opens then stretches into a bright smile. Snow! By force of habit she scans the courtyard for signs of life.

She does a double-take as she sees the ghostly figure beside the pool. She stares intently, trying hard to tunnel through the darkness, gathering faint impressions with her peripheral vision. Cloaked man. Head down. Hands locked behind his back. Her smile widens with the recognition of his endearing pensive pose.

The endless forced separation launches a spark of urgency in her thoughts. Her heart begins to pound. Without engaging her instinctive mental decision-making checklist, she instantly knows she must see him. Alone. She does not light her lamp, but scurries about the room, slips out of her bed clothes, washes her face, cleans her teeth, then changes into warm clothes. She slings her winter cloak around her shoulders, extracts her hair with both hands, reaches to her side table for her brush and tames it.

She tiptoes to her bedroom door and eases it open, successfully squelching its preferred creak. She leans into the library, looks to the left. Her father's divan is empty. Normally he would be asleep amid his books. Odd. He must have been very tired tonight. She listens for Aisha. Nothing. She slinks across the room, carefully avoiding the two squeaky floorboards, arrives at the door. She takes a deep breath then delicately slides the latch, wincing at the final metal click that seems impossibly loud. She freezes. Nothing. She slips through the door and closes it without a sound.

As she steps into the courtyard, she stops to locate him. The air is thick with giant snowflakes, the courtyard a lovely white delineation of the hard angles of the dark water. Her breath fog is just discernible. He is facing away from her and is about to turn left at the corner of the pool, head down, arms locked behind him, deep in thought. He moves in slow motion. He turns left, then passes the fountain. She pivots to face him, stands perfectly still. He walks on, rounds the corner of the pool, turns toward her, oblivious. She beams. When he is ten paces away he abruptly stops and raises his gaze. He breaks into a huge grin, and without thinking, runs to her and wraps his arms around her, bear-hugs her. She bursts out laughing as he lifts her off the ground, swings her side to side.

He gathers his wits, sets her down, steps back a pace, suddenly self-conscious. After a long moment of silent smiles, he offers a sheepish, "My Lady." He tenders an exaggerated bow.

Her smile fades. She whispers, "My William."

He steps forward to within a foot of her, stares deeply into her eyes, and whispers, "My Layla. I have missed you terribly. I can think of nothing but you. Nothing."

"And I you."

"How do you feel?"

"Better. Thankfully, those ugly bruises are nearly gone. No more blurriness in my left eye." She hesitates. "I do still have nightmares."

He nods, a concerned expression settling onto his face. "I know. I would do anything to take that pain away." He reaches up and touches the sealed gash, still puckered and pink.

Her eyes well up. "You saved me, William."

He closes his eyes, and when he opens them, a single tear streaks down his right cheek. "I will never again let anyone harm you, Layla. Ever."

She smiles. "My William." She steps forward, halving the distance between. She tilts her head back slightly to look up into his eyes, parts her lips, her breathing shallow and quick. Her eyelids begin to droop as her smile evaporates. He leans forward and down, stops within a half inch of her face, then brushes his lips against hers. An electric tingle jumps between them. He lifts his left hand, cups the back of her head. The tiny contact point between them solidifies, lingers. He kisses her, tenderly at first, then more urgently. Molten lightning deliciously dances along her spine. An unfamiliar sensation of spreading, damp heat twines itself around her body.

As they continue to kiss, he slides his right arm to the small of her back, pulls her gently against him. Their nerve endings begin to throb in lock-step with their pounding hearts. A sustained moment more and their glistening lips part, their breathing matched, heavy. There are no smiles in the courtyard now; instead, their eyes remain glued on each other, faces three inches apart, their pulsing breath fog co-mingling. He leans back, reaches his left hand around her shoulder, fills his palm with her hair, then pulls her hip-length, chestnut curls to her chest. He leans down, buries his nose in her tresses, breathes her in. An exaggerated exhale of "Ahhhh..." is chased by his playful smile. "You have no idea how many months I have longed to do that."

She giggles, breaking the nerve-tingling tension. "Careful with my treasure, sir." He laughs loud, then bear-hugs her tight, lifts her off the ground again.

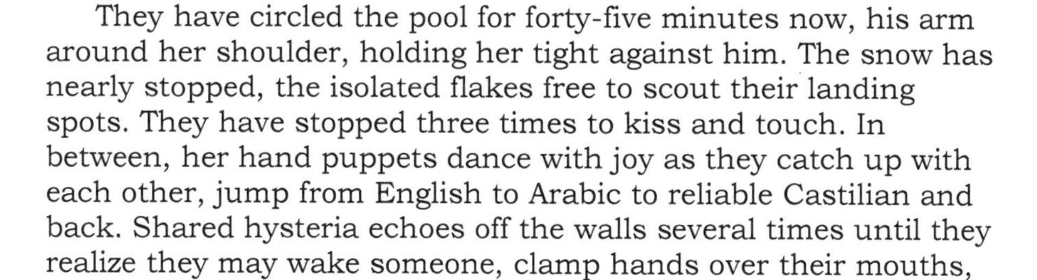

They have circled the pool for forty-five minutes now, his arm around her shoulder, holding her tight against him. The snow has nearly stopped, the isolated flakes free to scout their landing spots. They have stopped three times to kiss and touch. In between, her hand puppets dance with joy as they catch up with each other, jump from English to Arabic to reliable Castilian and back. Shared hysteria echoes off the walls several times until they realize they may wake someone, clamp hands over their mouths, double over to stifle the sound.

He stops and turns her, places both hands on her shoulders. “You are freezing.”

“I am fine.” Her shivers are uncontrollable now and obvious, her teeth starting to rattle.

He laughs, pulls her tight. “It is time for bed. Speak to your father tomorrow about re-starting our lessons.”

“I will.”

As they probe the depths of each other’s eyes, the silence stretches out comfortably and their giddiness melts away into serious. He swallows hard, resolved, and whispers, “Ana Behibek.” *I love you.*

Her eyes brim. “Ana Behibak.”

Their smiles widen in unison, fan out into giddiness. He leans down and kisses her tenderly, then hisses, “Now go to bed!” She flashes that smile, turns and skips up the stairs.

He looks up. The sky is beginning to clear, stars peeking intermittently between the charcoal-smudged cotton balls. His hands instinctively return to their stations behind his back and he circles the pool back to his room. He shakes his head in disbelief.

“Thank you, Lord. Thank you.”

Perseus leans forward, stretches for a better look. He smiles his approval then frowns as the gap in the cloud-cover closes. A moment later the clouds tear apart in a sliver and the Pleiades stand with him, anxious to offer a feminine opinion. The Seven Sisters elbow each other in their delight, giggle their approval, then erupt in a fury of whispers, all gossipy excitement. Perseus can only offer a half-hearted scold before he begins to beam. The rip in the clouds closes once more and the eight are gone.

Ibn al-Khatib steps from the tunnel linking the Palace of the Lions to the Comares Palace, stops to survey the dark courtyard. The barely perceptible hint of purple-gray sunrise allows him to appreciate the beauty of the snowfall set against the lines of the pool. As he turns to his left for his suite and the warmth of his bed, he halts, looks down, then frowns. His head scans, first right, then left, the footprints in the snow unmistakable. He closes on the entrance to his stairs, studying the tracks. Her partially filled prints lead out, then back in. He turns, looks at the stairwell entrance directly across the pool. More tracks. His eyes circle the courtyard. A well-worn path rings the rectangular pool. Ibn al-Khatib offers a deep, conflicted sigh as he puts two and two together, then shakes his head in amazement, the jumble of emotions rushing over him - happy, concerned, elated, worried.

He conjures Danah, awakens the games of love they played at the same age, then smiles.

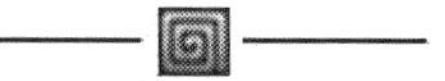

They have agreed to meet once a week in the deep of the night. They each use a candle to signal from their bedrooms, flash the all-clear. Their bold risks make them giddy. Kissing and touching exquisitely tortures their frayed nerve endings. Gentle words of love sustain them.

Her dreams have taken on a life of their own, her nightmares faded now, replaced with a delicious fitfulness to which she is unaccustomed. She wakes with a start, twisted in her covers, her body wound tight with a raw damp ache. She blushes when she revisits the feeling later in the day, but smiles. He paces his room at odd hours, a caged animal, releases his pent-up tension during his daily sparring sessions.

They have resumed their language lessons. To the casual observer not much has changed; grammar drills, word games, chess matches, history and geography lessons, the nuances of Sufism, shared meditation practice, the rudiments of calligraphy, poetry. They are careful, discreet. They quickly master the art of secretly projecting fiery passion, framing the mutual understanding of a shared thought, declaring unity of purpose, with the quick turn of an eye, a hint of a smile, a delicate hand gesture, a wink.

She has insisted on a return to the Maristan to resume her work. Ibn al-Khatib first attempted to fight it but reluctantly gave in to the inevitable after securing two conditions. Yazdan and Musa now linger in the courtyard by the pool, minus their weapons, while the two of them go about their work. She has agreed to remain in eyeshot at all times.

The days are beginning to warm at last, hints of spring, of birth, poking through in unexpected places. Buds swell with life as sap begins to flow. Birds break into song at odd moments, their vocal chords out of practice but their joy irrepressible. The white cloak of the Sierra Nevada retreats.

The star shine is breathtaking this night, the constellations ablaze, the palace a picture frame of young love. They walk together, hand linked in hand, circling the pool, quietly talking, enjoying each other's company. Merciful privacy. They fall into comfortable silence.

She seems pensive. Looking down, she says, "When we first met, you mentioned that you had loved before."

He does not respond.

"Tell me about her."

He offers a deep sigh, then says, "It is a sad, sad tale, Layla."

"Tell me, William. Please."

The silence stretches. "Very well. Her name was Sosanna. She was the daughter of the Bishop of Saint-Sauveur. My castle is about two miles east of the town. We were introduced at the summer festival, only a few months after I arrived. Almost four years ago now. The oldest of three girls. Bright, educated."

"Beautiful."

A weak smile. "Beautiful."

"She fell in love with you."

"We fell in love with each other. After nine months we were betrothed. Her father was happy; the town was happy. We were happy." He falls silent with the memory.

She waits patiently for him to continue.

"Do you remember Edward the Black Prince?"

"Yes. King Edward's son, your childhood friend. He arranged your first command in Brittany. You led those troops to victory at Auray."

"Yes. I owe Edward much. After Auray, Jean de Monfort renounced his allegiance to England, declared Brittany a part of France and swore allegiance to King Charles. Following my patron, I sided with de Montfort, and I, too, declared for France. Edward considered it a personal betrayal. Treason in his eyes." He hesitates. "I never thought of Edward as a bad man, though he does have a wicked temper. I came to discover that he can be merciless when he feels he has been wronged."

"What else could you have done?"

"To my mind, nothing. I do not regret the decision." He falls silent, then says, "But it had terrible consequences."

She whispers, "Sosanna."

A painful sigh, then he continues. "I was away when they came for me. It was a fine spring day. A raiding party, six of Edward's personal guard. They were to capture me, bring me back to England, where I would stand trial for treason and hang. But I was gone, seeing to the estate, making sure the spring crop was ready to set. They tortured three of my servants. The last told them about her." He hesitates. "They rode to Saint-Sauveur and found the Bishop." His voice begins to quaver. "Then Sosanna."

Her eyes well up. He stops to compose himself, but rage slips into his voice with the memory. He hisses, “First they beat her. Then they raped her. All six. In front of her mother and father.”

She gasps with horror, “Oh my...oh my...” Her tears begin to flow.

“Her father said they laughed while they passed her around, told him to relay a message to me from Edward, that ‘Traitors deserve no mercy.’ ”

More silence, then he continues. “When she awoke I was at her side. She was badly beaten. Her eyes were vacant, a shadow of who she had been just a day before. She kept whispering, to no one in particular, “I cannot bear the shame, I cannot bear the shame.” Over and over. Then her eyes would fly open wide with terror, not seeing me sitting right beside her, and she would shout, “Help me, William! Help me! Where are you, William? William! Help me!”

He grows silent, has to will himself to begin again. “Within a few days she stopped talking altogether, drew deep within herself, gone. I could not reach her no matter what I tried. Her parents did not know what to do, had no idea how to help her, what she needed. Her father could not deal with the idle talk, the whispers, the hateful gossip. I am sure he blamed me for what happened.” Chandon looks down. “And I suppose he should have.” Layla touches his arm to console him, but he turns away. “Sosanna’s parents withdrew from her. They tended to her physical needs, but little more. It was as if she had been irrevocably tainted, spoiled forever, and had no further value to them. I still do not understand it. After a while they barely acknowledged my presence when I came calling each day.”

They have stopped walking now and are facing each other. Tears continue to slide down Layla’s cheeks. She whispers, “I am so sorry. I am so sorry, William.”

He cannot make eye contact and instead stares into space, his face deeply pained; but he seems compelled to finish the story, purge the torment once and for all. “Over the next month she slowly began to recover, at least physically. But if I tried to touch her she recoiled. She flinched if I tried to kiss her. Words of love went unanswered. So instead we walked. Miles and miles each day. The most she would do was let me hold her hand. The walks seemed to help her, though. She began to talk again; bit by bit, a soft word here, a whispered phrase there. Birds, the weather, the scent of a flower, the color of the sky. Not much, but it was something. I began to grow optimistic that she might remember what we had together, who I was to her.”

He is silent for a long moment, then he takes a deep breath and continues. "But then, in the middle of the summer, her mood changed abruptly. She withdrew again from me, from the world. She stopped talking completely. I could not understand it. I pleaded with her to let me back in. Only silence. She began to cry constantly, whimper in her poisoned sleep, flinch when I stepped close to her, touched her cheek. She soon had the look of a whipped animal. Still, we walked. I held her hand, whispered words of love that went unanswered. It broke my heart to see her so."

He stops, gathers his strength, forces himself on. "On the morning of the last day of August we were walking across the high bridge that spans the Blavet River. We stopped in the middle, turned to admire the white cascade of water over the boulders below us. So beautiful..." The tense silence stretches. "I turned away only an instant to scan the horizon. She stepped up on the low rail and jumped. Without a word. Her body broke on the rocks."

Layla gasps.

His voice is quavering as he struggles on, "When we recovered her body it became clear that..." He stops, chokes back a violent sob. "It became clear that..." He tenses, can only whisper the words. "It became clear that she was...with child." He exhales, then shakes his head as he hisses, "God damn them! GOD DAMN THEM TO HELL!"

She steps forward and pulls him tight against her. With her hand she forces his face into her shoulder, cradles him. He does not resist. His shoulders sag under the weight of his grief, then his body begins to convulse, gathers momentum with his muffled sobs. She lets him cry, whispering, "I am so sorry. I am here, William, I am here. Let it out. Let it out."

Two minutes later the storm has passed. He lifts his head, wipes his eyes and looks at her. "A sad, sad tale, Layla. I did not imagine I would ever find love again." He shakes his head. "I was not sure I even deserved it." He looks up. "Then you." His lower lip starts to quiver.

She pulls his face to her and kisses him. "I love you, William. I will always love you."

He smiles weakly, then grows serious again. He whispers, "I would have killed the madrasa student who attacked you."

"I know. I know."

"Thank you for stopping me."

They stand silent, welded together.

Orion gazes down intently, sets his bow aside, mesmerized, a smile growing large on his face. He motions urgently to Perseus, Andromeda, Cassiopeia, Leo, Hydra, Virgo, Gemini and the others, who turn, drink in the scene, and rejoice.

# To Victory

6 March 1368. The seven men are seated around a large oak table in the expansive banquet hall in the Royal Palace in Zaragoza, the capital of Aragon. At the head sits King Pedro IV of Aragon. Moving clockwise, Enrique of Trastámara, bastard brother of King Pedro of Castile; Don Alfonso Méndez de Guzmán, aide-de-camp to Enrique; Sir Ernaud de Florenssan, papal liaison of King Charles V of France; Don Gonzalo Ruiz Girón, Aragon's ambassador; Antonio de Castrocario, Genoa's ambassador; and Bishop de Fonte, Apostolic Nuncio of Pope Urban V.

King Pedro IV lifts his tankard of ale and begins in French, "Gentlemen, a toast. With the arrival of Bishop de Fonte, the Pope's blessing, and the papal gold, we have secured all that is needed for Enrique's successful renewal of the war against his brother. To Enrique, future King of Castile!"

Tankards rise, then a bawdy, "Hear, hear! To Enrique, future King of Castile!" Clanks and smiles spread round the table.

After the cheer settles, Pedro IV turns to his left. "Tell us about your plans, Enrique."

"We now have all of the gold assembled to refit the army, make ready for war." He nods his thanks to Bishop de Fonte. "Twenty-one thousand gold francs. I am grateful to you all for your support. Your generosity will not go unrewarded when we are victorious. With this final installment of gold from the Pope we can now begin preparations for war. Our troop commitments are as follows: from Aragon, twelve thousand infantry, four thousand archers, two thousand cavalry; from France, eight thousand infantry, three thousand archers, three thousand cavalry; from Brittany, two thousand infantry, two thousand cavalry. From occupied Castile, five thousand infantry and two thousand cavalry. The Republic of Genoa will provide ships to sail up the Guadalquivir River to besiege Sevilla when the time is ripe. They will transport Aragonese occupation forces assembled in Valencia. While we engage Pedro in the field and his back is turned, Sevilla will be ours."

Heads nod in approval.

Ernaud de Florenssan says, "What about Edward the Black Prince and his longbowmen?"

Enrique continues. "There will be no repeat of the surprise at Nájera. Without Edward, Pedro has nothing. He will be lucky to mount twenty thousand against us." He pauses and looks around the room, his smile growing wider as his leer circles. "Gentlemen, I have it on good authority that Pedro has no gold to pay Edward for services rendered at Nájera. Edward's army is presently stranded in Aquitaine. It seems there is not enough money to even rent boats to cross the Channel. Edward will not fight without gold. No Edward, no longbowmen." He pauses to stoke the suspense. "Friends, Pedro does not have the gold to secure Edward." He beams as the others nod and crack smiles. "One of my spies in Aquitaine has confirmed that Pedro has offered Edward a token one-thousand gold pieces, as down payment, then promised him half of Aragon when the battle is over. Edward will not fight again on a promise." More nods of approval.

Ernaud de Florenssan clears his throat. "What of the Moors? Will they stay out of the fight?"

Don Alfonso Méndez de Guzmán interjects. "Unclear. But I remind you, at Nájera they only sent six hundred cavalry, and that number very reluctantly. Not be enough to be significant to the outcome."

King Pedro IV offers, "I am told that the Moors still hold William Chandon without ransom in Granada."

Enrique replies, "Indeed. Scandalous. We have had no news of Chandon since he was captured at Jaén, but we can assume he wastes away in a dungeon in the Alhambra, sad to say. I would much prefer to have him leading my Breton forces. C'est la vie." He ponders for a moment more, then says, "However, once we defeat Pedro, the Moors will be anxious to pacify us. I will see to it that Chandon comes back to us then as a peace offering."

Bishop de Fonte frowns. "There is to be no peace with Granada. The Moors must be driven from Spain."

Enrique responds, "Precisely, Excellency. Immediately after we defeat Pedro."

"Our secret weapon will be the Free Companies, our shock troops. Five-thousand heavy cavalry. We will use them to crush Pedro's flank. They remain encamped in Toulouse, awaiting our signal. And our gold. After we defeat Pedro, the Free Companies will be unleashed upon Granada, with the rest of the army in support. Gentlemen, mark my words, Granada will fall. We will all share in the spoils."

Antonio de Castrocario of Genoa adds, "A reminder that Genoa is to receive the spherical astrolabe."

"Correct."

Ernaud de Florenssan of France asks, "Who will lead the Free Companies?"

"As before, Bertrand du Guesclin and Hugh Calveley." Enrique ignores the grumbles and continues. "This time, however, I will be in command of the army, not du Guesclin. I will not repeat my mistake at Nájera. I have asked both men here today, to secure their commitment in your presence." He reaches over and touches de Guzmán's forearm, who rises and walks to the door, opens it, then motions the two visitors in.

Both men are dressed in flamboyant French finery, cold-blooded mercenaries starched and fluffed into court dandies. They approach the table, but are not offered a seat. Enrique begins, "Bertrand, Hugh, welcome." He introduces all at the table, each of whom grudgingly acknowledge the visitors. The two mercenaries offer amused grins, then perform a mock curtsey followed by exaggerated bows. "Excellencies, we are at your service."

Enrique ignores their impertinence. "Gentlemen, as you know, we are refitting the army to re-engage Pedro. Once again we require the services of the Free Companies."

Bertrand du Guesclin answers, "I am pleased to hear that, Enrique. But I am afraid the price for our services has doubled since Nájera. Ten thousand gold francs. In advance." Grumbles flare up.

Enrique remains even-keeled. "Our offer remains at five thousand, gentlemen. In advance, of course. However, we are prepared to offer an additional incentive to sweeten the deal."

The two knights raise their eyebrows quizzically, their attention secured.

"After you and your men help us defeat Pedro's army, you will turn south and lay waste to the Kingdom of Granada. By Papal Decree you will lead a crusade to rid Spain of the Moors once and for all. One-third of the spoils of vanquished Granada will belong to the Free Companies. One-third will revert to the Pope. And the rest will be split between myself and Aragon. You may rule Granada as you please, provided the mosques are burned and the Moors and Jews that remain either convert to Christianity or are expelled."

The two mercenaries turn to each other, impressed. "Might we examine the Papal Decree?"

Bishop de Fonte stands and offers them the parchment scroll. They unroll it and wade through the dense Latin script, then nod their heads, satisfied.

Hugh Calveley says, "And we will have the Papal Banner to fly with our colors?"

Enrique responds, "Yes."

The two dandies exchange a quick glance, then Bertrand says, "Excellencies, it is a bold plan. I congratulate you on your vision. The Free Companies are at your service."

Enrique smiles. "Good." He turns and locks eyes one by one with those present, securing their silent assent. "We will each prepare our forces through the summer and fall, then gather all of our troops in Zaragoza just after Christmas to begin final preparations for war. At the first hint of spring we will attack in force and end this civil war once and for all. Let us drink to victory."

"To victory!"

# Retraction

It is a glorious spring afternoon, angular and shiny in its newness; cloudless, the air laden with rebirth. Purposeful. The scent of damp, freshly-turned earth floats on the breeze, lounging. Intoxicating, sultry hints of orange blossom permeate the court, the intensity falling then rising with ebbs in the breeze. Horses chatter restlessly just outside the palace walls, followed by a perturbed whinny, an answering snort, finally a forceful "shush!" that ends the discussion. Swallows flit about in their spring fever. A trio of starlings pester a lumbering eagle just to kill the time, then offer taunting laughs as they beat him into retreat. Swollen oak buds begin to pop and unpack their dozen shades of green, stems wobbly as colts' legs.

The entourage enters the Courtyard of the Myrtles from the Palace of the Lions, rounds the western end of the pool. Their pace is quick, determined. First two bodyguards, then the Sultan, who is flanked on either side by two more bodyguards, followed by Ibn al-Khatib, al-Waziri, al-Bistami, al-Ghudari, and two more bodyguards. All in formal dress. The intense eyes of the bodyguards scan left and right, up and down, their hands resting on their sword hilts, arms spring-loaded, cocked and ready. They exit the Comares Palace to their right, wind their way into the Courtyard of the Mexuar. As he passes the fountain, the Sultan says, "A moment, please." The train halts. The Sultan pivots, motions Ibn al-Khatib to him, whispers into his ear, frowns, then whispers more furiously.

Ibn al-Khatib, makes eye contact, returns a somber nod, and says, "I agree, Sire."

After a resigned sigh, the Sultan says to the lead guards, "Please proceed." The entourage exits the southwest corner of the courtyard and passes into the Mexuar Council Chamber.

The Council Chamber is surprisingly small given the heft of their decisions, the lowest ceiling in the entire palace complex. The thirty-five crimson-robed members of the Mexuar Council are seated cross-legged on their white silk pillows in concentric semicircles about the south wall, lending an overstuffed, oppressive feel to the room. Fortunately, two small windows open onto the Court of the Machuca, enticing a pittance of fresh air.

The room's carved stucco walls have been recently redecorated and detailed to match the rest of the palace complex. Ornate silver oil lamps deliver a rich, serious hue. The Mexuar Council is not known for frivolity.

The chorus of hushed whispers fall silent as the Sultan enters, heads turning in unison to track his movements. The bodyguards assume their stations at strategic points as the Sultan and his viziers seat themselves at the center of the Council's neat semicircle. The silence stretches out.

Abd al-Hamid, the Grand Imam of the Mexuar Council, rises, bows to the Sultan, then turns to face the gathering of imams, theologians and judges; Granada's religious elite. He opens the meeting with a short prayer of thanksgiving, followed by a communal recitation of, "May Allah bless the Mexuar Council's thoughts, words and actions, and may He protect Granada from its foes." The Grand Imam sits back down, lifts his up-turned right palm to the Sultan and says, "Let all present hear to the voice of Sultan Muhammad, may Allah bless his reign." The circled council bow their heads as one body.

All eyes are on the Sultan; some kind and supportive, others combative and challenging, some neutral, eager to be convinced. Mexuar Council meetings are rarely dull. The Sultan does not rise, but instead speaks from his pillow, lending a calculated casualness to the exchange.

"Members of the Mexuar Council, I am grateful as always for your support and guidance. I wish to inform you of recent events, as well as answer any questions you may have." He pauses to allow whispers to be discreetly exchanged, then continues. "As you know, some months back the Marinid Empire sent a diplomatic delegation to Granada. Fez desires a new and expanded treaty between our kingdoms. I have agreed to this. We will expand our trade with Fez, lower the barriers to travel for citizens of both kingdoms, and seek to improve dialogue on both religious and state matters. In exchange, Fez has pledged military support for Granada in the unlikely event of a Christian invasion of the kingdom. Grand Vizier Ibn al-Khatib has drafted the treaty and it is now in the hands of the new Sultan in Fez. We have just received word that the document has been signed." The Sultan pauses to allow the room to absorb his words. All but the last sentence is already common knowledge at court. A low buzz commences, composed mostly of approving whispers and head bobs, but also laced with a small chorus of grumbles and a few vigorous disapproving side-to-side head shakes.

Unity of opinion has never defined the Mexuar Council. In recent years tensions within the Council have worsened, exacerbated by deep divisions between those members of Arab ancestry, the more tolerant Nasrid majority, and those of Berber ancestry, the more hardline African minority, whose numbers have slowly but steadily increased.

After a few moments silence returns. The Sultan scans the room to see if any hands are raised to voice a question or comment. None.

The Sultan presses on. “We have also been in contact with King Pedro of Castile.” Grumbles flare up then slide away. “It seems certain that his illegitimate brother, Enrique of Trastámara, is re-arming in Zaragoza for another attempt at conquest. Should war be engaged, Granada will again be asked to contribute troops in support of Pedro. I intend to provide this support.” Growls and grumbles erupt in a vigorous drone, dominate the room, then dissipate. A hand shoots up and the Sultan nods in the direction of the senior Berber voice on the Council. “Yes, Imam Abd al-Malik?”

“Sire, Muslims must NOT fight beside Christians. It is forbidden in the Quran.” He shakes his head violently. “Forbidden!”

The Sultan remains stone-faced. “I understand your concern. However, as vassal to Castile, Granada has no choice in this matter. Just as at Nájera, we must honor our alliance with Castile. It is very important, for obvious reasons, that Pedro prevail against his brother. Castile is our ally, Aragon our enemy. Enrique is aided by both France and the Pope. Granada’s military support is deemed essential by Castile. That said, we will send only a token cavalry force, led once again by Prince al-Bistami.” A hand shoots up, another Berber. “Yes, Imam Abd al-Salam?”

“Is it true, Sire, that Granada has agreed to provide financial support to Castile for this new campaign against Enrique?”

Ibn al-Khatib’s eyes track to the Berber. The Sultan’s eyes smolder, but his face remains blank, unreadable. He is silent for a split second longer than needed, then says, in his most casual voice, “No. Only our normal tribute. And the troops I mentioned.” Another Berber hand. “Yes, Imam Abd al-Rahim?”

“Sire, many on the Council are gravely concerned that a Christian infidel roams the palace. This is a grave insult to us all.” A chorus of approval rings out.

The Sultan sighs. “William Chandon, the Christian knight, has been deemed invaluable to Granada in our defense against reconquista. He is an asset to the kingdom. An attempt was made on his life, and I felt it best to bring him into the Comares Palace. For his own safety. I can assure you that he remains under close guard at all times."

Abd al-Rahim's hand goes back up, and the Sultan nods. "I fail to see how he is an asset, Sire."

"I am afraid I am unable to disclose those details at present." Grumbles circle the room. "I will say, however, that he is being instructed in Arabic and taught our ways and culture. And we are learning English from him. That said, he is only a pawn to be played when the time is right." Several approving nods.

Abd al-Rahim motions to speak once more. The Sultan nods.

"Sire, many on the Council are also concerned about the Grand Vizier's daughter. She is given free reign at court, like a man. She refuses to wear hijab. Even after her attack at the Maristan, she continues to study at the madrasa with the young men. It is forbidden. It is unwise. And it is blasphemous." He lowers his voice for emphasis, then says, "It is rumored, Sire, that she has been immodest in her...dealings...with the Christian." The Council roars. Imam Abd al-Malik continues to stare into his lap, a thin smile slicing his face.

Ibn al-Khatib face is instantly beet red as he angrily blurts out, "How dare you!" The Grand Imam is livid. The Sultan raises his left hand to silence the crowd, his eyes now steely, dangerous, as he bores into the Berber. Tense quiet reluctantly returns. He whispers to accentuate his words, "Imam Abd al-Rahim, your comments are both inappropriate and misguided, and they are unworthy of this Council. Retract them immediately."

The Berber remains defiant, but soon appreciates his untenable position and mutters, "I apologize, Sire, Grand Vizier, and Grand Imam, if you were offended by my words."

The Sultan nods, but Ibn al-Khatib continues to fume. The Sultan has clearly had enough, and says, "This Mexuar Council session is ended." The Sultan stands, followed by his viziers, then the entourage departs.

As the last bodyguard exits the room, the roar of angry voices flares back up.

# Confessions

The piercing morning sun climbs up and over the scalloped roof ridge and spills its white-gold beams into the far end of the Courtyard of the Myrtles, unleashing its impish smile. The air is still cool, refreshing, but it will be a warm day, humid. The fish surface from the dark water to primp, flash their iridescent reds and oranges. They blow bubbles, mock each other, ravenous as unfed tiger cubs.

Chandon turns and glances over his right shoulder, squints into the bright light, then smiles. He turns to his left, asks in quite-passable Arabic, "Yazdan, are you prepared to defend yourself, sir?"

The bodyguard smiles and answers, "My only hope, sir, is that your skills have improved since last week. I grow tired of easy victories." They both laugh. Musa stands, arms crossed, grinning.

Chandon is dressed in a fitted white robe, sashed at the waist, his wooden battle sword at his hip. He extracts it silently from its jeweled scabbard. Yazdan draws his own sword with a crisp metallic hiss, two-hands it to Musa hilt first. A matching wooden sword is returned. The two men turn to face each other, taking their positions four paces apart. Both grip their wooden broadswords with two hands, raise their blades to the sky and bow.

All frivolity has vanished, smiles evaporated, both men now deadly serious. The tension builds as they hold their positions, focus their energy to a point. Musa shouts "Fight!" and it begins, quick as a lightning bolt. Chandon double-steps forward, slashes left then right then left then right in rapid fire, matching the cadence of his stride. Yazdan steps backward to absorb the onslaught, parries the blows one by one, finally standing his ground. He then double-steps forward, mirroring Chandon's earlier moves. Chandon retreats as he parries. Both men test the other for any obvious weakness. None offered.

They begin to circle one another. Chandon suddenly releases a fury of blows. Thrust, parry; swing, parry; pivot; lunge, thrust. Step forward, slice right, parry; slice left, parry; lock swords. Thrust, parry; swing, parry; lunge, thrust. Chandon's daring grows by the day as he reawakens his sword skills. The duel continues for ten minutes more, a lesson in professional swordsmanship.

Both men stand gasping for air, armpits soaked. Sweat beads dot their foreheads. They look into each other's eyes long and hard, then burst out laughing. Chandon bows, "Excellent, Yazdan, excellent! A draw, sir?"

"Indeed, sir, a draw. You are improving, Chandon. I am starting to worry." He grins. "Another week and you may be able to best Musa." The three men share a boisterous laugh.

Chandon nods, then beams. "Thank you, Yazdan. I am enjoying this immensely."

Yazdan says, "Show me that move where you thrust then pivot then lunge."

Chandon rehearses the move in slow motion. Yazdan and Musa nod their approval. Lightning quick, Chandon dramatically slices the air in wide arc, first left then right, then cackles. "I would like to begin practice with both a sword and a dagger. Could you arrange that, Yazdan?"

"Full battle gear? I will see what I can do."

"Good, thank you. Gentlemen, shall we head to the baths?" Both bodyguards nod.

She stands at her window, grinning, watching his elegant, fluid movements, his taut muscles, his obvious expertise; the easy camaraderie with Yazdan and Musa. Her face blossoms as she calculates the days before their next midnight rendezvous. Two. A spine tingle of anticipation flares up, stretches from her neck to her toes, then settles into the pit of her stomach where it pleasantly gnaws. She tenders an annoyed grimace, tries to shoo it away, but eventually gives up and smiles again.

She continues to watch as Chandon demonstrates a unique sword move in slow motion. Both guards nod appreciatively. Chandon slices up the air in front of him, then laughs, now the showman. As she sighs, her smile fades, traded for concern.

The two friends play chess by oil lamp, a favorite evening ritual. Their foreheads are furrowed, eyes squinted and locked to the board, deep in thought. These two are well-matched and as usual their first four losses have been dead-even swaps: knight for knight, bishop for bishop, two pawns each. Several moves later, however, Chandon makes a serious miscalculation, loses a castle, then is forced to exchange his queen for a lowly bishop. He shakes his head in disgust, mumbles to himself.

Salamun scans his friend's face, first puzzled, then troubled. He exhales. "My eyes are tired tonight, Young Knight. I am not sure I will be able to finish our battle."

Chandon seems relieved. "I am sorry to hear that, Wizard. Somehow I am not able to concentrate this evening. My apologies." The silence stretches.

Salamun grins. "And how is our girl?"

Chandon's usual playfulness has vanished. He avoids Salamun's eyes. "Layla is fine. Our days together are joy-filled, happy." More silence. He looks up. "She has become my best friend, Salamun. We talk and talk, for hours and hours; about everything, about nothing. Neither of us tires of it. Her hands dance as she speaks. I do not think she is even aware of it." They both chuckle.

"She is an amazing young woman, Salamun. Unlike any woman I have ever known. Beautiful. But there are many beautiful women in the world. Layla seems almost ashamed of her looks, does not want to be judged for a thin veneer. She does not want to be dismissed as an ornament, put into a box." He smiles as he considers her, then continues.

"She blushes constantly, adorably. She is smart, by God, and knows more about most things than I do. She is far more skilled at language than I will ever be. She has twice the English vocabulary that I have of Arabic. She beats me at chess more than I beat her. Never has a woman beaten me at chess!" He gives up and laughs. Salamun joins in. "Oh my, does she have a temper; a will of iron. And strong opinions about everything! She likes getting her way, that much is sure. But this all suits her perfectly and I would not change it for the world." He smiles into empty space.

"She is connected to her spirituality in ways I have never even dreamed of, Salamun. The Sufi Way calls to her, makes her so happy. I have learned so much from her about God, about life. She introduced the Maristan to me, helped me to learn many things about myself that have opened my eyes, softened my heart. Who would have thought that I would wash and feed the outcast, and enjoy it? I have watched her while she works with the babies. She will be a wonderful mother, Salamun, so loving and tender." A weary sigh. He shakes his head. "I have never known a woman quite like her, Salamun. I feel like I can tell her anything. Anything."

Salamun raises his eyebrows. "Even Sosanna?"

"Even Sosanna. It was Layla's gentle tug that drained the wound's venom and healed me." Chandon locks eyes with his friend, his expression turning serious. "We cannot bear being apart, Salamun. Our love deepens by the day. I can think of nothing but her, of us, our future. I ache for her." He hesitates, then says, "I will see her again this evening."

Salamun offers a concerned look. "Yes, the weekly rendezvous. You must be cautious, Young Knight. The world watches, waits for a mistake. Between the two of us, Lisan al-Din has told me that accusations have recently been made within the Mexuar Council. He also told me that you should be wary of Zamrak. The Berbers on the Council are a minority, but a dangerous minority. Be careful, Young Knight, please."

Another weary sigh. "Yes. That is what weighs upon my heart, Salamun. I cannot bear putting her at risk. Yet, we cannot imagine not being alone together." His eyes fill. "I love her, Salamun. With my body and soul I love the woman. And she returns my love. It is killing us to be apart."

The grin fades from Salamun's face. "I know, Young Knight, I know."

"I need to ask you a serious question."

"Certainly."

"What would have to happen in order for me to marry Layla?"

"My, my, that is a serious question." He considers. "Well, first and foremost, her father would have to approve. But you have Lisan al-Din's blessing. He is very fond of you, Young Knight, and he respects you. He knows that you love his daughter, that she loves you. He will honor her wishes. But I am afraid that neither the Mexuar Council nor the Sultan would ever permit marriage between a Moor and a Christian at court. Ever. It simply cannot be."

Chandon looks pained. "Yes, I know. Layla and I talk a great deal about religion. Our one God, the Sufis, tawhid, Muhammad, Jesus. She reads the Quran to me, recites her favorites from the hadith. I have learned so much that I did not know."

Salamun nods. "That is good, very good. And?"

"I have never been an especially devout Christian, Salamun." Mock horror lights Salamun's face, followed by a chuckle. Chandon can only tender a weak smile. "I was raised by the friars, so I know Christian dogma. I attended Easter and Christmas Vigil Mass my whole life. I pray. I try my best to avoid sin, to be a good person. But the greed of the Church and its lust for power nauseates me. I believe in God. I believe in the truth of Jesus' message." He stops. "But Islam shares that God and holds Jesus in the highest esteem. The Sufi's search for mystical truth, direct union with God, just as the Christian desert fathers do." He hesitates. "What exactly is involved in conversion to Islam?"

Salamun raises his eyebrows, but remains silent. He inhales deeply, holds it, then exhales. "Quite simple, really. All one needs to do is testify with sincerity and conviction the *Shahada*, which states 'There is no god but Allah, and Muhammad is the messenger of Allah.' Generally this is done before an imam or an assembly in the mosque, but under certain circumstances it can happen in private. Once the testimony of faith has been professed, then one must simply commit to following the five pillars of the faith: reciting the Shahada; *salat*, prayer, five times a day; *sawm*, fasting during the month of Ramadan; *zakat*, almsgiving and charity for the poor; and *hajj*, pilgrimage to Mecca at least once in your lifetime. And, of course, reading and studying the Quran and the hadith, as a sign of commitment to the faith."

"Yes, Layla has told me of the five pillars. She has even shown me how to pray. Formal, but appealing. Fasting and almsgiving are nothing new to me."

The silence stretches once more. "Young Knight, there is more at stake here, surely you recognize that." They lock eyes again. "If you renounce your Christianity, the Moors will indeed embrace you, accept you as one of their own. You would be free to marry Layla. But no Christian would ever understand that choice, even if it was made for love. The Pope's death warrant is issued for any Christian that converts to Islam. They are forfeit in the eyes of the Church. In battle converts are not taken prisoner or ransomed, but are killed on sight. You could never return to Brittany or England. Ever. That life, that world, your family, your friends, your estate, would all be lost to you."

Chandon's head sags as he nods to his lap, then whispers, "Yes, Salamun, I know, I know. My heart is heavy." He looks up, his eyes brimming. "But I could never leave Layla, even if the Moors decided to release me. I cannot lose her, I will not lose her."

Concern creases Salamun's forehead. "I understand, Young Knight, I understand."

She cradles Maryam in her arms, staring into the baby's dark brown eyes as she noisily suckles the bottle of warmed milk. Layla's gentle rhythmic sway is matched to the melody of an ancient nursery song she hums. Mother and child. Constancia stands one cradle over, ladling porridge into Nafi's open mouth, his arms bouncing with joy between spoonfuls. When the bowl is empty, she wipes the boy's face, tickles him into giggles and then pats his head affectionately. She turns and begins to study Layla, her smile widening on her face.

"Love suits you."

Layla looks up, startled, blushes deep scarlet, but despite her best effort, cannot restrain the smile that spreads across her face.

Constancia laughs. "Some things are impossible to hide, my dear. But do not worry; it is not obvious to the casual observer. I have never seen you more joyful and radiant. I am very happy for you, Layla. Chandon is a good man and he has a good heart."

"We have become best friends."

"Yes. Good." Constancia's smile widens. "He clearly loves you, Layla."

Layla beams. "Yes, and I him."

The older woman grows more serious. "I am sure that your relationship has presented some interesting...challenges...for you both."

Layla's smile collapses into a heap. "Yes..." She edges closer to Constancia, lowers her voice to a whisper. "We see each other late at night, once a week, at great risk. But we must be together. We see each other daily at court under chaperone, and at the Maristan, but keeping our distance, pretending there is nothing between, is pure torture. We want to be together, we must be together, but we cannot. We are watched by the Africans. I fear for William's safety, and my own, and especially Baba's. We are tired of pretending, Constancia. We feel trapped."

"I understand perfectly. I have never told you my story, Layla." They find each other's eyes. "My late husband, Yusuf, may Allah grant his soul peace, was a knight of Granada. As a young woman I was nanny to the children of Dinar Abu Ishaq. We lived in a carmen house in the Albayzín, not far from here. Even though I was a Christian slave, I was treated well, made to feel part of the family. Yusuf was Dinar's younger brother. Such a handsome man; a good man. He would come for mid-day feast on Saturdays when he was not on campaign, to play with his nephews and nieces. We began to talk.

"Within three months we had fallen in love. His visits became more frequent, more urgent. Soon we were arranging secret meetings when I was out with the children. It was indeed torture. Finally, we could stand it no more. Yusuf confided in his brother, who in the end was supportive. I converted to Islam and we were married, with the family's blessing. Those next eight years were the happiest of my life. Sadly, we were not blessed with children, a fact that pains me to this day." She hesitates, her eyes welling up.

"Yusuf was killed in battle at Montejicar, four years ago. By Christians. The cruel irony still haunts me."

"Oh my..." Tears begin to slide down Layla's cheeks. "I am so sorry, Constancia. I had no idea."

"As his brother's widow, Dinar was obligated to care for me, but I was a constant reminder of the family's loss, the pain we all shared. A great sadness settled upon the home, with me at its center. Those were terrible times. Master al-Khayyat is Dinar's cousin, and when he was asked by Sultan Muhammad to oversee the Maristan, they found a position for me. The Maristan saved my life, Layla. My pain has slowly ebbed. The babies have brought me happiness once more. They are the children Yusef and I never had."

They grow silent. "You gave up your religion to be with the man you loved."

"Yes. While it was a difficult choice, it was one that I do not regret, even now. Sometimes one must sacrifice great things for great love."

"Yes."

"We had eight wonderful years together, and a lifetime of memories. Does your father know about your relationship with Chandon?"

"We have not discussed it, but Baba is a smart man. Surely he realizes. I am sure he likes William." She pauses. "Baba adored Mama. He must know what we feel."

They find each other's eyes again. "You must confide in your father, Layla, and seek his help."

Layla only responds with a pained nod as she chews her lower lip.

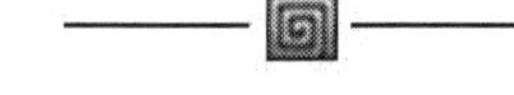

A textured riot of green brushed broadly upon a nut brown palate spills out across the plain, stretching to the mountains rimming the horizon, ten miles distant. Chandon sits atop Blue, palm shading his eyes, scanning the Vega. He breathes in the cool, fresh air as he studies the verdant landscape with a farmer's eye. To his far left, dense orchards of lemon, cherry, apple, orange, pomegranate, apricot and almond huddle side-by-side. The trees roll up and into the low foothills to the south of the Alhambra, heavily laden with white, pink and orange blossoms, exhaling their ridiculously fragrant scents into the light breeze. Bees busy about, their greedy snouts yellowed with pollen.

Tracking right, he sees acres of grape arbors thick with the spiky tendrils of young vine shoots. A spider web of irrigation channels crisscrosses the Vega, many still dark with the life-giving diversion of the Genil. In front, there are rectangular fields of foot-high spring wheat, tender shoots of barley, flooded paddocks of rice spindles. Turbaned workers dot the fields, spades and hoes working the rich earth. In the distance there is a small dust storm. Chandon squints, sees fifty mounted horsemen riding in formation under a blue banner. Cavalry patrol.

Further to his right, he sees a chess board of vegetable plots; chard, carrots, beets, celery, asparagus, onions and radishes. The plenty of the Vega never fails to impress Chandon. Being able to ride Blue along the cart paths has become the high point of his afternoons. His first ride with Layla is slated for next week, and he grins with the rich anticipation.

Chandon turns in his saddle and smiles. "Yazdan, Musa, ready for a race?" The two bodyguards return the smile, nod, ease their horses up alongside Blue, challenge accepted. The trio begin to walk their stallions forward as the tension builds. The horses' ears flick and pivot, tails twitching nervously. One-by-one they jostle for position, attempt to intimidate with a half-rear, are forced down by their riders. Three coiled springs. Blue stamps his left front leg then shakes his head and snorts, ready to race. His challengers both answer in turn.

Chandon searches for a target, points down the road a half mile. "See the small oak tree on the right? First to it wins." Yazdan and Musa nod, grip their reins tightly, lean forward in their saddles, and rise up on the balls of their feet. Chandon yells, "GO!" and the road erupts into thunder and dust as the stallions leap to a full gallop. The three Andalusians are neck and neck for the first one hundred yards but soon it becomes apparent that Blue has the superior stamina, and he begins to ease ahead of his rivals.

Yazdan and Musa urge their horses on, shouting Arabic encouragement, to no avail. As they pass the oak tree Blue has a twenty yard cushion. Chandon laughs loud as he rises up in his stirrups and begins to rein Blue in, allowing him to coast. They slow to a trot, then stop. The horse continues to gulp and blow, his body slick with sweat. Both horse and rider know that he could have easily done another half mile. Chandon leans forward, whispers to his stallion, "A fine ride, Blue. Fine ride! Good boy, good boy!" He pats his neck affectionately, strokes his right ear. Blue whinnies, signaling his confidence, his conceit.

Yazdan and Musa ease up beside him. The two stallions eye Blue warily, painfully aware of their place. Musa says, "Nice ride,

Chandon. You have a fine stallion." Chandon smiles, laughs again. They ride on into the lush expanse of the Vega.

She sits on the white cushion, back straight, legs crossed in front of her, up-turned palms resting in her lap. Her breathing is even and shallow and her head is bowed in deep meditation. Apart from the long white beard and grizzled skin, Mansur al-Mussib is a mirror image. They sit facing each other, three feet apart; twenty minutes, forty minutes, an hour. Without any change in posture, he begins to intone a whispered Sufi prayer. She joins him. When complete, master and disciple take a deep breath in unison, exhale, open their eyes, lift their heads and smile.

"It is good to share muraqaba with you, Layla."

"Yes, Master, it is very good."

The silence stretches out comfortably. "Tell me how you are feeling?"

"I am well, Master, thank you."

"You are keeping up with your practice?"

"Yes, Master, of course."

He nods, then more silence. "How long has it been now since the attack at the Maristan?"

Her smile fades. "Nearly six months, Master. My injuries have completely healed. Life has returned to normal."

He raises his eyebrows, then nods again. "I see. I am glad to see you back working at the Maristan. It clearly has been good for you to return to your duties there."

The smile returns. "Yes, Master. I cannot imagine my life without it." She searches for the right words. "My heart softens while I am there. I am able to see the world through the eyes and ears of my heart. I think more about others and less about myself. My compassion for the residents wells up, then overflows. Caring for them makes me happy, Master. The hours, even the chores, they fill me with great joy and great peace. Love."

"Mmmm...love...good, good." More silence. "I have noticed a change in you, Layla. A change which has grown increasingly obvious these past few months." She blushes scarlet, studies her lap. He grins. "A new kind of love. Such love cannot be hidden, my dear, nor should it be. It is nothing to be ashamed of."

She looks up to find his gentle eyes. Her lower lip begins to quiver as her eyes well up. She takes a deep breath to steady herself. "Yes, Master, I am in love."

"Chandon."

"Yes."

"Tell me what you are feeling, Layla." She looks uncertain. He warmly smiles. "Go on, my dear, tell me. Please." He raises his eyebrows expectantly, lifts his palms to coax her on.

She searches to connect the right words to her feelings. Her heart begins to spill over; a dribble at first, then gushes. "The feelings I have experienced these past months have been new and exciting, surprising and confusing, Master. Sometimes they are so strong and irresistible they scare me." She stops until he shoos her on. "My heart pounds when I see him. I cannot stop smiling when I think of him. We talk non-stop, for hours, about everything. We laugh, we read poetry, we play chess, we watch the world." She smiles.

"He is my best friend, Master. I teach him Arabic, he teaches me English. He teases me, I tease him. He talks on and on about gardening, farms, livestock, irrigation. Suddenly I am fascinated by such things, even though they have never once interested me." They both laugh.

"Go on, Layla."

"We talk about religion, Master. He thinks it is wonderful that I am training to be a Sufi. We share the same joy in serving at the Maristan. We talk of such things often. Sometimes I find myself crying for no reason at all, but they are tears of joy, not sadness. Somehow when I am with him I feel complete, whole. Safe. I feel like I am my truest self when we are together." She sighs. "My heart aches when we are apart and I have trouble concentrating." She hesitates, then lowers her voice to a whisper, "We take foolish risks that we should not, just to be alone. We cannot help ourselves."

He nods to his lap as she speaks to give her ample space. When she stops he looks up, mock serious, then breaks into a broad grin. "Yes, yes, I remember those feelings very well; very well, indeed." She looks surprised. "What, you think this old man never loved a woman?" He projects fake horror.

"Layla, Layla, when I was your age I fell hopelessly in love with a desert beauty in Fez. It was many, many years ago, but the feelings have never faded. We talked, we kissed, we laughed, we desired, we took stupid risks. Such is young love." He chuckles with the memory. "We were married for thirty-two wonderful years. My Ulla, my desert flower. May her soul rest with Allah."

"Master, I did not know." She is buoyant with the revelation.

Silence. "Your father tells me that Chandon is a good man, Layla, a man of integrity and courage. A man with a good heart.

Your father likes him." Al-Mussib hesitates. "You may have also noticed that he is a Christian?" He lifts his eyebrows in query.

Her bright smile slips off of her face. "Yes. We talk of it often, Master. There is much about Islam that appeals to him."

He nods approvingly. "Good. There is no rush, no rush at all. Let Chandon learn. He must come to that decision on his own, Layla." The old man turns serious again. "Tell me what else troubles you, my dear."

Her lip quiver begins anew, grows in strength. "Master, I do not want to give up my training. My heart is Sufi. I want to continue the Sufi Way." A tear breaks loose, then another.

He offers an affectionate smile. "Layla, Layla, all is love. There is no difference between your love of Chandon and a Sufi's love of Allah. They are simply different manifestations of the same Truth. In fact, our friend Master Rumi says that the easiest path to tawhid, perhaps the best path to tawhid, is through the love of another. Your love of Chandon has opened a gate to your union with the Beloved. Learning to give yourself wholly to another prepares you for giving yourself wholly to Allah. There is no conflict, my dear, nothing to worry over. All is love. Remember, Layla. The Sufi Way is the way of love; no more, no less. And I, for one, would be gravely disappointed in you if you gave up your Sufi training."

She beams as she wipes her eyes. "Thank you, Master, thank you. You have made me very happy."

"My sole aim in life, my dear, is to keep my disciples happy." He laughs. "Off you go now. Remain true to your practice and work hard. Embrace your flowering love, Layla." Now comes the wry smile. "And Layla? Please keep the risks to a minimum."

The Sultan and Zamrak sit together on a stone bench beside a bubbling fountain in the expansive gardens of the Generalife. The long shadows thrown by the skinny cypresses in the late afternoon sun zebra the landscape. There are a dozen bodyguards within twenty paces, tucked discreetly into the tall, manicured hedges, ever watchful. Even though it is within a long bowshot of the Alhambra's north wall, the Generalife, the Sultan's summer palace, feels like a distant land, a luxurious country estate set among plush gardens and carefully tended orchards.

On his lap, Zamrak cradles a stack of rectangular clay molds that will be used to fabricate his stucco poetry ornamentation for a new Water Garden Courtyard being installed in the Generalife. One by one he holds them up for the Sultan to read and admire, then moves to the next. The Sultan silently nods his approval. An ode to nature.

Zamrak sets the pile down, lifts a collection of different shaped ceramic tiles with bold green and red and gold and brown fired glazes.

"My thought, Sire, was to surround the poem with an arrangement of tiles and color patterns not found anywhere else in the Alhambra. To set it off and make it unique."

"Good, good, yes, I agree." The Sultan is pensive, seems preoccupied.

The silence stretches. Zamrak says, "I understand that the Mexuar Council has been up to its normal mischief again, Sire. I am sorry for the distraction."

The Sultan looks up. "Distraction? Yes, well, sometimes it seems as if the sole purpose of the Mexuar Council is to be a thorn in my side. Their pettiness grows tiresome, more bold."

"I hear that the Berbers actually challenged Master Ibn al-Khatib...over Layla, Sire."

"Yes, it was not pretty. Lisan al-Din is still fuming."

Zamrak admires the setting sun for a moment, calculating. "May I speak freely, Sire?"

"Certainly, Zamrak. What is on your mind?"

"Sire, I wonder about the wisdom of Master Ibn al-Khatib letting Layla spend so much time with Chandon. Perhaps learning English is not worth the aggravation, the personal risk to the Grand Vizier's reputation."

"Perhaps."

"Rumors abound, Sire."

The Sultan frowns. "Rumors, always rumors."

"I like Chandon, Sire. He is a good man. Ultimately, however, he is a pawn to be played for the glory of Granada. He is expendable. It seems to me that keeping him at a...proper distance...will make that easier, Sire. When the time comes."

"Perhaps you are right."

"I also fear for Layla's reputation, Sire. She spends far too much time with the Christian. She is a beautiful Granadine maiden, Sire, and her purity must be jealously guarded."

The Sultan stares somberly into the smoldering red-orange sunset. "Yes." The Sultan muses, then says, "It is odd. Layla seems even more ravishing these past few months." He sighs heavily. "That girl is bewitching. I cannot stop thinking about her."

Zamrak grimaces, looks away. "Has Prince al-Waziri made any progress tracking down the assassin?"

"Very little, I am afraid. A hint here, a clue there, but so far nothing definitive. He conducts regular surprise room-to-room sweeps of the entire palace complex. Not a trace. It is as if the assassin has evaporated into thin air. It looks as though I will remain in the Generalife for some time. With the warm weather coming soon, perhaps that is just as well. In truth, Bashir is as frustrated as I am. He has vowed to not give up the hunt until he has a head to place on a platter before me."

The Sultan claps his hands to his knees and rises. "Come, let us retire for prayer and dinner. Afterwards, perhaps some chess."

"Certainly, Sire."

## Slash of Crimson

A steady, warm drizzle falls through the night, ending just after daybreak, slaking the thirst of the magical garden. The lush terraced earth exhales, refreshed and jubilant. The cypress roots sense their opportunity and begin anew to worm vertically into the softened soil. Their coffers bulging, the wind-tilled reflecting pools offer a warm welcome to their long-lost cousins. The gray and purple marbled sky has split open in several rough patches, the sun's streaky yellow rays brazenly stretching through down to the earth, brushed in with egg yokes. The bird-gossip is boisterous, bawdy, an avian shouting match almost deafening in its enthusiasm. All is dark, damp and new. Glistening. Beads of sweat cling stubbornly to the canary rose petals and ruby cannas lilies, who luxuriate in the humid air, resisting the urge to dog-shake them to the ground.

Aisha's leisurely crunch upon the pea gravel path is echoed by Musa and Yazdan. The two bodyguards walk to either side of her, a half pace behind, as if she is their worry. Their eyes gauge the fog-tinged landscape, sweeping the garden for any hints of mischief, signs of danger. Aisha's eyes lazily track about as she day-dreams. An especially generous buffer of thirty paces separates the three chaperones from their charges, ample space to enable the cacophony of fountain splash and birdsong to render the lovers' conversation private.

To their left are rose beds in voluptuous full bloom, dozens of interspersed red, yellow, white and pink blossoms. A pleasing musky, spicy, citrus scent hangs heavy in the moist air. To their right a head-high, sculpted cypress hedge lines the gravel path, marked by periodic keyhole-shaped privacy niches.

They walk deeper into the Partal Gardens, listening to the birdsong and basking in the garden's simple harmony. Chandon is the first to break the silence.

"Your father told me that we may ride together on Wednesday. Provided, of course, our favorite twosome accompanies us." He grins.

She answers with a smile. "Yes, he mentioned it last night. That will be fun. I miss my riding. Before my Sufi training began, I used to roam the Vega several times a week."

"The Vega is a wonderful place to ride. Blue is a fine stallion, fast and proud. I have never ridden his equal."

"He was one of my father's favorites. He has ancient Arabian blood lines, you know, one of the finest Andalusians in the kingdom. However, I must warn you, sir, that my Afán has never been bested."

He laughs. "We shall see, my Lady, we shall see. Your Afán has yet to challenge Blue." He offers a coy, mock frown. "I am afraid for poor Musa and Yazdan. I suspect their stallions will not be able to keep up with us." They share a knowing look, simultaneously grin, stroll on in silence.

As they approach the third keyhole entry in the cypress hedge, a head-high boxwood hedge springs up on their left, providing the cover he has been seeking. Chandon snatches Layla's arm, pulls her into the concealing cypress niche. The chaperones' eyes immediately track to the disappearing movement. Instead of issuing an alarm, however, both men grin in unison. Aisha turns to check behind them. No one. The three do not alter their pace, knowing that at best the lovers will have only two minutes of privacy.

Her spontaneous squeal at his daring vanishes as he begins to kiss her. With no time for tenderness, this kiss is impassioned, urgent and wet. He bends his knees to equal their heights, circles both arms around her waist and pulls her tight against him. She lifts her right foot from her sandal, slides it beneath his robe and hooks it behind his left calf, warm flesh deliciously caressing warm flesh. He pulls her tighter still, kisses her harder. Tender, muted pleasure murmurs seep from her into the air surrounding them. Thirty seconds more then he abruptly releases her, pushes her back in self-defense. Their faces are flushed and serious, their bodies now throbbing in lockstep with their panting. As they catch each other's eyes, they break into hysterical silent giggles, doubling over to keep them hushed. She takes a deep breath to steady herself, steps back into her sandal, smoothes her robe, looks into his eyes and whispers in English, "I love you". She then waggles her finger in mock anger and hisses, "You are bad!"

The returns a sheepish grin, shrugs helplessly and whispers, "I am in love. What can I do?" They both laugh.

They emerge from the niche with the chaperones still ten paces out, as if nothing happened. They do not make eye contact with the inquisitive trio, but simply turn right, begin to pick up their pace to re-establish some distance. The lovers exchange wicked smiles, begin to wind their way through the Partal maze. The sun is beginning to break through the lifting fog. Soon their hearts are beating normally once more, the throbbing still coiled dangerously, but with fangs mercifully withdrawn.

The conversation floats over a range of topics; her lessons at the madrasa, their many grace-filled moments at the Maristan, his never-ending questions about Granadine culture. They settle into a tranquil quiet. She takes a deep breath, holds it, then exhales. He turns, lifts his eyebrows and says, "What?"

She sighs again, decision made. "I have been thinking about you and Sosanna."

Chandon swallows. "I see. What were you thinking about?"

She looks up into his eyes, uncharacteristically timid, then looks back down, but does not speak.

"What, Layla? Ask."

"I find myself wondering what it was about Sosanna that you fell in love with. I know that is silly."

"It is not silly. If you had loved another before me I would be curious; or more likely, jealous."

"You said she was bright and educated. What did she look like?"

He looks at her but her eyes remain glued to the gravel path. "She had long, straight, light brown hair; fair skin, dark brown eyes. A wonderful smile. She was a little taller than you. Breton women, of course, have a different style of dress than the women of Granada."

"Yes, I can imagine. Tell me about her."

"Well, let me see. I met Sosanna soon after the Battle of Auray. By then I was weary of war. Suddenly I had land, an estate, modest wealth, but what I desired most was a normal life. Peace. Our love grew quickly. It was fresh and exciting, a new experience for both of us. I found her very easy to talk to, with none of the normal awkwardness so typical between men and women when they first meet." Layla nods to the ground, expressionless.

"Sosanna was unusually knowledgeable, a gift from her father. She understood me when I talked about farming techniques, fertilizing the land, crop rotation, irrigation. She grew up in the Breton countryside. That may sound boring, but it pleased me. She seemed like the perfect person to build a life with. Somehow she could draw me out, lift me from my weariness and all the ugliness I had seen. And she made me laugh. She helped me see that a different path for my life was possible." He muses. "She loved children and wanted to raise a family, and suddenly that seemed to make so much sense to me, even though I had never before thought much about it. We planned for our future together. It was a good time, a happy time."

"Was she religious?"

"Well, her father was a Bishop, of course, but even so, she was not overly religious, no. Neither was I, despite my time with the friars. We went together to Mass on Sundays, of course, with the rest of the family. She knew her prayers, and she was pious. But most of all, Sosanna had a good heart. A pure heart. She never had a cross word for anyone, and she always put others before herself. She would have been a good mother."

"Yes, I would have expected that." A long pause. "Did she play chess?" That beautiful coy smile.

Chandon laughs. "No, no chess. Thankfully. I am still trying to get used to being bested by a woman." They share a laugh, then the silence lingers.

More serious now, she says, "I am very different than Sosanna, William."

"Yes, yes you are, Layla, wonderfully different. You have not been shy since that first day we met. Remember?" She grins. "You engage me in conversation as an equal, something I have never encountered in a woman, and certainly not with Sosanna. You question my opinions, and you tell me when you think I am wrong. I value that, Layla, even though it did take a little getting used to." They both laugh.

"I respect your spirituality, Layla, your strong commitment to your Sufi training and your heartfelt desire for peace. I have learned so much from you about who God is and what love is, and who I want to be, how I want to spend my life. Working with you at the Maristan has opened windows into my heart that I never knew existed, never dared to imagine were there. You possess such goodness, Layla, such purity of heart, such insight into the true meaning of life." His voice thickens as he says, "When I am with you, Layla, I feel like I am finally the man that God intended me to be. I feel like I am a better person because of you, because of the love we share. You are a beautiful human being and my best friend. And a ravishingly beautiful woman, though you seem so unaware of it, a fact that is so endearing. I cannot imagine my life without you, Layla. We were meant to be together, destined to love each other. I truly believe that. I thank God for you, my love."

She looks up, her eyes brimming, then flashes that smile. "It is a feeling I share, William, to the depths of my soul, to the marrow of my bones. I have come to know Allah so much more fully by loving you. I have come to know myself so much better, what I want from my life. I never imagined I would ever yearn to be a wife, or a mother, and now it seems like the most natural desire I have ever had." Tears roll down her cheeks. "I never imagined love would find me, William. I had given up on it. Then you. I thank

Allah for that Grace each day." They stare deeply into each other's eyes. "Thank you for sharing Sosanna with me, William, that meant a lot."

He edges closer to her, allows his fingers to discreetly brush against hers as they stroll. They bask in the moment, lapse back into a comfortable silence. "I understand why you took up your sword again and returned to war."

He sighs heavily. "Yes. I believed that a normal life for me died with Sosanna. When I learned that Edward would fight beside Pedro of Castile, I gathered the Bretons, joined our ranks with Enrique. I dreamed of revenge, and could not get it out of my head. I am not proud of that, but there it is. My blood lust poisoned my soul, Layla, it tortured me. Ironically, our paths never crossed at Nájera. No doubt it was for the best." He looks at her. "You helped rid me of that awful poison, Layla. Our love has healed me. For that I will always be grateful." She smiles.

They lapse into silence again as they stroll slowly on, admiring the flowers and water features, the bird song. "I had an interesting conversation with Constancia. She knows of our love. She approves and is happy for us." They lock eyes, grin. "She told me her story. Heart-wrenching."

"Tell me." Her hands begin to lift and dance to help tell the tale.

When she finishes, she says, "She told me that I should talk to my father about us and solicit his help."

He nods. "Yes. I have come to the same conclusion. I sense that he knows." He hesitates. "I believe that he approves."

"Yes." A long pause. "Master al-Mussib also knows."

He turns to look at her, raises his eyebrows. "Are we that obvious?" He grins.

She laughs. "Evidently only to those that have known the love that we know."

His grin fades. "We must be careful, Layla. Salamun says that there are many eyes watching us, waiting for a mistake." He hesitates. "Perhaps we should stop our late night meetings."

Her head whips around, anger painted bright upon her face. She shakes her head violently, "No, William, NO!" Her emerald eyes burn as her bile rises. "We cannot allow the Africans to dictate the rules of our love. I will NOT allow it! NEVER!"

She cools her temper by force of will. "I am sorry, William." He grins his forgiveness. She begins again. "We will be careful." He nods. "Master al-Mussib told me that our love will not affect my Sufi training. He encouraged me to embrace our love. He said that true love will help me better understand the Sufi Way, aid me in my journey to tawhid. Master Rumi agrees."

"Good, good." Chandon falls silent. "I have been thinking, Layla."

She turns, concerned by a note she detects in his voice. "What is it, William?"

He considers his words, then says, "I am going to ask your father if he would begin to teach me the ways of Islam."

She stops and faces him, her eyes widening. Incredulous, her heart begins to pound. "Really? Really, William? REALLY?"

"Yes. I have thought about it long and hard." He swallows to gain his nerve, then finds her eyes. "Layla, we will never be able to marry unless I join your people's faith. I want to begin my own training, learn more about Islam. For myself, for us."

Her eyes brim. Without thinking she leaps forward, bear hugs him, a tangle of smiles and giggles. He laughs loud, swings her in the air.

The three chaperones start with alarm, frown as one, begin to anxiously scan the garden for prying eyes. Thankfully, none are found. Yazdan raises his voice just enough to be heard, "Chandon, we should be getting back to the palace."

Too late, the lovers realize their mistake. She blushes dark, and he frowns as they back away from each other. "Yes, Yazdan, I agree. My apologies."

As they depart through the entrance to the Partal Gardens back onto the Lower Royal Road and begin to move towards the Comares Palace, a slash of crimson dashes between two cypress hedges, moving quickly in the opposite direction.

They occupy their usual spots, the room flush with comfortable silence. The windows are open to invite the fresh breeze. He reclines on his divan, medical books scattered about, his small writing table on his lap, quills and ink pot to the left, tea cup precariously balanced above dark stains. She leans over her neat desk, concentrating on her calligraphy, reed pen gripped loose but precise in her hand. A favorite prayer from the Quran torturously emerges in gold, black and blue arcs and swirls. The night settles in.

At a convenient stopping point he sets his quill back in its holder, frowns at his cramped hand as he flexes his fingers to limber them, then lifts his head to study his daughter. After a moment a smile eases onto his face.

"I had an interesting conversation with Chandon this morning. You two seem inseparable these days."

Her reed freezes, lifts a fraction of an inch from the paper, but her body does not perceptably move.

"Come, Daughter, sit with me." He lifts his writing table and sets it beside him, closes his books, pushes them aside, then pats his palm on the divan. "Come, let us talk, Layla."

She takes a deep breath to steady herself. She returns her quill to its holder, rises, turns and weakly smiles, heart now pounding. She comes and sits beside him, lowers her eyes to the divan.

He smiles at her uncharacteristic shyness.

"It was an interesting conversation." He pauses, waiting for her to look up, but she does not. He continues. "He seemed unusually nervous. He asked some perfunctory questions about irrigation, crop rotation, the usual, which I answered, of course. He then fell silent. Then he complemented me again on his stallion. More silence. Then he commented on the fine weather. Finally, he stopped himself and blurted out, 'Sir, I need to ask you something very important. About Layla.'"

Her heart is beating so hard it feels ready to leap from her chest. Still, she will not meet his eyes.

His expression grows serious. "He professed his love for you, my darling. He said that he loved you with his whole heart and soul, and that he wanted to spend the rest of his life with you, that he wanted to raise a family with you. Then he asked if I would instruct him in the ways of Islam, so that with my blessing he might marry you." His turn for silence now.

She looks up and into her father's eyes. Tears spill down her cheeks as her lower lip and chin quiver. She whispers, "I love William, Baba. With all my heart and soul I love him. I want to spend my life with him."

He smiles, his own eyes now welling up. "I know, my darling, I know. For some time now I have been aware of the love growing between you two." He stops. "Chandon is a good man, Layla, and he will make a fine husband and father. You two have my blessing and support." She bursts into a thick sob, hugs him tight.

"Thank you, Baba, thank you."

He spills his own tears now, then wipes his eyes. "You and Chandon remind me so of my early days with your mother. My Danah. We were so in love, Layla, so inseparable." He beams. "A flood of beautiful memories has visited me these past months, reminded me of much that I had somehow forgotten. I am happy for you, Layla. Such love is rare, my dear, surely you must sense that." They exchange a warm look. "I was not sure I would ever see the day my Layla's heart was tamed by a man." They laugh.

The silence stretches. His face grows serious. "Chandon told me that his decision to convert to Islam was his own, freely made. That is good. You both must fully appreciate, however, what he is giving up. He will be a marked man, Layla, with a price upon his head. In the eyes of the Christians his life will be forfeit, exchangeable for gold. He will never be able to return to England or Brittany. He will be at extreme risk in battle. He will forever be a...Moor...to them." He searches her brimming eyes. "He knows this. You must know this, Layla. You must understand what he is giving up for you." He hesitates. "With great love comes great sacrifice."

"Yes, Baba, Constancia said the same thing to me."

He nods. "I will fight to protect you both from the Africans, but please help make my job easier. You take too many risks, Daughter!" She blushes, looks down. "The fact that he is converting to the faith will quell the fire temporarily, but I fear that it will flame up again. The Africans grow bold and ambitious. They will oppose your union."

"I understand, Baba; we will be careful."

"Let us keep this strictly between the three of us until I can arrange a private meeting with the Grand Imam. Until I secure his blessing, Chandon's training, and the love you share, must remain a secret. Once I have the Grand Imam's support, I will approach the Sultan for his permission."

"Yes, Baba, I understand." She hesitates, then reaches for his hand, brings it toward her. She leans forward and tenderly kisses the back of his palm, touches her forehead to the same spot, looks up into his eyes. "Thank you, Baba, you have made me very happy." She lunges to hug him tight, his little girl once more. "I love you, Baba."

He whispers through his tears, "I love you, too, Daughter, I love you, too."

The days are warming, a presage of Granada's infamous summer swelter. Chandon sits atop Blue just outside the Royal Stables, waiting for her. As Yazdan and Musa ease up behind him, Blue casts a backward glance to remind the two stallions of their proper place, then whinnies for emphasize. Tails swish tensely, ears pivot and dart, an uneasy truce. Several stable workers lift their heads to admire the stallions, then return to their work.

Stable sounds and smells lay heavy on the air. Metallic jangles sing out as tack is taken down, sorted and fitted. The groan and flex of straining leather speaks as a saddle girth is cinched tight, then playful knickers, a stomped hoof, irritated whinnies. Next comes an angry 'shush!', a coaxing 'whoa...', a smart rump slap to garner attention, then a no-nonsense whip crack. Nearby, the crisp, metronomic ping of a heavy hammer on glowing orange steel as a horseshoe is shaped and sized on an anvil. The heady, organic mélange of fresh manure and oiled saddle leather, hay and sweat, is so thick in the still air it is almost visible; yet familiar, homey, pleasant somehow.

Chandon looks skyward, scans, then calculates. Loose cotton balls above, infant thunderheads loitering on the far western horizon. Clear to the east. He positions his eye between a cloud and a tree top to gauge direction and speed. Approaching, but no chance of a storm until at least late afternoon. He turns to Yazdan, "A good day for riding, sir."

Yazdan nods and grins.

He hears horseclop and without turning knows it is her. He reins Blue around to face her approach.

"My Lady." He offers an exaggerated bow of his head.

She flashes that smile. "Sir." She dips her head.

His eyes are instinctively drawn to her mount. A dappled buckskin stallion with wavy ebony mane and tail, matching legs. Intelligent eyes assess the assessor. Well-muscled, but sleeker than Blue. Certainly fast. Almost sixteen hands. Impressive. He holds his head arched high and tucked, proud. Chandon grins. This one has an attitude. His grin widens. To match his rider.

Horse evaluated, he returns to her. Her chestnut curls are loosely braided, then train down behind her to rest on her saddle. No head covering, a real treat. Her riding outfit consists of loose-fitting, cobalt blue cotton pants and shirt. She looks lovely against the dappled buckskin. Mid-calf, dark leather boots, matching riding gloves. He sighs. Ravishing. His grin returns as he notices that she uses a man's saddle. Unheard of in Europe for a lady at court, but in retrospect he realizes he should have expected it. She holds the reins like she knows what she is doing. He nods his approval, clearly pleased.

"A fine stallion, Layla."

"This is Afán. He is Lusitano, an Andalusian breed especially prized in Portugal."

"What does his name mean?"

She grins. "Spirited, filled with passion."

He laughs. "I notice that you ride a man's saddle. I am impressed. Women in Brittany only ride side-saddles."

"The Berbers taught me to ride, sir. In Fez, there is only one kind of saddle, one kind of tack. Thankfully, it allows me to ride Afán as Afán was meant to be ridden. Fast." A coy grin.

He nods appreciatively, returns her grin. "No doubt." He raises his palm up the road to the east. "Shall we enjoy an easy canter to the Vega, my Lady?"

"We shall, sir." She raises up in her stirrups, leans forward and whispers into her horse's ear. Afán acknowledges their agreement with a single ear cocked perfect, a slight head tilt as he readies himself. She tightens the reins, turns to Chandon, shouts, "Bettawfeeq!" *Good luck!* and explodes to a gallop up the road leading to the Vega, chestnut braid stretched out and dancing behind her, dust cloud in hot pursuit.

Chandon turns with raised eyebrows in mock disbelief to Yazdan and Musa, who shrug then grin. He grips his reins, shouts, "Run, Blue, run!" and the three give chase.

# Moonlight

The Sultan has been anxious, unsettled all afternoon, barely touching his supper. His servants wear discreet, worried looks as they remove his meal, wondering if they have somehow erred in the evening's preparations, perhaps done something to offend him. They frown and shake their heads, puzzled, then furiously whisper once out of sight. A mystery.

Resigned and sullen, he retreats to his suite in the Generalife for some privacy, then dismisses his bodyguards. They too share a concerned glance as they exit to take up their stations just outside the door. The Sultan paces back and forth, clearly troubled by something. He stops and turns, then sits back down at his writing desk, eyeing the letter. He sighs, reaches to pick it up, then examines the broken seal. Al-Khatib. He unrolls the parchment and begins to read for the fifth time the elegant Arabic script.

*My Dearest Sultan, most favored by Allah. I realize it has been some time since we have talked, but I think of you often. Since my attack at the Maristan I have been reflecting on my life and my future. I have reconsidered your invitation to join the Royal Harem. I am willing to submit to your desires, provided you agree to my one request. I will not become your concubine. Instead, I will become your wife. I will bear you the sons that you require to ensure the safety of your lineage and the kingdom's prosperity. My father does not yet know of my decision, but I am confident that we will have his blessing. If my offer is acceptable to you, I invite you to join me at midnight tonight in the Hall of the Ambassadors, so that we might come to know one another better under the beauty of the full moon. I will be dressed in a gold-laced white cotton gown, with a white silk head scarf. Please come alone. May Allah's peace be upon you.*

*Layla al-Khatib*

He sets the letter down and rests his chin in his hands while he ponders the words for the hundredth time, weighing his options, assessing the repercussions, searching for any hints of danger. All of this is interlaced with a pleasantly tortuous swollen ache he cannot ignore. Ten minutes, twenty minutes, a half-hour pass. He exhales, shakes his head side to side and chuckles, then rises, his decision made. His heart begins to race with anticipation. He walks to the door, opens it, and whispers to the bodyguard. "Please tell Zyad to join me. I will be visiting the palace later this evening."

The bodyguard nods curtly, "Certainly, Sire," then departs.

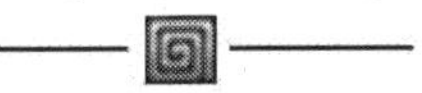

"Thank you for seeing me, Qasim."

"My Lord, I am at your service." The eunuch bows.

"Qasim, the Sultan has an unusual request. He would like the green-eyed concubine dressed in a particular manner and brought to the Hall of the Ambassadors at midnight tonight." The man pauses. "By me. Evidently the moon is full this evening, and he desires to enjoy her company in that grand space. I will arrange to have a divan delivered." The silence stretches. "The Sultan has sent the clothes with me that he would like her to wear for the occasion." The man hands the folded bundle to the eunuch, who accepts them.

"A most unusual request, my Lord."

"I agree, Qasim. Nevertheless, I told the Sultan that I would make the necessary arrangements." He searches the eunuch's eyes. "I assume I may depend upon you to carry out his wishes, Qasim?"

The eunuch bows. "The Sultan's wish is my command, my Lord."

"Good. The Sultan also instructed me to ensure that she does not wear the Royal Perfume, else she may attract attention as she passes through the palace. And no jewelry."

"I understand, my Lord."

"Qasim, I know that I may depend upon your discreetness in this...delicate...situation. No one must know of the Sultan's visit or the presence of the girl in the Hall. No one."

The eunuch nods. "Of course, my Lord, I understand completely."

"Good. Shortly before midnight I will knock three times at the door to the Royal Harem to collect her. I will see that she is returned when the Sultan's visit is complete."

"Very good, my Lord."

The man exits the Hall of the Abencerrages, looks both ways, then turns left towards the Partal Gardens.

As the Sultan and his two bodyguards approach the entrance to the Palace of the Lions, he raises his hand and the three come to a stop. As usual the Sultan is dressed in a plain robe, turban masking his face.

The Sultan turns to his right and whispers, “Ziyad, you are sure that all of the interior guards in the Palace of the Lions have been reassigned?”

“Yes, Sire, I checked everything an hour ago. The guards have all been moved to the outside exits of the palace complex. No one will enter or leave. You will see no one between the palace entrance and the Hall of the Ambassadors. You will have complete privacy, Sire.”

“Good. Thank you, Ziyad. I would like you two to wait for me just outside the Hall of the Abencerrages. When I am finished, I will rejoin you there and then we will return to the Generalife.”

“Understood, Sire.”

The Sultan glances over his left shoulder at the rising full moon and grimaces. The old man’s round, ghostly stare seems especially haughty tonight, mocking his weakness for beautiful women. He shrugs off the judgment.

It is a warm, cloudless night. The moonlight is bright enough to cast a sharp shadow. The Alhambra under a full moon offers unparalleled splendor, the intricately carved stucco walls and the smooth white marble floors magically coming alive, levitating, dancing like an eager bride on her wedding night. The Sultan’s pleasant gnaw of anticipation returns, settles into his groin. His heart begins to pound as the three move forward.

The entrance guards step aside to allow the trio to enter the Palace of the Lions. They halt and observe the scene. Satisfied, the Sultan nods to his bodyguards, who turn to the right towards the Hall of the Abencerrages. The Sultan turns left, keeping to the edge of the courtyard to remain out of sight, making his way to the tunnel connecting the two palace complexes.

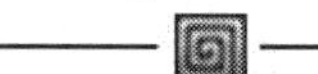

Chandon is fully dressed and already pacing his darkened room, anxious as usual. He gave up on reading long ago, unable to concentrate. His nerve endings are frayed after a week of close proximity with virtually no privacy. A quick angle of the eye, a knowing glance, a wink, a discreet brush of fingertips, a touch of knee to knee. This is the most they have dared risk. Their cherished time alone has finally arrived after an eternity. The weekly rendezvous.

He and Layla meet at an hour past midnight. She will first signal the all-clear by candle, he will confirm it, then they will slip out to meet by the pool. He stops pacing and cannot help but smile. They will ease back into the shadows, press tight against each other, and profess their love as they kiss and touch. Later, they will hold hands, circle the pool twenty times as they chatter on about all manner of things. Then they will sit and dangle their bare feet in the cool dark water, and talk about religion, plans for their future. Kiss and touch some more. She will cry when they depart just as the dim gray touches the eastern sky. His smile widens. Their touching has grown exquisitely familiar, bold. Pure delicious torture. He shakes his head as he marvels, then chuckles.

He steps to the window to survey the courtyard. Empty. He cannot see the full moon high to his right, but the courtyard is well-lit, glowing already in ghostly shadows, the reflections dancing off the white marble and the shimmering mirrored surface of the pool. The scene is ethereal, haunting but delightful. He knows that Layla will love the full moon, but the knight in him forces an unconscious tactical calculation. Too bright, too risky. He glances up to her window. Dark. As he pivots to resume pacing he discerns movement in his peripheral vision, turns back to the window and stares.

He sees a figure exit the tunnel between the Palace of the Lions and the Comares Palace, then stop. Short, feminine. White robe trimmed with gold lace, white head scarf. He recognizes the outfit. Layla. He squints to be sure while he wonders why she is early and why she would not have lit her candle. He frowns. He stares intently now, puzzled. He registers the shadowed figure standing to her right. Long black robe, a black hood pulled over his head, concealing his face. Tough to discern any detail in the moonlight.

He sees that the man has his hand at the small of her back, apparently guiding her. He lifts his palm to his right, and they turn, walk towards the far end of the courtyard and disappear into the Hall of the Ambassadors. The frown has not left his face. He looks back to Layla's window. Dark. He is uncertain what to do. For some odd reason Zamrak's face jumps into his mind's eye, but is chased away by his smirk. An uncharacteristic indecision settles upon Chandon. An exaggerated exhale as he considers his options, none of them good.

His eye is drawn to the tunnel once more as he sees a robed man with a turban covering his face enter the palace by the same route, stop and scan the courtyard. After a moment, he also turns right, begins to walk to the far end of the courtyard, disappearing into the Hall of the Ambassadors.

Decision made, he walks to his bed, pulls his jeweled scabbard from the wall hook, straps it on, walks to the door, unbolts the latch, and steps into the dimly lit hallway. His two bodyguards sit on their floor pillows, heads leaning back against the wall, mouths propped open, snoring.

Chandon touches their shoulders at the same time. "Alonso, Nasr, I am going to walk the courtyard."

The two open their eyes, close their mouths, blink themselves awake. After a moment they exchange a knowing glance. Nasr grins, says, "Say hello to the princess for us, Chandon."

Chandon offers an easy smile. "I will."

He whispers, "Auria, I would like you to stand in the moonbeam coming from the high window. Right here. Perfect. I want you to face away from the entrance. The Sultan will be here momentarily. When he speaks, no matter what he says, you are to remain silent, face away from him. Do you understand?"

No response.

A more forceful hiss, "Auria, do you understand me?"

"Yes, my Lord."

"Good. The Sultan has great plans for you, my dear. You are his favorite. It is important that you do exactly as I say. These are his wishes."

"Yes, my Lord."

"Once I am convinced that all is well I will depart and leave you two to enjoy the moonlight together."

"Yes, my Lord."

She is positioned now. Satisfied, the black-robed man slides back into the shadowed nook, invisible. The room is quiet as a tomb. They wait.

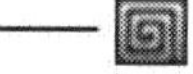

He slips through the entrance to the Hall of the Ambassadors, stopping just inside to let his eyes adjust. She is lit beautifully from behind by the moonbeam from the high window. She stares at his throne across the room, unaware of his presence. The vision of an angel. His sixth sense warns him to scan the room for any hint of mischief. Nothing. He listens. Not a sound. Reassured, he eases forward, stopping just behind her, close enough to reach out and touch her shoulder. She still seems unaware of his presence.

He licks his lips and whispers, "The moonlight complements your beauty, Layla. You look lovely."

She stiffens, but does not turn.

"I received your letter. I have come to grant your request, Layla. You shall join the Royal Harem. You shall be my wife."

He reaches for her shoulder, slowly turns her to face him.

The smile on his face freezes in place, then vanishes. First he looks confused, then troubled. He helplessly says, "Auria? What are you doing here? Why are you dressed like this? What is going on?"

From behind him, near the entrance, a menacing voice announces, "Caught like a fly in a spider web. My, my, all too easy. Funny, is it not, how the lure of lust, the promise of a beautiful young virgin, can fell the mighty?"

At the first words, the Sultan whips around, backs away several paces out of the moonbeam. Auria is frozen in place, a mute statue. She trembles. The black-robed man glides towards her, dagger drawn. He eases beside her into the ghostly light, then slips his left arm around her waist as he menaces the air with his sleek blade. Auria stares at the Sultan, eyes wide with terror.

The voice is familiar but muffled by the hood pulled across his face. The Sultan asks, "Who are you?"

"Ahhh...the question of the hour. Who am I, indeed? Your friend, your confidante, your assassin." He reaches up and removes the face covering, then pushes his hood back onto his shoulders. "Behold."

The Sultan is incredulous. "Bashir? How? Why? You are my most trusted vizier. What is going on here?"

"Alas, the hour of your death approaches, Sire." With a lightning-quick flick of his arm al-Waziri reaches around the girl, draws the dagger across her throat, the thin dark sliver stretching ear to ear. Auria's eyes open wide with surprise, then her mouth begins to open and close as if she cannot breathe, a fish out of water. She tries to speak but only gurgles emerge. The thin line erupts violently and begins to spill out a torrent of crimson, darkening the entire front of her white robe. She raises her hands and begins shaking them wildly in disbelief, uncertain what exactly has happened. Her hands flit about her neck as she tries futilely to staunch the flood.

Within a few seconds her eyes take on a confused, empty look, then her lids begin to flutter. Her knees buckle and she slides to the floor in a heap, the blood pool circling her head growing rapidly in diameter under the astonished gaze of the full moon. Al-Waziri carefully steps to his right to avoid the slippery mess. "Do I have your attention now, Sire?"

The Sultan hisses, "She was an innocent child, Bashir. She did not deserve to die."

"She is a symbol, Sire, of all that is decadent in your realm. You soil yourself with a Christian whore. You offend Allah. Shameful, Sire, very shameful. Blasphemous." He shakes his head with disgust.

"Why, Bashir, why? You have been with me from the beginning. You have known me all my life. I trusted you!"

Al-Waziri barks his laugh, sneers, then says, "I am settling an old family score, Sire. My line traces back to Sultan Abdallah al-Adil, a Maghrebi Almohad. A Berber."

"Yes, yes, I know that. That was one-hundred fifty years ago, Bashir!"

"My grandfather was Prince Abd al-Wadud, Military Vizier to your grandfather, Sultan Ismail. Your grandfather had my grandfather assassinated, Sire, a blatant move by the Nasrids to secure power by suppressing the Almohads of Granada, and eliminating the Berbers of consequence at court." He hisses, "As a result, my father, a Berber prince, was forced to live his life as a servant in the Royal Stables. He sacrificed everything he had to see me climb back to power. On his death bed, I swore to my father I would avenge that insult and restore our family honor, return the rightful rulers to Granada. That is about to happen."

"My grandfather? Bashir, that had nothing to do with me!"

"I am afraid we Berbers take such insults personally, Sire. You must pay your family's debt. With your blood."

The Sultan is silent. "I assume you have had help from the Berber Imams on the Mexuar Council?"

"Oh, indeed, indeed. Imam Abd al-Malik is behind me, as are Imam Abd al-Rahim and Imam Abd al-Salam, and others. Imam al-Malik will be my Grand Vizier when I am Sultan." A rueful smile. "Imam Abd al-Rahim will be the new Grand Imam. I am afraid the sun is about to set on the Nasrids. Granada will be absorbed into the Marinid Empire. It is the only way to secure a lasting future for the kingdom. Berber rule will be restored once and for all."

Al-Waziri lifts his dagger and begins to step towards the Sultan. "It is a shame that you are unarmed, Sire. I would have enjoyed the fight, though sadly, you would have lost." The Sultan steps back and tries to circle toward the entrance, but al-Waziri positions himself to seal the exit.

"Submit to me, Sire, and I will reward you with a quick death. Resist me, and I will watch you bleed in agony for an hour while your life slips out through a thousand cuts."

Chandon steps into the hall, sees her on the floor and cries out, "Layla!"

Al-Waziri snaps about, startled. He stands halfway between Chandon and the Sultan. Chandon sees the two men and freezes.

"Chandon, that is not Layla, it is a slave girl! This man is an assassin! Help me!"

Chandon draws his wooden sword, raises it high with two hands, and assumes a battle posture.

Al-Waziri laughs derisively. "A Christian knight defending a Muslim Sultan with a wooden play-sword. How precious!" His vicious laugh echoes. "I will enjoy watching you beg for mercy, infidel, before I cut your heart out and bathe in your blood."

Without warning al-Waziri launches a lightning quick move, instantly cutting the distance between them, his dagger slashing side to side. Chandon barely has time to react. He does his best to parry the flurry of dagger thrusts, but it is difficult to see the thin blade in the moonlit room and the last slash slices into his left forearm. Chandon winces, tries to shake the pain out of his bloodied arm.

A sinister laugh. "Hurts, does it not, infidel? I shall enjoy watching you suffer, Christian." The two circle one another. The Sultan backs to the wall, an impotent spectator.

Chandon is ready for al-Waziri's second barrage, retreats backward one step, two steps, three steps to absorb the furious volley of slashes that whoosh the air a dozen times. As he successfully parries, his blood spatters the white marble. The two come to a stop, eye each other, begin to circle again.

Al-Waziri readies himself for an expected forward thrust at his chest, but Chandon instead steps forward and pivots on his right foot out of dagger reach, pirouettes, then swings his wooden sword down hard upon al-Waziri's left knee. The older man yelps, attempts to step back but instead is forced to limp his retreat. Chandon matches step, swinging hard left to right at the assassin's chest, but the dagger meets the wooden blade, slicing off the top six inches of the broadsword, the sword tip sliding to the wall.

Chandon does not hesitate but continues to rush forward, swinging at the assassin's right shoulder, is parried, thrusts at his chest, is parried again. Chandon stutter-steps to put al-Waziri's timing off balance, charges, but instead of swinging at the man's torso, whips the sword at the man's head. Al-Waziri is expecting another thrust to his chest and cannot respond quickly enough to block the blow. The sword catches him squarely across the ear, crushing his jaw socket and bursting his eardrum. Al-Waziri is dazed, stands momentarily weak-kneed and vulnerable.

Chandon moves in for the kill, swings heavy left to right into the assassin's side, breaking three ribs. Al-Waziri gasps, doubles over in pain. Chandon steps forward, shifts his sword to his left hand, then swings a massive upper-cut to the man's chin. Al-Waziri's head snaps back. A second blow breaks his cheekbone. The assassin crumples to the floor, unconscious, dagger hilt resting in his open palm.

Chandon is panting, drenched. He steps forward and with his foot prods al-Waziri's leg. He does not move. Just as Chandon is about to turn and check on the Sultan, al-Waziri uncoils his body, thrusting his dagger upward, quick as a rattler's strike. At his maximum reach the dagger point comes within two inches of Chandon's gut as he tries desperately to lean away from the on-rushing blade.

Chandon reacts instinctively with a fluid motion, pivots to his right, two-hands his sword and with all his might strikes hard where al-Waziri's shoulder meets his neck. The crisp snap tells it all. Al-Waziri's body folds into a heap, his eyes still open in surprise. His legs twitch once, twice, then still. Blood leaks from his mouth and ear, his neck already purpling. Chandon watches his chest for movement but sees that he is not breathing. He steps forward and kicks him hard in the groin to be sure.

Chandon exhales, shifts his sword back to his right hand, leans over to catch his breath. His left arm hangs limp by his side. He drops the sword. Blood is steadily dripping now to the white marble. He raises up, determined, moves to the entrance, cups his right hand to his mouth and in his loudest command voice shouts, "Royal Bodyguard, ALARM! ALARM!" He turns to check on the Sultan.

A special-toned iron bell begins its aggressive clang, screaming that the Sultan is in immediate danger; then a second, a third. Muffled commands are barked, swords and daggers drawn and readied. A distant cry echoes. "To the Sultan! To the Hall of the Ambassadors!" Heavy foot traffic reverberates into Courtyard of the Myrtles from three directions as the palace guard mobilizes and converges. As members of the Royal Bodyguard storm into the hall, the Sultan stands close beside Chandon, cradling his injured arm, bloodying himself as he applies pressure to the wound. The two are quickly surrounded. Lamps are lit, revealing the blood spattered floor and carnage.

As the guards secure the room, the Sultan says, "Zyad, I am fine, but Chandon is injured. Find Salamun and bring him. Make haste!"

"Yes, Sire!" Zyad hand-signals and two bodyguards run from the hall.

As the palace awakens and the hall begins to fill as word spreads, guards first, then viziers, then court attendants and administrators. Musa, Yazdan, Nasr, and Alonso ring Chandon, comforting him. His bleeding has eased some. Chandon is quietly describing what happened. The Sultan is surrounded by his Royal Bodyguard, fielding frantic questions in hushed whispers. The hall echoes with a hundred conversations and hasty queries.

Yazdan smiles at his friend. "Chandon, I told you that you needed practice protecting that left arm from a dagger thrust." Chandon grins weakly, nods.

Salamun is escorted into the hall, trailed by Layla, Ibn al-Khatib, then Aisha. All restraint vanished, she runs to him, envelops him. "Tell me you are not hurt, William! Tell me!"

"I am fine, Layla, fine. Just a little unexpected sword play by moonlight." He sheepishly grins. She answers with a frown, heavy with worry.

An expectant hush settles over the room as heads turn to observe the two together. Whispers then murmurs begin to echo into the upper reaches of the hall.

The Sultan surveys the two, then the crowd. He proclaims, "People of the Alhambra, my viziers, knights of the Royal Bodyguard." Heads turn collectively to his voice. He pauses to let the commotion settle, then continues.

"Let it be known to all that William Chandon saved my life this evening. He defended your foolish Sultan with his life. May Allah's favor shine upon him forever. He is a hero of Granada, a champion of the Alhambra." Whispers of surprise and cries of amazement ring out. He indicates al-Waziri's body. "Let it also be known that my Military Vizier, Prince Bashir al-Waziri, was an assassin and a traitor to his people. He killed a member of the Royal Harem. His days of eternal pain are just beginning. Before he died, he named Imam Abd al-Malik, Imam Abd al-Rahim and Imam Abd al-Salam of the Mexuar Council as his co-conspirators. They will be arrested this evening. They too are traitors, and their lives are forfeit. This Berber conspiracy will be settled tonight, once and for all. Peace and order will be restored to the palace and to the kingdom." The shouts of approval ring out.

As the Sultan speaks Salamun is tending to Chandon's arm. Layla hovers beside them. He cuts away the sleeve, examines the wound, frowns. He places a thick cloth on the deep gash to staunch the bleeding, takes Layla's hands and guides it to Chandon's arm. "Keep hard pressure on this. Both hands." She nods, obeys. "Harder. Good." Salamun continues to examine the arm, gently twisting it side to side, then flexing the wrist to test the integrity of the tendons. Chandon winces as he works.

Salamun says, "How do you feel, Young Knight?"

"Faint. Cold."

The old Jew nods. "You have lost a lot of blood." Salamun uses cloth strips to tie the bandage tight and instructs Layla to relax her grip. He wraps his cloak around Chandon's shoulders. "I will need my sewing tools to fix this properly. We must get you to the Royal Hospital." Salamun looks at Chandon, shakes his head, then chuckles. "Young Knight, what are we going to do with you! Another injury!" The wizard shakes his finger in mock anger. Chandon laughs.

Salamun continues, "Thankfully, this one is a clean cut of muscle, no damage to your tendons or bone. The two dozen stitches will hurt you, I am afraid. And we need to get some fluids into your body. But you will heal nicely I should think." Layla relaxes her worried expression. "I know just the person to nurse you back to health." The wizard beams as Layla blushes and looks down.

Ibn al-Khatib approaches to offer Chandon his best wishes for a speedy recovery, clasps both shoulders and looks into his eyes. "You have done a great deed today, Chandon, a great service to the kingdom. Granada is in your debt."

At leisure now to survey the scene, Layla drifts over to the bloody heap in the middle of the floor, trailed by Ibn al-Khatib and Chandon. Her mouth slides open as recognition then shock sinks in. She turns to her father, "Baba, why is she wearing my clothes?" Ibn al-Khatib stares at the dead girl, looks to al-Waziri's body, calculates, then glances at the Sultan. He does not answer, but instead frowns, begins to sadly shake his head from side to side. She turns to Chandon. "William, why is this poor girl wearing my clothes?"

"I thought she was you, Layla, I thought she was you." He wraps his good arm around her shoulder and whispers, "Come, Layla, we must go. Come." She looks at the floor, remains silent, but allows him to lead her out.

The Sultan motions Ibn al-Khatib, al-Bistami and Ziyad to him. The four step back to the wall and huddle for privacy. As the Sultan whispers his instructions, all three men nod in unison. Ziyad turns, gathers a half-dozen men and departs.

# Rendezvous

3 June 1368. The two men sit side-by-side on silk pillows in front of the twin key-hole windows forming the exquisite mirador at the northern end of the Hall of the Two Sisters. The silence stretches comfortably as they sip their mint tea, pensive, both staring down into the inviting lush green of the Garden of the Lindaraja, the Sultan's enclosed private garden retreat within the Palace of the Lions. The Lindaraja fountain, the largest in the Alhambra, produces a pleasing sound of pearl on stone, the beads of cool sparkling water throwing diamonds into the late morning sun. When they weary of the dance, the diamonds slide down the white marble and drop into the collecting basin, a refreshing summer rain.

Three cypresses, slender as young girls, tower above them to their right. Flower beds are swollen with a riot of reds and yellows, whites and blues. A pair of orange trees stands to their left, with fruit the size of walnuts. A solitary lemon nestles in the foreground, lonesome. A shock of iridescent-pink bougainvillea scales the corner of the courtyard then rests its elbows on the roof-line with a contented grin, proud of its climbing skills. The birdsong is loud, insistent. The rich tangle of trills and sharp whistles, gawks and coos, betrays a dozen species, perhaps more. The garden's harmony is unmistakable, intensely soothing. No human is in sight; nothing but organic sounds of the Earth, of paradise, of al-Jannah.

Ibn al-Khatib is the first to break the trance. His words are soft, just above a whisper, so as not to disturb the tranquility. "Sire, I have given Chandon and Layla my blessing to marry." The Sultan remains silent, his eyes fixed on the garden. "Of his own free will, Chandon has decided to embrace Islam and join the faithful. I am instructing him in the ways of the Prophet. He is a quick learner, eager. Chandon will soon be Andalusi, Sire, a knight of Granada." He hesitates. "I have spoken to the Grand Imam, Sire, and I have told him of these plans. He approves. He will preside over Chandon's conversion ceremony and their wedding." The Sultan stares into space. "They are to be married by the beginning of the fall." The silence stretches out.

"Chandon is a good man, Lisan al-Din. I owe him my life. He will make a fine knight." He hesitates, searching for the right words. "Chandon and Layla have my blessing. May Allah's grace be upon their marriage, and may you be granted the joy of many grandchildren."

"Thank you, Sire, I will let them know. They will be very happy."

The Sultan seems troubled by something, and once again the silence stretches, but now with an edge of tension. Both men's eyes remain glued to the garden. The Sultan sighs. "Lisan al-Din, I owe you an explanation."

"There is no need for you to explain anything, Sire."

"There is. I received what I believed was a letter from Layla, telling me that she had reconsidered my offer to join the Royal Harem. She insisted that she would not be a concubine, but instead wanted to be my wife. She told me to meet her in the Hall of the Ambassadors. At midnight." He shakes his head with disgust. "Like a stupid fool, I did not see the obvious trap. I dismissed my guards and went to see her." He hisses, "I am a lustful idiot." He pauses, then continues. "I am the one responsible..." He halts as his voice starts to quaver, then composes himself and begins again. "I am the one responsible for my sweet Auria's murder. She was only a child."

Ibn al-Khatib's reply is barely audible. "I see."

"I am ashamed of my actions, Lisan al-Din. I have dishonored you, my friend. Please forgive me. Had Chandon known why I was there, he would have thought twice about saving me."

Only a whispered, "Perhaps."

"I have instructed Qasim to remove all of the concubines from the Royal Harem. I am recommitting myself to my three wives. I will focus on being a better husband, a better father. A better Sultan. I wanted you to know that."

"Thank you, Sire. There is no ill will between us. You have repaid the debt by giving Layla and Chandon your blessing."

The two men turn and look into each other's eyes, exchange silent understanding. Both men nod, smile weakly.

"Good. Thank You, Lisan al-Din."

Ibn al-Khatib moves on to matters of state. "Tell me about Bashir's family, Sire."

"Our prince was left outside the city gates for all to see. His body swelled tight in the sun then split like a gourd and rotted, a traitor's fate. The vultures picked him clean, and his bones were scattered in the hills. May Allah bring him an eternity of torture in hell. His entire family, any that carry his name or blood, will be exiled."

"I see. The Berber conspirators?"

"Yes, our Berber conspirators. The Mexuar Council passed judgment yesterday. The trial was refreshingly quick. The three imams will be executed next week, their heads displayed above the city gate, a message to any who may still consider meddling profitable. To those Berbers remaining on the Council, the conditions for their sustained membership have been...clearly explained... Peace and tolerance will return to the Alhambra."

"Good."

"I may even get to enjoy a glass of wine from time to time." Both men grin.

"Have there been any repercussions yet from the Marinids, Sire?"

"We have heard nothing. Complete silence from Fez. But I suspect they value our new trade agreement too much to make waves. The treaty will hold."

"I agree."

The Sultan's mood lightens and he breaks into a smile. "I have a surprise for the Alhambra, Lisan al-Din."

"Sire?"

"In celebration of the end of this Berber conspiracy, I will throw a grand feast in the Generalife. At the next full moon. I have already begun preparations. Food and music, poetry and dance. A proper party." He offers a coy grin. "And wine. The entire court will be invited. It is time the palace enjoyed itself a little. I will also honor Chandon for his service to Granada."

Ibn al-Khatib nods his approval. "An excellent idea, Sire."

"It occurs to me, Lisan al-Din, that perhaps you might announce the betrothal of Layla and Chandon at the feast. It would be fitting."

Ibn al-Khatib's smile grows. "A fine idea, Sire. Yes, a fine idea. They will be very pleased."

She stands frozen by the open window, hands on her hips, grinning, mesmerized by the scene in the courtyard. The two men sit on pillows in the shade at the edge of the pool. Ibn al-Khatib holds the open Quran in his left hand, right index finger tracing the elegant Arabic script. He reads a single line aloud then stops. Without looking up, he lifts his right palm, inviting Chandon to repeat the line, which he does. Ibn al-Khatib corrects the pronunciation of one word then a second. Chandon tries it again. Satisfied, Ibn al-Khatib's index finger returns to the text and he reads the next line, lifts his palm, inviting Chandon to follow. No correction this time, just a subtle nod of the head. “Jayed, jayed.” *Good, good.*

Chandon smiles, proud of himself. “Shokran.” *Thank you.*

They continue. After three more lines, Chandon interrupts, asks for a clarification of meaning. As Ibn al-Khatib lays the book in his lap, his hands begin to dance in explanation.

Her smile relaxes with the realization that his practice will continue for at least another hour. Her usual morning lessons with Chandon have all but evaporated on these days, her presence replaced by her father. The two men have recitation practice three mornings a week, followed by an afternoon of open discussion on a wide variety of topics on alternating days; various Hadith, an exploration of the nuances of Sharia, dissection of obscure Islamic protocols, the contrast of European and Arabic culture. Any and all questions are fair game, though Ibn al-Khatib insists Chandon begin all questions in Arabic, switching to Castilian only when he is desperate.

Chandon’s knowledge of Granadine culture is advancing rapidly, and his Arabic, under constant scrutiny, is honed to a fine point. By the end of their afternoon sessions they inevitably transition to agriculture, medicine, architecture, science, topics of great interest to both men. From time to time Chandon will unexpectedly ask a question about Layla as a young girl, or her mother. Ibn al-Khatib indulges him, but feeds him only tiny morsels. They laugh often. Both men have come to enjoy their time together, a source of great satisfaction to Layla.

Chandon’s arm has healed, the four-inch long pink ribbon tattoo is all that remains of the now-famous moonlit duel. He has eased back into sparring lessons with Yazdan and Musa, a welcome diversion for the three friends. Chandon is invited now to share the al-Khatib evening meal and he joins Ibn al-Khatib, Layla and Aisha for sunset prayer in their suite, an irresistible teaching moment for Ibn al-Khatib.

Layla remains silent and meek during these instructions, then beams Chandon a wicked smile when her father is not looking. Always observant, Aisha frowns at the boldness of her mistress, scolds her with her eyes, but cannot suppress her grin. She has warmed to Chandon, likes him, and has begun to relax in her role as chaperone, allowing the two a bit of space when there are no prying eyes about. His evening bodyguards have been reassigned.

Chandon and Layla ride in the Vega several days a week now, Yazdan and Musa in attendance but discreetly remaining out of earshot. As Chandon walks about the palace people stop and whisper, nod their amazement, and for most, voice their approval.

The midnight rendezvous? As inevitable as the sunrise, as necessary as blood to the body, rain to a garden. Intimate and bold and tortuous as ever, perhaps more so, but with an overarching ease now, a certain sense of trajectory. Ibn al-Khatib has made his peace with it and arranges to not fall asleep on his couch on those evenings. He smiles as he hears her light footstep deep in the night, the door latch click shut. He conjures Danah to share an ancient memory.

Layla smiles with her sudden realization, turns and races from the room to have Aisha put water to boil. A few minutes later she emerges with a tray of hot mint tea and dried fruit. She opens the door, descends the stairs, pauses for a moment to let her eyes adjust to the brightness, then turns left and approaches the two men.

Chandon is mid-sentence when he sees her. He botches the next three words, then halts. Ibn al-Khatib frowns, puzzled, then he looks up, sees his daughter, glances to Chandon and reluctantly grins.

"Daughter, you are distracting my pupil."

"Baba, I thought you two might enjoy some tea and fruit."

Chandon smiles. "Thank you, Layla. The distraction is a blessing. Your father has already taken me through half of the Quran this morning. We may be finished by sunset." Both men chuckle.

She bows, sets the tray down in front of them, coyly grins, then says, "I will leave you to your studies, Sir William." She winks as her father looks down to pick up his book. "Baba, if his Arabic is getting sloppy, just let me know and I will add more lessons to his study list." The two men laugh.

"Certainly, Daughter. Now leave us, Layla, we have work to do. Shoo! Shoo!" He grins at her as he waves her away.

As Ibn al-Khatib returns his eyes to the book, Layla flashes that smile, then chases it whimsically by sticking the tip of her tongue out. Chandon beams and winks, then drinks her in as she walks away. Ibn al-Khatib reads the next line then waits patiently for Chandon to follow. After a protracted moment he does so.

# Fireworks

The dusk exhales, reluctantly yielding to the insistent night, the laden palate of orange, crimson and purple only a thin jagged rim now on the distant mountains at the western edge of the Vega. The old man's greedy gaze above the eastern horizon is already impossibly large and luminous in its perfect spherical symmetry, a golden ghost done with patient waiting, ready to come out and play. Not a wisp of a cloud blemishes the blackening sky.

With the day's last gasp, the Granadine swelter relinquishes control to the cool, refreshing breeze that tiptoes in from the snow-capped Sierra Nevada. Birds gawk and bicker, fidget in their roosts, youngsters complaining as always about their early bedtimes, refusing to hush and settle in. The anxious bird-chatter evaporates as darkness seeps into the landscape and stills the scene.

Ibn al-Khatib, Salamun, Layla and Chandon have left the palace and strolled leisurely through the Partal Gardens, arriving at the Spiked Tower just above the Outskirts Gate on the northern wall of the Alhambra.

They are dressed in their most formal court attire, Ibn al-Khatib in a full length Granadine blue robe, white silk sleeves and gold mantle, thick gold cording looping shoulder to wrist, intricate patterns of Arabic gold embroidery splayed diagonally across his chest. Colors of a Grand Vizier.

Salamun looks like a caricature of his wizardly self, his flowing turmeric-yellow robe a pleasing backdrop to his long white beard. A large embroidered Star of David rests proudly over his heart. Two serpents twine a winged staff on both shoulders in royal purple, the Caduceus of Mercury, the unmistakable stamp of the medical arts.

Chandon is dressed as a Granadine knight of the court, in light tan breeches, thigh-length white short-robe with Granadine blue trim, red sash, a dark brown short-cape over his shoulders, wooden sword in its jeweled hilt at his side. Dashing.

Layla wears a fitted, full length cream-colored cotton gown, twelve gold buttons running in front from neck to foot, a thin strip of emerald silk trim just covering her fine leather shoes. Swirls of gold stitching rest delicately upon her shoulders and two-inch thick rings of emerald alternate with cream as they flow down her sleeves to her wrists, wonderfully accenting her eyes. A small, ornate piece of sheer silk lace is elaborately woven into her hair, but her chestnut curls spill full and loose down to her waist, bunched only twice with a thin emerald ribbon, once below her shoulder, and once in the small of her back. Tiny gold hoop earrings hang from her ears. Chandon has to will himself to keep his eyes off her. Unsuccessfully. She is absolutely radiant.

The four stand at the edge of the wall, admiring the sun's dying breath. They turn to survey the Generalife. It is already obvious this will be no common night. A deep ravine separates the Alhambra from the expanse of Generalife. After exiting the Outskirts Gate beside the Spiked Tower, the narrow road, protected on both sides by five-foot high stone walls, hugs the palace for a short stretch then bends around the eastern end of the ravine and wraps back to the west, entering the expansive terraced gardens of the Generalife from below. The road winds up the slope, leading to the entrance into the palace complex. This is the preferred transit path between the Alhambra and Generalife for the Sultan, the Royal Family and his special guests. Off-limits to all others.

At the far western end of the Generalife, perched high over the Darro valley to catch the cool breeze, is the Sultan's summer palace retreat, a compact set of buildings with enclosed garden spaces and water features. The palace has predictably plain exteriors, exquisitely ornate interiors. Several of the new water gardens have been completed just this week with decorations of with Zamrak's latest poetry.

As the gardens climb the gentle slope, the voluptuously flowered terraces transform into a maze of sculpted cypress privacy hedges, niches and fountains, then give way to progressively larger trees, transitioning finally into a line of thin, tall cypresses. Above this begins the Royal Orchard, which rises on up the high ridge beyond, wraps around the mountain and continues on. The lower half of the gardens of the Generalife are well lit, which is highly unusual. Torches line not only the road, but also the major paths through the garden maze, inviting people to roam and explore.

A large central gathering square at the western end of the garden just in front of the entrance to the palace complex is dotted with tall, multi-tiered oil lamps. Low-slung tables filled with food and drink line two edges of the square. Dozens of large Persian carpets cover the ground, a menagerie of pillows spread out upon them. Rows of servants stand just beyond of the scene, ready to begin their work.

Music can just barely be heard, a whisper on the horizon. Granadine blue and gold banners wiggle in the light breeze from the tops of the buildings, and large blue, white and red silk banners hang from the walls. The palace complex is well lit, as are the enclosed gardens. The scene is inviting even from this distance.

Only the most priviledged of court have ever been inside the gardens of the Generalife, fewer still the palace complex: the extended Royal Family, the Sultan's viziers and their families, select imams, trusted advisors, close friends.

The gardens of the Generalife have been a private fiefdom for Layla for a substantial portion of her youth. Since returning from Fez, she has roamed the intricate maze ceaselessly, a soothing balm to her restlessness, her loneliness, and the fierce hormone-tortures of puberty. It is a place to hide, to crack open a volume of forbidden knowledge without fear of discovery, to daydream. She knows the softest places to lay hidden and nap, the best spots from which to spy unseen. She has memorized the garden's deepest secrets.

As the foursome look down upon the scene they see that the well-dressed crowds are already starting to fill the narrow road heading towards the palace complex, the lead elements just now approaching the square. Knots of unmistakable crimson robes of the Mexuar Council dot the crowd. The deliberately plain, repressed attire of the Berbers stands out, their tightly wound turbans, their sullen bearded faces, their curtained wives. But the Berbers are in the minority.

Most of the crowd is dressed in their very best court finery, excited and ready to feast, to celebrate and laugh. Furtive, hushed whispers buzz about the women. Truncated giggles ring out, followed by quick, knowing smiles, mouths ovaled with delicious gossip, eyes widening with disbelief as a juicy tidbit is offered then chased by a furious propagation of cupped whispers. Children let out to play. The sense of excitement, of anticipation, is palpable. Most of the men walk in indulgent silence, formal and stiff, absorbing the scene as their plump wives chatter on.

In the distance an assembly of trumpets begin their shrill proclamation, announcing the guests. The insect-like buzz flares in intensity. Suddenly all eyes are drawn upward as a dozen streaks of gold sparkle arc high against the black sky, chased by a series of sharp pops. Oooohs. Another round. Ahhhhs. Fireworks to commence the festivities.

Ibn al-Khatib turns to Salamun, grins, then looks admiringly at Chandon and Layla, beams his approval, and says, "Children, shall we?" They both laugh, bow with mock seriousness, and the four head to the stairs to exit the Outskirts Gate.

Most of the court is seated now on their pillows in the garden square, filling the rich carpets in thick clusters. There is an unstated but obvious pecking order to the arrangement, a careful but subtle delineation of social strata. Courtiers discreetly inquire name or rank as the guests arrive, directing them to their appropriate places. A special carpet placed closest to the palace is reserved for the Sultan and his viziers. Radiating outwards in a broadening half circle are special carpets for the viziers' wives and their extended families, a single large carpet for the Royal Wives, the Sultana, and their attending eunuchs and servants, who relish the time outside their sequester even though a thin rope and several guards cordon them off from the crowd.

There are four carpets for the Mexuar Council and their families. Berbers sit with Berbers, then wealthy patrons and silk merchants and their wives. Al-Mussib and several of the Sufi masters from the madrasa recline with a handful of their most promising students. Majahid al-Khayyat and Constancia from the Maristan are present, as well as an assortment of ambassadors, various military attaches, political officials from nearby towns, high-level court administrators and functionaries of all shapes and sizes.

There are perhaps one-hundred fifty all told. The Sultan is nowhere to be seen. There is not a single child anywhere. The members of the Royal Bodyguard, as always armed to the teeth, stand stiff and expressionless at a dozen strategic points, eyes predictably darting about.

As the guests finish settling, servants sporting large trays of delicacies begin to busy about, stopping to lower their wares to gawking eyes, short excited laughs, giddy ooohs and ahhhs of surprise. Other attendants carry large amphora of cool, crisp watered wine. Most of the imams and all of the Berbers frown their answers and shake their heads vigorously with disapproval, but many of the court indulge in the revelry for a taste of scandalous luxury, a welcome respite to years of fundamentalist tension. No harm in a cup, perhaps two.

As the crowd settles in to enjoy the food and festivities, an ensemble of musicians seated at the edge of the square launches into Andalusi folk songs. A lute, two guitars, a flute, a pipe, three hand-drums, a cymbal, and a lap harp. The crowd quiets and heads begin to nod with warm familiarity as their smiles widen. The male cantor eases forward all stiff and serious, squeezes his eyes shut, then begins to weave his sweet, sad, melodic chant into the folds of the music. An ancient dream of Damascus, a palm-lined oasis rich with flowing water, the glory of a cool, star-studded desert night, the sweet, tender promise of a Arabian maiden.

After three songs, the singer stops, bows to the approving applause, and withdraws. There is a quick tic, tic, tic of the cymbal as the music resumes, shifted up-tempo, the fury of drums stepping forward with purpose and weaving a dense pattern into the air. A trio of veiled dancers bursts from the shadows to rousing applause. The young women begin to theatrically sway their taut, nubile bodies to the music, their movements choreographed and timed to perfect precision. There is a confluence of flowing sheer veils, billowing pants, lithe arms and legs. Their beautiful faces are only hinted at, coyly layered just beyond recognition. The dancers seductively bend and curve to the plush rhythms. All but the Berber men beam their approval in silence. A few of the boldest whoop and holler. The wives sit hushed and admiring, some wistful for their lost youth.

As the music begins to methodically accelerate and energize the deepening night, the dancers' generous hips suggestively swing and sway beneath their stationary bellies, their outstretched hands and bare arms stretching elegantly in tandem, producing hard swallows in even the most stoic of the men.

Two more veil-dances and the music ends to a loud chorus of approval. As the dancers leap back into the shadows, the food and drink attendants return to their stations. A quartet of unseen trumpets blare, lending an air of crisp formality. A double line of the red-robed Royal Bodyguard, each carrying a torch, exits the palace gate, entering the apex of the garden square, where they halt. All rise as the whispering ceases. Eyes track to the Sultan, who steps forward in his regal splendor, an explosion of blue, red and gold. A handsome man. Regal.

The courtier opens with a hypnotic chant, "Bismillah ir-Rahman ir-Rahim." *In the Name of Allah, Most Gracious, Most Compassionate.* The air is still. The courtier commences in a loud, formal voice of announcement, "People of Granada. His Royal Highness, Muhammad V, son of Yusef, ruler of al-Andalus, eighth

Sultan of the Kingdom of Granada, builder of the Alhambra, elder of the Nasrid clan, defender of the faith, welcomes you!"

The crowd bows in unison, then erupts in a massive cheer. The Sultan breaks into an easy smile as he nods his welcome. After the noise dies away, he beckons them to sit. When the crowd is settled, he raises his hands, palms up, and says, "People of Granada. My people. Today we celebrate the glory of al-Andalus, the many triumphs of our ancestors, our bright future. Let us thank Allah for the many blessings he showers upon us." Another rousing cheer.

After a pause to let the air clear, the Sultan begins again in a more serious tone. "My friends, as you know, the kingdom has recently endured the betrayal of a close and trusted man. My vizier, my friend. But the conspiracy he wrongly championed has been defeated. Never shall it raise its ugly head again. His Berber co-conspirators have been executed by mandate of the Mexuar Council, and their families exiled. The stain of their sin has been washed from the Vega forever. Granada has returned to peace. Tolerance now prevails and a lasting order has been restored." Another massive cheer. Before this dies out the Sultan looks skyward and cries, "Allahu Ackbar!" *Allah is Supreme!* The crowd echoes him.

The Sultan continues. "As many of you know, a foreigner at court, an English knight of Brittany, Sir William Chandon, risked his own life to save mine. He single-handedly thwarted the conspiracy and preserved my reign, the Nasrid lineage of the Kingdom of Granada, and the splendor of the Alhambra. I owe this man a great debt. Granada owes this man a great debt." The Sultan turns to face Chandon, indicates that he should come forward. Chandon stands, looking uncomfortable in the spotlight, then begins to weave his way through the crowd to join the Sultan. Layla, Salamun, and Ibn al-Khatib beam their approval. As Chandon walks forward, the Sultan turns, motions Zyad to him and whispers a few words. Zyad turns to an attendant, retrieves the object and comes forward to stand beside the Sultan.

As Chandon arrives, he stops and bows. The Sultan smiles. "Friends of Granada. Months ago, Chandon asked a favor of me. He asked for a wooden sword, a play sword, so that he might sport with my bodyguards to sharpen his skills. It was with that same wooden sword that he vanquished the traitor and saved my life. Today, friends, I present Chandon with the sword of my grandfather, Sultan Ismail, may Allah rest his soul. Behold 'Barq' (*Lightening*), treasure of the Nasrid clan."

Zyad two-hands the Sultan the priceless, jewel-encrusted broadsword, the crescent-shaped hilt emerging from the scabbard unmistakably Granadine. Ancient steel. The Sultan holds the scabbard with one hand and with the other draws the blade with a crisp metallic tear and lifts it high for the crowd to see. The steel is engraved with elaborate Arabic script. Muted 'oooohs' and 'ahhhhs' erupt. The Sultan returns the blade to its bejeweled home, pivots and with two open palms presents the sword to Chandon, who bows, accepts the prize with the wide-eyed expression of a surprised child.

"Never again will Chandon carry a wooden sword in my court. Barq shall stand ready by his side wherever he goes."

Chandon grips the sword, extracts it six inches, then looks up to scan the crowd. He smiles and re-sheathes the blade. "I am deeply honored, Sire. I place my life, and this precious sword, in your service." He bows as the crowd roars.

The Sultan proclaims in a loud voice, "The only victor is Allah!" The crowd echoes him, "The only victor is Allah!"

As the crowd quiets, he says, "Friends of Granada, there is another piece of joyous news to share this evening." He motions Ibn al-Khatib and Layla forward. The crowd turns, puzzled, and tracks father and daughter as they approach the Sultan. The two formally bow, then take their places to Chandon's right, turn and face the crowd to a background drone of whispers.

"Granada's Grand Vizier, Lisan al-Din ibn al-Khatib, polymath of al-Andalus, my most trusted counselor, has an important announcement to make." The Sultan takes a half step back.

Ibn al-Khatib clears his throat. "People of Granada, these past weeks I have served as teacher to William Chandon. I have carefully observed his mind and his heart. He has learned to speak Arabic. He can recite many passages of the Quran. He is learning the Hadith." He pauses for effect. "Friends, Chandon now desires to embrace Islam. He will join us in faith at the end of the summer under the blessing of the Grand Imam." Murmurs of shock, then slowly accelerating head nods, then a delayed, loud chorus of approval rings out. Chandon reaches for Layla's hand to steady her.

Ibn al-Khatib waits for silence to return. "In addition, Chandon has declared his love for my daughter, Layla. She returns his love. I am pleased to announce the betrothal of Chandon and Layla. They will marry early this fall, with my happy blessings for a wonderful life together, a life filled with love. May Allah bless them with many children." Stunned silence, then a spontaneous eruption of applause, loud cat-calls and shouts of approval. The two find each other's eyes, beam.

As calm returns, the Sultan motions to Prince Farqad al-Bistami, who stands ten paces to his left. Layla and Ibn al-Khatib step to the side, but the Sultan touches Chandon, indicates he should stay. The imposing gristled knight moves forward, bows, and takes his place beside the Sultan. The Sultan smiles then rests his left hand on al-Bistami's shoulder and his right hand on Chandon's shoulder and begins scanning the crowd as he lets the anticipation build.

Chandon is clearly puzzled. The Sultan continues. "I have one final announcement, friends. Prince al-Bistami will from this day forward assume the duties of Military Vizier of the Kingdom of Granada." Al-Bistami smiles, nods his acceptance. The Sultan turns to his right. "And from this day forward, William Chandon, servant of Granada, knight of the court, bearer of Barq, defender of the faith, soon to be husband of the most beautiful maiden of Granada, will assume the duties of Military Vice-Vizier of the kingdom." Stunned silence.

Chandon's eyes widen. He turns to make quick eye contact with Layla, whose bright smile collapses. She shakes her head side to side, a portrait first of concern, then of anger. As Ibn al-Khatib tracks Chandon's eyes to his daughter his own smile recedes. The Sultan and al-Bistami turn and face Chandon, expectant. The crowd holds its breath. Chandon hesitates just a moment too long, then bows. "Sire, I am pleased to serve Granada in any means you see fit. I am your humble servant." He bows again. The Sultan raises both arms to the crowd to elicit a thunderous applause.

"People of Granada. Let us join in a feast the Alhambra will remember for many years to come. Please make yourselves at home and explore my spectacular gardens. Dip your hands and feet into the cool water. Enjoy the fireworks. Our court poet, Zamrak, has been locked away, composing, all month. He will be reciting his new ghazal in the restored Water Garden Courtyard at midnight. Do not miss it! Enjoy yourselves, my friends!"

As the Sultan steps to the harem carpet to greet his wives, the musicians resume their playing. The servers return in droves, now bearing platters of freshly grilled game, an assortment of vegetables, piles of steaming loaves, fruits of all kinds, delicate sweets, more watered wine. To round out the meal, a refreshing icy slush of neon-pink pomegranate juice cut with wine is served, made from cut ice hauled in at great expense from the peaks of the Sierra Nevada. The garden is quickly enveloped in a hearty, dull roar.

The stars sparkle their approval. The old man's ghostly grin widens, high in the sky now, as he throws his ethereal twilight glow upon the scene. Every few minutes, golden sparkle tails of rockets arc high across the black sky, chased by a sharp retort.

As Chandon approaches Layla, her expression is serious, tense. Her temper stands close by, cocked and dangerous, and he knows from experience to tread lightly. He lifts her chin to connect their eyes. He leans forward, kisses her cheek, then whispers into her ear, "You are so beautiful." She frowns. He presses on. "There was nothing to be done, Layla. I could not refuse the Sultan's wishes. Surely you see that."

She pleads with her brilliant emeralds, then adds, "I understand, William. But this will bring you closer to war and death, not closer to love and Allah. Me. You must appreciate this."

"I do. But I had no choice. Look on the bright side. This new status will allow us to establish ourselves at court, have an apartment of our own in the palace."

"Where we live is of no consequence to me, William, so long as we are together."

He sighs. "Yes, I agree. I am sure my role will be only advisory. I know European tactics, and I can aid Granada's armies with planning and preparations for defense."

She is unconvinced. "I know them, William. No matter what they say or what promises they make, there will come a time, a week from now, a year from now, a decade from now, when you will be called upon to fight. That is what scares me. That day will surely come, William, mark my words."

He inches closer to her, turns serious, and whispers, "I will never let anyone or anything harm you, Layla. Ever. I will always be by your side, Layla. I promised you." He lifts her chin again. Her eyes are full now. She tries hard to smile but can't quite manage it.

Their privacy is interrupted as a small crowd converges around them, pushes tight to wish them well. Hands are pumped, backs are slapped, formal kisses applied to Layla's cheeks. In a few moments she is smiling once again. She laughs loud as she blushes bright scarlet at some bawdy advice offered by her elder cousin.

Yazdan, Musa, Nasr and Alonso, all sporting wide smiles, approach the congratulatory crowd surrounding the couple. Yazdan announces, "Chandon, you dog! Holding out on us, eh? How did you manage to snare the fairest maiden in all of Granada." Heads pivot in unison, then loud laughs.

The crowd parts as Yazdan approaches Layla, kneels before her and kisses her hand. She flashes that smile to a chorus of "ooohs." Chandon laughs. "Easy, Yazdan, easy, she is spoken for, sir."

Yazdan grins. "My Lady, the Royal Bodyguard requires the presence of your betrothed for a special ceremony. May we borrow him for a short while?"

Layla looks to Chandon, eyebrows lifted. "Certainly, sir. Provided he is returned to me in one piece."

They all laugh. "Of course, my Lady, of course. Consider it done."

She turns and bows to Chandon. "Sir."

He returns the bow. "My Lady." He steps close to her, whispers, "Do not worry. I will meet you a little later at the palace water garden. Before the poetry recital."

She offers an impish smile, says to the crowd, "Do not be late, sir, or I may have to find another's company." A chorus of laughter.

He winks, then turns and follows Yazdan.

Ibn al-Khatib has sought out al-Bistami. He waits until the crowd clears, then steps close for a word. "Congratulations, Farqad, I am happy for you. You are very deserving of this new role and I know you will serve Granada well. I am pleased."

"Thank you, Lisan al-Din. It is an honor I do not take lightly. I look forward to serving with you."

Ibn al-Khatib searches for the right words. "I must say that I was surprised by the Sultan's decision regarding Chandon. He had not told me of this."

"Yes, I know. He wanted it to be a surprise for you both, a fitting honor to lay upon Chandon's and Layla's betrothal."

"I see. You approve of Chandon as your Vice-Vizier?"

"Of course. Chandon and I did not get off to good start, but that was an unfortunate consequence of war. I have come to see that he is an honorable man, a good knight. He is brave and skilled with a sword. A fine leader. He will be a formidable asset to the kingdom."

"No doubt." There is an awkward pause before Ibn al-Khatib continues. "But Farqad, you realize that as a Christian converting to Islam, Chandon will be at great risk in battle. A price will be upon his head, and no ransom will ever be offered if he is captured. I have no desire to see my daughter, your niece, taste the cruel fate of the widow."

Al-Bistami nods. "Yes, yes, I know. The Sultan and I discussed this, Lisan al-Din. We agreed that Chandon's role will be confined to an advisory capacity. He will not lead troops into battle."

"Good. Thank you, Farqad, you have put my mind at ease."

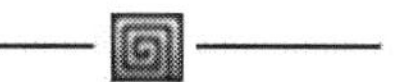

Despite the joy of their betrothal announcement, the unexpected news of Chandon's new position weighs heavily on Layla. Alone at last, she slips into a pensive mood, craving solitude, some space to think. She wanders to the Water Garden Courtyard, but at the entrance she stops, sees the assembling poetry crowd, and instead opts for privacy. She turns, walks past the entrance, angles left, then right, then left again, winding her way through the garden beds, finally entering the compact, walled Cypress Courtyard via a small, key-hole door. She has been here many times, and it is pleasingly empty. A lone torch stands in each corner, producing rippling four-cornered shadows in the diffuse light. Thankfully, the courtyard remains undiscovered by the festive crowd.

A lone cypress, ancient and proud, stands to her right just inside the wall, lending the space its name. She tracks upward along its trunk to its full height, the very top lost in the blackness of the night. The massive tree leans out and over the courtyard, protective, possessive. In front of her, at the far end of the courtyard, is the northern-most palace building, a two-storied structure with a double portico and columned horseshoe arches. The primary housing for guests and servants.

The courtyard has two inset scalloped fountains at either end of an elegant, L-shaped reflecting pool. Bougainvillea climbs the walls and there are several orange and lemon trees, sculpted myrtle hedges, all manner of roses. The space is wonderfully fragrant. She steps further into the courtyard to the edge of the pool, breathes the refreshing night air deeply into her lungs, holds it, then exhales. She is transported to her childhood, carefree days spent wandering the Generalife's gardens. The muted fountain murmur is soothing. Peace begins to sink its roots into her bones, unkinking her worry. Time stretches out pleasantly.

Then, a soft, "You look stunning tonight."

Layla starts at the voice. Heart racing, she whips around, then tries to compose herself, force a calm demeanor. "Zamrak."

He is eight paces away and cutting the distance between them. He scans her head to toe with an air of entitlement. "I have a few minutes before the recital. The crowd is just too much to bear."

She settles herself and answers in a casual voice. "Yes. For me also."

He stops just in front of her, closer than decorum would allow, but she holds her ground, locks onto his gaze.

Silence. He sighs and offers a resigned, "You are betrothed now."

"Yes."

"I could have made you very happy, Layla. I would have cherished you, given you anything you desired, even celebrated you in my poems. We were meant for each other. You are all that I have ever dreamed of, Layla."

She sees the torture, softens. "Zamrak...I do not doubt your feelings for me. But I love another."

"Yes. Another." He shakes his head then grimaces. "A Christian knight. Your children should be Arab, Layla, not English."

Her emerald eyes harden. "Careful, Zamrak."

He senses the danger and backtracks, adjusts his tone. "I wish you well. But I will not stop loving you, Layla. Ever."

"That would be a real shame. You deserve happiness, Zamrak. There are many maidens in Granada who would welcome your advances."

"But not you."

"No."

A tense silence stretches out.

"You should come listen to my ghazal. I have labored hard on it. I think it is my finest work yet. It is a poem of beauty and desire, of ecstasy and torture, of unrequited love. It is a song of lament for a beautiful woman." He locks onto her eyes. "It is about you, of course."

Softly, "I see."

"Do not worry, you will be the only one to recognize it for what it truly is. And perhaps your father. Chandon will not."

"Chandon will not what?"

They both turn and see him enter the courtyard, Barq by his side. Zamrak steps away from her. Layla walks quickly to him. She says, "Darling, I have missed you." She kisses his cheek, but he is not smiling.

Zamrak is silent now, his face cold stone.

Chandon's expression is serious, dangerous even, his gaze fixed on the other man. "Zamrak, there something you wished to say to me?"

Stubborn silence. "No. Nothing. I was just offering Layla my congratulations on your betrothal." He bows.

Still no smile. "We thank you. I look forward to hearing your poem."

"Yes, well, I should be going. I need to prepare."

Chandon nods as the other man passes. Chandon tracks his movements until he is gone, then turns to Layla, concerned. "Layla?"

"I am fine." She considers her words. "Zamrak is not a bad man, William. But he has much to learn about women. And love. I feel sorry for him. But do not worry, he will cause us no trouble."

"Good. Then I will let it rest." His mood brightens and he beams.

His smile is contagious. She asks, "Yazdan's surprise?"

Chandon chuckles. "I am now officially an honorary member of the Royal Bodyguard, complete with my own red robe and a special dagger." He lifts his cloak to reveal the jeweled sheath. "And they want to celebrate our marriage with a feast in our honor. With your permission, of course."

Her smile widens. "Certainly."

It simultaneously occurs to both of them that they are alone for the first time this night. They both glance to the entrance, then, satisfied, exchange a knowing look. She slides forward into his arms, followed by a lingering kiss.

After a moment they part, all smiles. Chandon says, "So, my Lady, may I escort you to the recital?"

"It would be my pleasure, sir."

The Water Garden Courtyard is packed. The Sultan stands beside Zamrak at the far end of the long, narrow reflecting pool. The crowd buzzes, waiting for the recital to commence. Having arrived late, Chandon and Layla stand side by side under the arched portico just inside the courtyard entrance, at the far back of the crowd.

A nearby bell gongs twelve times, signaling midnight, and the crowd begins to hush with anticipation.

Chandon has to tiptoe to see. Layla is hopelessly too short, and instead finds herself staring at Chandon. She enjoys observing him when he is unaware of being watched. Her heart swells with love. He looks to the end of the courtyard with an eager smile, oblivious. As the moments pass, her gaze turns more intense as she continues to contemplate him. Her heart starts to pound. Decision made, a hint of a mischievous grin eases onto her face. She edges closer to him, slips her arm into his, leans in and whispers into his ear.

"William?"

He turns to her. "Yes, Layla?"

"Come with me. I have something to show you."

His eyebrows lift. "Right now?"

She flashes that smile. "Yes, right now. Come."

Puzzled, he shrugs and they retreat from the courtyard. She leads him left and they are gone.

They hold hands as they walk towards the Cypress Courtyard, but bypass the entrance and instead walk through the twists and turns of the garden maze, then turn left. There are no lit torches here, but the full moon allows them to see once their eyes adjust. She stops at the base of a flared staircase. The pleasing sound of rushing water surrounds them, the cool breeze refreshing.

Chandon's mouth falls open.

Layla says, "The famous Water Stairway."

Rising up two flights is an elaborate stone and brick stairway, white-washed walls three-feet high on either side, but instead of handrails, a trough of cool water rushes down.

"Amazing."

"Yes. It has always delighted me. Few have seen it."

He slides behind her. They admire the moonlit scene in silence for several minutes. Without touching her, he leans down and breathes into her ear. She shivers. As he tenderly kisses the nape of her neck, he wraps his arms around her, eases his hands onto her belly and pulls her tight against him. They stand motionless, enjoying the view.

"I am glad you brought me to see this."

"There is more. Come."

They join hands and climb the stairs. At the top they turn right, enter a compact garden, now two stories above the palace. Delightful aromas and pleasing sounds of fountain gurgle envelop them. They stop at the small reflecting pool to admire the orange fish as they rise to the moonlit surface to greet the lovers with their syncopating kisses. She leads him to a mirador at the edge of the garden. To their right they can see the tops of the hushed crowd in the Water Courtyard, the entire Generalife palace complex, Zamrak's unintelligible voice. She points.

"Magnificent."

Straight ahead the Alhambra stands in all its glory a half-mile distant. Predictably understated, unadvertised. They drink-in the scene in silence.

"There is more. Come."

He grins and follows her.

They wander east through the garden maze, turn left up a narrow stairway adjoining a brick garden building set deep into the slope. The stairs end at a small landing at the roofline of the building, then continue on up the hill. There is a small, gated entrance on the right cut into a stone wall on the landing. She creaks the gate open and they enter a tiny courtyard ringed on three sides by a dense cypress hedge. In the center is a small, elevated marble fountain graced by a subdued, feminine pearl tinkle. There are four wooden meditation chairs, one in each corner of the courtyard. She leads him past the fountain to the back left corner. She lifts the chair and places it to the side. In the moonlight he can tell that there is a hole in the cypress hedge at ground level, just big enough to crawl through.

She giggles. "One at a time, follow me. As you come through pull the chair back over the hole."

He chuckles. "Your wish is my command, my Lady."

She hikes up her gown, leans low so she doesn't catch her hair, then crawls on all-fours through the opening and disappears. He shakes his head, laughs, then follows, tugging the chair back into place.

As his head pokes through he sees that they have entered a miniature secret meadow, no more than fifteen feet square, bounded on all four sides by the dense cypress hedge running down to the ground. Impenetrable. The square is covered with a plush, thick grass. Soft and inviting.

He stands and surveys the scene, then declares, "Your secret hideaway."

She smiles. "My secret hideaway. I found this while exploring as a young girl. It has been my favorite hiding place in the Generalife ever since. I have not been here in over a year, but it has not changed a bit. As far as I can tell, no one knows of its existence. I have spent many happy times here. I used to lay and watch cloud sculptures drift by, read forbidden books, daydream about my future, even nap. The fountain in the meditation space provides a pleasing backdrop. I have laid here undiscovered while secret politics was discussed next to me, while lovers kissed and wooed. It is my hidden treasure, my secret place. Now yours." She smiles. "Look up."

The moon's leer is blocked by the tops of the cypress hedge, muting the light to a deep dusk within the enclosed space. The stars sparkle, thousands of bright diamonds.

She points. "Look, Cassiopeia." She points again. "And Cepheus. The queen and her king."

The silence stretches out comfortably as they continue to scan the sky. She nestles against him, lays her ear to his chest and listens to his heartbeat. He folds his arms around her. She looks up into his eyes, her expression now serious. Her heart is racing.

"My William. You are my love, my joy and my life. All that I have is yours. Everything."

He smiles. "My Layla. I love you so. We are richly blessed."

More silence. She whispers, "William. We are betrothed now. We will be married very soon. Let us love each other as we desire."

Finally understanding, he swallows hard as his expression turns serious. "Layla. I desire nothing more. But there is no rush."

"I want to be one with you, William, body and soul. Tonight."

He smiles and nods. He leans down and tenderly kisses her. He steps back, removes his cloak and short-robe, places them end-to-end in the grass. He then unstraps Barq, lays the sword down. The dagger next. He takes his shirt off. She stands rigid, her eyes first glued to the ground, then shyly rising to watch him disrobe.

She flips her shoes off with her toes, then stops, suddenly unsure of what she should do next. He smiles then steps to her, kneels, begins to unbutton her gown from the ground up, inch by inch. As he rises her heart pounds. When he reaches her neck, the gown folds open. He slides forward, pushes his hands under the gown and around her back, her silk undergarment all that separates them. They kiss. He eases her gown off, makes a quick, clumsy attempt to fold it, then drops it on the grass. He then lifts her silk slip over her head, tosses it. His hands are shaking now as he first fumbles awkwardly with her bosom wrap then wrestles it. Unsuccessfully. She giggles and helps him unpin it, then steps out of her undergarments. He takes a step back to remove his trousers and loin cloth.

They stand two feet apart looking into each other's eyes, lips parted by their quickened breathing, hearts racing. He cannot prevent his gaze from dipping lower. He gushes, "My God, you are a beautiful woman!"

Her face darkens in the moonlight. Softly, she says, "I am yours, William."

The distance between them narrows then closes as they press against each other, hold each other tight. They kiss again.

He leads her down to the cloak. As she lays back, he settles beside her and rests on his elbow. He leans in over her and smiles. "I have dreamed of this day for so long, Layla."

She reaches up, runs her fingers through his hair. "As have I." She pulls him to her and they kiss again. As he makes his way to her breasts she arches her back, curls her toes.

What for months has been a passion urgent and frantic, now turns on a knife's edge, becomes instead slow and deliberate, methodical, a simmering of their pent-up desires suspended long and close over hot crimson coals.

They break from their wet kiss. He whispers into her ear, "You are perfect, so beautiful." He eases himself across her, slowly lowers his weight upon her. She instinctively parts. He whispers, "Are you afraid, my love?"

"No." She hesitates. "A little."

"Relax, my angel." Their eyes remain joined as he slowly eases into her. A sharp gasp, then a clinched exhale, then an exaggerated pleasure-sigh, finally a soft, feminine groan. He echoes her. She wraps her arms tightly around him, locks her feet around his ankles.

All motion freezes. Their desire rests delicately suspended in the air above them, expectant, then winds around them, between them, inside them, an almost visible aura surrounding the young lovers. Their eyes remain glued to each other.

She whispers, "My beloved."

"My beloved."

They remain perfectly still for what seems like an eternity. Finally, their interlocked throbbing and the heat of the liquid silk becomes too much to bear, issuing its own silent demands they can no longer bear to restrain. He begins to slowly move. Their soft moans join hands, follow along close behind, the pace quickening.

Her eyes close as the fever builds between them, but his eyes remain open, never leaving her face. Her eyes suddenly open wide with surprise, unfocused, pleading. She tenses, arching her back as she inhales sharply, squeezes him tighter, then softly cries his name. He does not stop, but instead accelerates very slightly. As she senses another wave looming close on the horizon her eyes involuntarily close again as she braces for the onrushing surge.

A moment more then he whispers, "Layla. Look at me."

She forces her eyes open and they lock onto each other as the waves build around them, rise to crazy heights and crest.

He whispers more urgently, "Layla, Layla, look at me." Her giant emeralds are fixed and dilated, and never leave his now. "I will always love you. Layla, I will always love you. I will always love you." He continues to repeat the mantra as the waves begin to crash down over them, roll around and over and through them for what seems like forever.

They lay still as the flood waters begin to recede. He studies her, but she isn't smiling. Instead, her eyes well up and her lower lip begins to quiver. Tears begin to slide off her face.

His concern grows. "Darling? Layla?" The tears are flowing steady now. She struggles to say something, but cannot. She tries again. "Layla? What is it, darling? What?"

She tries once more. On the third attempt he finally hears it and understands. A faint, "Tawhid."

"Yes, Layla, tawhid. Yes, my beloved, tawhid, yes."

She smiles through her tears, her lip-tremble easing. He rejoices now that he knows these are tears of joy. His chest swells tight with love, threatens to burst.

She whispers, "William, it is just as Rumi said. I experienced union with the Beloved through union with my beloved. When you and I became one body we each were annihilated. No Layla, no William, only Layla and William. One. Allah came to us then, William. We were joined together, our hearts and souls linked with Allah. One heart, one soul, one body. Tawhid. Tawhid, William!"

"Yes, Layla, yes."

They kiss again, exchange soft murmurs of love. Finally he slides from her with a shared gasp, and they lay in silence under the stars. She rests on her side, leg draped across him. He is on his back, her head nestled upon a cushion of her chestnut hair in the crook of his arm, his fingers tracing the soft warm curve of her hip.

Perseus leans into Virgo, points. The two watch, mesmerized, satisfied smiles spreading broad across their faces. Pegasus sees them and approaches, then the Great Bear, who motions over Orion, Vega, Libra and Scorpio. Young love writ large upon the stars.

After fifteen minutes of perfect peace, they hear the distant voice of the announcement bell. Three slow strikes. A pause. Three more. Again.

Layla says, "The bell marks the close of the feast. We should return. Father will wonder where we are; he will worry."

He sighs. "I do not want to leave our secret place."

"Nor I, but we must. Come."

They kiss again, then rise and dress, their shared knowledge of the great mystery of life producing a rich glow impossible to extinguish or hide.

Sparse throngs of revelers continue to make their way out of the garden maze. They converge on the square to exchange last laughs and goodbyes, then begin to head back to the Alhambra to sleep. The old man is low in the sky now. He seems disappointed but resigned that the end of the festivities has arrived.

As Layla and Chandon near the square, they see Ibn al-Khatib and Salamun standing and talking, arms folded, faces serious. The lovers compose themselves and approach.

Salamun sees them first. He raises his eyebrows as he gauges their appearance, then smiles broadly and chuckles. “Here they are now, Lisan al-Din.”

Ibn al-Khatib looks up, his concern obvious. “I was beginning to worry, Layla. You have been gone for some time.”

Layla goes straight to him and hugs him. “I am sorry, Baba. I wanted to show William the view from the gardens above the Water Stairway. We got caught up talking.”

Salamun can’t stop grinning. Ibn al-Khatib remains serious, looks intently at his daughter as he weighs her words but remains silent. Finally, he makes a decision and his mood lightens. He says, “And so, children, a very special evening, yes?”

Layla answers, “Oh, Baba, the best evening of my life!” She lifts his hand, kisses the back of his palm, then touches her forehead to the spot. “Thank you, Baba, you have made me so very happy.”

He smiles. “You are loved, Daughter.”

Unexpectedly, Chandon steps forward, lifts then kisses the back of Ibn al-Khatib’s other hand, touches his forehead to the spot. “I am grateful, sir, for all you have done for us.”

Ibn al-Khatib is clearly moved by the gesture, becomes endearingly tongue-tied for a moment, then whispers, “You are loved, Son.”

Salamun looks on as he beams. “My, my, young love is such a wonderful thing. A wonderful thing!” The wizard chuckles once more. “Shall we, children?” He lifts his palm.

The four join the last elements of the crowd heading back to towards the palace and begin casual talk of the wedding plans.

## Brothers

22 September 1368. "Damn him! Damn him to hell!" King Pedro paces, fists balled at his side. His face is flushed a deep red. "Damn Edward! DAMN HIM! COWARD!" His counselors know better than to speak. The king's barrage hovers above the floor, the storm cloud dense and dark, the room tense, oppressive. Pedro continues to pace. He comes to a halt, turns and says, "Read it again, Don Sancho. READ IT!"

"Certainly, Majesty." Don Sancho unwinds the scroll.

*"To King Pedro of Castile, on the third day of September 1368, from Edward of Woodstock, Prince of Wales, Duke of Cornwall and Prince of Aquitaine.*

*Greetings, Pedro. I trust you are in good health and that your kingdom is in order. I wish to thank you for the one thousand gold florins you sent some time back. I anxiously await your payment of the balance of your debt to me. As Lord Templeton must have told you, my troops remain in Aquitaine, stranded for want of ships to carry them home. They miss their families, and England.*

*Lord Templeton relayed your offer for my assistance with defeating Enrique. While tempting, I have decided not to join you on your campaign. May God grant you success."*

*Yours,*<br>*Edward of Woodstock*

Thankfully, a semblance of calm begins to settle on Pedro as he starts to explore his options. He sighs. "Where does this leave us, counselors?"

Don Alfonso says, "In a precarious position, Majesty, very precarious. Without Edward, we lose the longbowmen the French so keenly fear. We lose the lions-share of our men-at-arms, half of our cavalry."

Don Juan offers, "Majesty, we have it on good authority that Enrique's forces will converge on Zaragoza by Christmas, perhaps sooner. He is backed by Aragon, of course. And supported by the rebel Castilians from the south, and the meddling French. He has Genoese ships. And, of course, Papal backing. We have just learned that Bertrand du Guesclin and Hugh Calveley have committed the Free Companies to his service, a surprising and troubling move. I can only guess at how much gold they were promised."

"French swine."

Don Sancho joins the fray. "Agreed, they are swine. But formidable swine nonetheless, and a force to be reckoned with. By my estimate, Enrique will be able to field at least thirty-five thousand against us, likely more. I remind you, Majesty, that they had nearly sixty thousand at Nájera."

Pedro sneers. "Yes, and look what good it did them. Nothing." He sighs. "And Castile? How many can we field?"

"Without Edward? Perhaps twelve thousand, maybe fifteen."

"Not enough."

"No, Majesty, not enough."

"The Moors?"

"Muhammad has again pledged to send six hundred of his best cavalry. But that is far too few to carry the day, and they will not send more. As you know, we do have their gold in hand. Last year's tribute as well as the loan. This year's tribute is due next month. If they are on time."

"I see. How much do we have presently in the treasury?"

"After refitting our troops? Perhaps four thousand florins. Precious little."

Pedro frowns as he ponders their desperate situation. He looks to his left. "Don Ruy, why the silence?"

"Thinking, Majesty, thinking. I believe there is an additional option to consider."

"Go on."

"We could enlist the help of Portugal, Majesty."

All eyes turn to him.

"Go on."

"As you know, Majesty, your elder son now sits on the throne."

"Precariously sits on the throne. And Fernando hates me, Don Ruy. He has made it abundantly clear that he has no desire to aid me in my fight against my bastard brother. Why would he help us now?"

"Fernando is pragmatic, Majesty, and ambitious. We will offer him gold, gold we know he needs. And we will promise him Galicia, Trastámara, and western Asturias. Portugal would then own access to the northern sea. They crave this access, Majesty. For such a prize I suspect the Portuguese nobles would support Fernando."

"The entire northwest corner of my kingdom? That seems a hefty price to pay, Don Ruy."

“We have little choice, Majesty. Without more troops we have no hope of besting Enrique on the field of battle.”

Pedro stares at the floor, thinking.

Don Ruy presses his case. “Majesty. When we defeat Enrique we will have all of Aragon. We stand to gain much more than we lose. We cede northwestern Castile to Portugal, but at the same time we expand to the east.”

Silence settles in as they each consider the ramifications.

Don Ruy adds, “If Portugal has direct access to the northern sea, Majesty, Aquitaine will be threatened. Portugal will bear down on Edward, on England.”

Pedro nods. “Yes, I would enjoy slapping Edward.” Rueful smile.

“I would want at least three thousand men-at-arms, five thousand heavy cavalry and three thousand archers. More would be better. Would Fernando accept our offer?”

Don Ruy tips his head. “Unclear. But I suspect so, Majesty. With your permission I could send a query...discreetly, of course...to gauge his interest.”

Pedro considers for a few minutes more then turns to the three other counselors. “What say you?”

“I agree with Don Ruy, Majesty.”

“Agreed, Majesty.”

“A wise course of action, Majesty.”

“Good, then let us proceed. If Enrique gathers his forces by Christmas they will march on us at the first sign of spring. We must be ready to field an army to meet him straight away, settle this once and for all.”

Enrique of Trastámara, King Pedro IV of Aragon, Don Alfonso Méndez de Guzmán and Sir Ernaud de Florenssan circle the oak table. They lean forward on their hands pouring over the map laid before them. Enrique slides his finger to a village just outside the walls of Zaragoza, beside the river. “The French troops will garrison at Santa Isabel, Ernaud, east of the city.”

Ernaud nods, “Good. I know the place. It is nicely suited to our needs. The French forces will gather and depart in November and should begin to arrive here by mid-December.”

Enrique nods then slides his finger again. “The Bretons will garrison in Cuarte de Huerva, southwest of the city, and the Castilians in La Arboleda, between the Bretons and the French. They should both be settled by Christmas at the latest.”

Ernaud asks, “And the Free Companies?”

Enrique slides his finger once more, taps the map. "They will soon leave Toulouse to cross the Pyrenees before the weather turns. They will winter in Zuera, well away from Zaragoza. It is twelve miles to the northeast."

King Pedro IV nods. "Good, the further away the better. I want no trouble from them, Enrique, is that clear?"

Enrique looks up. "Perfectly. They will remain at arm's length until we march." The four continue to study the map. "We will train during January and February as a united force, here, between the two rivers."

Ernaud de Florenssan says, "What are the present troop tallies we can expect?"

Don Alfonso Méndez responds, "Close to what we originally envisioned. Twenty-seven thousand infantry, seven thousand archers and nine thousand cavalry, not counting the Free Companies. They should bring five thousand heavy horse. Forty-eight thousand all told, give or take a few hundred."

Ernaud nods his approval. "Good. Less than at Nájera, but still formidable."

Enrique stands and the others follow suit. "It is better than you think, Ernaud. My spies in Sevilla have just learned that Edward the Black Prince has refused to join forces with Castile." He offers a rueful smile. "It seems there was not enough gold to go around." All four men chuckle. "If you can believe it, my brother even promised Edward he could have Zaragoza." King Pedro IV frowns. "Without England, gentlemen, we will not face the longbow again or their heavy cavalry. It is not clear yet how many men my brother can field, but it cannot be more than twenty thousand, if that."

Ernaud says, "Our strategy?"

Don Alfonso Méndez reaches to a table behind him and hands Enrique a scroll. Enrique unrolls the map of Iberia, orients it, then the four lean back over the table. "My intent is to make this a short campaign." He taps Zaragoza then slides his finger towards Sevilla. "A direct assault. We head south from Zaragoza and enter Castile through the regions sympathetic to our cause. That way we will face no early resistance and can easily resupply as we move. Then we march a straight line to Sevilla, as fast as we can ride. My brother will have no choice but to engage us directly on the field of battle. No cat and mouse flanking games like before. We should clash somewhere south of Ciudad Real." He taps his finger. "With our superior forces and the Free Companies as our battering ram, we will crush my brother. Then we move on Sevilla." The three men nod their approval.

Ernaud asks, "When do we march?"

Enrique answers, "At the first hint of spring."

"Good. The French forces will be ready. Do we have the Papal Banner yet?"

"It is in route as we speak. It should arrive by the end of the month."

"Excellent."

"The Genoese?"

"They will place forty ships at our disposal. They are scheduled to arrive in Valencia in early February. We will send a portion of the Castilian infantry to meet them. When we march, they will set sail for Sevilla."

Ernaud responds, "To victory."

They all smile. "To victory!"

## Promises

The day is warm and bright, but already the summer swelter wrestles with the changing of the seasons, its white-knuckled grip pried loose finger by finger under autumn's steady advance. A refreshing hint of cool dampness nestles in the whispering breeze, teasing the senses.

The small entourage stands circled around the mihrab inside the Great Mosque: Chandon, Ibn al-Khatib, Yazdan and Musa, Ziyad, al-Bistami, al-Mussib, the Sultan, and a half-dozen imams and qadi from the Mexuar Council. No Berbers. Even Salamun has been invited, perhaps the only Jew this century to adorn this sacred space. As betrothed, Layla has received special dispensation to attend the ceremony, which normally would exclude females. All are dressed in their most formal court attire.

Chandon, by contrast, is dressed in the simple white cotton robe of a convert. He has meticulously performed his ghusl at the fountain outside. Chandon has not been back in the Great Mosque since his attack there well over a year back. His expression is serious and strained, tense.

The atmosphere is expectant, with an undercurrent of suppressed excitement. Several conversations are conducted by whisper. Most stand silent, waiting for the Grand Imam to arrive and the ceremony to commence.

Layla can barely contain her tactile self, cannot keep her hands from fussing over him, touching him, though the occasion demands solemnity. Her father discreetly whispers in her ear to remind her of her place. Her scolded hands reluctantly fold themselves by her side as her smile slides away, only to spring to life a moment later, seemingly of their own volition. Her smile is captivating as always and several of the men, the Sultan included, attempt to steal an admiring glimpse of the Arabian beauty. There is no denying that the young couple basks in the rich-toned glow of love.

As the Grand Imam arrives, he offers a formal bow to the Sultan, a kind word of welcome to Ibn al-Khatib and Chandon, then one by one he warmly greets the others. When he gets to Layla, radiant and fidgety, a hint of a grin slides onto his face as he fondly recollects his own daughters during their betrothals.

The Grand Imam lowers his head, then lifts his palms and begins. "In the name of Allah we gather as one. All Praise is due to

Allah, Lord of the Worlds, the Beneficent, the Merciful, Owner of the Day of Judgment. You alone we worship and You alone we ask for help. Show us the straight path, O Lord, the path of those whom You have favored." The group collectively echoes an "Amen."

The Grand Imam motions Chandon forward and lifts his hands over him in blessing. Chandon bows his head. "William Chandon, do you come to this assembly before the witness of Allah of your own free will, with a desire to enter the true faith of Islam?"

"I do."

"Allah desires your submission, your surrender and your obedience to his Holy Will. Will you embrace Islam?

"I will."

"The Prophet Muhammad, peace be upon him, has given his followers the five articles of faith: We believe in Allah, who is alone in His divinity; we believe in Allah's angels; we believe in Allah's books and in the Holy Quran as his last book; we believe in Allah's prophets and in Muhammad, His last and final messenger; and we believe in life after death. Do you believe as we believe?"

"I do."

"Do you swear to be faithful to the five pillars of Islam, steadfast in your practice of salat, sawm, zakat, and hajj?"

"I do."

"Do you swear to be faithful in your reading of the Quran and hadith and to abide by the *Sunnah* and laws of Sharia?"

"I do."

The Grand Imam nods, then says, "Please recite the Shahada."

Chandon closes his eyes, mentally rehearsing his pronunciation for the hundredth time, then melodically intones, "Ash-hadu an laa ilaha illa-llaah wa ash-hadu anna Muhammadan rassulullah." *There is no god but Allah, and Muhammad is the messenger of Allah.* Chandon opens his eyes.

"Excellent. Do you wish to choose an Arabic name?"

"Yes. Shahab."

"Ahhh...shooting star. Shahab and Layla. The shooting star that lights the night. Good, very good." Layla is grinning ear to ear.

The Grand Imam smiles at the group. "Shahab Chandon, welcome to the faithful. May Allah's peace and blessings be upon you." As those gathered burst into applause, Yazdan and Musa rush forward with back slaps and shoulder shakes. Layla glides beneath his arm to hug him tight. Ibn al-Khatib and Salamun are beaming and al-Bistami, the Sultan and the clerics are clearly pleased. Chandon's easy smile returns as the laughter and cheers circle round the room.

The man looks up from his weeding and furls his eyebrows, puzzled. He exchanges a quick, concerned glance with his daughter working three rows away. He hears the distant rumble of thunder on the horizon, but the sky is a clear, piercing blue. He tilts his head and pivots to scan all directions just to be sure. Confirming the weather, he cups his ears and listens. His quizzical expression hardens as the sound grows louder, more insistent. Riders. Heavy horse.

The man is still considering his options when the cavalry exits the tree line in double-file a hundred yards away.

The man turns and says, "Alays, run to the house and tell your mother and brother to hide in the room beneath the floor. Go quickly! Run, girl!" She dashes for the house but does not vanish before the cavalry draws up to the edge of the garden, the horses sucking and blowing.

The officer walks his mount forward as he surveys, with no regard for the vegetables he is trampling. He removes his plumed hat, bows with mock ceremony and says in formal French, "Sir. I am Guinot de Diagon, Lieutenant of the Free Companies. We ride with Bertrand du Guesclin and Hugh Calveley for Zaragoza. A crusade against the Moors. My men require food for the journey across the great mountains."

The farmer bows. "You are welcome here, sir. Please water your horses in the stream." He points to his right. "There is good grass for grazing. Unfortunately, sir, you see that I have only a small farm. I have no food to spare beyond what feeds my family and pays my taxes."

Silence. A smile eases onto the knight's face. "And who, pray tell, is your Lord?"

"Galhard Cadona of Lourdes."

"I see. And where is his castle?"

"About three miles south, sir."

"Good. We will visit him next. What food do you have for us, serf?"

"As I said, sir, I have no food beyond what feeds my family and pays my taxes."

The knight's expression hardens into a death mask as he hisses, "Careful, old man, or I will have my men search the farm. If they find any hidden treasure I will personally enjoy your daughter's sweet body and then burn your farm to the ground. Do I make myself clear, scum?"

The farmer withers. He stammers, "I have a dozen salted hams...in my cellar. To feed my family...this winter. And some honey. You are welcome to them. I also have...a dozen sacks of grain in the store shed. My taxes for the year."

The lieutenant smiles and nods his head. "Good, good. I would be happy to accept your kind hospitality, thank you." Quick hand motions launch six riders towards the barn. "Now, if you would be so kind as to introduce me to that pretty daughter of yours."

Panic frames the farmers face. "But you said..."

Mock surprise from de Diagon, then an evil sneer. "I said nothing, scum. You deserve a lesson for your insolence. Fetch the girl, before I change my mind and put your farm to the torch. NOW!"

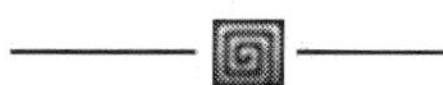

Chandon and Ibn al-Khatib sit cross-legged on white silk pillows three feet apart, facing each other. Layla sits erect beside her father on a meticulously placed white wedding divan, gold pillows behind her.

The wedding party occupies a terrace on the upper level of the Partal Gardens, overlooking the large reflecting pool in front of the Tower of the Ladies. The betrothed are arranged on a small square of bright ceramic tiling bounded by white and black stone pavement sculpture then ringed by two compact L-shaped pools. A closeby fountain gurgles pleasingly. The iridescent orange fish are surfaced and attentive amid the luxurious white and yellow blooms of the water lilies. The party is spare: Salamun, Aisha, Constancia, al-Khayyat, al-Mussib, al-Bistami, the Sultan, Yazdan and Musa, Zyad, and the Grand Imam, who presides.

Chandon is dressed in the formal attire of a Royal Bodyguard, sans sword and dagger, red robe over red shirt and a gold sash. Layla is stunning in her gold-embroidered white silk gown, her chestnut curls elaborately woven and tied with emerald silk ribbons and lace. Her hands and feet are decorated with bronzed henna art that twines around lines of Rumi laid out in tight Arabic script. Hanging around her neck at the end of a delicate gold chain is a giant white pearl set in gold, her *mahr*, the formal wedding gift from her husband to be. The two cannot keep their eyes off one another. Their faces are radiant with love and barely contained excitement.

The Grand Imam clears his throat, then begins the ceremony with the *khutbah*, the wedding speech. "Praise be to Almighty

Allah, the Sustainer of the Worlds from whom we ask help and pardon. We seek refuge in Allah from the evils within ourselves. He whom Allah guides no one can lead astray. We testify that there is no deity but Allah and that Muhammad is His servant and His messenger." After a pause, he continues. "Almighty Allah has created humanity, male and female, each in need of the other, and has established the institution of marriage as a means of uniting their souls in a blessed bond of love leading to their mutual pleasure and happiness. The Quran says, 'It is He who created man from water. Then He established relationships of lineage and marriage, for your Lord has power over all things.' The Quran also reminds us of His great favors: 'And among His many signs, He created for you your spouses, that you may live in joy with them, and He has set between you love and mercy.'"

The Grand Imam stops and smiles at the gathering, lifts his palms to the couple, then says, "Brothers and sisters, today we are uniting in the bonds of marriage our brother, Shahab Chandon, and our sister, Layla al-Khatib, who desire to live together as husband and wife, sheltered with the blessings of Almighty Allah and His divine benevolence. May Allah fill their lives with much joy and may He grant them peace, health and prosperity. May their union be blessed with many children. May their love never diminish, nor their tender regard for each other. Peace be upon them."

The gathering collectively intones, "Peace be upon them."

Ibn al-Khatib, as *wali*, legal guardian of the bride, now lifts both palms to Chandon and begins the formal wedding rite.

"In the name of Allah, the Merciful, the Mercy-Giving, praise be to Allah, Lord of the Worlds, may prayer and peace be upon the Prophet Muhammad, his family and his companions. I marry you, Shahab Chandon, to my daughter, Layla al-Khatib, whom I represent, in accordance with Islamic Law and the tradition of the Messenger of Allah."

Chandon bows his head in acknowledgment then lifts his palms to Ibn al-Khatib and responds, "I accept in marriage the young woman you represent, Layla al-Khatib, in accordance with Islamic Law and the tradition of the Messenger of Allah."

The Grand Imam faces Chandon. "Shahab, do you accept Layla as your beloved wife."

"I accept Layla as my beloved wife."

The Grand Imam now faces Layla. "Layla, do you accept Shahab as your beloved husband?

"I accept Shahab as my beloved husband."

Al-Bistami, as uncle of the bride, steps forward and presents an inked quill and the *nikah*, the wedding contract, to Chandon, which he signs. Al-Bistami repeats the procedure, first with Ibn al-Khatib, then with Layla.

Ibn al-Khatib, Chandon and Layla stand and face one another. Ibn al-Khatib bows his head, then takes Layla's hands and places them in Chandon's and steps back. Husband and wife ease to within a few inches of one another. Their hands are joined, and their eyes are welded to each other. Tears slide down both their cheeks. As the men beam their approval, Aisha and Constancia sniffle and dab tears.

Ibn al-Khatib closes the ceremony by intoning the wedding blessing. "May Allah bless this union with all that is good." The crowd responds with a loud "Amen!" and the scene erupts in thunderous applause and a high-pitched, undulating feminine trill, courtesy of Aisha and Constancia. Chandon and Layla remain locked to one another as they kiss. The crowd closes in to interrupt and the barrage of hugs, shoulder slaps and vigorous handshakes commences.

After the commotion settles, Ibn al-Khatib announces, "My friends, please join us for *walimah*, a feast to celebrate Layla and Shahab's wedding." Another round of cheers rings out. The wedding party begins to make their way back to the Comares Palace.

She is snuggled tight to him, her head nestled to his chest as she listens to his heartbeat, her left leg scissored across his belly, her heel locked beneath his thigh. The covers of their bed are jumbled, haphazardly kicked back to the floor. A single candle burns in the corner, spilling a warm, soft glow into the room. He traces a single fingertip along her thigh from hip to ankle and back again, admiring her feminine curves. Her eyes are closed as she basks. He lifts his hand and begins to slide his fingers down her back. He slows and lightens his touch as he sinks into the delicious inward arch at the small of her back, then rises back out again, continuing to move down her body, exploring. She tenses then shivers then laughs, causing him to grin.

She lifts her head then begins to finger the large pink scar on his left shoulder. She moves to another older jagged scar across his breastbone, then a third on the far right side of his abdomen. "You have so many scars, William."

"Yes. I need to learn to be more careful." They both laugh, then grow silent as they find each other's eyes and share a long, wet kiss.

"Wife."

"Husband."

He squeezes her tight to him. "My beloved."

"My beloved."

They kiss again. "It hardly seems real, William, that we are finally together, that we do not have to worry over prying eyes as we steal a glance or a quick touch. I am so happy." She tightens her arms around him.

"Yes. I never thought this time would come. I do miss our midnight rendezvous, but this new arrangement has its...advantages." He chuckles. "So what do you think of our new apartment, wife? Adequate?"

She laughs. "I feel guilty, William. It is larger than Baba's suite. The view of the Garden of the Lindaraja is wonderful."

"When will Aisha join us?"

"In three days. But I will worry about Baba without someone to attend to his needs."

"We will find someone to stay with him, though I am sure he will fight that. He will join us, of course, for dinner and prayers each evening."

She smiles. "Thank you." A moment of silence follows, then with mock seriousness she says, "William, you will have to be quieter once Aisha is here. These walls are thin."

He laughs loud. "I could say the same for you, my darling. Perhaps you could put your hand over my mouth?" She laughs, but grows instantly serious as he eases her over on top of him, pulls both of her knees forward, then cups the back of her head with his hand, pulls her down to kiss, her chestnut jumble curtaining their faces.

The coming winter's chill has begun to slink into the palace, insinuate its icy tendrils along the floors and into crevices, chilling the water in the basins. The glowing brazier in the corner of the room casts a pleasant hue as it chases away the intruding pall. As the night deepens, they each sit on their divans, oil lamps towering over them. She is reading Rumi, he is reading Ibn al-Khatib's new medical treatise. Aisha has retired for the night.

She closes her book, turns and begins to study him as he reads. After a moment she offers a soft, "William?"

He looks up and smiles. "Yes, darling?"

She grows silent, looks down, then back up, then back down, tentative.

"What is it, Layla?"

She hesitates. "We have been married almost three months now and still I have not conceived our child." Her lower lip starts to quiver and her eyes well up. "I am not sure what is wrong with me." She looks down again.

With a tender smile he closes his book, rises and comes over and slides in beside her, pulls her head to his chest. "I know that weighs on you, my love, but all in God's time, all in God's time."

"I know, I know, I keep telling myself that. But somehow having a baby is all that I can think about these days. It seems such a natural extension of the great love we have been given and the many blessings we share. I sometimes feel that our love is too big to hold within my heart, William, that Allah wants our love to spill over into another life, a new creation. I can feel it, I know it."

"Yes, He does, darling, I am sure He does, but according to His time, not ours. When God wills it to happen, Layla, it will happen, of that you can be sure. Be patient, my love." He lifts her chin to look into her brilliant emeralds. "Besides, think of all the fun we are having trying." He beams. She smiles weakly, then grins, finally laughs.

Out of nostalgia they have decided to resume their late evening jaunts around the Courtyard of the Myrtles. It is past midnight, the moon bright and full in the cruel cold, the winter sky cloudless, the stars ridiculously gaudy in their brilliant sparkle. Their breath fog is exaggerated, the steam clouds stretching rhythmically from their mouths. They are wrapped tight in blankets against the brutal chill.

They hold hands as they quietly talk, a fond recollection of days past, but with none of the tense paranoia. They stop and kiss, hug each other tight, then resume their stroll in silence.

She says, "I have been thinking."

"You are always thinking, my love." He grins.

She looks up and smiles. "Yes, well. I have been thinking about our future."

"Ahhh...our future. Tell me."

"Well, I was talking to Majahid al-Khayyat yesterday after I finished my work at the Maristan. He suggested you and I consider starting a new hospital. Like the Maristan, for the outcasts of the city."

"I see. Interesting. Where?"

"Somewhere in the city. There is an obvious need for more space than the Maristan can offer. Perhaps in the Jewish quarter? I am sure Salamun could suggest a location. We would need the Sultan's financial support, but with Baba's help I am sure he would be willing." Her excitement level rises. "I took the liberty of having the conversation with Master al-Mussib." He lifts his eyebrows but remains silent. She continues, "He suggested that perhaps we could start a small madrasa as a part of the hospital building itself. For females. It would be a service-oriented madrasa and focused on the training of young women in the ways of Sufism. Master al-Mussib feels, as do I, that service is essential for a true education." She smiles. "I could teach at the madrasa and you could run the hospital." She grows quiet and waits for his response.

"I would have to give up my position as Vice-Vizier."

"Yes." She sighs, sensing the exasperation edging into his voice. "William, we have talked of this many times. Your role as vizier must be temporary or you will never find peace. I do not want to raise our children with the cloud of war hanging over their Baba's head."

His turn to sigh. "No, neither do I. Though in fairness, Farqad has not once suggested I take part in any military maneuvers. My role has been purely advisory, as they originally promised."

She frowns. "Do not be naïve, William. You and I both know that your role will change at the first hint of an invasion threat. You know my uncle well enough to know I speak the truth. He will be the first to remind you of your duty as a Granadine knight, your loyalty to the Sultan."

He considers her words. "Yes."

She continues, "Will you at least think about it? For me?"

His mood brightens. "Certainly, darling. The idea speaks to my heart." He thinks for a moment more, then says, "Perhaps we could make it a hospital just for orphaned children."

She hugs him tight. "Thank you, William, thank you."

They stop once more and kiss. "You are cold, Layla. We should return to the Lindaraja so I can warm you up properly." They lock eyes, offer each other a devilish grin, then turn and head back to the Palace of the Lions.

## Secrets

4 January 1369. Layla lays curled in a tight fetal position on her bed mat, sobbing hysterically, her face buried in her hands. Aisha sits beside her stroking her hair, offering a maternal "Shhh...shhh..." over and over. A blood-soaked rag lies bunched on the floor, the tight circle of crimson on the bedding unmistakable.

Her sobbing ebbs, begins to be punctuated alternately by heaving inhales, rattling exhales, and wet sniffles. She opens her eyes, looks up at Aisha.

"How many bleeding moons have you missed?"

Layla sniffs. "Only one. My second would have been in two weeks."

Aisha raises her eyebrows, skeptical. "You are positive you were with child?"

"Yes, Aisha, I could feel the changes in my body. I am certain."

"Tell me about this morning. What did you feel?"

"I was fine when William rose before dawn and dressed. I drifted back to sleep after he left, then I woke with a start to a violent cramp in my stomach. Soon they were coming in waves, worse than any I have ever felt." She sniffs. "Then the bleeding started. But not my normal flow, worse. I called you when I could not get it to stop." Her voice quavers as she says, "Why would I lose my baby, Aisha?" She chokes back a sob.

Aisha nods her sympathy as she continues to stroke her hair. "It is hard to understand, but these things happen. It is not uncommon." She pauses. "Did William know you were with child?"

"No. I was going to surprise him after the second moon."

"Good. Keep this between the two of us. There is no need to worry him."

"Aisha, I feel like I have lost a part of me. My heart aches." She draws her knees tighter to herself and begins to rock as she starts to cry again.

"Shhh...shhh... I know, I know. You must trust me, Layla. You will soon be with child again. Be patient." Aisha slides her hand under her shoulder, urges her up. "Come, let me clean you up and change these bed covers. Come, Layla, up, up."

The orange-rimmed orb of burnished gold wrestled free of the Sierra Nevada's jealous clutches just a half-hour back, the euphoric light angular and sharp, forcing a hard squint on any eyes looking east. The day is cold and clear but the air is still, lending a refreshing crispness to the biting winter chill.

It is too early for anyone from the medina to have ventured forth and instead the expanse of the parade ground in front of the Alcazaba is occupied by elite troops, a cadre each of the Royal Bodyguard and the Royal Infantry, both units forty strong. Training exercises. Two dozen infantry and cavalry officers observe the proceedings from the sidelines, all eyes and ears.

Al-Bistami and several of his adjutants stand close by as they watch Chandon bark instructions, the troops rushing about in response. He is a natural leader. Satisfied with his arrangement, each cadre facing the other in two lines of twenty, Chandon begins to pace between them as he lectures them: the nuances of European heavy cavalry tactics against infantry; the weak points of armored plate on European knights; how the mace is most effectively defended; the differences in bow construction and arrow length between French and English archers, on and on. Several questions are raised then dispensed with. All eyes are glued to Chandon. The hint of an smile rests on al-Bistami's face.

Chandon draws Barq, two-hands it up and steps into a battle stance. He calls out Musa, who comes forward, smiling sheepishly. Chandon has no time for games, however, and commands his friend to draw his weapon. Musa's smile fades as his sword is pulled and locked into place. Chandon commences his lesson, steps forward in slow motion, demonstrating a move a French knight would use against them. Chandon feigns a chest-thrust, pivots then swings Barq unexpectedly downward at Musa's exposed knee, stopping just shy of contact. He lowers his blade and elaborates on why the tactic is so effective. Several heads nod. They have witnessed this move in battle.

Chandon instructs Musa to perform the identical move, at full speed. Eyebrows are raised as nervous grins are exchanged. Chandon steps back with the assault and pivots, easily parrying Musa's swing at his knee, then launches a pirouette counterattack, which Musa cannot fend off. Barq stops just shy of his friend's neck. Heads nod appreciatively as furious whispers are exchanged. Musa doesn't appear amused.

Chandon looks about for questions. Satisfied, he smiles and shouts, "Knights of Granada, pair up and show me!" The field erupts with activity. A thin smile marks al-Bistami's face.

King Pedro sits atop his white Andalusian stallion surveying the parade ground beside the Guadalquivir River just outside of city walls of Sevilla. To his counselors' chagrin, Pedro could be easily confused with a Moorish prince, choosing to forgo the customary full body armor of a Castilian noble and instead donning the much lighter chain-mail and boiled leather preferred by Granadine knights. His jeweled scabbards for his crescent-hilted Granadine sword and needle dagger are Moorish, gifts from the Sultan. A heart-shaped leather Granadine shield hangs from his saddle. Don Ruy and Don Sancho flank him atop their own horses, gleaming in their steel-plate cocoons.

The field is occupied by several hundred cavalry executing close-order drill, the steam clouds rhythmically pulsing from the horses testimony to the unusually cold winter.

Pedro turns in his saddle to Don Sancho. "What do you hear from our spies in Zaragoza?"

Don Sancho replies, "Majesty, troops have been assembling since early December. They are being quartered for the winter in separate towns surrounding the city. Large contingents of French, Breton, Castilian troops are settled in. They join ranks for weekly training exercises of their coordinated forces."

"How many?"

"Estimates range from forty to forty-five thousand, possibly more."

Pedro sighs. "So many." He ponders this for a moment then turns to Don Ruy and says, "When are Fernando's troops due to arrive from Portugal?"

"They are promised by early February, Majesty."

"Good. How many?"

"Twelve thousand, Majesty. Three thousand men-at-arms, six thousand infantry and three thousand archers."

"Don Sancho, how many will that give us all together?"

"Twenty-three thousand, Majesty."

Pedro nods as he considers, then says, "Similar to the odds at Nájera. I can live with that, assuming my brother is still as ignorant of battle tactics as he was then. Any news of the Free Companies?"

Don Sancho answers, "I am afraid so, Majesty. As you know, since they crossed the Pyrenees late in the fall, they have been rampaging through extreme northeastern Castile. They taunt us, Majesty. They arrived in Zaragoza two weeks back, loaded down with Castilian booty. They are being wintered far from the city, in Zuera, well to the northeast of the city. They are as unruly as ever."

"I assume du Guesclin and Calveley are with them?"

"Indeed, Majesty."

"Don Ruy, when can we expect Enrique to march on us?"

"Not before spring, Majesty. With this year's unusual cold, I should think it unlikely before March."

"We must be ready, gentlemen."

Both counselors nod.

"Any opinions on my brother's strategy?"

Don Sancho answers, "If I were him, Majesty, I would strike due south. He has sympathy in our southeastern lands and will find easy resupply as he moves. He will then strike southwestward towards Sevilla."

Don Ruy seconds the opinion, "I agree, Majesty. With his superior forces he will march directly for Sevilla, forcing us to engage him. He will push for a quick, decisive action."

Pedro considers this for a moment. "Yes, I would do the same. Let us be ready to move at full strength by the first of March. And send word to Granada. I want their cavalry prepared to join us at a moment's notice." Don Ruy nods. "Don Sancho, I want weekly reports from your spies in Zaragoza. I must know the instant Enrique musters for battle."

"Certainly, Majesty."

The invitation has an intriguing formality to it. A cryptic note penned in Ibn al-Khatib's fluid hand, in Castilian, delivered the day before, not to his apartment, but passed discreetly by al-Bistami. "Shahab, I require your presence at my suite at eleven tomorrow morning. I wish to introduce you to a special visitor. His presence here, and this meeting, is of the utmost secrecy. Shahab, I request that you not mention this to Layla. Baba." Ibn al-Khatib's formal seal just below his signature.

Chandon knocks then enters Ibn al-Khatib's suite. He stops to observe. The room is well-lit. There are six pillows arranged in a tight circle. On four of them sit Ibn al-Khatib, al-Bistami, the Sultan, the Grand Imam. The fifth is occupied by the one man he has never seen. The sixth pillow, to Ibn al-Khatib's right, is vacant.

The visitor is not Anadalusi; nor Berber. Ancient. His face is wrinkled, with an oiled-leather complexion; heavy lids, ebony eyes, a long gray beard. Elaborate white turban and a flowing black robe.

No one rises to greet Chandon. The room feels serious, pinched. Ibn al-Khatib lifts his palm to the open pillow and says, "Welcome Shahab, thank you for joining us."

Chandon continues to puzzle over the man's ancestry as he moves to take his place. It comes to him as he crosses his legs. Persian. Chandon notes that in the center of the circle lies a black cloth draped across some object.

Ibn al-Khatib begins, "Shahab, we have invited you here to seek your advice on an important matter. While you are a Granadine knight now and Military Vice-Vizier to the Sultan, we seek a European perspective on the topic in question, one that you can uniquely provide." Chandon nods. "As I intimated in my note, this meeting is of the utmost secrecy. All contents of this discussion represent a secret of the kingdom and must remain forever sealed in this room. Do you understand?"

"Certainly."

"Good." Ibn al-Khatib continues, "As you can see we have a visitor with us today." He lifts his palm to the man, who nods.

Chandon returns the nod, then says in flawless Arabic, "Yes, a visitor from Persia. Welcome to Granada, sir."

The man lifts his eyebrows, exposing a twinkle in his ebony eyes, then the barest hint of a smile touches his features.

Ibn al-Khatib continues. "Indeed. From Maragheh, in northwestern Persia, the famous astronomical observatory. May I present Ibn al-Shatir, an astronomer from the east. He is a disciple of the astronomer Nasir al-Din al-Tusi, may Allah rest his soul, inventor and perfector of the revolutionary object before you."

Chandon glances at the cloth.

"We have been in possession of this remarkable object for nearly one and a half years now. It was sent to us from Maragheh for safe keeping against the forces growing in strength in Baghdad. It seems that small-mindedness and intolerance are not unique to Africa. The object has been guarded in Granada by a Muslim secret society, the Ikhwan al-Safa, the Brethren of Purity, defenders of knowledge and truth. Those seated before you are members of that brotherhood."

Ibn al-Khatib leans forward and removes the cloth, then lifts the heavy orb and places it into Chandon's waiting hands. "Two months back matters took a turn for the worse. The Caliph in Baghdad sent troops to forcibly close the Maragheh Observatory. They arrived without warning and confiscated all of their instruments and imprisoned the astronomers. It seems that they are to be tried for blasphemy. Ibn al-Shatir was away making observations in the desert the day the troops arrived. He escaped. These past two months he has traveled to us at great risk via Damascus and Egypt, through the Maghreb, aided by our brothers there in the Ikhwan al-Safa. He arrived in Granada last week." Ibn al-Khatib falls silent.

Chandon's eyes fall to his hands as he examines the instrument. He has never seen anything like it. "It is beautiful." He rotates the brass sphere in his hands, noting the gradations and Arabic script on the gold and silver bands that circle the object. There are gold inlays for lines of latitude and longitude, various calculating arcs with marked numbers and a collection of symbols he does not recognize.

Ibn al-Khatib says, "Can you tell us what it is?"

Chandon continues to study the object as he rotates it in his hands. "Some sort of navigational instrument I would guess, but nothing like anything I have ever seen."

The Sultan frowns at the easy recognition.

The astronomer speaks, his voice thin and raspy, "It is a spherical astrolabe. It possesses a precision far exceeding that of any astrolabe known to mariners, Muslim or Christian. It is capable of guiding a ship over a thousand mile journey with an error of no more than ten miles." Chandon's eyes widen. "It is the first navigational instrument with sufficient accuracy to enable safe passage across the great western ocean."

Chandon absorbs this fact. "Remarkable. Such an instrument would change the balance of power in the world."

Al-Shatir continues. "Indeed. It breaks my heart to know that it is the last of its kind, an orphan. Three were made. One was sent to Granada for safe keeping. Its two brothers were melted down at Maragheh on the Caliph's orders. The machinery and calculations used to produce them were destroyed. They will not soon be re-created, if ever."

Chandon says, "I see. Who knows of its existence?"

Ibn al-Khatib answers, "We had assumed no one beyond the brotherhood. We took great pains of secrecy during its transport to Granada. Alas, two months ago we learned that the captain of a trading vessel from Genoa was offering bribes in Málaga for information on a 'golden sphere' rumored to be in Granada. Large bribes. We can only surmise that the brother that brought the astrolabe to us was captured after he delivered it. We have been unable to locate him. We must assume that the Genoese know of the spherical astrolabe's existence. How much they know of its power remains unclear." The room falls silent.

The Sultan finally speaks. "Shahab, we would like your perspective on whether Genoa will appreciate the implications of such an instrument."

Chandon considers the question. "Yes, Sire, they will. Genoa has the largest and best sailing ships in Europe, far superior to any Muslim fleet. They control the Mediterranean Sea, Sire. And it is well known in both England and France that Genoa lusts for the fruits of the lands across the great ocean beyond the Strait of Gibraltar. I am afraid they would make good use of the spherical astrolabe if they obtained it."

Ibn al-Khatib responds, "I share Shahab's opinion, Sire."

Al-Bistami says, "Genoa does not possess the land power to directly threaten Granada, Sire, even if they wanted to. They could never take the astrolabe by force."

The Sultan turns to Chandon. "Shahab?"

"I agree with Farqad, Sire. However, Genoa is allied with the Pope, and the Pope with France, and France with Aragon. When France sided with Enrique and Aragon at Nájera it was more than evident that the Pope was in the background, with a papal agenda resting south of Castile. Here. The Papacy pines to renew reconquista, Sire." The heads in the room begin to shake side to side with disgust. "What the Pope desires, Sire, France will support. The Pope is French, after all. Enrique will have no choice but to grant France's wishes, since he cannot muster an army without their help. Sire, if Genoa knows that such an instrument exists in Granada, they will find a way to side with Enrique as a means to obtain it. Perhaps as payment for the use of Genoa's ships for transport. This civil war will not end in Castile, Sire. It will travel southward to Granada."

The Sultan has a troubled expression on his face. He inhales, holds it, then exhales. "Yes. I would guess that the Pope will appreciate that this new world to the west is ripe for conquest and forced conversion. What then should we do with the astrolabe, gentlemen? Send it out of the kingdom?"

Ibn al-Khatib replies, "Too risky, Sire. It must remain hidden."

Chandon says, "We should destroy it, Sire."

All eyes turn to him, but the room remains silent.

Finally, the Grand Imam says, "Shahab, the Pope may desire to use the astrolabe to convert the new world to Christianity, but think of the lands that we could claim for Islam. Destroying this astrolabe, now that there is no chance to create a duplicate, eliminates that possibility forever."

"I understand. Perhaps it could remain hidden by the brotherhood in the Alhambra unless Granada is directly threatened. But if there is any risk of its capture, even remote, it must be destroyed."

Al-Bistami says, "Make no mistake. Even if Pedro somehow manages to win this civil war, and I remind you that he is heavily outnumbered, Granada will be threatened. It is just a matter of when, how and by whom. Reconquista is no illusion, I am afraid, it is inevitable. If Pedro loses, the direct threat to Granada will come very soon. As you know, Sire, Sevilla is already asking for our cavalry and Enrique's army is now encamped in force in Zaragoza. He will march as soon as spring arrives."

The Sultan sighs. "I agree, Farqad. We must ready Granada's defenses and make ready for war." He turns to Ibn al-Khatib. "Lisan al-Din, let us return the astrolabe to its hiding place. For now. But please put the plans in place to destroy it at a moment's notice if the need arises."

The Sultan stands, the meeting concluded. The other men follow suit. The Sultan turns to al-Shatir and says, "You will be my honored guest in the Comares Palace for as long as you desire."

Al-Shatir bows. "I am grateful, Sire."

The late winter downpour seems to go on forever, the incessant dampness somehow sharpening the rawness of the cold, a chill which defiantly refuses to disperse even under the glare of the glowing brazier. Chandon's shoulder and thigh bother him in this weather, the skill of the bath attendant's kneading hands the only foil for his deep aches. Two days of steady rain and counting. The palace is restless for sunlight and the promise of spring.

They sit on their pillows an hour before dinner, each a mirror image of the other; elbows to knees, chins to interlaced hands, faces concentrating on the chess board. The advantage rests on a knife's edge, as usual, a knight, a bishop and three pawns huddled lifeless on both sides of the checkered battleground. Layla's hand reaches decisively for her queen, which she slides diagonally forward seven squares. "Check." A wisp of a devilish grin tickles the corners of her mouth.

Chandon's eyes shift from the board to her face and back to the board.

"Nice idea." He waits. "Though anticipated." As his grin widens, her face hardens with concentration, fearing a trap.

Thirty minutes later the match is ended. Another draw. She rises with a feline stretch then adjourns to the divan. He joins her. Aisha sets hot mint tea beside them then sets off for the Royal Kitchens to secure dinner for the four them.

They curl up together and twine their bodies tight, elbow-in-elbow, leg-in-leg, hand-in-hand, their standard divan posture. She leans her head against his shoulder. He breathes in the pleasing scent of her hair, kisses the top of her head.

After a few comfortable moments of silence, she begins, "I meant to tell you. Salamun says he believes he has found a suitable location for the new hospital. In the Jewish quarter, just above the silk market. There is a two-story building that can be renovated to suit our needs."

"Mmmm..."

"He says there is even room for the madrasa."

"I see."

"You sound uninterested, William."

He straightens his back, shifts his leg. "I am sorry, Layla. I am interested, I was just thinking."

"About...?"

"About my role as vizier."

She lifts her head, turns to appraise him. He continues to stare straight ahead. Her voice stiffens, "That again?"

"Things have changed, Layla. Farqad believes the war between Pedro and Enrique will commence this spring, perhaps within the month. Enrique has assembled his army in Zaragoza and readies to march on Castile. Granada will send six hundred cavalry to fight with Pedro, under Farqad's direct command. I will be acting Military Vizier in his absence. The Sultan has instructed us to prepare for war, Layla."

"I see." The silence stretches, the tension slipping in to surround them. "More the reason to resign your position, William, before the fighting begins."

"It is not that simple, Layla. I possess knowledge of European tactics that Granada's armies desperately need."

Her voice rises, exasperation seeping in between the syllables. "It is that simple, William."

He shakes his head, "No..."

"IT IS THAT SIMPLE!" Her emeralds open wide, a fiery flash. She hesitates, then says, "The longer you delay the more likely you are to get pulled into this fight, William. Do not be a fool, if Granada goes to war, you will not be an advisor. They will insist that you command troops. They will shame you into it. You risk our love, William, us, our future."

He turns and meets her eyes, his expression hardened. "The two of us are more important than the safety of the kingdom, Layla?"

She looks down, falls silent. She whispers, "I am sorry I raised my voice."

"My love, I am trying to balance my desires, our desires, for a life of peace and service, with the needs of the Sultan and the demands of the kingdom. With my duties and loyalties. I cannot ignore my responsibilities, Layla. My heart is heavy with the struggle. But I cannot deny who I am, surely you can see that."

"I know who you are, William, better than you do." More silence. "And what about our...our...our..." Her voice begins to quaver in cadence to her chin-tremble. She chokes back a sob and manages to get it out. "Our children."

He looks at her tenderly, pulls her tight to him. "Layla, our children will come, you will see. Many children." He smiles. "Little girls with giant emerald eyes and chestnut curls, as beautiful as their mother."

The flood commences. She looks down as she whispers, "William. I...I...I...lost our baby." She sobs into him.

He lifts her chin, looks into her brimming eyes. "What? What do you mean, 'our baby?' What happened, Layla? Tell me."

She heaves it out a gasp at a time. "I was...with child...nearly two moons... I woke...with cramps...and bleeding...our baby is gone, William, gone." Her sobs break out again.

"Oh my God, Layla. I am so sorry. Why did you not tell me, darling?" He smothers her with his hug, holds her head to his chest. "Shhh...shhh... Look at me, Layla. Look at me." He lifts her chin and they lock eyes. "We will have a baby, Layla, I promise. Do you hear me? We will have a baby. We will." She nods through her sniffles, buries her head in his chest.

At that moment there is a soft knock as the door angles open. Ibn al-Khatib enters, sees the mayhem on the divan and halts. He averts his eyes and begins back-pedaling. "I am so sorry, I should have knocked before I entered, forgive me."

Chandon rises. "There is no problem, Baba, just give us a few minutes."

# Bargains

14 March 1369. The rolling thunder of the six hundred cavalry is deafening. They ride hard for the enemy's flank, skirting behind the low hill to the south of the battle, hoping against odds for surprise. Al-Bistami prays that the distraction of the raging battle will provide some measure of cover for the billowing dust cloud that dogs their movements, else this will be a wasted opportunity. The cavalry ride eight abreast and stretch backward a quarter of a mile. The Granadine-blue banners carried high by the first two riders whip and snap, the gold embroidery ironically proclaiming to the opposing Christian armies, "There is no victor but Allah."

As they complete their flanking movement and begin to climb the hidden side of the low hill, al-Bistami raises his right hand without looking back and circles it in the air. On cue the cavalry slows, gathers into a compact, four-pronged formation, then halts. The knights begin to ready their weapons. Al-Bistami and three of his officers walk their horses to the crest of the hill.

The battle stretches to the low ridgeline a half-mile distant. The flat golden farmland makes for easy maneuvering and long lines of sight. Deforested centuries back, the patch of fields are decorated with a splash of green stubble from the two-inch high spring wheat seedlings. A tangle of scrub marks the stream that meanders across the plain. Small olive groves are scattered sporadically and several farm buildings dot the scene, dice cast upon a gaming table. To his left, at the western horizon, al-Bistami can just see the castle clinging to the treeless, rocky hill. Castillo de Montiel.

He studies the scene unfolding before him with a practiced eye. The brutal mayhem that defines medieval warfare spills its grisly carnage over the entire plain. Pedro's army is to his left, west, Enrique's army to the right. In the center, tens of thousands of infantry are massed together in an enormous clot, their unit lines obliterated, an intermingled free-for-all of swords, maces, pikes and crossbows. Hundreds of dead and dying litter the ground. The collection of colored banners dancing about the plain announces the combatants; red and yellow stripes for Aragon, blue castle on red for Castile, red and green for Portugal, blue with gold fleur-de-lis for France, and oddly, at the extreme right, the unmistakable crimson-on-white Jerusalem cross, the

Crusader's Cross, the infamous Papal Banner of reconquista. Al-Bistami frowns.

A low, hushed groan of desperation envelops the fields of death. Al-Bistami cups his hands to his ears, hears the macabre sounds of crisp metal on metal pings, exhausted grunts, the soft moans and begging of the maimed and mortally wounded, all punctuated by staccato blood-curdling screams. He hears the unearthly wailing of wild-eyed, pike-gutted horses hobbled on their own slippery entrails as they scramble about, riderless. Dozens of vultures patiently circle, certain of their evening's meal.

Throngs of heavy cavalry knife into the carnage at a dozen points from both sides, broadswords and maces slicing the air to devastating effect, trampling any that get in the way, friend or foe.

As Al-Bistami widens his view, the difference in numbers between the two armies becomes striking. Discouraging. He sighs with the recognition. Pedro was foolishly overconfident in challenging Enrique's superior force on such an open battleground. The odds are not in their favor.

Al-Bistami's eyes are drawn to a fuzzy cloud that leaps into the air from a tight, squared formation to his right, arcs high as it lengthens, then descends upon the helpless infantry. Dozens crumple to the earth. French archers. Another volley, then a third, finally an answering volley from behind Pedro's line. He looks at his target now, the enemy's left flank at the base of the hill. Several hundred cavalry gathered in disorganized bands anchor the infantry line and seem oblivious to their imminent danger. Aragonese banners.

Al-Bistami barks at his officers for their attention then slices the air in the direction of their quarry, saying, "Bakr, you will swing west and attack from their front. I will lead my column down the hill to crush their flank. Jalaf and Muhallab, you will slide in behind them to block their escape." Each man nods an acknowledgment. They turn their horses to join their columns and pass final instructions.

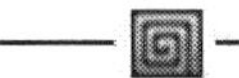

Pedro and a half-dozen of his adjutants sit on stools under the command tent set on a low rise within an olive grove a quarter mile to the rear of the main battle lines. The Castilian banner snakes in the breeze. Pedro sips wine from a silver goblet as the battle unfolds. He pauses every few moments to query an officer on the status of this or that planned action, the health of this or that cadre of infantry, the location of a cavalry unit. He seems at ease, pleased at the battle's progress despite his brother's superior numbers.

Riders periodically arrive in a dust cloud, drop to the ground to make their reports. The officers confer with the King on the information delivered, but Pedro personally issues all final commands, which are hastily scribbled and passed to the rider, who remounts and darts back to find his commanding officer in the battle lines.

Pedro turns to his left and asks the adjutant, "Has the Moor cavalry begun its attack yet?"

"No, Majesty."

Pedro stands and searches the low hill to his right, then begins to pace. "Damn al-Bistami! We need to turn Enrique's flank while we have the momentum. What is holding them up?"

"They should be in place at any moment, Majesty. They circled wide behind the hill to avoid detection. They should attack from the top of the rise."

Pedro's frustration is mounting. "The Moors need to hurry or my brother will close ranks and the opportunity will be lost."

Just as he finishes saying this the faint blare of trumpets sounds far off to his left. Pedro and his adjutants turn as one and study the scene, confused by the unexpected announcement.

An adjutant's arm whips up and points, alarm edging into his voice. "Majesty, there! The dust cloud at the ridgeline."

As Pedro squints, his frown hardens. A line of heavy cavalry two dozen wide is spilling over the ridgeline en masse. "Can you make out the flag?"

"Crusader's cross, Majesty." He continues to study the scene. "Wait, there is a second. Black skull on white."

The timbre of Pedro's voice shifts. "Are you sure?"

"Yes, Majesty, positive. Black skull on white."

Pedro can only offer a weary sigh. He shakes his head. "God damn them! The Free Companies. Under Papal Banner, no less. I wondered why we had not seen them on the battlefield. I should have guessed they were being held in reserve. GOD DAMN THEM!"

"Our spies said that they were five thousand strong, Majesty. We have no reinforcements to send. They will turn our flank."

"Yes..." Pedro whips back to his right, squints at the hill. Still nothing. He turns back to the left. Already the Free Companies are engaging his thinly protected flank as they continue to hemorrhage from the ridgeline unchallenged. He knows his cavalry at the flank will be no match for the Free Companies. His gaze returns to the battlefield in front of him as he locates the

Aragonese banner and Crusader's cross atop the distant tent. "God damn you to hell, Enrique!"

Pedro begins pacing again, then halts. "The day is lost, gentlemen. It seems my brother has improved his tactics since Nájera. We must retreat while there is still time. We make haste for Castillo de Montiel."

"Majesty, there is not enough room to house our army there."

"What do you not understand? There will be no army to house. The Free Companies will roll up our flank and crush us from the rear. There will be no escape for the infantry or archers. Send word to the cavalry units to disengage and ride for Montiel. They are to protect our rear as we retreat." Shocked silence ensues, followed by grim nods of understanding.

"Should we send word to the Moors, Majesty?"

"Damn the Moors! They are on their own now. Make haste!" The scene erupts into frantic activity.

It is deep in the night before Pedro has a moment to collect himself, breathe. He looks exhausted, shaken, the whites of his eyes ghost-like, his hair disheveled. The retreat was panicked, awful, the Free Companies dogging the limping army the entire four miles to the castle mount, methodically separating the slow and the weak, then casually executing them. No prisoners were taken between the battlefield and the castle. None.

Of the twenty-three thousand men that stepped on the battlefield at Montiel with Pedro on the fourteenth day of March 1369, only forty-two hundred make it to the castle, all cavalry. Only a few hundred can be fit inside the castle proper. The rest are hastily bivouacked inside the outermost defense walls of the compact town of Montiel which is edged tight against the southwest base of the castle mount. An unmistakable concentric ring of thousands of campfires dots the night a quarter mile out from the hill. Surrounded.

Pedro is joined in the castle keep by Don Ruy and Don Alfonso, his counselors, Don Perro Carrillo, commander of the Portuguese forces, and Don Sánchez de Velasco, the commander of Castillo de Montiel.

"Any news of Don Sancho and Don Juan?"

Don Ruy answers, "None, Majesty. They were forward with their cavalry units when the Free Companies turned our flank. Hopefully they were captured and will be ransomed."

Pedro nods, remains silent. "Your castle has excellent fortifications, Don Sánchez, and is easily defended. My brother will not capture it by direct assault. Tell me about your stores."

"Water is no issue, Majesty. The river flows inside the town walls at the base of the castle mount and we have full cisterns within the castle. But the wheat harvest is still two months away. We only have food for three months, possibly four, Majesty, and only for those in the castle. I am not sure how we will feed the cavalry settled in the town."

"Can the town's defenses hold off a direct assault?"

"Unlikely, Majesty, not from an army of this size. The town's outer walls are modest. The castle has the only serious defenses."

The room falls silent.

Don Alfonso says, "Majesty, we must attempt to fight our way out before Enrique settles in for a siege."

Don Perro adds, "I agree, Majesty. We will be eating our horses within a month."

Pedro appears lost in thought. He looks up. "Fight our way out to where exactly? Even if we could break out, the Free Companies would be on us in an instant. You saw what they did to us during the retreat. Sevilla is two hundred miles. My brother will take the town, capture the cavalry, then lock us in the castle and starve us into submission. That is what I would do."

The foul-smelling pall of desperation drifts into the corners of the room unobserved. The torch light seems to dim perceptibly in response to the lack of good air.

Pedro kneads his chin as he begins to pace. The others exchange wary glances but remain silent, unwilling to risk his rage. Pedro stops and turns. "I see only one option, gentlemen. I will try and bribe the Free Companies for safe passage out of the castle. They are the worst kind of mercenaries, after all, and gold is all they really want. They could care less who conquers Castile or Aragon. Knowing my brother, he will have paid them a bare minimum for their services. I will sweeten the deal."

Don Ruy counters, "Majesty, we do not have the gold to pay them."

Pedro's impatience infuses his tone, "They do not know that, Don Ruy!" He lowers his voice. "Besides, I will offer them land as well, and noble status. That, they definitely covet."

Don Alfonso offers, "Risky, Majesty, very risky. These mercenaries are not to be trusted."

"No argument, Don Alfonso, but we have no real choice, do we? If we delay, my bastard brother will tighten the noose, and Castile will be his. Desperate times demand desperate measures."

Pedro turns to Don Sánchez and says, "Can you manage to slip a man out of the town with a guide that knows the land?"

"That should be no problem, Majesty."

"Don Alfonso, remind me. I recall that there was an officer in your cavalry that knows du Guesclin."

"Correct, Majesty. Juan Rodríquez de Sandóval. A distant cousin, I believe."

"Did he make it to the castle?"

"He did, Majesty."

"Good. I will compose a letter and suggest a secret meeting to discuss my offer. He is to personally deliver it to du Guesclin. We will all pray, gentlemen, that God's fortune might shine upon us once more."

The answer from du Guesclin has arrived at last, the letter suggesting a meeting with Pedro just outside the town wall at midnight. The letter is emphatic that Pedro come alone.

The King and his entourage have arrived at the wall. Their hoods are pulled tight around their faces to obscure prying eyes.

Don Sánchez indicates the bolted door at the base of the stone wall. "When you slip through the door, Majesty, you will emerge behind a large bush that will provide cover. But do not move unless you see the signal."

"Yes. A single rider on a white horse will remove his plumed hat and replace it three times." Pedro looks skyward. "There should be plenty of moonlight."

Don Sánchez continues. "We will watch from the wall. When you return, Majesty, two knocks, a pause, then two more." Pedro nods.

"It could be a trap, Majesty."

"I have little choice, Don Alfonso, precious little choice." He turns to his counselors, tries to exude some confidence. "Wish me luck, gentlemen." He fingers his sword hilt as the door is unbolted, then checks his dagger for the third time. Pedro nods to the counselors then slips through the wall. The door is bolted behind him.

Pedro freezes, listens for any hint of movement. Nothing. He eases to the edge of the bush and stops, letting his eyes adjust. The ground is flat for a hundred yards in front of the wall, then dips to the river, rising again on the other side into low rolling hills. Hundreds of campfires dot the horizon. He scans left to right with his peripheral vision, looking for a horseman. None. He crouches to wait. Five minutes. Ten minutes. His eye is drawn to movement in front of him. A plumed hat, then a black cloak, then finally a white horse rises into view as the rider walks his stallion up the bank from the river. When in full view, but still beyond the range of any archers on the wall, the rider stops, removes his hat, then replaces it. Again. Once more.

Pedro pulls his cloak tight, rechecks his dagger, then begins a brisk walk towards the rider, his eyes continuing to scan for any hint of danger. When he is within twenty paces, the rider sees him and dismounts. Pedro draws within three paces and stops.

The rider removes his plumed hat and offers an exaggerated bow.

"Bertrand du Guesclin, commander of the Free Companies, at your service, Majesty." His honeyed Castilian is perfect in form but dusted with a hint of a French accent.

"It is a pleasure to meet you, Bertrand."

The knight bows again. "The pleasure is mine, Majesty. I received your intriguing letter, Majesty. You mentioned a desire for my services. May I inquire as to the nature of that request?"

"Indeed. As you may have noticed, Bertrand, I have experienced some acute...misfortunes...over the past two days."

An exaggerated frown from the Frenchman. "I am afraid I did indeed notice that, Majesty. Let me apologize for the...transgressions...of my troops during your retreat. Sometimes my men just seem to forget the rules of war. I have since reminded them that mercy brings God's Grace."

Pedro chokes back his bile, continues in an even voice. "That is in the past, Bertrand. I require safe passage out of Montiel and a guarantee that the Free Companies will not pursue me."

"I see. How many men, Majesty?"

"Two dozen, no more."

"Forgive me, Majesty, but why would I do you this service? You are the one, after all, holed up in a squalid castle, surrounded."

"Let me be frank, Bertrand. You are a mercenary. My brother despises you. Whatever he paid you I will double."

A thin smile. "I see. A generous offer, Majesty. It may interest you to know that Enrique secured my services for ten thousand gold francs, Majesty."

"Then I will give you twenty thousand for safe passage."

Bertrand nods appreciatively. "Forgive me, Majesty, but there are those who might be skeptical that Castile possesses that much gold."

Pedro considers his words. "It is true, Bertrand, that Sevilla's coffers have been emptied by the refitting of my army." He hesitates. "What is not known, however, is that Sultan

Muhammad of Granada has offered to loan me as much gold as I require to win this war. The Moor coffers are chock-full. Twenty thousand pieces of gold will be available within a month of my safe delivery to Sevilla."

Bertrand's eyes widen with this knowledge. "I see, Majesty, that is indeed interesting news." He thinks for a moment, then says, "I must tell you also, however, that in addition to gold, I desire...oh, how should I say...some regal legitimacy. A noble title perhaps, maybe some land."

"That is a small matter, Bertrand, easily accomplished. Perhaps something in Galicia?"

"Oh, I was thinking of a Dukedom in the Navarre, Majesty. Pamplona, perhaps? You see, I love a mountain view."

"Consider it done."

Bertrand falls silent as he thinks. "I have a counter offer for your consideration, Majesty. A better bargain."

"Oh?"

"Majesty, forgive me for saying, but your brother is scum. I take his gold, and I fight, but he does not have my allegiance, nor does he deserve it. The same is true of Pedro of Aragon. A pompous old man. He had the nerve to banish the Free Companies from Zaragoza. Imagine. An entire winter in the moth-eaten farm town of Zuera. No women, no wine, nothing. Despicable treatment, I am afraid, for those whose services he so desperately requires. Enrique is lucky we lasted the winter. And as you well know, Majesty, without the Free Companies you might have carried the day. The Aragonese and French are worthless in a good fight, cowards that they are. We all saw that firsthand at Nájera, Majesty, did we not?"

"What is your proposal, Bertrand?"

"You will surrender to me, Majesty." Pedro's eyes widen. "I will take you to my command tent a mile from here. I will invite Enrique to come and gloat over our victory." He licks his lips with anticipation, then continues, "When he arrives I will slip you a dagger and allow you to slit your brother's throat." He lets his words trail off. "The price would be the same, of course, twenty thousand pieces of Moor gold. And I become the new Grand Duke of Pamplona.

"Think of it, Majesty. If I help you escape to Sevilla you still have to rebuild an army and defeat Enrique. This way you end the war here. Now. As soon as Enrique is dead, the Free Companies will ride north and settle in the Navarre. Aragon will have learned a valuable lesson about how to treat the Free Companies. Aragon and France will have no choice but to retreat. And you still have your cavalry in Montiel to help persuade their exit from Castile." Bertrand opens his hands expectantly and smiles.

Silence.

"Your reputation for cunning strategy is not exaggerated, Bertrand. I like the idea. Snatch victory from the jaws of defeat. What guarantees can you offer me?"

"Guarantees, Majesty? My word of honor as a knight, of course." He extends his right hand.

After a tense moment of anticipation, Pedro reaches out and firmly shakes Bertrand's hand. "I accept your offer on your word of honor."

"Good, Majesty, good. I will arrange things. Let us meet here tomorrow evening at midnight. Come alone." He flicks his eyes at Pedro's sword, "Unarmed this time," and remounts. "Until then, Majesty." Bertrand tips his hat, turns and canters back towards the river. Pedro's eyes do not leave the man as he considers the risks of the deal he has just agreed to.

As Bertrand and Pedro canter their horses over the low rise the massive tent comes into view, the black skull on white prominently displayed on each vertical panel is highlighted by the moon's jealous gaze. The same insignia flies above the three tall central poles used to lend vertical height to the spacious interior. The two men dismount, give their reins to an attendant, then walk past the six heavily-armed guards posted outside the entrance. Bertrand nods but does not speak to them.

He parts the canvas, lifts his palm and says, "After you, Majesty." Pedro steps inside, then stops to absorb. Two bodyguards stand to either side of the entrance, otherwise the tent is empty. He turns to observe Bertrand in good light. The Frenchman is dressed as a court dandy; ruffles and frill, lace and bright colors. A handsome man. Long blond hair, steely blue eyes. Pedro has no love of French knights or their finery.

The interior of the tent is palatial, even by Pedro's standards. It is well-lit by a dozen oil lamp stands. Persian carpets, an oversized feather-stuffed poster bed with a lace canopy, French tapestries, a pillowed lounging couch, a gaming table set with an exquisite chess set and two decks of cards, an oak dining table with silver place-settings for eight, and an ornate silver tea service. The requisite wine cask. Two full suits of glistening armor stand in the corner beside a long table covered with a priceless collection of swords, daggers, and maces displayed on crushed red velvet.

Bertrand says, "As you can see, Majesty, I prefer to travel in comfort when I am on campaign." Pedro remains silent. "You will forgive me, Majesty, but I do not allow weapons inside my personal tent. Vitalien, can you please ensure that the King is unarmed?"

Pedro sneers as the bodyguard steps forward and begins to pat him down, but does not resist. No sword or dagger, but as the man's hand slips into the edge of the King's left boot, he extracts a jeweled, four-inch needle dagger tucked into the leather. The bodyguard hands the dagger to Bertrand, who flips it over in his hand and smiles. "A beautiful dagger, Majesty. Moorish?"

"Yes. A gift of the Sultan."

"Ahhh...good. It will have a place of honor in my collection, Majesty. Thank you." He hands the dagger to Vitalien then raises his palm and indicates the game table. "Shall we sit, Majesty, while we wait for Enrique?"

Pedro moves to the table and pulls back the chair, sits.

"Vitalien, a goblet of wine for each of us. The finest Bordeaux, Majesty, you will like it."

Pedro nods.

After they each have a sip, Bertrand says, "Remember, Majesty, when Enrique arrives, I will have Vitalien and Arnaldus stand at your side, pretending to guard you. This will put Enrique at ease. I will see that he is disarmed when he enters, as I did you. Sad to say, his bodyguards will not be allowed to enter the tent. When he comes forward to gloat and stands before you, I will draw my dagger and hand it to you. I am afraid the rest is up to you."

Pedro turns and studies the man. "I am up to the task, Bertrand."

"Indeed, Majesty, of that I have no doubt." He smiles.

Riders. Bertrand rises and indicates where Pedro should stand. Vitalien eases beside him, draws his sword and rests its point on the floor. Satisfied, Bertrand turns and moves to the entrance. He nods to Arnaldus.

Enrique parts the canvas and steps inside the tent. Bertrand comes forward, smiles then kisses Enrique on both cheeks. "A pleasure, as always, Enrique."

Enrique does not return the smile, but instead strains to look past Bertrand at the man standing near the back of the tent.

"As you know, Enrique, I do not allow weapons in my tent."

"Of course. I left my sword and dagger with my bodyguards."

Bertrand smiles. "Arnaldus, please ensure that Enrique is unarmed." The bodyguard moves forward and methodically pats him down. Nothing. He flicks his head then takes his place beside Pedro.

"Thank you, Enrique, for indulging me." Bertrand smiles, then says, "I suppose you wish to behold my catch? Come, say hello to your brother, come." The Frenchman seems to be enjoying himself.

Enrique follows Bertrand across the tent. Enrique sizes Pedro up in silence. "You have changed, Brother. You look old and tired."

"You are a bastard, Enrique, the son of a whore. I do not acknowledge you as my brother, and I never will." A thin smile forms on Enrique's face as he continues to study Pedro. "Pedro the Cruel. Time has not softened your heart, Brother." Bertrand grins. He is enjoying the spectacle. Enrique continues, "Still playing at becoming a Moor, Brother? You make a mockery of Castile and all that Father accomplished during his reign. All of Europe laughs at you, Pedro, roars behind your back. Shameful." He shakes his head side to side. "Very shameful." Pedro's eyes burn with hate, but he remains silent.

Bertrand interjects, "Enough, brothers! Time for some fun."

Both men turn and look at Bertrand as he reaches into his vest and withdraws a ten-inch needle dagger. He grips the blade between his thumb and forefinger and taps his palm with the handle. Both men's eyes widen. Pedro's heart is pounding. Bertrand says, "My, my, decisions, decisions." He turns and hands the dagger to Enrique, then bows. Pedro lunges forward and grabs for the blade, but Vitalien and Arnaldus step in front of him, swords ready. Pedro seethes. The smile on Enrique's face grows wide.

Bertrand says, "My apologies, Majesty. It seems that Enrique had a better offer after all. Not only do I get gold and land a plenty, but he has given me Granada. Imagine, Majesty, Bertrand du Guesclin, Grand Duke of Granada! More gold and more land than Aragon or Castile could ever hope to offer. So you see, the decision was out of my hands, I am afraid. I must think of my men." A giant smile.

Pedro hisses, "You are scum, du Guesclin, a knight with no honor. What of your word, scoundrel?"

Bertrand waggles his finger, "Now, now, do not be angry, Majesty. It was a business decision, not personal."

"You will never conquer Granada, du Guesclin, and you will never see Moor gold."

"Oh, do not be so sure. We are on a Crusade, Majesty. Reconquista! With the Pope and God behind me, how can I lose?"

He doubles over as he cackles. "Arnaldus, you and Vitalien take the King's hands, hold him fast. Bertrand raises both his palms to Pedro, then turns and says, "Enrique, may I present the King of Castile."

Pedro struggles but cannot move. Enrique steps forward, halving the distance between them. His face has drawn tight with purpose. Pedro becomes frantic as he sees a killer's eyes staring back. He blurts out, "I demand ransom! By God, I am entitled to ransom by the rules of chivalry!"

Enrique smiles. "Oh, there will be no ransom this day, Brother, none whatsoever." The dagger shoots forward into Pedro's gut and withdraws, eliciting a surprised gasp as he doubles over in agony, a sharp moan slipping from his mouth. The bodyguards do not let go of his hands, however, and force him back up.

Enrique turns to Bertrand. "Tell me, Bertrand, how long can a man live with his bowels sliced open?"

The Frenchman beams, "Oh, easily a few hours. Though the wicked stink from your leaking shit is pure torture. Or so I am told. And the thirst, oh my, the awful thirst. Slake your parch with a fine wine, and I am afraid it will leak right out your belly."

The dagger shoots into Pedro's gut again, but this time Enrique does not withdraw it and instead jerks it side to side, eliciting a sharp scream. The bodyguards let Pedro slide to the floor.

Enrique bends down and lifts Pedro's head by the hair, stares into his brother's pleading eyes with smoldering hate. Pedro gasps, "Please, Brother, mercy."

Enrique hisses, "Brother, Castile is mine now. My troops will be arriving in Sevilla by ship any day. When you die, I am going to enjoy flaying you and staking your skinless corpse to the ground and watching the vultures pick your Moorish bones clean. No funeral for you, dear Brother. I will scatter you in the hills. A dozen years from now, no one in Sevilla will even remember what King Pedro the Cruel looked like, who he was or what he did. Goodbye, Brother." He lifts Pedro's head higher to stretch his neck, then slips the dagger underneath, draws it ear to ear. Pedro's eyes widen as he tries to speak, but he can only gurgle as his blood erupts onto the carpet. Enrique drops the head and stands. He turns to du Guesclin and says, "I am in your debt, Bertrand."

"Indeed you are, King Enrique, indeed you are. Do not forget our arrangement, Majesty."

# Booty

16 May 1369. The Vizier Council has been convened in the cool anteroom of the Royal Baths, the bath eunuchs and the Royal Bodyguards dismissed. Gathered around the Sultan are Ibn al-Khatib, al-Bistami, Chandon, al-Harish, al-Mubarak and al-Ghudari. Despite the Sultan's attempt to inject calm, the cool, moist air remains tense, the palpable sense of foreboding heavy in the hammam.

Al-Bistami rode through the city gates late the evening before, his cavalry exhausted. A disturbing number of the horses were riderless. Even without direct knowledge of recent events, a general sense of alarm has settled upon the palace.

The Sultan begins, "Gentlemen, the kingdom is in grave danger. I have called you together for your counsel. Farqad, please bring everyone up to date."

Al-Bistami is uncharacteristically haggard, for once looking his age. "King Pedro of Castile is dead." To a man, the eyes of the group widen. The nervous glances pick up steam, betraying a rising discomfort. Al-Bistami continues, "Pedro engaged Enrique's army on the open plains just east of Montiel.

Ibn al-Khatib interrupts. "Montiel? Remind me."

"Seventy-five miles to the northeast of Jaén. It was a foolish decision. Enrique's army had nearly a two to one numerical advantage. Pedro was overconfident, as usual. He ignored his senior military advisors, who sought a more defensible position from which to engage the enemy. Pedro kept touting his victory at Nájera. Ridiculous given the absence of Edward and the English longbowmen. So battle was waged despite the protests. Still, things seemed to tip to Pedro's advantage late in the day. He sent my cavalry to try and turn Enrique's flank to seal the victory. As we were beginning our attack, however, the Free Companies moved up behind the far ridge and emerged in force on Pedro's left flank, a complete surprise. They were under Papal Banner, no less. The Free Companies crushed Pedro's flank, then circled behind the army, producing predictable panic. Pedro deserted his infantry and archers and retreated with his cavalry to the castle at Montiel."

Al-Bistami snarls, then hisses, "He left me hanging on the right flank, with no word. By the time I realized what was happening, the Free Companies were on us. I lost eighty good men by the time we managed to disengage and escape." He pauses. "The Free Companies pursued Pedro all the way to Montiel, executing any they could catch. The rest of Pedro's army was annihilated. Many thousands were killed, more captured. My cavalry retreated into the hills, then circled wide to Montiel under cover of night to see what would happen. Two days later we learned that Enrique personally murdered Pedro. In du Guesclin's tent. Somehow du Guesclin convinced Pedro to come unarmed to parley with Enrique." He shakes his head side to side. "Stupid fool." He looks around the room. "Enrique sent Castilian troops by Genoese transport up the Guadalquivir River and they have now taken Sevilla. A bold move. That happened a week ago. Enrique was crowned King of Castile two days back. They have already signed a treaty of alliance with Aragon and France."

Chandon says, "Where is Enrique's army?"

Al-Bistami looks up. "Unclear. I would imagine it remains assembled at Montiel. For now. Enrique is not fool enough to let the Free Companies get too close to Sevilla." He weighs the possibilities. "My guess is that they will refit, then turn south towards Granada." He turns to the Sultan. "I have heard rumors, Sire, more than once now, that Enrique promised du Guesclin and the Free Companies the lands of Granada in exchange for their support."

"Yes, that would make sense."

Ibn al-Khatib says, "They will have French and Papal backing to renew reconquista, Sire. It is no secret that Pedro of Aragon desires nothing more than the collapse of Granada. I am sure he would be more than happy to send troops south in support of their cause. And Genoa has clearly taken sides." Ibn al-Khatib exchanges a quick glance with Chandon, then continues. "Enrique has made no secret of the fact that he hates Granada and all that we represent. He will support any move that involves reconquista."

The Sultan responds, "Farqad, what of our garrisons at Jaén, Baeza and Úbeda?"

"They are well fortified and supplied, Sire, particularly Jaén, but they cannot hold back an army of that size for long without support."

Chandon says, "I agree, Sire. Farqad, what is your estimate of Enrique's strength?"

"At least forty thousand, perhaps more."

Chandon shakes his head side to side.

Al-Harish chimes in. "With Pedro dead, Sire, any Castilian troops that survived the rout will turn and fight behind Enrique. They will have no choice."

The Sultan turns to al-Mubarak and says, "Will the Marinids honor their treaty and send troops to support us if we are invaded?"

Al-Mubarak sighs. "Unclear, Sire. They continue to send mixed messages. The Sultan is weak and his viziers are strong. They have their own internal politics to deal with."

Al-Bistami glances at the Sultan. "Sire, we must prepare for a Christian invasion. We cannot count on Marinid support."

The Sultan queries Chandon with his eyes. "I agree, Sire."

The rest of the men nod their heads in agreement as the Sultan looks from vizier to vizier. Ibn al-Khatib nods his 'yes', then frowns at the floor.

The Sultan somberly says, "Farqad, see to it."

The Sultan reclines on his white divan in the Hall of the Ambassadors. To his right sits Ibn al-Khatib and to his left Prince al-Bistami. They sit silent and watchful, expressionless. Four red statues stand behind the Sultan, intimidating as usual, their weapons prominently displayed.

The entourage approaches behind the courtier, then stops ten paces in front of the Sultan. Muhammad's face remains unreadable but his eyes sparkle with amusement as the visitors's eyes dart about to take in the magnificence.

The courtier begins, "His Excellencies, ambassadors of Castile, Aragon, Genoa, France, and the Pope." He pauses for effect. "His Royal Highness, Muhammad V, son of Yusef. Ruler of al-Andalus, eighth Sultan of Granada, builder of the Alhambra, elder of the Nasrid clan, defender of the faith. May Allah bless and protect his reign." The echo lingers. The visitors seem quite uncomfortable in these alien surroundings, as if ghosts hide behind every door.

The Sultan says, "Welcome, gentlemen, to the Alhambra." He introduces his viziers.

The man in the center responds, "Sire, I am Don Alfonso Méndez de Guzmán, representative of King Enrique of Castile. Thank you for agreeing to see us." He lifts his palm to his right. "May I present Sir Ernaud de Florenssan, papal liaison of King Charles of France, and Don Gonzalo Ruiz Girón, ambassador to King Pedro of Aragon." Each man bows as his name is announced. Don Alfonso moves his palm to his left. "Antonio de Castrocario, ambassador to the Republic of Genoa, and Bishop de Fonte,

Apostolic Nuncio of Pope Urban V." The bishop is dressed in royal purple shoulder to ankle, complete with gold ring, miter hat, and large gold pectoral cross hanging from his neck. Quite a spectacle. The Sultan struggles to suppress a smile.

The Sultan nods. "And how may I be of service, gentlemen?"

Don Alfonso continues. "Sire, perhaps you have heard that Pedro of Castile is dead. His brother, Enrique, is now King of Castile."

"I am afraid I had not heard that news, Don Alfonso. Word travels so slowly in Granada these days. Please offer my best wishes to King Enrique."

Don Alfonso smirks. "My understanding, Sire, was that Granadine cavalry fought beside Pedro at Montiel." His eyes track to al-Bistami, who remains stone-faced.

"That is true, Don Alfonso. Granada is diligent in honoring its treaties with its neighbors. But during the battle at Montiel, our cavalry broke off and returned to Granada before the battle was concluded. We were unsure of the outcome."

"I see." Don Alfonso considers his words, then says, "Sire, our combined forces are encamped south of Ciudad Real. Eighty miles north of Jaén."

The Sultan raises his eyebrows quizzically but does not respond.

"Sire, King Enrique intends to respect the borders of your kingdom, but he does have several...suggestions...that he would like to make in order to seal our friendship."

Ibn al-Khatib and al-Bistami lock their eyes on the ambassador. A thin smile creases the Sultan's face. "Do tell, ambassador."

"King Enrique suggests that a fitting tribute as vassal to Castile would be twelve thousand gold dinars, delivered annually to Sevilla."

"I see. You do appreciate, Don Alfonso, that that is double the tribute that we paid to Pedro."

"Indeed, Sire. King Enrique feels strongly, however, that it is fair price for a sustained Castilian-Granadine alliance and protection against Granada's enemies."

"I see. And which enemies would those be, Don Alfonso?"

"Whomever, Sire. Granada's enemies would be Castile's enemies." Bishop de Fonte grins.

"I see. And?"

"Sire, King Enrique wanted me to remind you, respectfully, that Jaén, Baeza, and Úbeda belong to Castile, not Granada. They must be returned. With their gold."

"I see."

Don Alfonso adopts a awkward expression, as if unsure of the correct word choice; clearly a practiced pose. The Sultan indulges the obvious ploy. "Continue, please, Don Alfonso."

"Sire, it has come to King Enrique's attention that a golden orb, a metal sphere with the curious markings of the Orient, resides in the Alhambra." Ibn al-Khatib's eyes widen. "King Enrique collects such trinkets and would look upon Granada...favorably...if the object in question could be displayed in the Alcazar museum in Sevilla."

"I am afraid, Don Alfonso, that I am not familiar with the object you describe. I would be happy, of course, to try and locate it for King Enrique's collection."

"Thank you, Sire. Securing the object is of high priority to the King. As you may know, he is a collector of unusual artifacts." The Genoese ambassador licks his lips.

The Sultan nods, his expression hardening. Don Alfonso appears to search for a misplaced thought in the air. "Oh, and one final request, Sire."

The Sultan raises his eyebrows but does not speak, his eyes narrowing.

"Sire, it seems that a English knight, one William Chandon, Viscount of Saint-Sauveur in Brittany, was captured by your forces at Jaén two years back. Chandon commanded the Breton cavalry in King Enrique's army, and was one of his very best officers. He is a personal friend of mine. King Enrique was deeply troubled that no offer of ransom was made in accordance with the established rules of war. Sire, Chandon must be returned to Sevilla. Today." Don Alfonso's smile broadens. The Royal Bodyguard tense in unison, their fingers flexing over the tops of their sword hilts. The Sultan lifts his hand into the air to calm them.

"I am afraid that is quite impossible, Don Alfonso." All heads turn to the voice that enters from the side entrance. The shock is universal among the ambassadors. Mouths fall open, but no words are uttered. Don Alfonso is obviously rattled. Chandon is attired in the full battle dress of a Granadine knight, Barq strapped to his side. "You see, Don Alfonso, some things have changed since we last met."

Don Alfonso wrestles for control. "Chandon? What is the meaning of this?"

"I am a knight of Granada now, Don Alfonso. My allegiance and my sword rests here. With the Sultan." Chandon stands beside al-Bistami, arms folded.

Bishop de Fonte blurts out, "With these infidels? You must be joking, Chandon!" The bodyguards ease forward a step, hands now gripping their sword hilts, their scowls menacing.

Chandon's face hardens. He hisses, "I am a Muslim now, Bishop. These are my people. Refrain from insulting my brothers or there will be a bill to be paid." The Bishop closes his mouth as he blushes bright scarlet.

The Sultan stands, lifts his palms in the air. "Ambassadors, please. As you can see, Chandon is here by his own choice. You may tell King Enrique that I will consider his requests for additional tribute and the return of our cities. And I will scour the palace for signs of the...orb. But Shahab Chandon stays. Have a safe journey home."

Ibn al-Khatib and al-Bistami rise. The Sultan exits, followed by his viziers, then two of his bodyguards. The other two bodyguards remain as they were, eyes deadly serious. Shocked expressions are all that the ambassadors can manage. The courtier steps forward into the confusion.

"Gentlemen, may I show you the way out?"

The Royal War Council sits circled around the Sultan in the Hall of the Kings. Al-Bistami, Ibn al-Khatib, Chandon, and two dozen of the highest ranking Granadine officers. Garrison commanders from the major cities of the kingdom have each sent representatives.

Al-Bistami begins, "Gentlemen, the threat of war from the combined forces of Castile, Aragon and France is upon us, the most serious threat to the kingdom in the past one hundred years. Enrique's army lays camped outside Ciudad Real, north of Jaén. My riders have confirmed this. They estimate a force of forty thousand. The Free Companies are with them, five-thousand strong. The army marches under the Papal Banner. I am afraid reconquista once again knocks on our gates." Glances are exchanged among the officers, chased by several grumbles. Al-Bistami continues.

"We have decided to vacate Baeza and Úbeda. They are indefensible against an army of that size. The troops will retreat to the garrison at Castillo de Santa Catalina and dig in. We stand and fight at Jaén." He pauses to look around the room. "Granada will muster twenty thousand troops. Loja, Montejicar, Guardix, Mojácar and Almería will each send three thousand. That will leave you with sufficient reserves to defend yourselves should that prove necessary."

One of the representatives raises his hand. "When are the troops needed, my Lord?"

"We have arranged watchtowers with signal fires on the mountain tops throughout the kingdom. The signal fires trace a line from Jaén to each of the your cities. When Enrique breaks camp you will know within the hour. Your troops must be ready to march at a moment's notice. All but Montejicar will converge at Granada, then march north. They will join us at Jaén. That could be tomorrow, it could be a month from now. But the day will come, rest assured. Make ready."

The representative from Málaga raises his hand. Al-Bistami nods. "What of Málaga and Ronda, my Lord?"

"We have other plans, gentlemen. I will lead five thousand cavalry from Granada to Málaga, to join forces with the three thousand troops sent from Ronda and those from Málaga." Quizzical expressions appear on the faces of the officers. Al-Bistami smiles. "Then we will attack Algeciras in a lightning strike, seize its gold and raze it to the ground. Gentlemen, we aim to send a message to Enrique he cannot misinterpret. Threatening Granada has repercussions." Excited whispers circle the room.

"What of the defenses at Algeciras, my Lord?"

"Weak. A garrison of no more than two thousand troops, and we have the element of surprise. With Enrique camped on our northern border it will be impossible for him to reinforce. We will burn Algeciras and be back in Granada within three weeks, perhaps less. Bearing Castilian gold."

The representative of Guardix says, "And what if Enrique's army moves during your absence?"

The Sultan interrupts. "It is a risk worth taking, gentlemen. Algeciras will be a wakeup call for Enrique. It will force him to reconsider his plans. It also will open a port for receiving troops from the Marinids, should that turn out to be necessary. I will lead our combined forces against Enrique."

One of al-Bistami's officers says, "When do we ride for Algeciras, Sire?"

"In three days. Make ready for war." Faces harden. The Sultan continues, "Gentlemen, we fight for the life of the kingdom, for Granada and her peoples. For the Prophet." Heads nod. "We will defend our land with our lives. May Allah's favor shine upon us."

The officers and representatives rise and depart, leaving the Sultan, Ibn al-Khatib, al-Bistami, and Chandon, who remain silent until the hall is cleared. The Sultan begins. "Farqad, Algeciras must fall quickly."

"It will be so, Sire."

The Sultan turns to Ibn al-Khatib and says, "Lisan al-Din, two things. Please craft a message to Sultan al-Aziz in Fez. Coded. Inform him of the situation and that Algeciras will soon be ours. Drop the hint that we may need Marinid troops to support our defense. But be discreet. Farqad will take the letter with him and send it across the sea by courier from Algeciras. I also think it would be prudent to...melt down the astrolabe. We must destroy it." Lisan al-Din first frowns, then sighs, then reluctantly nods.

"I understand, Sire. I will see to it."

Chandon turns to the Sultan and says, "Sire, I will accompany Farqad to Algeciras. My knowledge will be valuable for a quick victory." Both Ibn al-Khatib and al-Bistami turn to Chandon, Ibn al-Khatib with a concerned frown, al-Bistami with a slight smile. The Sultan remains silent for a moment as he considers the offer, then says, "No. I need you in Granada, Shahab. To help prepare the troops for battle."

The midnight air is warm and heavy, the new moon's jealous black veil drawn tight around the Alhambra, the only sound the soft movement of wind through the tops of the trees, and an odd, repetitive panting pulse of air. A rhythmic red glow leaks from the windows of the Partal Oratory. Inside, the eleven hooded men are seated in a circle, deep in meditation, flattened open-fingered right palms fixed to the tiled floor, left hands balled, thumbs fitted into the curved index fingers and rested in their laps.

In the center of the circle a small ceramic smelter has been assembled, the large cotton bellow manned by the attendant, who levers it as precisely as a metronome, up then down, up then down, inhale-exhale, inhale-exhale. The bright red glow of the coals spilling from the slit in the top of the furnace brightens then dims in perfect time to the bellow's breath. The pulsating light reclaims the men's faces folded deep within their hoods, surrenders, then tries in vain once more to capture them, a desperate wrestling match between light and dark, truth and ignorance, life and death.

As the muraqaba ends, Ibn al-Khatib reaches down and picks up the book in front of him. The bellower does not break his rhythm; inhale-exhale, inhale-exhale. Ibn al-Khatib opens the book to the marked page, lifts his taper close and reads, "It is written in the *Rasail Ikhwan al-Safa,"*

> *"Turn, brother, from the sleep of negligence and the slumber of ignorance."*

The familiar rhythmic cadence begins.

*"We are the Ikhwan al-Safa, the Brethren of Purity.*
*We are the guardians of truth.*
*We are the defenders of inquiry.*
*We are the protectors of sacred knowledge..."*

When finished, Ibn al-Khatib looks from person to person, then says, "Brethren. It has been decided that the spherical astrolabe sent to us by our brothers in Persia must be destroyed. We dare not risk it falling into Christian hands. This is a sad day for us all, for the Truth. May Allah, in His Grace and Wisdom, resurrect this great scientific instrument at a more favorable time. Are we in agreement, Brethren?"

The group chants together, "Allah alim." *God knows best.*

Ibn al-Khatib nods, then leans forward and touches the shoulder of the bellower. The man picks up an iron rod with a hook on its end, fits it into the notch on the door of the smelter and opens the furnace. Those facing the door feel the heat on their faces as the fire's red glow fills the room. Ibn al-Khatib removes the black shroud and lifts the astrolabe from the floor in front of him and passes it to the attendant. The man places the sphere in a crucible, then takes a hinged iron tool and lifts it into the furnace. He closes the door of the smelter and returns to his bellow, doubling the pace now of his companion's breath.

Ibn al-Khatib lifts his palms and says, "Brethren, let us together recite the dhikr, the remembrance, while the refiner's fire does its work." He begins and they follow.

*"Ar-Rahman - The Compassionate.*
*Ar-Rahim - The Merciful.*
*Al-Malik - The Sovereign Lord, Our King.*
*Al-Quddus - The Holy, the Pure, the Perfect..."*

Two weeks later, just outside of Ciudad Real. King Enrique has convened his War Council. The map spread on the table inside Enrique's large tent is circled by Don Alfonso Méndez de Guzmán, Ernaud de Florenssan, Don Gonzalo Ruiz Girón, Antonio de Castrocario, Bishop de Fonte, Bertrand du Guesclin, Hugh Caveley, and the commanding officers of the Castilian, French, Breton, and Aragonese forces.

Enrique begins. "Gentlemen, as you know, we sent a delegation to the Moors to present our demands. They met with the Sultan in the Alhambra. We learned several interesting things. First and foremost, Granada is rich beyond our wildest dreams." Appreciative nods. "In addition, Don Alfonso is confident that the spherical astrolabe exists and still resides within the Alhambra. Capturing it remains a key goal for us." The Bishop and de Castrocario smile. "Finally, and I must say, most interestingly, it seems that William Chandon, commander of Breton forces at Nájera...is now a Moor. It seems that our famous English knight has gone native, renounced his Christian birthright, and even married himself a Muslim whore."

Shocked silence.

Enrique sneers, "Chandon's life is forfeit, gentlemen. I will deliver five hundred gold florins to the knight that presents me with his head."

A thin smile crawls across du Guesclin's face. "I lay claim to that wager, Majesty."

"Good, Bertrand, good. I look forward to paying you." Enrique continues, "Gentlemen, the plot has thickened. I received word yesterday that Algeciras has fallen, razed to the ground by the Moors. Our merchant ships are sunk; our gold has been seized." He waits for the fury of whispers to subside, then pushes on. "An unanticipated move, I will grant, and a good reminder that the Moors do appreciate strategy. Still, our plans remain unchanged. The Moors have vacated Baeza and Úbeda, and I have already sent Castilian troops to occupy the towns."

Caveley asks, "I assume they have retreated to Jaén and dug in, Majesty?"

"Indeed they have, Hugh." He drops his gaze to the map and slides his finger from Ciudad Real to Jaén. "Our goal will be to march south from Ciudad Real, surround Jaén, then crush Granada's forces when they attempt to reinforce, as they surely must. We are already constructing a siege engine. Jaén will not stand long." He slides his finger southward and begins to tap it on the city of Granada. "We then march due south into the heart of the Moor kingdom, surround Granada and starve them out. Capture the Alhambra and there will be no need to assault the other Moor cities. Cut off the head and the body dies."

Approving nods circle the room.

"Gentlemen, I will not rest until the Alhambra is burned to the ground, its palaces reduced to dust. I will spit on the grave of the infidel Sultan. Then I will build a giant cathedral upon the ashes of their mosque. Mark my words, gentlemen, the infidel kingdom will cease to exist." He turns and locks his eyes on each person. One by one they offer their approval.

Du Guesclin asks, "Will Granada be reinforced by the Marinids? That would greatly complicate matters, Majesty."

"Indeed it would, Bertrand. I have anticipated that possibility." He turns to de Castrocario. "Genoa has kindly agreed to anchor their fleets outside of Algeciras, Marbella and Málaga. The Marinids will have no landing should they be foolish enough to attempt to cross the Strait. In addition, we will patrol their coast to remind them of our presence. Our spies are already planting seeds to this effect in Fez. I can assure you that the Marinids will remain in Africa where they belong. Granada is on its own."

"Good. When do we march, Majesty?"

"We strike camp in three days. Sharpen your swords and make ready for war."

## Radiant Blue Flame

He eases into the apartment, trying not to disturb her. As he closes the door, the only sound is the soft click of the latch. Without moving he turns to study her. He inhales, holds it, then releases. The room is lit by two tall candelabras beside her desk, their swaying golden flames lending a pleasing undulation of light and shadow upon the walls. She faces away from him, her head bent in concentration over her calligraphy, one of her favorite evening Sufi meditation practices. She wears a white silk evening robe. Her chestnut curls spill loose and unruly down her back.

At the sound of the latch she lifts her quill from the parchment but does not otherwise indicate a break in her concentration. She speaks just loudly enough for him to hear. "The signal fires from Jaén."

Silence.

"Yes."

"My uncle has still not returned from Algeciras."

More silence.

"No."

The tense quiet stretches out now, but still neither of them moves a muscle.

"When do you leave?"

"In two days."

He hears only her muffled gasp. Her head wilts and her shoulders begin to shake. He hears the unmistakable slow, soft plop of tears on parchment, a sad rain. He crosses the room to her and raises her up, turns her and buries her in his arms. He squeezes her hard against him, holding her head tight to his chest. Her crying intensifies and then she breaks into a constricted sob and begins to groan.

His eyes well up as his heart breaks. "Shhh...shhh...do not cry, my love. It will be fine. Layla, it will be fine. Layla, shhh...shhh..."

She lies on her side nestled into the crook of his arm, her body molded tight to him as he rests on his back, eyes open in the pitch black. He strokes her hair. Her sniffles have thankfully eased. They lay in silence listening to an owl's lonely song mingling with the faint fountain-tinkle from the Garden of the Lindaraja.

She whispers, "Tomorrow is our anniversary, William." She raises her eyes to his face, but cannot see him.

"Tomorrow? September, my love."

"I mean the anniversary of our...first time together. The Generalife."

"Ahhh..." He calculates. "Yes, you are right. My most treasured memory."

Silence.

"I want us to spend tomorrow evening in my secret space. Can we? Please?"

He smiles. "I will arrange it for midnight."

"Thank you."

His tone turns serious. "Do you remember the way?"

She tickles him and he laughs loud. Mercifully, she giggles. "Yes, I remember the way."

Her white and emerald gown from a year ago lies folded in the grass beside them, his clothes tossed haphazardly in a heap. She lies on her side on the blanket, glued to him in her usual position, her head cushioned in the crook of his arm. Her hand strokes his chest. They lie in silence admiring the night sky, enjoying the solitude. The night is cloudless, the moon's thick sickle low on the horizon, making ample room for the brilliant diamond sparkle above them. The Milky Way is a bold, creamy brushstroke from horizon to horizon. In the distance they hear the lonely cry of a wolf. A moment later his lover answers. They both smile. A meteor streaks its long fiery red plume off to their right. They simultaneously offer a soft "Ahhh..." as their smiles widen.

He reaches over, and starting at her shoulder, he uses his fingers to feather down her bent arm, pausing to explore the soft crevice of her elbow. When he reaches her fingertips, he lifts her hand and brings it to his face, inhaling her scent. He touches his tongue to her palm, traces a tight circle. She shivers.

He whispers, "Wife." He kisses the pad of each finger one by one, then rubs the back of her hand across his cheek.

"Husband."

He hugs her tighter to his body and they kiss, then relax back into silence, staring up at the stars, content to make the moment last.

She whispers, "I had a dream last night. So vivid I could reach out and touch it."

"Tell me."

"I dreamed of this secret space, our space, on this day, under these stars. We made love. Allah came to us in our union, as so many times before. But this time I was certain, positive beyond all doubt..." She hesitates.

"Certain of what, Layla?"

Silence.

"That we had conceived our baby. Allah's Grace will smile upon us this night, William. I know it. I can feel it."

He turns his head to look at her, concern marking his face. "Layla, please. You cannot know that, no one can. You must be patient."

"No, William, it will happen tonight, I have seen it. I know it. I can feel it."

He sighs. "Subhanallah." *Glory to Allah.* He whispers, "I believe you, my love."

"Come to me, William."

He rolls his wife onto her back, lifts her hands above her head and drinks in her delicious curves for a long moment in the dim twilight. Her eyes are closed. She licks her lips as her breathing quickens and her heart begins to race. He kisses her closed eyes, then raises up and pauses, letting the anticipation billow. He runs his finger down the inside of her arm, up across her neck. She smiles. He leans down, breathes softly into her ear and whispers, "I love you," as he simultaneously traces a wide arc with his finger tip from her shoulder, down her side, then across her belly. She tenses, then squirms, then softly groans. He grins. He eases himself on top of her and they tenderly kiss, begin to walk hand-in-hand into the sacred space so familiar to them.

Time slows to the careful step of love's convulsed dance. Senses are exquisitely teased, then stretched and tortured. The lidded caldron steams, begins to boil over.

"Look at me, Layla. Layla, look at me." She opens her eyes, sees the white-capped waves perched dangerously high all around them, her dilated emeralds sparking bright with love's fire. His eyes are locked onto hers. He urgently whispers, "I will always love you. Layla, I will ALWAYS love you. I will ALWAYS love you." Her tears are already streaming off her face as he whispers his mantra, the waves crashing crazily down upon them, rolling them about, singeing their nerves, setting their senses ablaze with love's radiant blue flame.

At that very instant, the star twinkle abruptly stills, the approving smiles of Orion, Vega and Scorpio freeze hard to their faces, Perseus's arm locked awkwardly mid-air as he urgently motions the Seven Sisters to come quick to witness the miracle.

The world ceases its rotation, time collapses, stops to a point, sacred eternity folded close and tight around these two, the brilliant pin-prick of light both infinitely small and infinitely large at the same time.

## Midnight Sky

An hour past sunset, the pleasing cool of the evening offers a refreshing antidote to the oppressive heat of the day's hard ride. Chandon exits his tent and stops, captivated by the large, ghostly orange orb easing its prying eyes over the distant sawtooth of the Sierra Morena. The moon is full, glorious. He bows. "A good evening to you, sir." He pivots and squints to the northwest, studying the darkening scene with his peripheral vision.

The grayed, angular outline of Castillo de Santa Catalina can just be made out high above the city, two miles distant. The faint twinkle of hundreds of campfires ring the base of the mountain to the west, stretch round past the city gates and on to the northeast until they bend back to the west and out of sight. Surrounded. He turns back to the south, to Granada, and has to will himself from conjuring her face, her body.

He gazes down into the valley, calculating. The cooking fires of the Granadine army cover the slope in thick knots, stretching a good half-mile down the ridge, safely obscured from their enemy. Chandon fingers Barq's hilt as he mulls over their options.

The Sultan's tent is sparsely adorned, modest in size; a sleeping mat tucked in the corner, a low table, a circle of pillows atop a large Persian rug in the center of the room. A trio of oil lamps produces a rich, warm glow. Four bodyguards stand at attention behind the Sultan, the dozen officers already seated.

The Sultan is studying a map spread out on the rug in front of him. He looks up and says, "Welcome, Shahab." Chandon bows then seats himself on the last remaining pillow. "Shahab, we have just received a rider with news from Jaén. Harun is an adjutant to the castle's garrison commander, Muflit al-Nasr." He turns to his left and lifts his palm. "Harun?"

The man's eyes circle the tent before he begins. "Certainly, Sire. Enrique's army of forty-thousand arrived three days ago at dusk. Jaén is surrounded. Two assaults on the castle have been pressed already, the last this morning at sunrise. Both were repulsed with heavy losses to the Christians. They are not likely to capture the garrison, Sire. More worrisome is the siege engine the Christians are assembling opposite the city gates."

Chandon interrupts, "Describe it to me, Harun."

"The engine is as tall as the city wall and thirty feet wide, my Lord. Wheeled. The top, front and sides are covered with thick planks, but the wood is lined with metal plate to protect against flaming arrows. There are slots for archers at the top, providing cover for a hinged gangplank to be dropped onto the wall. In the front of the engine there is a large hole four feet from the ground, which can only mean a battering ram."

Chandon nods. "A French Belfry. How close to completion?"

"As early as tomorrow, the next day at the latest. The major pieces must have been assembled in Ciudad Real then transported whole to Jaén."

"How many trebuchets does the city possess?"

Silence.

"None, my Lord."

Chandon frowns. He turns to the Sultan. "Sire, the Christians do not mean to starve the city out. I have seen a French Belfry in action. With no trebuchets, Jaén will not stand against it." He turns back to Harun. "How heavily guarded is it? Would it be possible to send a small force in the dark of night to burn it?"

"Impossible, my Lord. They have infantry camped around it."

"How large is the city garrison?"

"Five thousand within the walls, another two thousand on the mountain."

The Sultan says, "Even if the castle holds, the battle will be decided if the city falls."

Chandon nods. "I agree, Sire. At all costs we must break the siege before the gates are forced or the wall is breached." There is whispered agreement about the room.

"What do you suggest, Shahab?"

"Sire, we must drive at the city gates and destroy the Belfry, split Enrique's forces in half. Half of the city's garrison will join us to help hold the north end of our line against counterattack. We then turn and seal the east end of the valley below Santa Catalina, trapping Enrique's forces. Our flanking cavalry will swing wide to the south and come in undetected on the west end of the valley. The castle's troops will link up with our cavalry and together they will push east down the valley. Enrique's forces will be trapped between hammer and anvil. We annihilate them there. With half his army gone, Enrique will be forced to retreat.

The Sultan considers this. "What of the Free Companies?"

"At Montiel they were held in reserve. When the battle was fully engaged and all troops committed, they emerged to crush Pedro's flank and rout his forces from the rear. I suspect Enrique will follow a similar tactic here. I would. My guess is that they lurk in the woods behind the low hill east of the city gates. When Enrique sees us make for the Belfry, the Free Companies will swing round behind us to try and turn our flank."

The Sultan sighs. "Yes. How do we counter?"

"Sire, we must hold cavalry in reserve. We will remain hidden behind the ridge so that Enrique does not suspect a trap. When he gives the word and the Free Companies attack, we will surprise them, reinforce our flank from their assault. If we hold the flank, we carry the day."

"If only we had Farqad's cavalry. Where is my vizier when I need him most?"

Chandon continues. "He cannot be more than a day or two behind us. Sire, we cannot wait for Farqad's cavalry to rejoin us. Delay and the city will fall. We must attack tomorrow morning at daybreak while Enrique is not yet aware of our position and strength."

Silence settles in as the Sultan thinks. "I agree. We attack in force at daybreak. Harun, take word to the garrison. They must be ready. I will send a dozen of my Royal Bodyguards with you to assure safe passage." He turns to his officers. "Shahab will draft battle plans for each commander. We will strike camp an hour before sunrise."

Chandon says, "Sire, I will ride with you."

"No, Shahab. You will command our reserves. I will leave you two thousand of the Royal Cavalry. You will hold our flank." He turns to his right. "Mujahid, you will be second in command to Shahab." The officer bows. "Shahab, Musa and Yazdan will serve as your bodyguards." Chandon opens his mouth to offer protest, then closes it.

"Gentlemen, this day we fight for Granada's life, for our children. There can only be victory. Make sure your troops understand this." Curt nods. "Let us convene here in three hours. Make ready for battle."

The solitary candle placed on the floor in front of her lights the still room, the gentle rhythmic movements of the golden flame producing a soothing sway of shadow dance upon the whitewashed walls. She rests on her knees upon her prayer mat, back straight, up-turned palms floating in her lap. Her mind and heart meld as she focuses on the sacred breath of life. In, then out; in, then out. She whispers, “Allah, tawhid; Allah, tawhid.” A shimmering golden aura dances lightly upon her, touching her skin here and there, settling into her welcoming hands. The peacefulness in the room, the exquisite harmony, is at once ethereal and tactile, her mind, heart and soul sharing the same bounded space, encased in the radiant glow of the love that swells her chest.

A half hour later, her intonations cease. She remains silent for a moment more, then her hands rise from her lap. She joins palm to palm, fingertip to fingertip and whispers, “Glory and praise to you, Allah, maker of the universe, origin of all goodness, source of all love. May your Grace rest upon my husband. Keep William safe, protect him from harm. Bring my beloved back to me, O Lord.”

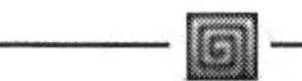

Final orders issued and gone over twice, Chandon heads to his tent and begins to dress. He dons the blue on white of a Granadine cavalry officer; white cotton robe, high leather boots, ring-mail vest, heavy felt tunic. His jeweled dagger is tucked into his belt. He eases Barq halfway out of its scabbard, the crisp steel on steel hiss reassuring. "Do not let me down this day, friend. Stand firm by my side."

As Chandon exits the tent, a bundle of nervous energy, he turns sharp right to head down the ridge, and plows into Salamun, who is standing tall and still, opaque in his flowing blue robe.

"Young Knight, you nearly ran me over!" The old Jew chuckles.

Chandon smiles. "Wizard, how is it that you are always sneaking up on me?" He laughs.

Salamun looks his wizardly self, except that his eyes are perhaps a bit more tired than usual. His shock of white hair and his flowing white beard lend an ancient, timeless presence. As their chuckles fade, the two friends stand silent, smiles still lighting their faces, as they gaze into each other's eyes.

"We fight for Granada's life this day, Young Knight."

Chandon's smile fades. "Yes, Salamun, we do."

"Where will you be?"

"I command the Royal Cavalry held in reserve."

Silence.

"Do you like our chances?"

Chandon hesitates, then says, "Yes. With a little luck."

Salamun smiles. "Ahhh...luck. You have always been lucky, Young Knight." Chandon grins. The silence stretches out. "Our girl made me promise to look after you. Please do not make me search for you, Young Knight."

Chandon laughs. "I would never do that, old friend."

Salamun steps closer. As he reaches up to clasp Chandon's shoulders, his eyes well up. He whispers, "Please be safe, William. Please."

Chandon nods. "I will, Salamun, I will."

"May our God watch over you."

"Yes, may our God watch over us all."

Chandon straddles Blue, Musa and Yazdan to either side of him, surveying the scene. The Royal Cavalry are assembled in four attack formations just below the crest of the ridge, checking their gear. The main Granadine force, commanded by the Sultan, departed a half hour earlier. They are heading due north for the gates of Jaén, as quietly as possible, a march that will consume at least an hour. The flanking cavalry has three times the distance to travel and have angled wide around the mountain to the south of Santa Catalina to avoid detection. Still no sign of al-Bistami.

Chandon looks to the east. The hint of gray allows him to make out the jagged outline of the Sierra Morena. He looks back to the north, but it is still too dark to see the army or the gates.

Yazdan asks, "Shahab, where are the Free Companies hiding?"

"Good question, my friend. My guess would be the low hill to the east of the city gates. Close enough for striking distance to the siege engine if it is attacked and still safely out of sight. That is where I would be." He points, though it is still too dark to make out exactly where he means. "They will swing round the hill and try to slip in behind the Sultan and turn his flank.

Musa joins in, "How many, Shahab?"

"Five thousand, give or take. Heavy cavalry in full armor."

"Two and a half to one. Our numbers are weak."

"Yes, Musa, but we have the element of surprise, and we bring battlefield tactics they have not seen."

"Yes..."

"May Allah protect us this day, my friends."

"We will defend you with our lives, Shahab."

Chandon locks eyes with first one then the other, nods. The silence closes in around them as they wait for the dark to lift.

The plains of Jaén are awash in an eerie gray, as if the world is devoid of all life-giving color. The sun has still not broken the Sierra Morena, but they can finally make out Santa Catalina and the city walls in the distance. Chandon can see the smudge of the Granadine army as he squints. Still unchallenged, perhaps a quarter mile now from the gates. He points. "Mujahid, do you see them?"

"Yes, my Lord. They are in place."

"Ready the men, but keep them below the crest of the ridge."

"Yes, my Lord." He turns his stallion and canters to the rear.

Chandon sees a cavalry formation break from the main army and race at full gallop towards the wooden behemoth. Chandon's voice hardens. "Gentlemen, it begins." He cups his hands to his ears. Granadine battle horns begin to sound, followed by an unmistakable chorus of thousands shouting in unison, "Allahu Akbar! Allahu Akbar! *God is great! God is great!*

The surprised enemy camp erupts in mayhem as they race about for their weapons and armor but are overrun. Answering trumpets begin to blare in a wide arc across the plains as the Moor presence is made known and the battle is pressed.

Chandon points. "Look, the Belfry. Good, good!"

Thick knots of black smoke are rising from the base of the scaly monster as it is engulfed, a giant's funeral pyre that can be seen for miles.

A half-dozen throngs of Granadine cavalry splinter from the main army, some aiming for the city gates, some turning to seal the eastern end of the valley below Santa Catalina. The infantry force splits into three, one moving to claim the gates, one angling to the northeast towards the burning Belfry to defend their flank, the third turning west to help seal the valley below the castle.

Resistance is still light but growing in intensity as the sleeping giant awakens. A tight collection of blue banners marks the position of the Sultan in the center of the line as he moves with the infantry to claim the city gates. He is surrounded by the tight ranks of the Royal Bodyguard.

The sun breaks its golden beams over the lip of the Sierra Morena, splashing a palette of yellows across the grayed-hued battlefield. The world bursts into color. Castillo de Santa Catalina stands bold in outline against the bluing sky, looking formidable in the brilliant spotlight.

The infantry have arrived at the gates unchallenged. Chandon can see a sliver of black as the city gates split open, spewing infantry out to join the Sultan. Wheeled wooden barriers are pushed forward to fortify defensive positions against the coming counterattack from the north. Chandon nods, pleased.

Over the next hour the battle intensifies along the quarter mile arc from the gates to the burning siege engine, the bulk of the

Christian army to the north of Jaén finally assembled and attacking the Moor lines. The Christian infantry have charged the Granadine line repeatedly, repulsed each time with heavy losses. The Granadine infantry stand shoulder to shoulder, a dozen men deep. Then pikemen, crossbowmen, standing knights, light cavalry, and at the rear, reserves to recharge the dead and wounded.

The Christian heavy cavalry have punched through the Moor lines twice, only to be met by reserves of Granadine crossbowmen, whose withering bolts force hasty retreats. The Christian archer companies have mobilized and every two minutes a black cloud of arrows floats lazily upward, arcs high over Granada's lines, then descends like terrible lightning. The Moor officers look skyward, shout to their men to raise their heart shields above their heads, but they are too small for adequate coverage. Dozens drop with each volley. Confused miscues launch the arrow barrages while the Christian infantry engage Granada's lines, indiscriminately felling troops on both sides.

The eastern end of the valley below Santa Catalina has been sealed, the Christian army split in half. Chandon searches the far end of the valley. He cannot see the action, but a promising dust cloud is growing, a hint that the flanking cavalry has arrived and is pressing the hammer to the anvil, as planned. He can see troops continuing to move down the western slope of the mountain from the castle to support the action.

Chandon reins Blue around to face his officers. "Gentlemen, it will not be long before the Free Companies attack." He turns and points at the low hill a mile distant. "Remember, timing is everything. We will not show ourselves until they are committed. I will lead the first company. Mujahid's company will support me. We have the angle. We gallop as fast as the wind to reach the Sultan's flank before they can. We must break their momentum there, hold our line at all costs. Salim, your company will strike at their center to cut them in half and prevent them from supporting the attack.

"Ali, you ride in support of Salim. When he cuts their line, you break east and turn their tail so their rearguard is forced to retreat." The officers all nod. "Gentlemen, today's battle will be won or lost by our actions. Stand tall and proud for Granada, my friends. Hold the Sultan's flank and we will have victory." He pumps his fist into the air. "There is no victor but Allah!"

The officers raise their fists and shout in response, "There is no victor but Allah!" They canter back over the ridgeline and give the command to ready weapons. The hearts of the most fearless of the knights pound in their chests.

Chandon scans the desperate battle for the gates, the quarter-mile long line now thick with bodies on both sides. Granada's lines are holding. His eyes move left. The battle in the valley rages, but the angle prevents him from seeing who has the upper hand. His eyes track round to the eastern hill. Nothing. He begins to wonder if perhaps he guessed wrong on their location.

At that instant he sees two large banners ease over the angled line of the hill. The Crusader's Cross dances beside the black skull on white. Free Companies. The heavy cavalry comes into view as they swing wide round the hill, their approach obscured from the city gates. The tight gleaming column is twenty horses wide and stretches back around the hill. Cantering, not galloping; unhurried, confident.

Chandon takes a deep breath, holds it, then exhales. He raises his right arm, turns in his saddle back towards the cavalry and shouts, "Knights of Granada, we ride!" Hoof-thunder erupts as the two-thousand horses move as a single organism.

Blue puffs and blows as he cuts the distance to Granada's flank, Musa and Yazdan to either side. Chandon's eyes alternate between the advancing column to his right and his target in front of him. The Free Companies have clearly seen them by now, but have not altered their trajectory or pace, a mark of confidence. Chandon's practiced eye scans for the best defensive position. A hundred yards east of the smoking rubble of the Belfry he sees what he is after. Flat ground with a slight rise to the front. He signals to Musa and Yazdan, who nod their understanding.

He pulls up Blue and looks to his right. A quarter mile out. Three minutes, maybe four. As the rest of the company arrives, the horses' legs tighten straight as they brake, churning up an obscuring cloud of dust. The knights slide from their saddles, reins in their hands, and whisper soft words into their stallion's ears. The horses drop to their knees then collapse to their sides, backs facing the on-rushing charge. Distant thunder rumbles on the horizon.

With the sloping ground, the attackers will not see them until they are on top of them. The dismounted horsemen load bolts into their massive crossbows, then kneel behind their bedded Andalusians and wait, hearts pounding. They offer reassuring pats and soft words to their mounts, arrange extra bolts and their cocking levers at their feet. Chandon, Musa and Yazdan have taken positions behind the cavalry crossbowmen, swords drawn.

Mujahid's company arrives, but remains mounted, forming itself into a wide arc five riders deep behind the bowmen, blocking the path to the Sultan's exposed flank. Instead of their broadswords, they lift their crossbows in unison.

The Sultan sees the action and shouts to an officer for infantry support from his reserves. One crossbow company and one pike company are all that he can spare, but they begin in double-time to close the distance.

Chandon strides behind his men shouting. "Do not fire until you hear my signal! Do not fire until you hear my signal! No bolt will be loosed before you see the whites of their eyes! Aim for the horses! Aim for the horses! Stand strong, knights of Granada, stand strong, my friends!" The rolling thunder grows louder as the Free Companies accelerate to full gallop.

The gleaming cavalry has broadened to a hundred wide as they bear down on the entrenched Moor line. They are fifty yards out but still cannot see the bedded horses over the low rise. Broadswords are withdrawn from their scabbards and raised, studded maces and killing tools unhooked and lifted, then visors tipped closed, as the Christian knights ready to wield their carnage.

"Steady! Steady, men! Wait for my command! Steady! Wait for my command!" As the lead element tops the rise and sees the peril they frantically try to rein-in their horses. Chandon screams, "NOW!" The massive volley of twelve-inch bolts bury themselves to their feathers in the chests of the on-rushing stallions, dropping all but three in the lead wave. Dust chokes the scene but cannot suppress the sustained awful crunch of metal-on-metal, flesh-on-flesh, intermixed and overlaid with piercing screams as the trapped riders are rolled upon and crushed by their mounts. The galloping riders just behind them cannot stop in time and trample dozens of knights now flat on the ground. Horrible screams of terror and agony ring out to the sickening sound of horseshoes dancing on armor plate.

The attack devolves into panicked and confused pandemonium. The second row of crossbowmen rise in unison from behind their mounts to shoot. As the next set of mounted knights break free from the dust and their trampled companions, the bolts are loosed, to devastating effect. Another hundred knights drop. The remaining dozen riders still visible are picked off one by one by marksmen.

By now the attacking cavalry recognizes that something is terribly wrong and try to veer away from the carnage. The tattered column bunches up then billows out and slows to a canter, then circles back to regroup for a second assault.

Chandon turns and signals Mujahid, who barks commands to his cavalry. His company moves now, circling wide around the attackers in a closing pincher action. As the reserve pike and crossbow company arrive they move forward to support Chandon's men.

Salim's attack on the center of the column has not faired as well. As soon as the Granadine thrust severs the column, the Christian knights in front and behind the cut line simply circle round and surround the attacking Moors. The Granadine light cavalry is no match for armored heavy cavalry in close-quarter fighting and Salim's men begin to drop like flies.

Ali, whose cavalry company is riding in close support, sees this, and instead of launching the planned flanking maneuver to try and turn the tail of the advancing column, decides he cannot abandon Salim and instead rides straight at the raging battle. Their combined actions prevent most of the Free Companies from advancing on the Sultan's flank, a victory in itself, but it comes at a terrible cost. The methodical slaughter of the surrounded and out-numbered Granadine light cavalry ensues.

Now that the Free Companies recognize the peril to their front they abandon any further organized charge of the Moor line. To keep his men in the fight, Chandon urges his troops to recock their crossbows and move forward on foot. The infantry join in behind them. They weave their way through the blood-drenched clot of dead knights and horses. At the top of the rise, Chandon stops and studies the battle raging in the distance. He grimaces. Salim and Ali will not last long.

Mujahid's circling cavalry stays wide of the Christian knights, avoiding close-in fighting, drawing near enough only to make accurate crossbow shots. Each rider has to dismount to recock his weapon, so the flanking attack comes in waves, one group firing then retreating as another comes up to take its place. The effect is devastating and the Christians begin to fall on the lethal outer edges, causing them to bunch back to the middle of the field where they cannot maneuver.

As Chandon's men move forward off the rise, the Christians facing him decide in desperation to renew their frontal assault. The officers form the knights into ranks. Chandon instructs his men to kneel and make ready to receive the attack. He shouts orders to the pikemen to anchor their flanks. The smaller crossbows of the infantry are no match for iron plate and are held in reserve.

As the Christians begin to move forward they dismount and begin to use their horses as shields against the awful bolts.

Chandon frowns. He shouts, "Only the first row fires, the rest hold for my command. Take down the horses. NOW!"

The bolts find their marks, dropping dozens of horses, but as each knight loses his shield he simply joins with the knight next to him and they continue to move forward. It is apparent to Chandon that the Christian line will reach his in force before they are out of horses. Still, they continue to alternate firing lines, one group recocking while the other takes aim and shoots.

Dead and dying horses blanket the field, their awful screams unnatural and bone-chilling. Some stallions struggle to rise, wild-eyed, only to have their legs buckle and collapse. They try once more, unsuccessfully, then accept the awful truth and lay their heads flat to the earth and close their eyes. The knights of the Free Companies move steadily forward on foot.

When the Christians are fifteen yards out, Chandon yells, "When you fire your last bolt, drop your bows and pull your swords and daggers. We fight for Granada's life!"

The sharp pings of sword-on-sword ring out a hundred-fold as the armored knights crush into Chandon's line, bloodied swords and maces swinging furiously. Desperate point-blank crossbow shots take down two dozen more Christians. Most of the Moors toss their bows aside as instructed, draw their steel and prepare to defend themselves. Those that foolishly attempt to recock their bows one last time have their skulls crushed by maces or are run-through with broadswords. A dozen loaded bows drop to the ground before they can be fired.

The battle lines blur and the fighting turns hand-to-hand, ugly, the light chain mail and leather of Chandon's cavalry placing them at a serious disadvantage against armor plate. The Granadine troops begin to fall.

Musa and Yazdan, in their brilliant red, fight on either side of Chandon, the trio making a formidable killing machine, dispatching a half dozen Christian knights in quick order. Out of the corner of his eye, Chandon recognizes the distinctive glint of a French nobleman's ornate, engraved armor. The Christian knight dispatches two Moors as he makes his way towards Chandon, then a third, a fourth.

Musa sees the threat and steps forward to face the Christian, anchoring himself between the attacker and Chandon and raising his sword high. A furious duel commences, but Musa is at a disadvantage against the Christians' armor and can only fend off the heavy blows. Chandon tries to make his way to help his friend but is faced by another knight to his front and cannot move. Musa is overmatched and tiring, his sword swings slowing dangerously.

Chandon yells a warning to Yazdan, who tries to move to support Musa. At that instant the Christian swings down hard on Musa's sword arm, biting through the light mail, severing muscles and tendons. Musa screams and drops his sword. He stands frozen, helpless to resist, and curiously studies the man's other arm as it rares back then swings. Chandon and Yazdan turn just in time to see the slow motion arc of the spiked mace, helplessly watch it bury itself deep in Musa's brain. The Royal Bodyguard is dead before he hits the ground.

Chandon screams with rage. He dispatches his opponent with a dagger thrust up under the man's shoulder armor, then turns to face Musa's killer, who is now bizarrely relaxed, bloody sword and mace hanging limp by his side. Chandon approaches to within five paces. Yazdan moves to Chandon's side, ready to protect his flank, his eyes darting about. The mayhem stretches around them but is waning as the dead and wounded grow on both sides.

Chandon hears an odd sound, realizes that the Christian knight is laughing. Chandon says in French, "Prepare to die." The knight reaches up and unbuckles his helmet, pulls it off, and tosses it in the dirt. Even with his beet red face and matted hair Chandon recognizes the man and hisses, "Bertrand du Guesclin. I should have guessed. French swine."

The Christian laughs louder. "The infidel was a friend of yours, Chandon? I enjoyed watching his brains splatter."

Chandon hisses, "He was a finer man than you could ever hope to be, du Guesclin."

The French knight drops his mace and plants his broadsword into the earth. It continues to sway back and forth as he unbuckles his front and back chest plates and lets them fall with a heavy metallic thud. He pulls off his felt undergarment, baring his chest. Next come his arm scales, first right then left, then his lobster-gloves, finally his leg armor, metal boot covers. Chandon watches silently.

Du Guesclin says, "I challenge you, Moor, to a duel. Sword and dagger. A fight to the death. Or do Moor bastards not honor the rules of chivalry?" He spits on the ground. "Tell me, Chandon, did you become a coward when you married that Muslim whore?" He howls with laughter.

Chandon has never taken his eyes from du Guesclin. They are steely, deadly. Yazdan leans close and whispers, "No, Shahab. I will kill him. Musa was my friend before yours."

"No, Yazdan, he is mine." Chandon surveys the battlefield. Perhaps three dozen Christian knights remain within a hundred paces, but they are being overwhelmed and taken down by sheer numbers. It will not last long.

Chandon looks to the east. Mujahid's cavalry has continued to exact their terrible toll on the Christians. As they near the completion of their encirclement the Free Companies sense the coming doom. They panic and begin to ride hard for the narrowing valve to their rear, first one, then a dozen, then hundreds. Full retreat. He looks back to the city gates. The Sultan's banner flies, the line has held.

Satisfied, he turns to face du Guesclin. "I will fight you. Tell your men to give up and lay down their weapons. This battle is over." He slides Barq into its scabbard, lays it on the ground. Next his dagger. He pulls his cloak over his head, removes his chain mail, baring his chest.

The Frenchman smiles and nods, cups his hands to his mouth and shouts, "Free Companies! The battle is over, lay down your weapons. Time for some sport. Come, friends, come!" They turn and see the source of the invitation, then begin to disengage, drop their weapons, and walk zombie-like towards du Guesclin and Chandon. The Moor infantry follow, their crossbows and pikes trained and ready. A wide circle forms, ringing the two men in.

Each man lifts his broadsword and dagger. They begin to circle, looking for an opening. Chandon whips forward with lightning speed, lunging at the Frenchman's chest with his sword as his dagger slashes in from the left. Du Guesclin recoils and parries first the sword then the dagger in quick succession, then turns like a rattler and swings at Chandon's side, who parries with ease. They back away and begin to circle once more. The Frenchman charges hard and Chandon steps back with the advance. Swing, parry; lunge, thrust, parry; slice left, parry; lock swords, retreat. On the next charge the Frenchman pivots before his thrust and slices down hard at Chandon's hip. Chandon blunts the swing, but Barq's recoil clips his thigh, slicing it open. He winces and limps back two paces. The Frenchman smiles, begins circling once more.

Du Guesclin feigns a chest-thrust, pivots then swings unexpectedly downward at Chandon's exposed knee. Chandon steps back with the assault, counter-pivots, easily blocking the Frenchman's swing, then launches his own pirouette counterattack. The Frenchman backs away as Chandon presses. Swing right, parry; lunge, parry; swing left, parry; lock swords. Instead of retreating, however, Chandon charges anew, pivots then swings right once more, but as he does so stutter-steps and comes in low and unseen with his dagger as his broadsword swings high at du Guesclin's neck. The Frenchman is able to parry the sword but does not see the dagger, which enters his abdomen obliquely and buries itself to the hilt. The Frenchman doubles over, the surprise painted brilliant on his face. He actually chuckles, amused. Chandon rips the dagger forward and out as he withdraws it. As the Frenchman tries to rise, blood begins to spurt from the ugly wound. He looks down, baffled, then frowns as he attempts to stuff his stringy guts back into his opened belly. He looks up at Chandon and sheepishly smiles, then shrugs.

Chandon sheathes his dagger and two-hands Barq, steps forward and says, "Adieu, French swine," and with a whir and a breath of air the man's head sails wide. The Frenchman's body lingers in mid-air for a long moment then crumples heavily into the dirt.

As Chandon turns and begins to limp towards Yazdan, he mouths, "For our friend." Yazdan does not make eye contact but instead looks past Chandon and screams "SHAHAB!" The world drops into slow motion, silent, baited breath held tight. Chandon turns his head to follow Yazdan's gaze and from the corner of his eye sees the French knight pick up the loaded crossbow and aim it. He does not even feel the arrow, only a slight tug in his guts. He looks down, surprised, shocked even, to see the metal arrowhead sticking out six inches from his upper abdomen. The Christian is turned into a human pin-cushion.

The hue of the world shifts, taking on a dream-like, gauzy look, then becoming surreal and peaceful, the colors softening. The sounds of the battlefield become muted and hushed, blurry. Yazdan runs to him in slow motion and grabs his friend, his mouth open as he screams his name, but Chandon does not seem to hear him. Chandon looks confused, grimaces his disapproval, then mutters, "Yazdan, I am fine, I am fine." Oddly, his feet don't seem to want to be where he plants them. A moment later his knees buckle. His friend cradles him in his arms, eases him to the earth, sobbing his name, “Shahab! Shahab!”

A quarter mile away as he gives chase to the retreat, Mujahid hears a trumpet sound on the horizon, then two, a third. Confused, his looks south. The ridge is lined with cavalry, stretching a half mile end-to-end. The blue banners of Granada snap in the breeze. "Praise to Allah, al-Bistami has arrived!" The trumpets sound again as the cavalry launches as one mass and rides hard to harass the retreating Free Companies and rescue the remnants of Salim's and Ali's decimated cavalry.

She has been awake most of the night, tossing and turning with worry. After morning prayer and breakfast, the drowsiness becomes too much and she lays her head down on her divan to rest her eyes, muttering, “Just for a moment, only a moment.”

She wakes with a violent start forty-five minutes later, her emeralds wide with terror as she gasps then screams, "WILLIAM!" She heaves for air and tries to settle her racing heart. She stands, then sits, then stands, then paces, suddenly frantic, a caged animal. She chokes back a violent sob, wipes her tears.

Aisha rushes into the room and blurts out, "What is it? What is it, Layla?"

"Something has happened to William."

"How do you know?'

"I KNOW!"

"What should we do?"

"I am riding for Jaén. Go to the Royal Stables and have Afán saddled."

"Layla?"

Her emeralds blaze. "Aisha. Go! NOW!"

As she ties her waterbag to her saddle and checks the tightness of the girth, she feels familiar hands ease onto her shoulders from behind. She turns, "Baba."

"Daughter, Aisha came for me. What has happened?"

"William has been injured. I must go to him."

Silence.

"Layla, that is a forty mile ride."

"Afán and I will be there before midnight."

"Ride into the middle of a battle? Are you crazy, Layla? I forbid it."

Her emeralds flash with fury as her face hardens. In a crisp cadence she hisses, "I...will...go...to...my...husband."

He recognizes the expression, a mirror of her mother, and knows the debate is ended.

He sighs. "Very well. But I am sending four of the Royal Bodyguard with you."

"As long as they can keep up."

She begins to mount her horse, but Ibn al-Khatib restrains her, turns her to face him. His eyes well up as he whispers, "Daughter, I love you, please be careful." His chin quivers. "Bring my son back to me."

She hugs her father tight, looks into his eyes and says, "I will, Baba. I will."

Four red-clad bodyguards canter up and nod to Ibn al-Khatib. "We will guard her with our lives, my Lord."

Layla leans down and whispers furiously into Afán's cocked ear. She looks up and shouts, "Fly like the wind, Afán!" The stallion bursts from the stables up the Royal Road. The bodyguards thunder out, giving chase.

The rich orange glow of the sun is spectacular as it drops behind the mountain crag, the fluorescent pink cirrus clouds stretching halfway across the sky. The sounds of the camp are hushed and exhausted. The survivors sit around their fires, dazed. Very few speak. Thankfully, a pleasing coolness begins to slide across the landscape, soothing the dust and slaking the weariness of the blood-stained earth. The smell of death wafts on the faint breeze from the north, muted but unmistakable. By tomorrow the sun will swell the dead and split them like gourds, polluting the air with its vile brew of awfulness.

The white linen tent is warmly lit by oil lamps. The steaming cauldron rests in the corner, in its usual spot, the medicinal herbal aroma powerful, somehow pleasing. Chandon lies on his back on the padded table, a pillow under his head, a thin cotton sheet covering his body. His eyes are closed, his chest rising and falling. He is very pale.

Salamun stands in the corner, arms folded, gaunt. The Sultan and Yazdan stand with him, whispering.

"I have removed the bolt, Sire, but the surgery was long and difficult. He has lost much blood." He hesitates. "I fear that his organs were damaged...beyond repair." Salamun tries to steady himself, then continues, his voice quavering, "I have done all that I can do, Sire. I have reached the limits of my powers."

Yazdan places his hands over his eyes and softly cries. The Sultan nods somberly, then says, "I understand, Salamun. Shahab is strong. He will survive." The Sultan turns and looks at Chandon, then turns back to Salamun. "I want to speak to him." Salamun nods. They move to his side. Yazdan lifts Chandon's hand and folds it between his own two. Salamun takes a damp cloth and wipes Chandon's forehead, leans down and whispers, "Young Knight. Young Knight, the Sultan is here."

Chandon's eyelids flutter then work their way open.

The Sultan smiles. "You were right, Shahab. Your plan worked perfectly. We have carried the day. We have won the battle. Enrique's troops in the valley below Santa Catalina were annihilated. Our line at the gates held, attack after attack. And you, you, my friend, defeated the Free Companies. You held them off our flank and turned them. Al-Bistami arrived and helped finish the job. The Free Companies are no more. Enrique has fled north, and Jaén is secure. Granada's future for the next hundred years is intact."

Chandon tries to smile, but cannot quite make it. He swallows hard. "That is good, Sire, very good. Allah has blessed us. A lasting peace for our dear children and grandchildren." His voice is weak, strained.

"Yes, Shahab. 'There is no victor but Allah.' You must rest now and get well. I have need of you, Shahab."

"Yes." Chandon's eyes slowly close.

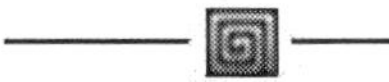

Blue is planted beside the entrance to the tent. The stallion has violently refused to be led to the paddock. The stablemen try to force the issue with a whip, but Yazdan scolds them and sends them away, then tenderly removes the horse's saddle and tack. The Andalusian remains silent, watchful, his head uncharacteristically bent low.

She arrives just before midnight in a cloud of dust. She dismounts before she comes to a stop, rushes to the entrance of the tent. Afán eases forward and nuzzles Blue's shoulder, who lifts his head to the sky and whinnies.

Salamun sits in a chair beside his bed, keeping vigil. He leaps up in surprise when she opens the flap and steps through. He rushes to her and folds her into his arms, holds her tight. "Thank God you came. Thank God. Thank God."

She looks up into the old Jew's face. She is remarkably composed, strong. She says, "It came to me in a dream, Salamun. I knew he had been hurt." She searches his eyes. "Tell me the truth, Salamun. Please."

Silence.

"He was shot in the back with a heavy crossbow. It exited his upper abdomen. I was able to remove the bolt, but he lost a great deal of blood. His organs are damaged, Layla...beyond repair." She gasps sharply only once but does not cry, grasps his arm to steady herself.

She whispers, "How much time do I have?"

The wizard begins to cry, "Very little. Precious little."

Her eyes well up but do not spill. She fights for control. "I understand. I must speak with my husband."

"I know. I will leave you. Call if you need me."

She moves to his side, takes his hand into hers, kisses it over and over. She bends down and kisses his forehead, then his eyes, then his lips.

His eyes blink open and a smile spreads across his face. "My Layla."

"My William."

His eyes well up, but she wills herself to stand firm. He whispers, "I am sorry, my love, I promised you I would stay safe."

"Yes, husband, you promised me."

"Do not worry, wife, I know a wizard that will fix me." He averts his gaze.

She stares at him, eyes full but mercifully not spilling, then reaches and turns his head to look at her. It takes all her strength to flash that smile. "Yes."

"I am glad you came, my love."

"I had to see you, my love. I have news for you, William. Wonderful news."

"Tell me."

She lifts his hand, smiles, places it on her belly. "My William, my love, our baby grows within my womb. Just as I dreamed."

He smiles, then whispers, "Our baby. Praise God." He swallows hard then continues. "A little girl with emerald eyes and chestnut hair, as beautiful as her mother. I can see her. Yes, I see her." He falls silent as tears begin to flow down his cheeks.

"Tell our little girl about me, Layla. Tell her. Do not let her ever forget the love I felt for her mother, that her mother felt for me, the tawhid we shared."

Her lower lip starts to quiver but still she stands firm. "Never, my love, never. You will always be in my heart, William, always beside me. Always."

He winces then gasps with the pain, tenses his arms and purses his lips, holding his breath until the agony passes. His eyes close with the exhaustion.

She leans down over him, kisses his tears then his lips. She pulls back two inches from his face, whispers, "Look at me, William. William, look at me." His lids slowly open. Their eyes lock together as they peer into each other's souls, one body, one heart, one mind. "I will always love you. I will always love you. William, look at me. I will ALWAYS love you. I will ALWAYS love you. I will ALWAYS love you." His eyes do not close as he exhales, his chest stills, his breathing stops.

Her blood-curdling scream, an equal measure of agony, of despair, of fury, of bone-crushing sadness, turns the eyes of those still awake for a hundred yards in all directions. As the echo dies away it is replaced by desperate, heaving sobs. Both stallions rear in unison, violently paw the air, then stamp and snort. The heads of the battle-weary Royal Bodyguard sag, begin to shake side to side as the pain burrows deep into their chests, curls around their hearts, and squeezes.

The heavens are inconsolable. Orion and Virgo and Vega and Libra and Scorpio collapse into a heap of sorrow, hysterical. The Seven Sisters hold each other tight as they sway, wail. Perseus weeps and weeps and weeps, his tears whipping up a fierce storm into the midnight sky, lighting the battlefield with dozens of fiery emerald streaks for Shahab and his Layla.

# Epilogue

She cradles the swaddled babe in the crook of her arm and slips her robe down off her shoulder, exposing her engorged breast. Eyes closed, the baby begins to suckle the air, instinctively rooting for her. She smiles and whispers, "Silly boy." She pulls him close and guides her nipple into his open mouth, the sucking sound loud, his pull surprisingly strong.

"Ouch! Careful, young sir." She strokes his wispy blond hair. A moment later the baby loses hold and desperately begins to suckle the air. In his frustration he opens his eyes wide and looks up at her, annoyed, his giant emeralds piercing and brilliant. She reaches down once more and with her forefinger helps him find his target. She closes her eyes and listens to his tender suckle-sighs, then conjures her husband's face and whispers gentle words of greeting and love, a contented smile easing onto her face.

After she finishes feeding him, she hands him to Constancia, who lifts the baby high into the air. "Shahab! How is my baby boy today? Look at my beautiful boy!" The baby smiles, then coos, his face already a haunting image of his father. She twirls him in the air then brings him down and smothers him with kisses, squeezes him tight.

They both look up as Salamun walks into the room. The old Jew bows, "My Ladies, Young Knight." Everyone smiles. Salamun says, "Layla, we added another infant and two toddlers this morning. Twenty and counting. The Atfal Hospital will be full by month's end. I already have drawn up plans for an expansion wing. Your father showed them to the Sultan yesterday. We have his approval."

Layla answers, "Excellent." She looks into his eyes as her face turns serious. "Thank you, Salamun. Thank you." He smiles and bows.

Aisha enters and greets them all, then turns to Layla and says, "They are waiting."

"Yes. I will be there in a moment."

Down the hall a dozen young women, aged thirteen to sixteen, sit cross-legged on their pillows in a wide circle. Nervous whispers run back and forth around the room, the girls tense and anxious, yet excited for what awaits.

As Layla opens the door, the room falls silent. Heads droop to the floor, eyes safely tucked out of sight. Layla cannot help but smile. "Welcome, ladies, to the Sufi madrasa." She pauses for effect. "Today we learn how to breathe."

## The End

# *Glossary*

***Adhan*** - The Muslim call to prayer.
***Al-Andalus*** - The lands of Iberia under Muslim rule.
***Albayzín*** - The dense, maze-like Muslim quarter of Granada.
***Alhambra*** - The walled fortress that clings to the long and narrow red-soiled ridge overlooking Granada. The Alhambra contains the Royal Palace of the Sultan, the complete functioning town that supports it, all of the judicial and administrative services required to run the kingdom, and a separately castled garrison.
***Allah*** - The Arabic word for "God."
***Almori*** - The ubiquitous savory-sweet, sunbaked Andalusi seasoning made of salt, honey, raisins, pine nuts, almonds, hazel nuts, and flour.
***al-Jannah*** - The Islamic walled garden, an image of paradise with its origins in the Quran.
***Andalusi*** - The people of al-Andalus.
***Baba*** - The Arabic word for "Father."
***Berbers*** - The native peoples of the Maghreb in North Africa.
***Brethren of Purity*** - A secret society of Muslim men, typically with Sufi roots and membership.
***Carmen*** - A traditional Muslim home of the upper middle class found in the Albayzín in the city of Granada.
***Dhimmi*** - Literally, "protected." The "People of the Book" (ahl al-kitab) are Christians and Jews, each of whom share the same biblical roots as Muslims.
***Dhikr*** - The Islamic prayer chanted as a "remembrance" or "invocation" of Allah.
***Fatwa*** - An imam's or qadi's pronouncement on matters of religious law and scriptural interpretation.
***Generalife*** - The Sultan's summer palace and gardens, located just outside the Alhambra.
***Genies*** - Jinn, or genies, are supernatural creatures in Arab folklore which occupy a parallel world. Together, genies, humans and angels make up the three sentient creations of Allah.
***Ghazal*** - An Arabic love poem.
***Ghusl*** - A thorough ritual cleansing with water before prayer. Ghusl is required by Muslim law after being in battle, or being in some general state of unworthiness.

***Hadith*** - The collected sayings and teachings of the Prophet Muhammad.

***Hammam*** - A Muslim bath house.

***Harem*** - Literally, "forbidden." The Royal Harem houses the Sultan's wives, his children, and his concubines. The harem is overseen by eunuchs and is strictly off-limits to all males.

***Hijab*** - Literally, "curtained off." Hijab consists of concealing, loose fitting clothes and a head scarf which completely covers the hair. Hijab is intended to protect a woman's modesty.

***Hajj*** - A pilgrimage to Mecca. Hajj must be performed at least once in a Muslim's lifetime.

***Ikhwan al Safa*** - Literally, the "Brethren of Purity," an Sufi secret society.

***Imam*** - The spiritual leader of the mosque and an expert in Sharia law. An imam leads the worship service at a mosque.

***Islam*** - The monotheistic religion articulated by the Quran, a text considered by its adherents to be the verbatim word of God (Allah), and the teachings of Muhammad, the Holy Prophet of Islam (called the Sunnah and composed of hadith). In addition to referring to the religion itself, the word Islam means "submission to God." An adherent of Islam is called a Muslim.

***Jihad*** - Muslim holy war.

***Khutbah*** - A wedding speech.

***Madrasa*** - A religious school.

***Maghreb*** - Land including the rugged Atlas mountains of extreme northwest Africa and the coastal plains of modern Morocco, Algeria, Tunisia, and Libya.

***Mahr*** - A wedding dowry.

***Marinids*** - The Muslim Marinid Empire of North Africa, with its capital in Fez (in present day Morocco).

***Maristan*** - The Sultan's hospital for the deformed and outcast of Granada, located in the Albayzín.

***Medina*** - The maze-like center of an Islamic town.

***Mihrab*** - The focal point of a mosque, precisely oriented towards Mecca.

***Minaret*** - The spire beside a mosque from which the muezzin calls the Muslim community to prayer.

***Mocárabes*** - The honeycombed ceiling structure made from thousands of individually molded stucco pieces of various prismatic triangular constructions. A key innovation in the architecture of the Alhambra.

***Moor*** - The name Europeans give to the Muslims of al-Andalus, regardless of ancestry.

***Mosque*** - A Muslim place of worship.

***Mudéjars*** - Muslims living in Christian lands in Iberia.
***Muezzin*** - The reciter/singer of the Muslim call to prayer.
***Muhammad*** - The Holy Prophet of Islam.
***Mullah*** - A Muslim theologian.
***Muraqaba*** - A Sufi meditation form.
***Nikah*** - A wedding contract.
***Oratory*** - A private prayer mosque.
***Order of Merced*** - The Order of the Blessed Virgin Mary of Mercy, or Order of Merced, was a religious order founded in 1218 by Saint Peter Nolasco of Barcelona for the ransom and exchange of Christian prisoners.
***Qasr*** - The Royal Palace of the Sultan.
***Qibla*** - The direction to Mecca, the holy city of Islam. Muslims face Mecca during their ritual prayers.
***Qadi*** - An Islamic judge.
***Quran*** - The Holy Book of Islam. The Quran is considered by Muslims to be the verbatim word of Allah, dictated (in Arabic) to the Prophet Muhammad.
***Ramadan*** - The ninth month of the Islamic calendar. Ramadan is the month of fasting, in which Muslims refrain from eating, drinking and sexual relations, from dawn until sunset.
***Salah*** - The time for Muslim prayer.
***Salat*** - Ritual Muslim prayer, conducted five times a day.
***Sawm*** - Fasting during the month of Ramadan.
***Shahada*** - The Muslim prayer of profession: "There is no god but Allah, and Muhammad is the messenger of Allah."
***Sharia law*** - The body of Islamic law and its interpretation.
***Sufi*** - A Muslim mystic.
***Sunnah*** - The Sunnah of Muhammad includes his specific words, his habits and his practices. The Sunnah addresses the best ways of dealing with friends, family and government.
***Sultan*** - The Muslim ruler of the kingdom.
***Tawhid*** - The mystical union with Allah sought by all Sufis.
***Vizier*** - An advisor to the Sultan.
***Wali*** - The legal guardian of a Muslim female.
***Walimah*** - The wedding feast.
***Wudu*** - The minor ablution. Before prayer a Muslim must at very minimum wash himself or herself; hands, hair, feet, face. All mosques provide a water source for this purpose.
***Zakat*** - Almsgiving and charity for the poor.

# *Reflections*

I am no historian. But I am passionate about historical fiction. And the timelessness of love. I believe that if you are determined, have a vivid imagination, and are willing to pay your dues and invest the proper amount of time and energy, you can enter history. Step into the action, awaken names and places, see what they saw, feel what they felt, think what they thought, love as they loved, die as they died.

Yes, you must locate some good reading material and digest those whole, chew them up and sometimes even spit them out. Wrestle with them. As I said, pay your dues. Then you must set aside all the facts you have so painstakingly made your own and go visit the darn place so you can absorb the sights and sounds and smells. Do all these things properly, toss in a little luck, and you can indeed bring a dead place to life, awaken a time long past, enter history, breathe it. I do believe that. Such is the magic of well-executed historical fiction.

During my sabbatical at Georgia Tech in the fall of 2010, following nine months of reading, hard thinking and obsessive straining of my imagination with all sorts of images of medieval Granada, I finally ventured to Andalusia, remarkable place that it remains to this day. I traced a big circular arc; Seville, Córdoba, Jaén, Granada.

I roamed the streets of Seville, slurped my delicious orange salmorejo (tomato soup topped with ham and egg) at the rowdy tapas bars as the dozens (hundreds!) of Iberian hams dangled above my head. I heard the distant Arab whisper buried deep within the rich, tortured sounds of flamenco, stared skyward in the Hall of the Orange in the Alcazar, traced the Arabic on the stucco walls Pedro copied from the Comares Palace.

Next I wandered the magnificent, unmistakable red and white columned arches of the fabulous Mezquita in Córdoba, for hours and hours, relishing the time alone before the inevitable tour buses arrived. I even attended Mass inside the Mezquita, sad irony of ironies. I chased steaming three-inch thick buttery potato tortilla with a cold cerveza. Daily! I sat in the Plaza de la Corredera and tried to conjure the terror of the burnings held there during the Inquisition.

I stayed in the exquisite Parador (state-owned luxury hotel) nestled beside the ancient Castillo de Santa Catalina, perched high atop the mountain towering over Jaén. I stood with Chandon, hand resting on the giant cross, as we scanned the battlefield together.

Finally, my bus wove its merry way among the rolling hills and endless olive groves, arriving at last in Granada, my heart pounding, pounding, as I craned to steal my first glimpse of my beloved Alhambra. I planted myself in a hotel off the Plaza Nueva, climbing over and around and through the Alhambra and the Albayzín, day after day, even absorbing the palace and Generalife by moonlight. Twice.

I climbed each morning from my hotel through the Pomegranate Gate and entered the Alhambra through the Justice Gate, just like Chandon. I secured my thimble of sweet coffee and made my way to the big chestnut tree that towers now over the hammam Salamun and Chandon luxuriated in off the Upper Royal Road in the medina. There I wrote.

I sneaked a snip of myrtle from the Comares Palace as I peered up at the jalousie windows on Layla's suite and then across to Chandon's room, visualizing their all-clear signals by candlelight. I awakened their budding love in my mind, smiled at the bravado of their midnight rendezvous, their secret kisses and stolen glances, transported back to my own delicious early years with my Maria.

I stood agape at the marvels of the Hall of the Ambassadors, the Hall of the Two Ladies, the Hall of the Abencerrages. It was easy to picture Sultan Muhammad in his element there, no more difficult for Ibn al-Khatib, Zamrak, the Royal Harem. I dipped my fingers in the fountains and pools of the Partal Gardens, witnessed the Brethren of Purity in all black and hushed and secret in the Partal Oratory under the new moon.

I climbed the Water Stairway in the Generalife, located the secret space of my young lovers' first encounter with tawhid under the starlight so many, many years ago. I was there. I even jumped the security fence and found the Royal Cisterns that powered the palace fountains those many centuries ago. It was a magical time of discovery for me, an awakening of six hundred years of silence.

The great service of historical fiction, it seems to me, lies in the bringing of a time and a place long dead magically back to life. This was my primary aim in writing this book. That, and to share my own small understanding of the truth and holiness and timelessness of the love I have come to know with my wife of 30 years, my Maria.

Al-Andalus desperately deserves remembering. This was no ordinary time or place. Our world aches for its memory, aches. Medieval Muslim Spain was a head-spinning intersection of three great cultures, three great religions, three great languages – Islam, Christianity, Judaism. Remarkably, for long stretches of time not far removed from our young lovers, all three religions lived together in something closely approximating harmony, following the enlightened Arab Muslim dictates of mutual respect and religious tolerance. *Convivencia* (coexistence). Tense, historical boundaries between the Muslim, Christian and Jewish peoples softened, then blurred. Languages were shared by all, cultural and intellectual achievements celebrated by all. Mutual acceptance and tolerance naturally blossomed with the lowering of time-honored artificial barriers. Love inevitably began to cross ethnic and religious dividing lines, just as in my book. Love always finds a way. Beautiful convivencia. If only we could recall that time.

To approach al-Andalus as a modern reader, you must put aside the common association of the word "medieval" with "Dark Ages," by standard inference a time of backward, unclean, uneducated peoples mired in a stagnate civilization. This pat answer has no value here. In al-Andalus, there was an unprecedented bubbling up of so much intellectual prowess and cultural sophistication as to make the lettered among us feel like bumpkins. There was rediscovery, translation and absorption of Greek and Roman and Far-East knowledge lost for a millennium, and the consequent rebirth of science, medicine, architecture, engineering and agriculture. There was enough poetry, music, song and philosophy to make the ancients proud. And books. My goodness the books. At the beginning of the 11th century, there were four hundred thousand volumes in the Great Library of Córdoba alone! The largest library in Christian Europe, at the University of Paris, held four hundred volumes! Dark Ages? I think not.

With predictable irony, surrounding all this cultural enlightenment was enough political wrangling, arm-twisting, court intrigue and diplomatic maneuvering to dizzy the most jaded, jet-setting, modern head of state. Political expediency was the only law of the land. Muslim was allied with Christian against Christian, Muslim against Muslim, brother against brother. Assassins prowled the Royal Courts. And war. Of course, war. Close-fought with clenched teeth and sweaty brow, with gilded sword, crossbow and ugly studded mace, the bloodied land cloaked in shocking, casual violence and death. War was waged then for the exact same reasons as today, these six hundred years later: Ego, power, greed, religious intolerance, misguided do-gooding, ignorance. As toxic then as now to the voices of reason, to culture, to civilization. Sadly, to love.

Al-Andalus, bright light of cultural and religious tolerance, intrepid explorer of the mind and soul, boiling caldron of enlightened thinking, place of song and dance and dazzling colors. Alas, she did not stand the test of time. Born in 711, subdued finally in 1492 at the hands of Isabel and Fernando, the Catholic Monarchs of Columbus fame. But consider - nearly 700 years of inspiration! Al-Andalus left a deep legacy that molded then fired the clay that was to become modern Europe, and by extension the Americas and her peoples.

In our so-called modern era, with its hurtful religious and cultural tensions, rife with terrorism of the innocents, suicide bombings and fanatical intolerance, ancient al-Andalus has much to teach us all – Muslim, Christian and Jew alike. Al-Andalus, a distant beacon of light, perhaps the world's greatest forgotten reminder that a peaceful future among us three is indeed a possibility, provided we make the difficult but necessary choice to set aside our differences and honor our shared sacred roots. Tolerance and mutual respect. Why is this such an impossible concept?

This is a six-hundred year old story of love, yes, but also a story of a largely unknown past we all need to remember, and memorize, if we are to place any real hope in an olive-branched world for our dear children and grandchildren.

# *Language*

To make the book more accessible to readers, diacritics and other accent marks, which abound in Arabic, have for the most part been omitted. For instance, I use *Quran* instead of *Qur'ān.*

I have chosen to have my Muslim characters use the Arabic word *Allah* for 'God' when they speak, but it is important to emphasize that a Muslim uses 'Allah' in a manner which is identical to how a Christian uses 'God' and a Jew uses 'YHWH'. That is, the words 'God', 'Allah' and 'YHWH' are simply the English, Arabic and Hebrew words for the Supreme Being shared by the three great monotheistic religions.

Muslim words with no conventional English equivalents appear in italics the first time they are used, but not afterwards. Most are included with explanation in the glossary.

I use the Spanish spelling for the major historical figures (e.g., Pedro and Enrique for Peter and Henry) and the Spanish spellings of the cities of Iberia (e.g., Sevilla, Córdoba, Zaragoza, Jaén).

There are times when my characters are speaking Arabic that I use a Romanized phonetic pronunciation of the Arabic words to lend dramatic effect. Such phonetic choices are obviously subject to interpretational latitude. It goes without saying that the Arabic spoken in fourteenth century al-Andalus clearly had some significant differences from modern spoken Arabic, and no attempt has been made to account for these nuances.

Some preferred pronunciations of places and characters:

***Abencerrages*** (ah-ben–cerr-rah-jezz)
***Al-Andalus*** (ahl-on-duh-luze)
***Alhambra*** (ahl-om-bruh)
***Chandon*** (shan-don)
***Córdoba*** (core-duh-bah)
***Generalife*** (hen-er-al-lee-feh)
***Granada*** (gruh-nod-uh)
***Jaén*** (hi-an)
***Layla*** (lay-luh)
***Lindaraja*** (lin-duh-rah-hah)
***Mexuar*** (mesh-you-are)
***Sevilla*** (say-vee-ya)

# *The Alhambra*

The following views of the fourteenth century Alhambra palace complex were made from photographs taken of the scaled model found in the Calahorra Tower in Córdoba.

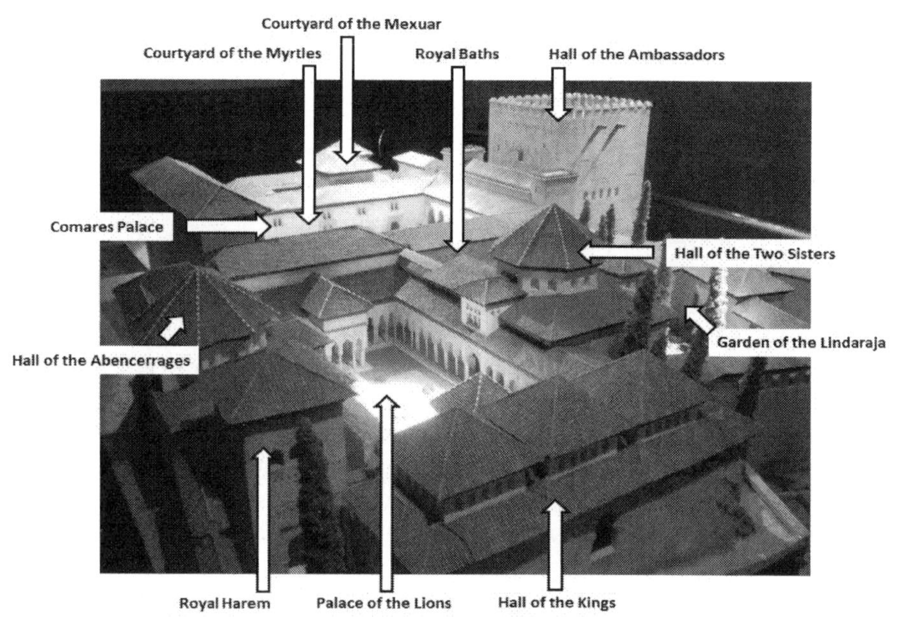


*View 1. The palace complex looking to the west. The Comares Palace is in the background and the Palace of the Lions is in the foreground. Various points of interest within the story are indicated.*

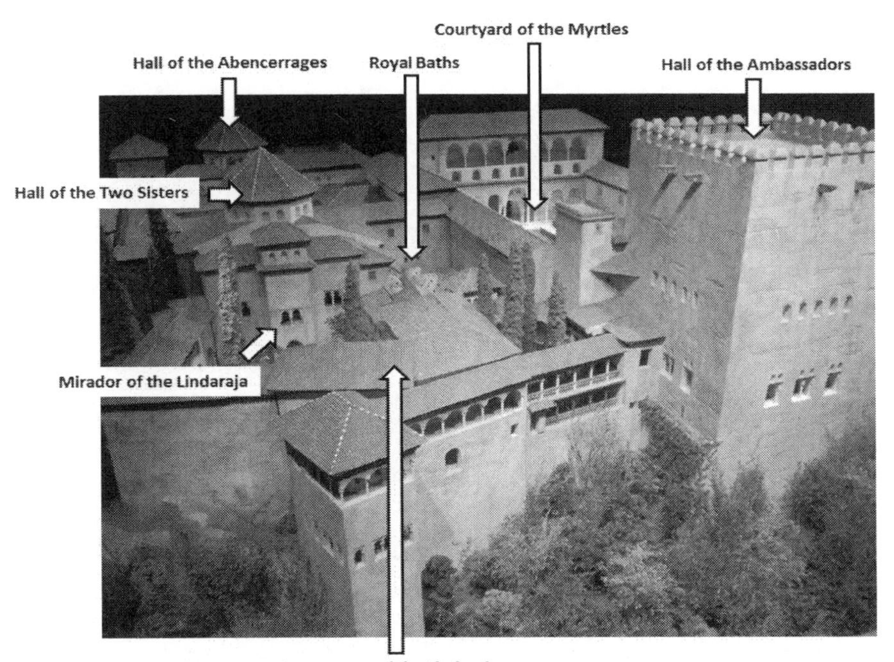


*View 2. The palace complex looking to the south. The Comares Palace is to the right and the Palace of the Lions is to the left.*

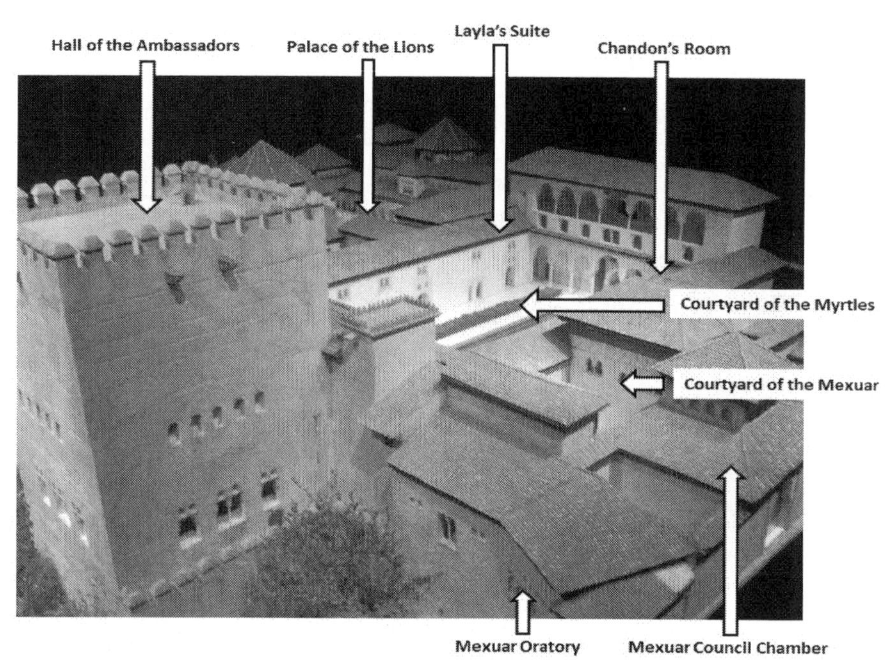


*View 3. The palace complex looking to the east. The Comares Palace is in the mid-ground, the Palace of the Lions is in the background, and the Mexuar Palace is to the right.*

# *Photographs*

*Photo 1. View to the north from the base of the mountain, showing the Castillo de Santa Catalina in Jaén. Note the cross to the right.*

*Photo 2. Looking east at the outer wall and central tower of the Castillo de Santa Catalina.*

*Photo 3. View to the southeast from the Castillo de Santa Catalina, looking down upon the location of the first and second battles of Jaén (in the distance, at the very center of the picture). The city of Jaén is immediately back to the left. Granada is forty miles to the right (south).*

*Photo 4. Looking east at the cross just outside Castillo de Santa Catalina. The city of Jaén is to the left and the battleground is to the right.*

*Photo 5. The Alhambra from the northwest. The square tower to the far left is the Hall of the Ambassadors. The towers of the Alcazaba are to the right. The large square building in the center (the Palace of Charles V) dates to the sixteenth century, as does the tall pointed tower to its immediate left, which is part of the cathedral built on top of the Great Mosque. The Sierra Nevada mountains are in the distance.*

*Photo 6. The ubiquitous Granadine columned horseshoe arch. This example is found in the Comares Palace.*

*Photo 7. The Alhambra's famous tilework and stucco poetry. This example is found in the Palace of the Lions.*

*Photo 8. The Alhambra's famous tilework. This example is found in the Comares Palace.*

*Photo 9. The ubiquitous Arabic carving (read right to left) of the Granadine motto, which translates, "The only victor is Allah." This example is found in the Comares Palace.*

*Photo 10. A column in the Mexuar Council Chamber, with background arabesque. The blue polychrome in the line of Arabic poetry at the top of the column is original.*

*Photo 11. A decorative wall niche in the Palace of the Lions.*

*Photo 12. The mihrab in the Mexuar Oratory.*

*Photo 13. View of the façade in the Courtyard of the Mexuar. Note the Arabic calligraphy framing the windows.*

*Photo 14. The interior of the Hall of the Ambassadors within the Comares Palace.*

*Photo 15. The Courtyard of the Myrtles within the Comares Palace. At the end of the reflecting pool is the entrance to the Hall of the Ambassadors. Chandon's room is on the second floor to the immediate left of the frame and Layla's suite is on the second floor to the immediate right. In the fourteenth century, the myrtle hedges were inset to ground level to avoid obstructing the view of the pool.*

*Photo 16. The entrance to Chandon's room in the Courtyard of the Myrtles within the Comares Palace.*

*Photo 17. The jalousie double window in Layla's suite in the Courtyard of the Myrtles within the Comares Palace. Note the repeated Granadine motto running above the windows.*

*Photo 18. The interior courtyard of the Palace of the Lions. Note the famous lion fountain in the center.*

*Photo 19. Columns in the interior courtyard of the Palace of the Lions.*

*Photo 20. Inside the Hall of the Two Sisters within the Palace of the Lions.*

*Photo 21. The entrance to the Royal Harem inside the Hall of the Abencerrages within the Palace of the Lions.*

*Photo 22. The ceiling of the Hall of the Abencerrages within the Palace of the Lions.*

*Photo 23. The view from the mirador in the Hall of the Two Sisters within the Palace of the Lions down into the Garden of the Lindaraja.*

*Photo 24. The ubiquitous black- and white-pebble street paving ornamentation found within the Alhambra.*

*Photo 25. The "warm room" of a Granadine hammam (bath house). The octagonal ventilation ports would have been covered with red glass.*

*Photo 26. The Alhambra's Justice Gate, the main entrance to the palace during the fourteenth century.*

*Photo 27. A view of the Albayzín looking north from the outer wall of the Alhambra. The fourteenth century city wall can be seen in the distance traversing the ridge.*

*Photo 28. A view to the west overlooking the city of Granada from the highest tower in the Alcazaba, at the western tip of the Alhambra.*

*Photo 29. A view of the Generalife from the Outskirt's Gate on the northern wall of the Alhambra.*

*Photo 30. The Water Garden Courtyard in the Generalife. The fountain jets are contemporary additions, as is the open portico to the left.*

*Photo 31. The Cypress Courtyard in the Generalife. The fountain jets are contemporary. The trunk of the giant cypress (sadly, now dead) can be seen at the far right.*

*Photo 32. The Water Stairway in the Generalife.*

*Photo 33. A view to the west from the upper gardens of the Generalife. The Alhambra is in the left background.*

*Photo 34. A view to the north from inside the terraced Partal Gardens within the Alhambra. The Palace of the Lions is to the left and the Partal Oratory is to the immediate right of the building in the background.*

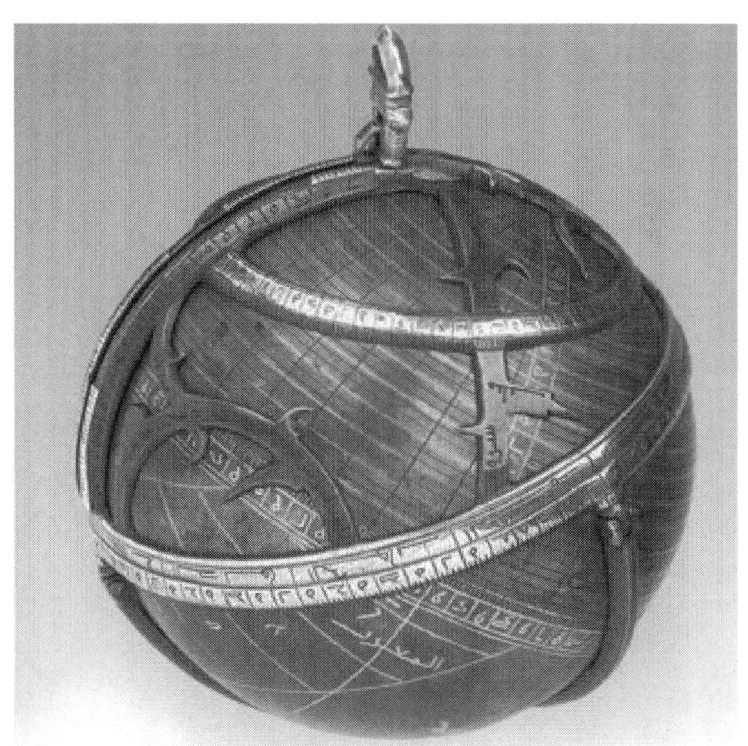

*Photo 35. A fourteenth century example of a spherical astrolabe.*

*Photo 36. The model for Chandon's horse, an Andalusian.*

*Photo 37. The model for Layla's horse, a Lusitano.*

## *Historical Primer*

In the Islamic world, the death of the Prophet Muhammad in 632 C.E. without a chosen successor led to several decades of bloody internal power struggle, the remnants of which linger to this day in Shiite vs. Sunni tensions. By 661, however, the Sunni Arab Umayyad clan prevailed and to solidify their power moved the Islamic capital from Medina (Saudi Arabia) to Damascus (Syria). A rapid swelling of Islamic culture, wealth and power commenced, launching a conquest of conversion reaching from the western end of the Mediterranean basin to the Near East.

By 711 the Maghreb was breached (land including the rugged Atlas mountains of extreme northwest Africa and the coastal plains of modern Morocco, Algeria, Tunisia, and Libya). An Islamic army, led by an Arab Syrian governor turned general named Tariq ibn Ziyad and comprised of a freshly-converted, capable warrior clan of local Berber tribesmen, invaded Iberia at Gibraltar. They rapidly conquered the Iberian peninsula under the banner of *jihad* (holy war), effortlessly absorbing the Visigoth and post-Roman era towns and peoples. *Al-Andalus*, the Arabic name for the (ever-changing) lands of Iberia under Muslim dominion, was born.

Al-Andalus survives 781 years, until the cold morning of January 2, 1492, when Fernando and Isabel, the “Catholic monarchs” of a newly unified Spain, ironically dressed in flamboyant Moorish finery and under the wind-taut Papal Banner of Christian reconquest (*reconquista* – their own brand of holy war), at long last defeat the Moors, the Christian name for the Muslim Andalusians, famously capturing the last great stronghold of al-Andalus, the exquisite Alhambra palace in Granada. Legend has it that the last Nasrid Sultan, Muhammad XII, Boabdil to the Castilians, riding out of now-Christian Granada, wistfully glances back at his lost treasure, the Alhambra, and utters the famous “Moor’s last sigh.” Muslim Spain is dead.

Several pivotal events in the history of al-Andalus are important to our story. In 750 C.E., the Umayyads in Damascus are slaughtered by the rival Abbasids, and the sole surviving Umayyad heir, Abd al-Rahman, a boy in his late teens, sets out on the twenty-five hundred mile journey to al-Andalus, to boldly reclaim his own slice of history in a forgotten corner of the Islamic empire – Córdoba, on banks of the Guadalquivir river in southern central Spain. The Umayyad regime re-emerges like a phoenix from the ashes with the crowning of Abd al-Rahman *Emir* (governor) of Córdoba in 756.

The fuse is lit, and al-Andalus soon rockets skyward. Abd al-Rahman's heir (the III) ultimately declares himself the rival caliph (from the Arabic *khalifa*, "successor" (to the Prophet Muhammad) – supreme ruler of Islam) to the Abbasid caliph in January 929. Now unified and under able and enlightened Arab leadership, al-Andalus rises to its full glory. *Convivencia* reigns. Córdoba becomes the largest and most prosperous city in Europe, the crown jewel of Western Islam, and a magnet of learning and intellectual fervor that equals Baghdad, the rival Abbasid caliphate's capital and the biggest city on the planet. Late $10^{th}$ to early $11^{th}$ century Córdoba is considered the cultural and intellectual zenith of al-Andalus.

Ironically, much of the knowledge that ultimately spawns European hegemony hundreds of years later will enter the continent through Córdoba and its neighboring Muslim cities (Toledo, Sevilla, Granada and Málaga). Sadly, by 1031, only a hundred years later, the Umayyad caliphate of Córdoba is gone, the sublime Royal Palace at Madinat al-Zahra razed to the ground. Mercifully, the great double-horseshoe-arched Great Mosque of Córdoba was preserved and still stands today. The Umayyad caliphate of Córdoba was a victim of its own internal power struggles, ego and weak leadership.

The post-Córdoban Umayyad caliphate dissolves into a loose collection of small *taifa* ("parties" or "factions") kingdoms, bitter rivals all, and suddenly without a unified front to present to the displaced Christian kings in the north who thirst for both land and power. Alfonso VI of Castile conquers Muslim Toledo in 1085, triggering panic throughout al-Andalus. A fateful cry for help to the fundamentalist Muslim Almoravids of the Maghreb is made. The Almoravids are fierce Berber clans with great disdain for the cultural accomplishments and the rich, easy life and religious tolerance of the Arab Umayyads. They are steadfast in their strict interpretation of Islam, loathing any perceived attempt to water-down the dictates of Muhammad. In 1086, the Almoravid Yusuf ibn Tashfin answers the northern distress call and invades al-Andalus. The Almoravids quickly halt the Christian advance, and after a cursory comparison of the rich, lush al-Andalus with their own unyielding, arid homeland, decide to stay, making quick work of conquering the Arab taifa kingdoms.

Al-Andalus passes from tolerant Syrian Arab rule to fundamentalist Berber Almoravid rule. The even more fundamentalist Almohads, also of fierce Berber stock but bitter enemies of the Almoravids, and with even greater disdain for moderate Arabs, defeat the rival Almoravids in the Maghreb in the late 11th century, and cross the Strait of Gibraltar to join the party. The Almohads transfer their capital from North Africa to Sevilla in 1170.

From that fateful day in 1086, al-Andalus transitions from enlightened, tolerant Umayyad rule to 150 years of stark fundamentalist Berber rule. Andalusian vs. Berber tensions smolder across Iberia. Jews once welcomed (prized!) at Umayyad court are now persecuted and segregated. Christians formerly living peacefully side-by-side with Moors are expelled from Muslim cities. Convivencia is dead. Christian vs. now-fundamentalist Muslim tensions flare, and with Papal encouragement, reconquista soon becomes the calling card of a crusading Christian north. War drums sound. Slowly but surely over the next two-hundred and fifty years, al-Andalus is pushed inch-by-inch, town-by-town, to the southern shores of Iberia.

The Ahmohads are resoundingly defeated on the 16th day of July, 1212 at the "Battle of Las Navas de Tolosa" by a unified force led by the Christian kings of Castile, Navarre, Aragon, and Portugal. The unprotected Muslim crown jewels begin to fall like dominos to Christian armies – Córdoba in 1236, Valencia in 1238, Murcia in 1243, Sevilla in 1248. The scent of blood is thick in the water for an Iberia free of Moors.

And so we come to Granada. Following the power-vacuum created by the collapse of the Ahmohads, Muhammad ibn al-Ahmar ibn Nasr (Muhammad I), of the Arab Banu Nazari clan (the Nasrids), contrives in 1232 to set up a small kingdom centered on the lovely, mountain-girded city of Granada. At its largest, Muhammad's kingdom is a mere one hundred mile wide swath of land at the extreme southeastern tip of Spain, stretching from the Mediterranean coast north of Almería, through Málaga, to Gibraltar.

Inevitably, in 1245, reconquista knocks on the door, and Fernando III of Castile lays siege to Jaén, the well-fortified northern-most Muslim stronghold only forty miles north of Granada. To make peace, Muhammad reluctantly surrenders Jaén in 1246 and agrees to become a tribute-paying vassal to the king of Castile, ensuring at least a temporary halt to reconquista in the region. In hindsight, this was a profoundly shrewd move. The Nasrid Kingdom of Granada is born, and will prosper, wildly, through twenty Sultans and two-hundred forty-six more years, the last great seat of Muslim power in Iberia.

The famed "Vega de Granada" surrounds the city, at once a source of the kingdom's pride and strength. The Vega is literally the floodplain of the river system emerging from the Sierra Nevada mountains. It becomes the fruit and vegetable and bread basket of Granada, flanked by miles upon miles of verdant grazing land, the envy of all of Europe in its culinary opulence. Stretching outward from the city walls far into the surrounding countryside, the mountain-rimmed Granadine Vega is breathtaking by medieval standards; flat, fertile, and lush. Irrigation is the lynchpin. Without it, Granada is practically a dustbowl. Sophisticated hydraulic systems lift and lower precious water at will from the convergent Darro, Genil and Beiro rivers. Irrigation dams within the fields channel water among the thirsty rows on a weekly rotation.

The splendor is remarkable: Wheat, barley, rice, sugar cane, cotton, artichokes, eggplant, beans, endive, spinach, chard, radishes, leeks, carrots, beets, celery, peppers, onions, asparagus, figs, cherries, apples, pears, grapes, olives, oranges, lemons, limes, pomegranates, apricots, dates, almonds, pine nuts, hazel nuts, saffron, hot peppers, cumin, aniseed, mint, cinnamon, nutmeg, coriander, parsley, garlic, mustard. A Granadine feast. Typical European fare stands bland by contrast, centered on roasted meats, breads, grain gruels, and roots; spices and seasonings are available only for the rich. Cattle, horse, goat, sheep and chicken dung recharge the Vegan fields (pigs are forbidden in Islam). Arab mastery of irrigation, fertilizer, crop rotation, and fallowing precedes Europe by centuries.

Bickering among the rival Christian kingdoms, predictable exhaustion of coffers, and the threat from the emergence of the Muslim Marinids, yet another set of Berber clans who in 1244 conquer the Ahmohads to rule the Maghreb from Fez (Morocco), stymie the Christian advance and reconquista comes to a grinding halt. Meanwhile, Granada thrives. Predictably, the Nasrids ally themselves with the Marinid Empire, and begin a long, slow, swaying dance as thinly sliced buffer between Christian Spain and the Muslim Maghreb, at the same time vassal of Castile and ally of the Marinids. Interesting times for the diplomatic corps.

Now to some specifics of our story. Enter Muhammad V in 1354, age 16, eighth Nasrid Sultan of Granada. In 1358 the Christian kingdoms of Castile and Aragon (in northeast Spain) bicker and finally come to blows, and Granada, as vassal to Castile, lends its support (both financial and naval) to King Pedro of Castile (later nicknamed Pedro the Cruel), earning great favor at the Castilian court in Sevilla. Aragon bitterly resents the meddling by the Moors in Christian politics.

The plot thickens. Young Muhammad V falls victim to a coup led by his brother Ismail II on a sultry August night in 1359; sadly, orchestrated by Muhammad's own mother, Maryam. Muhammad barely manages to escape with his life to Fez to live in exile with the Marinids. Ismail II is in turn assassinated in 1360 and replaced by Muhammad VI, their ambitious cousin. In 1362, Muhammad V, secretly encouraged and assisted by his unlikely ally, Pedro of Castile, crosses the Gibraltar Strait to reclaim his throne. Muhammad VI, in a painfully naïve move, races to Sevilla with his entourage and throws himself at Pedro's feet, begging for help. Pedro welcomes him with open arms and a slap on the back, feasts lavishly with his Arab guests, then promptly has all thirty-seven arrested, stripped of their valuables, and two days later Pedro personally executes Muhammad VI. Pedro the Cruel. Muhammad V reclaims his throne and receives a welcoming gift from Pedro – his cousin's head.

With Muhammad V successfully restored to power, a welcomed stability returns to the Granadine court and the kingdom flourishes under his benign rule. Muhammad V completes the glorious Alhambra, the lavish fortress-palace of the Granadine Royal Court. He even sends his masons to assist Pedro in remodeling his own palace in the Granadine style.

"Alhambra" refers to the entire walled fortress that clings to the long and narrow red-soiled ridge overlooking Granada. The red hill itself is the source of the palace's name (*al-hamra* is Arabic for 'red'). Unlike today, in the fourteenth century the towers and walls of the Alhambra would have been white-washed and the hill laid bare for defense, a stunning white on red contrast. The fortress is compact, as dictated by the terrain, about one hundred yards wide and seven hundred yards long, and is nestled within the walled and garrisoned city of Granada. The Alhambra complex contained the Royal Palace of the Sultan (*qasr*), the complete functioning town (*medina*) that supported it, all of the judicial and administrative services required to run the kingdom, and a separately castled garrison.

The Alhambra and the walled city of Granada itself were, for all intents and purposes, impregnable, and were never captured by force of arms, only surrendered (in 1492 to Isabel and Fernando, the "Catholic Monarchs"). The Alhambra's population in 1367, when our story begins, was roughly two thousand, including a garrison of perhaps three hundred elite troops, compared to about sixty-five thousand inhabitants in Granada proper, a very large city by fourteenth century standards.

Alas, in 1366, after only four years of calm for Muhammad V and Granada, Enrique II of Trastámara launches the Castilian Civil War, and with the support of Aragon, France and the Pope, attempts to wrestle Castile away from his brother, King Pedro. As vassal of Pedro, Granada is once again reluctantly thrust center stage, ironically pinioned between the dueling Christian kingdoms of Castile and Aragon.

# Fact and Fiction

When it comes to my creative writing, I am no slave to history. When the historical record needed some bending in service of the dramatic action or my characters, I did so. Freely. That said, I do believe strongly in full disclosure and I attempt here to differentiate between what is historical and what is fictional. My litmus test while writing was always: "Given what we know today, is this person's actions or that sequence of events or this plot twist plausible?" If that criterion could be passed, I went with it.

- Layla is purely fictional, but there are many examples of strong, well-educated women in the courts of al-Andalus, over many centuries. There is also historical precedence for women becoming Sufis. Layla's name is taken from the famous Arabian myth of Layla and Majnun (the Madman), a well-known story of the consequences of unrequited love dating to seventh century Arabia. Needless to say, Majnun falls head-over-heels in love with the beautiful Layla, but, sadly, goes mad when her father will not allow him to marry her.

- Parts of Chandon's character are loosely based on Sir John Chandos, an historical English knight of humble stock, who was born in Derbyshire and also happened to be a childhood friend of Edward the Black Prince. Chandos won the Battle of Auray and became Viscount of Saint-Sauveur in Brittany, just like Chandon. There the parallels end. Chandos fought beside Edward and Pedro at Nájera, not Enrique, and certainly never ventured to Granada. Everything else about Chandon is fictional.

- All of the proper names used in the book are historical, whether Muslim, Jewish, Castilian, French or English. They are taken from church documents, court records, and legal proceedings dating to the fourteenth century.

- Several of the major characters in the book are historical: Sultan Muhammad, Ibn al-Khatib, Zamrak, King Pedro, Enrique, Edward the Black Prince, Pope Urban V, Bertrand du Guesclin and Hugh Caveley. The rest are fictional. Some we know quite a bit about (Ibn al-Khatib, Sultan Muhammad V), others much less. We do not know if Ibn al-Khatib had a daughter, but it is certainly plausible (by convention, females rarely entered palace records or formal documents and thus inevitably became lost to history). Interestingly, Ibn al-Khatib eventually meets his demise at the hands of Zamrak (a story for another day). I could never quite get my mind around how this could have happened, given that Zamrak was clearly anointed by Ibn al-Khatib and groomed to be his protégé. One day it popped into my head that a woman might have been involved. Seems plausible. Certainly, all would agree (both then and now) that Ibn al-Khatib had one of the finest mind's on the planet. Ever. He knew it all and he wrote it all down, dozens and dozens of books, many of which survive. His interest in medicine and how he dealt with the plague in Granada is historical. He was an amazing individual. I like to think he would have educated his daughter and cheered her on.

- Salamun is fictional, though it was quite common in al-Andalus for Jews to serve as physicians to the Royal Court, even for the Sultan and the Royal Family.

- Al-Andalus was refreshingly multi-lingual by today's standards. Many Granadines, perhaps most, would have been conversant in three languages (Arabic, Hebrew and Castilian, the latter resembling modern Spanish), the educated of the court even more, including various Arabic dialects (Andalusi, Maghrebi), Persian (Farsi), perhaps French, other Spanish dialects beyond Castilian, even Latin.

- Sultan Muhammad's use of bodyguards of European descent is historical. As depicted, Christians placed bounties on the heads of converts to Islam and they were not offered ransom during battle. We have several accounts of Muslim converts captured in battle actually being used for target practice by Christian troops.

- The Maristan Hospital is historical, as are Layla's statements about Granadine medicine, which was far and away more advanced than the rest of Europe. The ruins of the Maristan still stand and it was indeed the first of its kind in Europe, the gift of Sultan Muhammad V to the people of Granada to serve the disadvantaged. My descriptions of the Maristan's residents come from my own experiences working with the poorest of the poor in the slums of Kingston, Jamaica beside the dear brothers of the Missionaries of the Poor.

• Several of the major battles are historical and happened more or less as described (Nájera, Montiel). Some are fictional (the second battle for Jaén, Montejicar). Pedro's betrayal to Enrique by du Guesclin at Montiel is historical (amazingly enough). The use of mountain-top signal fires by the Kingdom of Granada to sound the alarm when under attack (just like in *Lord of the Rings* when Gondor beckoned Rohan when Sauron's forces invaded!) is historical.

• The descriptions of the Avignon papacy are reasonably accurate. The fourteenth century was not an especially flattering period for the Catholic Church. In 1367 Urban V (Guillaume Grimoard from the Languedoc region in southwestern France) was in Italy trying to find a way to move the papacy back to Rome, and papal intrigue predictably blossomed during his absence. The French dominated the papal court, as presented, and the papacy actively supported reconquista in Spain. Whether or not they would have had the spare change to fund Enrique in 1367 is debatable, given that they had invested so heavily in building the Papal Palace in Avignon.

• The Free Companies (the origin of the word "free-lance") and their mercenary menace in France and Iberia is historical, and they did in fact extort gold from the Pope. Among their leaders were the French mercenary knights Bertrand du Guseclin and Hugh Caveley. The Free Companies did fight with Enrique at both Nájera and Montiel, but to our knowledge were never promised Granada by Enrique, and certainly did not fight at Jaén.

• The prologue mentions that Aragon invaded southeastern Castile in 1367, occupying Jaén. This is fictional. Castile still held Jaén in 1367. Even though Castile and Granada were allies, Muhammad V did in fact attack and seize Jaén, Baeza, Úbeda in the spring of 1367, in the manner told. Castillo de Santa Catalina is accurately depicted, although to my knowledge there is no evidence of a secret "backdoor" from below for the Moors to gain entry. Having been there, however, it is not implausible.

• When Enrique defeated and murdered Pedro at Montiel he immediately had his hands full as he struggled to unify Castile. He was thus in no position to immediately invade Granada as portrayed in the book. Granada's attack, capture and razing of Algeciras, which is historical, did not produce a substantive Castilian response, supporting this conjecture.

• The modern rules of chess did not evolve until the middle of the fifteenth century. Chess was highly prevalent, however, in both Christian and Muslim courts during the 1360s. In a Muslim chess set of the period, the vizier, not the queen, was the most powerful chess piece. The Sultan, not the King, was to be guarded. It is certainly plausible that the Sultan's court would have enjoyed the rich irony of playing on Christian chess sets.

• The details and layout of the Alhambra, Generalife, the medina, the Alcazaba, the Albayzín, and Granada proper are historically accurate as presented, with one exception. The Palace of the Lions may not have been finished by 1367. The exact date of its completion remains debated, but it was certainly between 1367 and 1369. Sadly, many of the names used by the Nasrids for the various palaces, halls, and locations within the Alhambra are lost to history. I have used the modern names to refer to them (Palace of the Lions, Comares Palace, Courtyard of the Myrtles, etc). The silk trade was indeed the cash cow of the kingdom. The food described is historically accurate, as are the bath rituals at the hammam. Do note that the "sweet orange" (the Valencia), did not come on the scene until the sixteenth century. In fourteenth century al-Andalus, the "bitter orange" (the Seville orange) was not eaten, but was instead prized for the scent of its blossoms and used primarily for medicinal purposes and perfumes. There is only one detailed record of a lavish party/feast held at the Alhambra (written by Ibn al-Khatib, no less) celebrating Muhammad V's victory at Algeciras. This party occurred within the Alhambra, not within the Generalife, but anyone who has been to Granada will readily agree that the Generalife would be a fine place for a party under the stars. It is well accepted that fireworks existed by this time in Granada, although the military use of gunpowder (firearms, canons) is still several decades away.

• While convivencia reined in al-Andalus during the tenth and eleventh centuries, by 1367 the tensions between Muslims and Christians were real and acute. For all intents and purposes the only Christians in Granada were slaves, as presented. Jews, however, continued to live in relative peace within the kingdom, although they were largely confined to the Jewish quarter of the city, and taxed.

• The spherical astrolabe is historical, although it is implausible that it could have actually revolutionized medieval transoceanic navigation. The astrolabe was held in high esteem by

Muslims and Christians alike. The spherical astrolabe, a late innovation, was a combination of the conventional disk astrolabe and the so-called 'armillary sphere,' enabling improved functionality and accuracy. It was clearly a sophisticated scientific instrument by any reckoning. By 1367, it was certainly known to Muslim scholars, and likely even to some Europeans, that the world was in fact a sphere and could be sailed around to reach the east, though this was not attempted due to the travails of navigation over such long distances. The role of the Republic of Genoa in a Christian vision of world conquest is fictional, although they did trade with Granada, dominate the Mediterranean trade routes, were allied with Aragon, and had influence with the papacy (their chief rival was the Republic of Venice). It would have been a plausible ambition to conquer the New World if they had secured an sufficiently accurate navigational tool (such as our spherical astrolabe) to make the long voyage safely.

- The Brethren of Purity, the clandestine Sufi society, is historical, having its origins in tenth century Baghdad. It was secretive, as described, and embraced science, mathematics, the medical arts and philosophy, as I have suggested. The Brethren did possess a written "Epistles," of which we have copies today. Knowledge of the details of their membership over the centuries remains a mystery. The statements presented of their "ideal man" are taken directly from the Epistles. Their creed is fictional. While there is no evidence that the Brethren were active in Granada at this time, it is certainly plausible, perhaps even likely.

- I have attempted throughout the book to be sensitive to Islam, to treat its traditions accurately and with respect. Do appreciate, however, that there were differences, sometimes significant, between Islam as practiced in medieval al-Andalus, and modern Islam. For instances when no firm historical basis could be found (e.g., my marriage ceremony), I have deferred to modern practice, which itself differs from region to region. It should be noted that Sufism, mystical Islam, was held in very high esteem by the Arabs of medieval al-Andalus.

- The Arabic poems and inscriptions that adorn the Alhambra are rendered accurately, within the natural limitations of translation.

- Rumi served as a convenient choice for my poetry needs, and certainly he is passionately concerned with love, the relation between the beloved and the Beloved, and tawhid. Rumi died in 1273 and almost certainly translations of his poems had made their way to al-Andalus by 1367, satisfying my plausibility criterion.

- The descriptions of medieval battle are historically accurate. In fourteenth century Spain, Christian knights favored the steel plate most of us associate with medieval armor. Muslim knights, however, favored much lighter armor (chain mail, boiled leather, heavy felt) for improved mobility on the battlefield. The crossbow was a heavily utilized weapon by Granadine armies in the 1360s, whereas Christian armies still favored the massed bow and arrow for infantry support. Muslim troops were famous for their superior riding skills and battlefield agility. The tactical use of heavy crossbows by mounted cavalry using their horses as shields is fictional, although it passes my plausibility criterion.

- The significant tensions between the fundamentalist Berbers of North Africa (the Maghreb) and the moderate Arabs of Granada are historical. Chief among those tensions would have logically been the role and rights of women, including, for example, whether women should be educated at the madrasa with men. One could argue that these fundamentalist-moderate Muslim tensions, beginning with the Berber Almoravids and worsening with the Berber Almohads, brought about the demise of al-Andalus. It was the fundamentalist African Muslims, not the moderate Arab Muslims, that first clashed violently with Christians, ultimately destroying convivencia and precipitating reconquista. That said, it is important to emphasize that my story is told from an Arab Nasrid viewpoint, with all of those implicit biases, and hence the Berbers in the book may at times come across as monolithic in their mal-intent, barbarian even compared with the Nasrids. Several things are clear from the historical record. The Berber Marinids had a well-developed civilization and maintained a love-hate relationship with Granada during the fourteenth century. As a reminder, the Marinid Sultan hosted Sultan Muhammad while he was in exile, and there is a school of thought that suggests that at least some of the innovative architectural designs of the Alhambra had their origins in Fez. It is also clear, however, that the 1360s were very politically unstable in the Maghreb, with various viziers vying for power, a rash of court assassinations, and a number of young puppet sultans. It is also true that the Marinids lusted after Granada's well-earned recognition in the Islamic world and its staggering wealth. Is it plausible that the Berbers were enough at odds with Granada to infiltrate the Sultan's court and sow seeds of discord and conspiracy in an attempt to bring down the Nasrids? I think so. Clearly, however, there are always two sides to a story and a Berber would very likely tell a different tale.

- A word about hijab. Interestingly enough, wearing hijab was not the norm in fourteenth century Granada, especially at court (nor were turbans). This represents a fascinating instance of differences between medieval and modern Islam. The fact that the fundamentalist Berbers on the Mexuar Council would have likely taken issue with this and insisted upon women wearing hijab, especially for young women moving about the city, is plausible. Knowing Layla as I do, and the way her father educated her, it seemed logical to me that she would resent hijab as a repressive badge of Berber conservatism, an affront to her more moderate and tolerant Arab Nasrid ancestry and sensibilities.

# *Bibliography*

The credenza in my office at home where I write is lined with over ten feet of references on all things al-Andalus. I have included below a selected list of the books that I found particularly helpful, some of which (starred) I circled round to time and again during the birthing of this novel.

[1] A. Ali (Translator), *Al-Quran*: Princeton University Press, Princeton, 1993.

[2] C. Barks (with J. Moyne, A.J. Arberry and R. Nicholson), *The Essential Rumi*: Harper Collins, 1995. ***

[3] C. Barks, *The Soul of Rumi - New Collections of Ecstatic Poems*: Harper Collins, New York, 2001.

[4] G. Brooks, *Nine Parts of Desire - the Hidden World of Islamic Women*: Anchor books, New York, 1995.

[5] O.R. Constable (Editor), *Medieval Iberia - Readings from Christian, Muslim, and Jewish Sources*: University of Pennsylvania Press, Philadelphia, 1997.

[6] G. Dardess, *Do We Worship the Same God? - Comparing the Bible and the Quran*: St. Anthony Messenger Press, Cincinnati, 2006.

[7] J.D. Dodds, M.R. Menocal and A.K. Balbale, *The Arts of Intimacy - Christian, Jews, and Muslims in the Making of Castilian Culture*: Yale University Press, New Haven, 2008.

[8] J.D. Dodds, *Architecture and Ideology in Early Medieval Spain*: Pennsylvania State University Press, University Park, 1989.

[9] R. Fletcher, *Moorish Spain*: University of California Press, Berkeley, 1992. ***

[10] A. Fernádez-Puertas, *The Alhambra - I. From the Ninth Century to Yusef I (1354)*: Saqi Books, London, 1997. ***

[11] J.S. Gerber, *The Jews of Spain - A History of the Sephardic Experience*: The Free Press, New York, 1992.

[12] A. Harvey, *Teachings of Rumi*: Shambhala, Boston, 1999.

[13] L.P. Harvey, *Islamic Spain - 1250 to 1500*: University of Chicago Press, Chicago, 1990. ***

[14] K. Helminski (Editor), *The Rumi Collection*: Shambhala, Boston, 2000.

[15] B. Hintzen-Bohlen, *Art and Architecture - Andalusia*: Tandem Verlag GmbH, Germany, 2006. ***

[16] W. Irving, *Chronicles of the Conquest of Granada*: IndyPublish.com, Boston 2008 (first published in 1829).

[17] W. Irving, *Tales of the Alhambra*: Everest, 2008 (first published in 1832).

[18] R. Irwin, *The Alhambra*: Harvard University Press, Cambridge, 2004. ***

[19] R. Irwin, *Islamic Art*: Laurence King, London, 1997.

[20] S.K. Jayyusi, *The Legacy of Muslim Spain, Volume 1*: Brill, Leiden, 1992. ***

[21] S.K. Jayyusi, *The Legacy of Muslim Spain, Volume 2*: Brill, Leiden, 1993. ***

[22] H. Kennedy, *Muslim Spain and Portugal - A Political History of al-Andalus*: Addison Wesley Longman, Essex, 1996. ***

[23] C. Lowney, *A Vanished World - Muslims, Christians, and Jews in Medieval Spain*: Oxford University Press, New York, 2006. ***

[24] M. McWilliams and D.J. Roxburgh, *Traces of the Calligrapher - Islamic Calligraphy in Practice c. 1600-1900*: Yale University Press, New Haven, 2007.

[25] M.R. Menocal, *The Ornament of the World - How Muslims, Jews, and Christians Created a Culture of Tolerance in Medieval Spain*: Back Bay Books, New York, 2002. ***

[26] M.R. Menocal, R.P. Scheindlin and M. Sells (Editors), *The Literature of al-Andalus*: Cambridge University Press, Cambridge, 2000.

[27] D. Nicolle, *Granada 1492 - the Twilight of Moorish Spain*: Praeger, Westport, 2005. ***

[28] D. Nicolle, *The Moors - the Islamic West, 7th - 15th Centuries AD*: Osprey Publishing, Oxford, 2001. ***

[29] J. Augustín Núñez (editor), *The Alhambra and Generalife in Focus*: Edilux S.L., Madrid, 1991. (Translated by J. Trout.) ***

[30] J. Renard, *101 Questions and Answers on Islam*: Paulist Press, New York, 1998.

[31] D.F. Ruggles, *Gardens, Landscape, and Vision in the Palaces of Islamic Spain*: Pennsylvania State University Press, University Park, 2000.

[32] J. Schacht and C.E. Bosworth (Editors), *The Legacy of Islam* (2nd Edition): Oxford University Press, London, 1974.

[33] A. Schimmel, *Rumi's World - the Life and Work of the Great Sufi Poet*: Shambhala, Boston, 1992.

[34] M. Sells, *Approaching the Quran* (2nd Edition): White Cloud Press, Ashland, 2006. ***

[35] H. Smith, *Islam - A Concise Introduction*: Harper Collins, San Francisco, 2001.

[36] D. Sutton, *Islamic Design - A Genius for Geometry*: Walker, New York, 2007.

## *Acknowledgments*

My heartfelt thanks to Lawrence Knorr at Sunbury Press for sharing my vision and opening the door for *Emeralds*. I am grateful for Allyson Gard, my editor, for 'getting it,' for Tammi Knorr at Sunbury for all her help with my launch, and for Stephanie Barko, my publicist, for her help in getting the ball rolling.

I am deeply indebted to a number of people who read my manuscript and provided me with valuable feedback, including: Maria Cressler, Christina Gawrys, Michael Gawrys, Matthew Cressler, Mary Ellen Giess, Joanna Cressler, Tracy Benden, Dick Gaeta, Bob Wilhelm, Dick Wilhelm, Tom Jablonski, Roger Meyer, Barbara Nalbone, Nathan Black, Denise Black, Sadahat Adil, Dave Webb, Amy Edwards, Anita Hall, Gerry Hankes, Beth Saba, Sylvia Hall, Jenan Mohajir, Shelly Case, Craig Johnson, Sachin Seth, Sharon Machek, Tom Nadar, Matt Saba, and Doug Davis.

Of this list, several folks deserve special mention because their feedback prompted me to make important changes to the manuscript.

Matthew Cressler loved my "chorus of constellations" and urged me to introduce them earlier in the story. He also gave my revamped first one-hundred pages a critical thumb's up.

Mary Ellen Giess thought I should expand the relationship between Chandon and Sosanna.

Barbara Nalbone said the book begged for a glossary and offered a number of thoughtful semantic suggestions.

Tom Jablonski helped me solve several logistical inconsistencies, and encouraged me to rethink my chapter titles.

Craig Johnson and Tom Nadar were relentless in helping me root out my verbal anachronisms and other word-quirks.

Roger Meyer smirked at my over-use of 'smirk' and suggested a cadre of word choice improvements.

Sabahat Adil reminded me of some of the subtleties in the relationship between the Arab Nasrids and the Berber Marinids, and the nuances of convivencia. She and Matt Saba corrected my Arabic in several places.

Joanna Cressler was my go-to source for all things horse related. She picked the breeds and the colors of Layla's and Chandon's horses and even named them for me. She insisted that

I bring Blue and Afán back in the last scene, and suggested a confrontation between Layla and a Berber imam.

And of course, my Maria. She saw each chapter before anyone else, and was the first to read the whole beast. I recall well how nervous I was tentatively slipping my very first pages into her hands for critique. Her criticisms stung a bit (okay, sometimes a lot!) when they flowed back my way, but once I got past my own ego (I have found novel writing is a very humbling business!), I came to appreciate Maria's terrific insights into my characters. To be fair, we did not agree on everything (smile darling!), but many changes were made that improved the book. And yes, my love, even your insistence that I tone down the sex scenes here and there was ultimately on target. But I must say, it did feel good when you said, "Oh, don't get me wrong, I LOVE what you wrote, so don't delete it, just don't put it in the book!" Perhaps we can pull those cut passages out from time to time and smile together. Thanks for all your help and support, my love.

# About the Author

John D. Cressler is Ken Byers Professor of Electrical and Computer Engineering at Georgia Tech, in Atlanta, Georgia, USA. He received his Ph.D. from Columbia University, New York, in 1990. His academic research interests center on the creative use of nanoscale-engineering techniques to enable new approaches to electronic devices, circuits and systems, especially as required to support the emerging global communications infrastructure.

He and his students have published over 500 scientific papers in this field and he has received a number of awards for both his teaching and his research. His previous books include: *Silicon-Germanium Heterojunction Bipolar Transistors* (2003), *Reinventing Teenagers: the Gentle Art of Instilling Character in Our Young People* (2004), *Silicon Heterostructure Handbook: Materials, Fabrication, Devices, Circuits and Applications of SiGe and Si Strained Layer Epitaxy* (2006), *Silicon Earth: Introduction to the Microelectronics and Nanotechnology Revolution* (2009), and *Extreme Environment Electronics* (2012). *Emeralds of the Alhambra* is his debut novel.

He and his wife Maria have been married for 30 years and are the proud parents of three: Matthew (and now Mary Ellen), Christina (and now Michael) and Joanna. His hobbies include hiking, gardening, bonsai, all things Italian, collecting (and drinking!) fine wines, writing, reading, cooking, history, and carving walking sticks, not necessarily in that order. He considers teaching/mentoring to be his primary vocation, with his writing a close second.

He can be reached at:

School of Electrical and Computer Engineering
777 Atlantic Drive, N.W.
Georgia Tech, Atlanta, GA 30332-0250 USA

E-mail: cressler@ece.gatech.edu
Web-site (research): http://users.ece.gatech.edu/~cressler
Web-site (books): http://johndcressler.com

# *Questions for Discussion Groups*

Were you aware that Muslims, Christians, and Jews lived side-by-side in relative harmony for several centuries in medieval Spain? How does that fact make you feel regarding the current state of extreme tension between Muslims, Christians, and Jews in our twenty-first century world?

For Christian readers, what did you learn about Islam that you did not know before? What was surprising to you? How do you feel about the role of the papacy in the history of medieval Europe?

For Muslim readers, what differences between medieval Islam and modern Islam struck you as interesting? Were you aware that significant tensions between moderate Islam and fundamentalist Islam existed in medieval Spain? What does it say about the origins of these tensions that they still exist today?

Contrast the role and treatment of women in al-Andalus with those in the rest of medieval Europe. This discussion might include clothing options, educational opportunities, marriage rights, legal rights, etc. How have these differences changed over the centuries?

Contrast the evolution of the rights and roles of Christian and Muslim women. How and why have they evolved in different ways?

How does it make you feel knowing that a substantial fraction of our modern understanding in science, technology, philosophy, agriculture, and medicine flowed into Europe through the largely forgotten gateway of al-Andalus? One could fairly argue that this knowledge was essential to the European Renaissance and ultimately the Enlightenment, which birthed modern science and with it technology.

Were you familiar with Rumi before reading this book? What do you think of the examples of his poetry presented and what he believed regarding the ability of earthly love and sexuality to connect one directly with the divine Other?

Did the medieval concept of chivalry among knights, Christian and/or Muslim, encourage or discourage the use of war as a means to settle disputes between countries/peoples/cultures?

How did the concept of prisoner ransom influence the way war was conducted? How has that changed over time, and why?

Can love transcend cultural and religious boundaries? If so, what is required for success?

In what ways is human love divine?

The notion of holding onto injustices, prejudices and grudges against "the other" figures heavily in the book, be it other family members, other clans, other religions and those from other countries. Have our attitudes of "us" vs. "the other" evolved much since the medieval period? Why or why not?

What do you think of Sufism? How has its relation to mainstream Islam changed since medieval al-Andalus?

What do you think of the Sufi concept of *tawhid*, the mystical union between a human and the divine? Note that this concept, even as experienced between husband and wife through their sexual union, shares common roots with all mystical traditions, Muslim, Christian and Jewish. Have you personally experienced tawhid? How do your own experiences compare with those of Layla and Chandon?

What do you think of the Muslim concept of *al-Jannah*, the walled, private garden, as a mirror of paradise? What do you think of the role water plays in Islamic architecture? What debt does modern Western art and architecture owe to medieval Muslim art and architecture?

How did the conception, execution and appreciation of architecture and art differ between Christians and Muslims in medieval Spain? How have those differences evolved over the centuries?

How did the role of sultan in a Muslim kingdom differ from the role of king in a Christian kingdom during the medieval era? How did religion play in those respective dynamics?

# ***Author's Note:***

Ten percent of the author's proceeds generated by sales of this book will be donated to organizations committed to opening dialogue and fostering mutual understanding, respect and tolerance between Christians, Muslims and Jews.

Made in the USA
Charleston, SC
23 August 2013